[See p. 23

HE CROSSED HIS ARMS ON THE BACK OF THE SEAT, RETURNING
STARE FOR STARE

THE PLANTER

A NOVEL

BY
HERMAN WHITAKER

AUTHOR OF
THE SETTLER

Fredonia Books
Amsterdam, The Netherlands

The Planter
(A Novel)

by
Herman Whitaker

ISBN: 1-4101-0098-7

Copyright © 2002 by Fredonia Books

Reprinted from the 1909 edition

Fredonia Books
Amsterdam, The Netherlands
http://www.fredoniabooks.com

TO
MY MOTHER

CONTENTS

CHAP.		PAGE
I.	SHOWING HOW THE WIND WAS TEMPERED FOR THE SHEARLING	1
II.	THE YAQUIS	12
III.	LOS ENGANCHADORES	27
IV.	LA LUNA	36
V.	IN WHICH THE SHEARLING FEELS THE WIND	59
VI.	NEW ENGLAND vs. THE TROPICS	76
VII.	A MAN-HUNT, AND—	87
VIII.	—THE MAN	103
IX.	A VISIT	117
X.	THE TROPICS vs. NEW ENGLAND	137
XI.	CANCER SWINGS, AND—	153
XII.	MR. DAVID GOES DOWN, AND—	177
XIII.	—TAKES THE COUNT—	189
XIV.	—BUT COMES BACK SMILING	210
XV.	CANCER SUSTAINS A REVERSE	225
XVI.	DAVID CASTS HIS BREAD UPON THE WATERS	253
XVII.	A SURPRISE	283
XVIII.	—ITS SEQUEL	296
XIX.	THE BREAD FLOATS OUT	318
XX.	A CHECK, AND—	338
XXI.	—HERTZER TRIES FOR "MATE"	355

CONTENTS

CHAP.   PAGE
XXII.   A Move in Another Game 360
XXIII.   The Move 380
XXIV.   The Girl Plays the Man's Game . . . 388
XXV.   The Shearling Develops Horns . . . 406
XXVI.   Wherein the "Queen" is "Castled". . 439
XXVII.   The Travail of a Night 470
XXVIII.   The Sins of the Fathers 491
XXIX.   The Realization of a Dream 516

PREFACE TO NEW EDITION

UNTIL the first edition of this book called forth expressions of incredulity from some reviewers as to the reality of certain phases of life which are portrayed, the writer had a very decided opinion as to prefaces, deeming them usually superfluous and often impertinent. By that criticism, however, this opinion has been modified till it now ranks as a belief that, while never fortunate, a preface may sometimes be expedient.

It has been truly said that we learn more history from our novels than our text-books. One might almost add that our fiction exercises a wider influence, is more powerful to mould public opinion, than the pronouncements of our parliaments. In view of this influence, it behooves a writer to go slowly over new ground, and to make certain that, while depicting life, his book reflects the truth. Never ought he to be more careful than when exaggeration or distortions may react harmfully upon living persons or enterprises still existent. Once sure of his facts, however, it is equally incumbent upon him to hew to the line, let the chips fall where they may.

PREFACE TO NEW EDITION

As to the view of the Mexican rubber industry given in this book, it may fairly be claimed that the failure or suspension of over two hundred companies in the last three years justifies the verdict delivered by Ewing—that the "rubber culture is individual business, and does not lend itself to company management." Such a disastrous record, involving loss to many thousands, might be accepted with a certain amount of philosophy had it rid us of its cause— the rascally promoter. Unfortunately, his failure in one field merely directs his steps to another. The rise of new companies proves that he is still with us, and will be until public opinion forces a law to end his baneful activities.

Turning from his fraud and chicanery to darker acts, it is no exaggeration to say that the "contract-labor system" on plantations owned by Americans is the worst form of slavery that this world has ever seen. Contrary to the opinion of the critic, who thought that its cruelties had been accentuated to procure an artistic effect, a very real indignation had to be continually repressed during the writing of this book in order that it might not read like a calendar of crime. The facts are unprintable; they transcend belief. The statement that every violent crime has been, is being, and will be again perpetrated in the *galeras* of American plantations comes well within the truth.

Worse even than the lot of the miserable *enganchar* has been that of the Yaqui—the Yaqui who, after

PREFACE TO NEW EDITION

centuries of struggle and for no other crime than patriotism, has been sold into perpetual slavery to the planters of Chiapas and Yucatan; sold to a servitude of so vile a reputation that fifteen men and women jumped overboard in transit to Campeachy from Vera Cruz last year, choosing death before its torrid rigors.   In the last four years five thousand Yaquis— farmers, laborers, miners — have been expatriated under conditions that were rendered unnecessarily cruel by the spite of brutal Mexican soldiers.   Rounded up in scores while their men were off at the mines, women have been taken away on the trains.   In the general round-ups, wives were separated from husbands, sisters from brothers, children from mothers— infant babes were torn from the breast and left behind on the ground while their mothers were driven away. The deportation was carried out with absolute brutality, and in accordance with a policy that aimed at the scattering of tribes and families.   Taken all in all, the tragedy of the Yaquis is perhaps without a parallel in American history.

In conclusion: Other critics have questioned whether, if aroused, an indignant American opinion could affect abuses that obtain across our southern frontier.   It could—in two ways: First, by the intervention of stockholders in American companies, who have been hitherto in ignorance of labor conditions upon their plantations.   Second, by reaction upon Mexican public opinion.   Nations which are rising to a higher plane are invariably exceedingly

PREFACE TO NEW EDITION

sensitive to foreign opinion, and this is especially true of Mexico, whose government and people keep always an imitative eye upon their northern neighbor. In that country at this late date abuses such as the "contract-labor" and Yaqui slave systems could only exist in a hole and corner. When the Mexican government realizes that they stand forth in the open light of day, it will speedily make an end by enforcing in the tropics the law and order that obtains all over the "Plateau."

H. W.

THE PLANTER

THE PLANTER

THE PLANTER

I

"IF the cub was only out of the way, J., I believe the widow would come in?"

Mr. Jarvis Osgood — "Osgood & Short, Banking and Farmers' Loans," as per gilt inscription on the plate-glass window — closed his ledger with a bang and looked at his partner across the office. Tall and stooped, in Mr. Osgood fiery red hair was associated with a cold eye which abundantly advertised the fact that the warmth of feeling popularly attributed to his colors was here entirely lacking; and as he leaned back in his chair, frowning, his lean fingers weaved in and out in a manner that always suggested surgeon's practice to those unhappy debtors upon whom he held financial post-mortem examinations. He was gnawing his thin mustache, too—a sign of unusual irritation.

"I called round there to-day," he went on, still

addressing the partner, who was short and gross as he himself was thin and long, "but I got the usual 'David thought this, and David thought that, and David believed t'other.' If he were *only* out of the way!"

"He's not," Mr. Short laconically answered.

"No, he's not, and I suppose it is foolish to think of it."

Frowning still, Mr. Osgood picked up a pamphlet from a pile at his elbow and began to idly turn the leaves. Emblazoned "Verda Rubber Company" in gilt on its back, it was one of a thousand that were pouring, just then, from the presses of the country which had been recently struck by the rubber craze. Rubber! rubber! rubber! The promoter's golden tongue was belling it full and free in Maine woods, swamps of Missouri, the cotton fields of the South. Every State—almost every town—had its company; and as Mr. Osgood was a particularly early bird with a keen eye for the very earliest worm, he had organized the first in Northfield, Maine—also the biggest and best, as was abundantly explained in the pamphlet.

According to this, the company held five thousand acres of land, choicest on the Isthmus of Tehuantepec, in the State of Vera Cruz, one thousand of which carried two-year-old rubber, also the finest of its kind. One share of the company's stock represented an acre of this land, and its price would be used to clear, plant, and bring it to bearing at six years old, when the first tapping would repay the shareholder his entire outlay. A rosy proposition; but there it was, worked out in plain figures, which never lie — so many trees to the acre, so much rubber per tree, at such a valuation; all you had to do was to reckon up the profits. Never was such an offer! The pamphlet declared it in bold type broidered with letters from eminent citizens, who knew the firm of Osgood & Short to be of spotless reputation, and enticingly decorated with photographs of "our manager, Mr. Meagher," posed beneath a rubber-tree. It was all so complete, compact, such a parcel of truth, that there was nothing left for the public but to believe.

And it had believed, backing its opinion so strongly that the firm had been compelled to move into larger offices and to add two typists to the establishment of one clerk, which had sufficed for the easy shaving of farmers. So far, however, the investors had all been "instalment people"—small fry, mere nibblers at the hook which Mr. Osgood had baited for whale. He had hoped to get Mrs. Mann, widow of a well-to-do lumberman, into the company; to which end—though not naturally of a religious temperament—he had interested himself in her Sabbath-school class for the past year, shepherding it forth upon many expensive picnics. But whereas, these solicitudes of his had undoubtedly won on the widow, David, her only son, had proved conservative beyond his two and twenty years. Returning to the marine simile, whenever Mr. Osgood had brandished his harpoon for a kill, the calf had rushed in between him and the mother whale.

"If he were only out of the way!" he again repeated.

"Ain't," Mr. Short affirmed once more. Then as a red shock of hair and underlying continent of Hibernian feature protruded from behind the creaking door, he said, sharply: "This is a private office, my man. If you have business with us, apply in the next room. The clerk will—"

But just then Mr. Osgood leaped from his chair. "Meagher!"

"Meagher?" Mr. Short echoed. "Not the—"

"—manager, yes." Mr. Osgood nodded irritably. "What in thunder are you doing here, Meagher? When did you arrive? Who did you leave in charge?"

"Aisy, aisy." The Irishman grinned. "Wan at a time. Why am I here? You'd better be askin' that av the Greaser that tried to hold an ante-mortem on me. 'Tis an inquest on his remains they held instead, wid so many witnesses I had to skip. Guadaloupe, the mandador, is in charge, an' Hertzer, av La Luna, promised to ride over every bit."

"But you can go back?" Short questioned. "I understand a little thing like that is easily settled down there."

"Not if thim thaving Jefe-Politicos have ye surecinched. Tin years' salary wouldn't plug the hole in that Greaser's head. No, sir; 'tis another climate for Andy Meagher."

HOW THE WIND WAS TEMPERED

Seating himself, he grinned again at the senior partner, who coughed uneasily, and said, after a minute's musing: "Um-m! It's unfortunate, very unfortunate, Meagher. We should like to have kept you in our employ. But if we can help you—letters of recommendation, and so forth," he hastily added, "command us."

"Faith, thin, 'tis kind av you to be saying it, 'specially as it's the very thing I'm to be seeing ye about. Just now I'm afther heading for Peru. There's gold there, on the plateau. Injuns bring it out to the coast be the ton. But the trip 'll take money—eh?"

Mr. Osgood's look of uncertainty settled in unhappiness, and he coughed again behind his hand. "Let me see: our last draft paid your salary to date, I think?"

The Irishman nodded. "But be way av a loan." Diving into a huge side-pocket, he fished out a Verda prospectus. "Picked this up in a barber shop, an' I was wondering if the local papers wouldn't like an interview from a man that had been down there?"

By way, perhaps, of a change, he looked at Short, who looked at Mr. Osgood, who broke an ominous silence. "Of course, we didn't intend to see you stranded, Meagher. If a hundred dollars—"

"Five hun'red for the outfit," the Irishman calmly interrupted. "Steamer fare an' incidentals, two hun'red more. Let's say—seven-fifty."

"Hell!" Short sprang up, his gross face shaded

5

from livid to black. "What kind of fools do you take us for? We'll shove you for blackmail!"

"Ye will, will ye?" Rising, Meagher shook the pamphlet under his nose, then·turned to the door.

But the senior partner interposed. "Don't go, Meagher. The sum you mention is out of the question. If three hundred—"

"Seven-fifty, an' no more words to it."

Mr. Osgood bowed to unkind fate. "Write a check for the amount, J." While the pen was scratching minutes of the Irishman's success, he ran on: "We don't want you to feel that this was obtained under duress, Meagher. You are very welcome to the accommodation. No, no! we won't hear of a note. Consider it as our testimonial to your faithful service. Good luck and good-bye."

"Might have been worse," he sighed, coming back from the door. "If he had the wit he might have bled us of thousands. As it is, he'll surely get killed in Peru. What is more, I rather believe that we can turn this to advantage. Why not make young Mann plantation manager?"

Short grunted. "That milksop?"

"Yes, he's been coddled to death. But he never took to the process, and I believe he'd jump at the chance to break mamma's apron-strings."

"Good and sickly down there, too," Short mused.

But Mr. Osgood, who kept the upper chambers of his mind swept and garnished, waved away the evil suggestion. "On the contrary, J., the climate is beautiful, or I wouldn't consider it. I think," he added, reaching his overcoat from its peg, "that I will drop in on my way home."

Though Northfielders spoke pridefully of their town as "the city," one could hardly pass the length of its principal street without coming under observation of a majority of the inhabitants. Wherefore, it happened that as Mr. Osgood paced along through dusk ladened with the odors of coming spring, his footfall penetrated to a parlor where David Mann was closeted with a pretty girl, and where, had the banker but known it, events were shaping themselves to further his philanthropic purposes.

"Why, David," the girl exclaimed even as the banker's footfall died, "I would as soon have thought of marrying—your mamma!"

The young man winced. For while not necessarily destructive of the suit he had just pleaded, her words, when delivered minus a blush and plus a giggle, hurt a self-esteem already too sensitive to its own deficiencies. Of medium height, his figure was slight — though *spare* described it better; for his frame predicated bulk and strength strangled by coddling from the cradle. Very religious, his mother had tried to force his youthful clay into ecclesiastical mould. He had had Joseph and Benjamin, in scarlet and ochre, for early companions, and had grown up in companionship of the apostles — goodly enough fellowship for bearded age, but somewhat depressing

to verdant youth. It speaks for some germs of jovial
sin inherited from the lumberman, his father, that
with such a start he should have fallen as far short as
a law-office of the ministry at which his mother aimed
him. Yet the print of her thumb showed in his
quiet reserve, studious air (that was accentuated by
glasses, which were due to her anxiety rather than any
real need), and a womanish texture of skin. But for
a jaw that was perpetually at outs with his otherwise
peaceful features, he might have posed as the arch-
type of the paragon known to old ladies as "a nice
young man"; but the prominence of this feature debarred him forever from that innocent company.

The said feature now took command of his face
as he rose and faced the girl. "I didn't ask you to
marry mamma, Kate. But since I'm so perfectly
ridiculous—good-night!"

Her giggles died, and she jumped up as he flung out
of the room. "David! David! I didn't mean to
offend—" Then, as the door banged in her face, she
gasped, stared, then broke into a little laugh which
yet expressed admiration. "My, what a look! If he
could live up to that, one might take him seriously."

Unconscious, however, that honors lay with him,
David flung down the street toward the fate the
banker had in kindly preparation. "I'm spoiled,"
he groaned — "a milksop, to be laughed at, spurned
by every healthy woman. I won't stand it any longer. I'll get out, I'll—I'd sooner be a tramp than a
softy—I'll leave home."

HOW THE WIND WAS TEMPERED

And while he fretted and fumed, Mr. Osgood was pursuing the even tenor of his own argument in the widow's parlor. "Why, my dear lady," he was saying, "it is a lazy dollar that will not turn more than four per cent. Invested with us, your capital would double, treble, quintuple, in as many years. You would be so wealthy that some of us who now enjoy your friendship would feel diffident about pressing our acquaintance."

Very pretty at twenty, at forty-five the widow was comely enough to warrant the simper she accorded to his sentimental look. "I'm sure no change of fortune could affect our friendship, Mr. Osgood."

Bowing, he ran on: "Then think what a power wealth can be in good hands — and our church so badly needs a Dorcas."

"I should like to — very much." She simpered again as bright visions of herself, a patron of home and foreign missions, floated through her mind. "I trust your judgment; feel that I may depend upon it—implicitly. But David is so stubborn. You see, I have always regarded the property as being held in trust for him, and I do not like to run altogether counter to his wishes."

"Exactly, exactly; and it does you credit." Mr. Osgood knew when to pause, and he turned to the second count in his argument just as the outer door swung under David's hand. "By-the-way, we need a manager for the plantation, and Short suggested that David might like the place. The salary is not very high. A hundred and fifty a month the first year, two hundred the second, and more later if he likes the life." He threw off the figures nonchalantly, as though a hundred a month were not a princely salary in Northfield. "If he doesn't, he'll be none the worse for the experience. Nothing like contact with the world for brightening a young man."

"But the climate?" the widow quivered. "I'm told—"

"Nonsense, madam." Mr. Osgood waved authoritative fingers. "Meagher, our late manager, just returned, is the picture of health, and actually recommends the climate for consumptives."

"Still—he would be so far away. I could never—"

Enough of the conversation had floated out to the hall, where David was doffing his coat, to inform him of the issue which jibed so well with his present inclination, and, entering, he interrupted her protestations.

"I'll take it. When shall I go?"

Neither had heard him enter, and the widow uttered a little cry of surprise. Mr. Osgood, however, was equal to the situation. He shrugged. "I don't wish to hurry you, but—the plantation is without a manager."

"Then I'll start to-morrow. It's no use, mother" (he anticipated objections), "I'm thoroughly sick of this life. Yes, you trained me for something else —that's the trouble; trained me as a French gardener trains a peach-tree, leading its branches over a trellis till he has made a creeper out of a tree that nature intended to swing free in the winds. I'm tired of it. I must—*will* go out and rub shoulders with the world."

"But," she complained, "who will keep you out of draughts? And there will be no one to air your sheets and warm your bed at night?"

But skipping her further protestations, along with Mr. Osgood's assurances that draughts were a blessing in the tropics, where beds needed hot-water bottles less than ice, the story jumps to the morning that a Ward liner brought Mr. David, with contained cargo of New England prejudices, orthodoxies, and beliefs, into Vera Cruz.

II

THE YAQUIS

FROM the beach north of the town the break-water of Vera Cruz throws a stone arm around and along encircling coral reefs, swells midway of its length into a huge biceps the island and fort of San Juan de Ulúa, then runs on to meet the second stone limb that comes sweeping out from the south. Builded of twenty-ton blocks and broad on its crest as the *camino real* (the royal highway), it fends the gulf swells and bridles the tides that sneak in to tug at the ships whose silver bells pace off the hot, damp hours.

Coming in as David did, the eye draws first to the fort, whose beetling emplacements mock the peace of smiling blue waters, nodding palms. Next he found himself looking down from the Ward liner's high deck upon the swarthy crews of diminutive Mexican gun-boats; nor did he fail to note that the gold in the officers' uniforms seemed to increase in ratio with the smallness of their craft. At first a veil of masts had hidden the water-front, but presently the mesh widened, and he saw, between red-

and-black bulk of many steamers, the town, a blaze of color, sitting in jungle country at the lip of the sea like a wonderfully blazoned cup in a wide green saucer. Save where some oaken grill - weathered portal supplied an ashen note, its adobe buildings burned in smouldering rose, saffrons, purples, gold (the latter predominating), glowing in the sunblaze the whirling dust, the skins of men, women, venders of sweetmeats, porters, and *cargadores*, who came running along the quay as the steamer drew into her berth.

Vera Cruz, city of the true cross, anciently haunted of Morgan, Kidd, and other famous freebooters! Magic name! it calls up galleons and plate-ships loaded with bars and ingots, jewels and rich vestments, sack and siege, buccaneer revels in a pestilential climate that spared not saint nor sinner, but snatched them alike from their prayers and their cups. What youth could fail to kindle at such fires? Surely not David, who was once caught in church with the leaves of a buccaneer romance neatly fitted into his Bible. As he looked down on the rabble, a sea of chocolate flecked with a foam of glistening eyeballs, memories came crowding. The rotten wharf and furry railroad tracks spoke to him of the climate, suggesting that Yellow Jack might be lurking at the corner of any one of the flaming streets, or had taken sanctuary and was peering from behind the green bells of the cathedral's yellow towers. The *cargadores*, who were quarrelling for possession of his baggage, were lineally descended from the Aztecs, who first fought Cortés, then dragged his boats and armament over those distant blue mountains to lay siege to Montezuma.

Under convoy of the two who survived the quarrel, he presently made his way through the rainbow streets to the station of a jerk-water railroad which advertised that its trains ran through "the heart of the tropics," a statement which he presently found needed qualification in that, a railroad in summer, it was navigable by steamers for half its length during the rainy season — if the conductor were to be believed.

It was after the train had bumped by a couple of stations that the functionary, a rubicund blond with a good-natured face, shed this piece of information. "Fact," he said, as he settled down for a talk. "Last rains we didn't run a train for three months, an' Pollard, of Plantacion Sol Suchia, poled a five-ton dugout eighteen miles up the right of way from Viga to La Soledad. Some of them tin railroaders up in the City of Mexico call us the 'canal,' an' ask why we don't feed our mules more hay to stop 'em from bolting the towpath? An' while I'm not denying that we hit the ditch too often, we're surely on the mend. On'y jumped four times coming up. What's more, we've got a future. Just t'other day Uncle Porfirio—Diaz, you know—grabbed about two-thirds of our stock, an' as he's clean cracked on beating out the Panama Canal with his cross-country lines, it

means that we'll be running Pullmans, tide-water to
tide-water, inside a year. So let 'em laugh. After
we've ballasted up an' shaken out a few kinks, we'll
make their pot-iron roads look like scrap in a nigger's
backyard."

Whatever magnificence the future might have in
store, half a coach yet sufficed for the road's first-
class travel, and this, in comfort, cleanliness, and
appointments, was a grade or two behind an American emigrant car. The cane seats were dark and
shiny, suggesting many perspirings; iron spittoons
stood in every section, and a heavy odor of stale
tobacco testified to their constant use. The passengers were few—a scattering of Spanish business men;
some half-dozen *rancheros* (farmers); a fat Mexican
woman with a daughter whose delicately pretty
profile instantly caught David's eye. The *rancheros*,
with their tight, bell-bottomed trousers, bolero jackets, peaked sombreros, interested him, though not
nearly so much as the *rurale* who stood on the platform without. Gray felt sombrero, gray jacket, gray
trousers, all striped or laced with silver, his brown
belt and bandoleer afforded the one touch of color
in his costume. A rifle swung by the latter diagonal-
ly across his back; a sabre and a revolver, full two
feet long, hung from his belt. His face, in its stern
immobility, reminded David of a picture he had once
seen of a bronzed Roman guard.

"The rurale?" The conductor answered his question. "One is detailed on every train to put the fear

of God—that's Diaz again—into the third-class peon's hearts, an' they do it, too, you bet. You have heard how the rurale corps was formed? Well, he issued a free pardon to all bandits who surrendered by a certain date, made officers of the chiefs, an' sent them out with their men to exterminate all that were left in the mountains. They did it, too. Beyond Ameca, t'other side of Guadalajara, you can see a hundred an' eleven graves, side by side, the toll of one village. Innocent or guilty, they shot every man they met on a mountain trail, an' when they finished you couldn't scare up a bandit in the whole of Mexico—except in the rurales. That fellow's undoubtedly cut throats in his time, an' now keeps the peace on this train."

The train stopped just then at a station—more accurately, a *jacale*, big hut, half store, half groggery, that stood in a green clearing dotted with tall feather palms. From its apex the roof of palm-leaves ran down and out over sidings of split poles to wide eaves, beneath which two peons were hulling rice with a churn arrangement, rude and primitive as those with which the captive Israelites winnowed out the scant Egyptian ration. At one end a burly Mexican was serving *tequila*, the fiery spirit of the country, to some *rancheros*, whose tethered ponies each carried a sheathed machete at the saddle-bow. At the other, his wife, equally brown and stout, was measuring gaudy cloth for two Indian women whose broad bosoms and limbs of bronze were revealed rather than hidden by sleeveless chemisettes and scant skirts of cotton. Their dark, wild faces fitted their primitive husbandry, and while David looked on, full of interest, there occurred that which bore in upon him the knowledge that he had passed the outer pale of civilization into a country where a man must take care of himself.

It happened too swiftly for him to grasp any details. He was aware of an angry shouting, saw the knot of *rancheros* open, and caught a glimpse of faces, one scowling blackly, the other writhing with passion. Then came a flash of a knife. A woman shrieked as she threw herself upon a fallen man— and the train rolled on, carrying with it a youth who, beneath a thrill of horror, was conscious of a strange stir of feeling, throb of primitive impulse.

"Yes, he killed him," the conductor said, returning. "But that don't count down here like it does up in the States. I could tell you stories—but 't'ain't worth while; you'll soon see for yourself. Look at the old lady over there. Now, you'd hardly call her savage-looking?"

David shook his head. But for its masculine strength, the woman's broad brown face might have served as the type of tropical motherhood.

"Well, after discounting the lies they tell about her, she can still show more nicks to her gun than a bad man in a Western story. She's the Señora Morales, widow of a labor contratisto, an' has run the business since his death six years ago. She delivers her enganchadores (contract laborers)—that is, thieves, jail-birds, the offal of Mexican cities—three an' four days' journey from the railroad to outlying plantations, an' does it all on her lonely. Any one of the thousands she's handled would cut her throat for a nickel, yet she's still delivering them like sheep to the shambles. The girl? Her daughter by a first husband, who was a colonel in the army. Pretty? Wait till you see her eyes. An' she's nice as they make 'em. Just look at the way she carries her head. Blood, sirree, for the colonel was tall timber —as she might be if she threw over her mother. You see, his folks never liked the marriage, and have tried again and again to get her away, but she just won't do it. No, she don't know a thing about the business. Came along, I guess, for a bit of a trip. But here comes the old girl—going back to her men in the third, I guess. Take a good look at her as she goes by."

This was the easier for, pausing opposite, she thrust out a pudgy hand. "Ola! Señor el conducteur, Gringo! Como le va?" (How goes it?) While rippling off a few sentences, she held David in the tail of her eye, then rolled on laughing—or, rather, her bulk flowed along the aisle like a flood of jelly.

"Wanted to know which of my wives was responsible for you," the conductor interpreted, grinning. "The old girl loves a joke, an' ain't too particular about its color, if you don't crack it before the girl. With her she lives right up to the colonel. By-the-

18

way, she told me that this bunch ain't no common or garden enganchars, but Yaqui Injuns that have been sold by the government to the plantations I'm going back now, so come along if you'd like to see them." Leading back through the train, he ran on: "The rurales uster shoot 'em in bunches—men, women, an' children—fast as they rounded 'em up; but that was sheer waste, with the planters aching to take 'em at eighty dollars a head, an' you can trust your uncle Porfirio to see a dollar without a microscope. Yes, they're sold for life—though you might call it two years, for what of calenturas, malarias, insects, an' sixteen-hour days' labor under a boiling sun, it's a poor planter that can't make a good Injun in less. Many of 'em die the first year." Opening the third-class door, he commented: "How's that for a jam?"

Besides the guard of armed *cabos* (overseers) at either end, fully two hundred Yaquis were packed like cattle in a car that was narrower and lacked a third of the length of those in use on American lines. Five, sometimes six, Indians, mostly women with bundles, crowded the wooden sections. A full hundred stood in the aisle, sweltering in the heat and the fetor of their own perspirings—would so stand throughout the day, with no other rest than that afforded by changing the weight from one to the other foot. Born of the mountains, free as the clouds that flit over the Sierra Madres, last of a race that defied Toltec and Aztec, that set limits for Spanish territorial lust and greed of Gringo miners, who had themselves fought the whole Mexican army for a generation, they lived up to their tradition, enduring the heat, crowding, tedium, with the same patient bravery they had accorded wounds and bruises. Nor could the livery of slavery detract from their stolid dignity; for all had been fitted with peon dress—straw sombreros, *guaraches* (leather sandals), cotton trousers girt up with a colored sash, shirts of the same material, that drew tightly across broad backs, deep torsos, and bulging breasts.

"What splendid fellows!"

The conductor indorsed David's opinion. "Prime lot. Look at that chap—six feet in his sandals, an' carries his two hundred pounds like a light-weight. A chief, I'll bet. The planter that gets him has his hands full, all right." With a shade of feeling, he went on: "Poor devils, none of 'em will look like that a month from now. All but fifty are sold to the tobacco an' sugar hacendados of the Valle Nacional, Spaniards, as cruel a lot as the devil ever spewed from the pit. Indeed, the Valle's known as 'The Hell of the Enganchador,' an' no peon will contract to go there—if he knows it. La señora could tell you both how he gets there an' whether or not the Valle's rightly named. She's told me tales that made my hair stand up, an' it don't naturally train that way."

"But have they no recourse?" David asked, as they made their way back to their own car. "Is there no law to which they can appeal?"

THE YAQUIS

The other grinned. "Law? There's mighty little, an' that's too much, for it's uncertain as lightning, an' you can only guess it won't hit a thousand miles from the longest pocket. If you get to feeling a hankering for law while you're down here, son, just fly back North an' let a nice American lawyer go through your pockets. He won't charge you extra for insults. T'other batch?" he said, answering another question. "Goes to a rubber plantation on the Amarilla."

Now, as Mr. Osgood's pamphlet had been prepared entirely for investors, David's single clear idea of Verda was that it lay on the Rio Amarilla. "The Amarilla?" he repeated, flushing. "That's where I'm going. You don't mean to say that they employ slave labor on American plantations?"

It was the conductor's turn to stare. "They work enganchars, mostly, though you'd hardly tell the difference. But say, young fellow, you surely haven't been investing in rubber? Why? Because there ain't any — not an ounce — in the Mexican tropics. There's experiments, yes, though none of 'em are what you could call a howling success. All along the Tehuantepec Nacional scores of the plantations are going back to jungle. Why? Overcapitalization, extravagant or fraudulent management, but mainly because rubber-planting, like any kind of farming, is individual business an' don't lend itself to company management. Mind, I don't say there's nothing in rubber. Any man who buys up one of them bankrupt plantations an' farms it himself ought to come out on velvet—if he has capital to run him along for six or seven years. But I don't see any of the managers, that ought to know, investing their savings in rubber. Steer clear of 'em—if it ain't too late. You're going to manage Verda? Oh, that's different. It's a new company, an' you orter be able to put a nice little roll in dry-salt before the stockholders quit on the instalments. You're new, so take my tip an' don't get too far behind your opportunities, for this climate ain't so damn nice that any of us are staying down for our healths."

This piece of worldly advice was delivered on the last platform, but before David could find expression for his dismay his companion stopped, pointing through the glass door. "Now, don't that beat hell! There's Mexican manners for you!"

In their absence one of the business men had reversed a seat of the section in front of the girl, and now sat ogling her. A gross man, stubby, his small pig eyes and brown chops were equally implicated in a grin so fulsome that David tingled to remodel it.

"The brute!" he exclaimed. "Ought to have his head punched."

"An' I'd do it myself—if she was American," the conductor agreed. "But she's Mex, an' 'tain't worth the risk of a knife in the ribs. Anyway, the old lady 'll be along in a minute to settle his hash. Here, where are you going?"

But David was already half-way down the aisle.

He hardly knew what he intended; was conscious only of the girl's red distress, of her glance which had touched himself. Dropping into the seat beside her, he crossed his arms on the back of the seat and leaned forward, aggressive chin thrust out, returning stare for stare at a range of a yard.

"Phew!" the conductor whistled. "An' me putting him down as a parson! By golly! Mexico's quitting already!"

A snicker passing around the car told that the passengers had noted the incident, and as, red and flustered, the man returned his seat to its original position, the *rancheros* burst out laughing. His defeat accomplished, David also rose, but before he could retire the girl jumped up, hand out-stretched, speaking rapidly in liquid Spanish. The conductor had praised her eyes. Now, while her soft palm rested in his, David saw himself twinkling in deeps of translucent brown, wide and tenderly soft. Conscious of a curious stirring beneath his ribs, he could only stand before her, red and confused, until the conductor came to the rescue.

"She's asking your name."

Repeated with her musical accent, his homely cognomen took an unsuspected grace, and while he was in full enjoyment thereof the door banged and the señora flowed up the aisle, a brown and threatening flood. Eyes one black glare under heavy lowering brows, she bore down on David evidently sus-

THE PLANTER

pecting an invasion of the faithless Gringo; but being informed by her daughter of his part in the affair, she whisked round on the starer, burst out in tropical stormings, under which the girl's pleadings ran like the patter of summer rain. The things she told him! David's blushes were saved through his lack of Spanish. Her threats! She would pistol him with her own hand! Call her *cabos* to throw him headlong from the train! But being dissuaded from this last and mildest intention by the *rurale*—whose single word sent the cowering starer to herd with second-class peons—she simmered down, the sun of her broad smile broke through her frowns, while she returned stately thanks to David. Also she bloomed with tropic flowers of hospitality. He must come over for a cup of chocolate! And while preparing the beverage over a tiny alcohol stove, she conversed affably and with a patrician ease that would have done honor to the colonel, inquiring solicitously both of his antecedents and present purpose in the *tierra caliente*.

As the conversation flowed through the mouth of the conductor, it took quite a serial flavor through his absences at stations, but the interruptions brought compensations in that they permitted private study of the girl. Seen *vis-à-vis*, her face proved every whit as delicate as in profile. A perfect oval in a frame of brown hair shot with a tangle of sunshine, its rich creams emphasized the scarlet of her mouth and added depth to eyes that were deep enough in their own right. It was one of those faces in which intangible mysteries dwell, tantalizing by suggesting unexplorable deeps of feeling beneath. Toned as yet by youthful ingenuity, it were easy to imagine its charm as developing into one of those remarkable fascinations which have, on occasion, set the world by the ears. For one, David already felt its force, and as the strange sights of the *tierra caliente* passed unseen in slow procession under the car windows, he came more and more under its spell.

Naturally this expression centred upon her eyes, and if he did not solve its puzzle it was not for lack of opportunity, for her glances freely met his, both during the lapses and while the señora was talking. A boyish frankness, however, robbed them of all taint of immodesty; nor were they more frequent than was to be expected, seeing that the fates had brought under their sparkling range a new type of the genus *homo*, one whose respectful timidity, after such gallant conduct, made his subjugation particularly enticing.

On his part, David displayed far more interest in the frequency and quality of said glances than was becoming to a disappointed suitor. If he thought of Kate Somers that livelong day, it was only to wonder what she would think could she see him now. For which piece of boyish conceit he was presently punished.

Nemesis took fat form in the señora. Gracious at all times, she passed, under the stimulation of the chocolate, from pleasant intimacy to motherly ban-

THE PLANTER

ter, and prepared David's undoing by asking the number of señoritas who must be lamenting the absence of such a fine young man. There was, of course, one in particular? She would undoubtedly be prettier than Consuela here, and possess a finer nose?

Now, as a matter of fact, Kate Somers' features, while pretty, would have appeared coarsely moulded in contrast with this girl's, and being suddenly struck with the fact David returned a vigorous denial to the latter half of the question.

So there *was* a fiancée? The young lady herself now took it up, nor could David's vehement denials, per conductor, dissipate a slight hostility that crept into her manner — the touch of disdain with which most girls regard a man who yields to the attractions of others than themselves. She developed, too, a penchant for teasing that kept him on nettles up to the moment when, after farewells that made him master of the señora's house in Ciudad Mexico, she left the car that evening.

While the Yaquis were being marshalled upon the platform she stood under David's window, and, had they known it, the same thought was in the minds of both. Her "Que importa? Si se ha ido," exactly complementing his "What does it matter? I shall never see her again."

As the train rolled on, however, she glanced up, softly smiling, and he took unnecessary comfort out of her parting salutation: "Hasta la vista, señor" (Till I see you again!).

III

LOS ENGANCHADORES

HITHERTO patches of tropical forest had alternated with open grazing country, the paradise of the *rancheros*, but within the hour the train plunged into the jungle proper. A ferment of life, it boiled and seethed on every hand, bubbling up from the fat, dank mould in endless variety of beautiful or fantastic forms. Creepers, climbers, parasites of a hundred orders twined, a mad arabesque, among the trees, which in turn shouldered one another away from light and air. A plague of orchids, like some beautiful leprosy, infested the latter in trunk and limb, burning unnaturally in mossy shadows, weighting the sickly air with cloying scents. The *bejuca*, strangler of the wilderness, ran everywhere, constricted its tough cables deep into the bark of wood of even the giant saber, from whose wide umbrella top it leaped hundreds of feet to the ground to writhe off and away after other victims. It was riot, vegetable war, plant against plant, tree against tree, and all against the railroad. Reaching out, monster briars clawed the car windows with curving thorns.

27

THE PLANTER

Like some ocean comber, the jungle curved over the right of way, roofing it with giant palms; hung, a perpetual threat, that might break at any moment and flood the tracks with greenery.

In open country the train had made fair time, approximating, perhaps, that of a third-class freight on an American mountain road. But here the trials and tribulations which had made the road's fame lay in wait. Twice did the train break in two, to be mended with ropes. Thrice the engine bolted the track, and was only persuaded back by the united prayers and work of passengers and crew. While graduating in train - wrecking, David learned, incidentally, how forcible one may be, on occasion, in such a liquid tongue as Spanish; also he scraped acquaintance with various insect pests. Through the muggy tropical night, lit only by the amethyst incandescence of myriad lantern-flies, the cars racked along, their wheels groaning curses at the execrable road-bed. Sleep was out of the question, save when the engine went into the ditch, and then he had to turn out and work. Daylight found train as tired as people. Withal, it clanked, rattled, or jerked through the heat of a second day, grinding rails and ties deep into the oozy soil, and at sundown pulled into the terminal.

While the conductor's conversation had tended to discount expectation, David had looked, at least, for a pocket edition of Vera Cruz, and, alighting, he stared dismally at the Chinese eating-house and the Mexican

groggery which with a few score *jacales* and dilapi-
dated wooden buildings made up the town.

A scant three years old, the feverish isthmus climate had so touched the place in thatch and wood
that in its combination of pioneer rawness and premature decay it resembled a degenerate youth who
achieves the senility of age before manhood's years.
Its palm-leaf roofs were sere and smoke-blacked;
weather blotches stained the unpainted station.
The Indian women squatting in split-pole doorways, their children golden blots in the dusk; the
peons drinking at the groggeries; even the pigs and
leaden vultures, helped to produce a composite of
heated squalor, of brown life, teeming and prolific
as the environing jungle. In vivid contrast he saw
Northfield amid its piles of scented lumber, sweet
and cool as a girl in a summer dress, and the memory
brought acute homesickness.

"Don't like the looks of it, eh?" A friendly hand,
the conductor's, dropped on his shoulder. "Well,
we can't take you any farther. Verda? Eleven
hours from here—muleback, you know. Too late
to start to-night. You can get a bed at the Chink's,
horses from Don Manuel at the store over there, an'
if you beat the sun to it to-morrow you orter make
Hertzer's, on the Amarilla, 'fore night. Come along
to grub." And, grasping the lad's arm with a friendly grip that almost squeezed out the homesickness,
the good-natured fellow led over to the store.

The horses arranged for, the "shakedown" proved

a *catre* (sheet of canvas nailed to a saw-horse frame and set up with two sheets, its complement of bedding, on the mud floor).   Hard as rock in comparison with his mother's feather-beds, David was so tired that, though reinforced by the quarrelsome gobblings of the Chinese waiters over a game of fan-tan, its hardness could not keep him from his sleep. The kindly conductor had bidden him good-bye ere he retired, and, as in a dream, he heard the cars roll away in the dark of the morning. It seemed, indeed, that he had barely closed his eyes before the Chinaman called him for breakfast. He was still eating when the Mexican *moso* brought his horse to the door, and an hour thereafter he was deep in the jungle, wrapped by the teeming life he had viewed from the car.

Having, as the conductor said, "beat the sun to it," travelling was, at first, very pleasant. Through dark temples roofed by curving palm fronds and hung with woven damask of creepers, the path now wound along a babbling *arroyo*, again emerged on an oak-studded clearing, to lose itself in a marsh. Twice they forded rivers—swift, silent streams that slid through tunnels of overhanging vegetation without ripple of laughing waters to give notice of their presence. A lurid gleam through thick foliage, a splash as a basking alligator took the water, and the horses would be in to the shoulder. Only the music of leaping fish spaced the heated silence.

The jungle, however, rang with life. Brilliant

birds flew, screaming, at their approach—noisy parrots and macaws; the *gaucamaya*, one flash of red and gold; a king vulture, raven black save for his scarlet crest. From the safe height of a saber, monkeys showered vituperations upon them. Once an *iguana*, great chameleon lizard, rose underfoot and dashed for the nearest water; again a python wound its slow length across the path.

Vegetation was equally gorgeous, always strange. He saw plants that stung more bitterly than insects, insects barely distinguishable from plants. Here a tree bore flowers instead of leaves; there flowers grew as large as trees. A "fly-catcher," the harlot of flowers, drooped like a white bell over the path with portals, pure as the snows of a virtuous woman, spread for unwary insects, and trumpet larynx leading down to inner chambers crimson as the halls of vice. Birds, beasts, flowers—all were strange, all wonderful; and as David rode along Romance peeped from the swaddlings in which his mother had smothered her, and illumed all things with her golden smile. Homesickness, pessimism, dropped away. Even the heat, that fell like a steamy blanket around him at noon, failed to damp his mood. He was still in the full flush of enjoyment when, midway of the afternoon, a high nasal chant rose in the jungle ahead.

"Los enganchadores, señor." The guide answered his look.

He now knew that the term stood for "contract laborer," and, remembering all that the conductor

had told him of the system, he turned anxious eyes
toward the long file, weird procession, which just then
came winding through the trees. Such men! Such
women! Peons of the upper Mexican plateau, they
lacked even a suggestion of the physical development of the Yaquis he had seen on the train. For
upon them the Isthmus had wrought its worst, rot-
ting them with its *calenturas*, thinning their blood
to a serum with its steam heat, poisoning them with
the venom of its myriad insect plagues. As they
drew nearer he saw not one face but that was pocked
or marred by eruptive disorders, not a body that was
straight and sound, neither a man nor woman that
walked uprightly. Yet though worn, wan, weary,
they sang as they flitted along like a trail of Doré's
dim ghosts, chanting, like the Israelites of old, their
deliverance from bondage.

For so the *moso's* next remark informed him.
"They are from the plantation of Señor Hertzer."
After a question addressed to the leader, he added:
"Their term is expired, and they return to Ciudad
Mexico, their pais."

Halting of its own volition, the procession had
turned yellow eyes on David in a look in which fear
was evenly compounded with the dumb pleading one
sees in the eyes of an over-driven ox. All were busily
searching through grimy, sweaty rags, and presently
the leading tatterdemalion fished out a paper which
the *moso* handed to David.

It read:

LOS ENGANCHADORES

"SE DA SU LIBERTAD

"Presecio Pena

"Por haber cumplido su termino de compriso con su trabajo personal en esta plantacion y para que no se la impido su camino, se le da este papel para constancia y su resguardo" (This gives to Presecio Pena his liberty for having accomplished his term of personal labor on this plantation, and he is given this paper in order that he may not be stopped on the highroad).

It hardly required the *moso's* interpretation to inform David that this was a manumittance from labor. The word "*libertad*" was sufficient. Liberty? What mockery of it was this when he, David Mann, but lately of Northfield, Maine, was detaining some thirty human beings upon the public highway. It was monstrous! Incredible! Yet the anxious faces plainly told that they felt their newly acquired freedom to be in jeopardy. Shocked, pained, he held the paper out to the *moso*.

"What have I to do with this?"

"It is the custom, señor." The man smiled, the greasy smile of the henchman the world over. "No enganchador may travel the camino real without a pass."

"Well, let them go on."

But the *moso*—but one remove from an *enganchador* himself, and liable to have that cancelled by sale for debt or crime—either misunderstood or was so inebriated by the unusual exercise of power that he did not hear. He was officiously pushing up and down the line when David spoke again.

33

THE PLANTER

"Let them go, I say!"

Still misunderstanding the words, the fellow placed his own interpretation upon the tone, and, leaning over, struck the nearest *enganchador* full in the face. "Carajo! will you keep the señor waiting!"

A light blow, scarcely sufficient to stagger a healthy man, it felled the miserable skeleton, and his cry, thin as that of an infant, yet pierced David to the heart, smashed through the ice with which Mrs. Mann had plated her son's emotions. Righteous anger flooded away the barriers she had built across his passions. Uttering a full-mouthed "Damn!" he rode at the bully and struck him behind the ear.

The first blow he had ever given in anger, he gave it with a will, thrilling to a gust of passion. But as he rose in his stirrups, swinging his fist, tingling to strike again, he glimpsed the *moso's* face beneath his raised elbow, and its ridiculous terror caused him to burst out laughing. Then suddenly realizing that the *enganchadores* were regarding his hilarity as another manifestation of his madness, and evidently believed themselves to be next for immolation, he quickly sobered.

Remembering the conductor's familiar cry at stations, he suddenly yelled: "Vaminos!" Incorrect in tense, the command yet proved efficacious. For, breaking into a shambling trot, the line vanished with the echoes.

But this was not the end, for the trail of thin ghosts had still its thinner stragglers. A half - mile

farther on David's horse shied at a foul bundle, which
proved to be a woman flat on her face in the mud of
a marsh. Her baby, a tiny brown attenuation, sat
a few feet away, up to its small waist in mud and
water. Yellow, fevered eyes, gasping breath, told
that the mother was nearly spent, yet the sight of
David was sufficient to inspire her with strength to
rise and stagger another mile. A second woman
fell as she turned from their path, and lay kicking
like a turtle, held down by the bundle across her
shoulders. Her ludicrous strugglings set the *moso*
laughing—that is, he laughed till David jumped down
and helped the miserable creature to rise.

"La calentura, señor," he then explained her gasp-
ings. "Has it very bad."

She was the last, nor was more needed to dispel
the smiles of romance, for thereafter the memory of
her rode like dull care at David's saddle-bow. With
the shadows of evening his doubts deepened, forebod-
ings grew darker, reaching their climax when, at sundown, he rode out on a sand *playa* and saw, darkly
outlined against a smouldering sky across the river,
the conical huts of La Luna, source of that stream of
misery.

He started as a voice, deep in its masculinity, answered the *moso's* hail: "Carmen! Carmen! Traiga
la canoa!"

IV

LA LUNA

RISING a hundred feet sheer from the water, the opposite bank loomed black against a fiery sky, and the *moso* had no more than stripped the horses before a cedar dugout, manned by an Indian, shot out of its shadow and ploughed a sable track athwart the blood-red reflections. Motioning David to sit with the *moso* in the bows, the Indian manœuvred the crank craft to bring the horses ahead of his pole and so drove them into deep water.

Now, though good swimmers, horses make heavy weather of it, and alarmed by the distressful snorts of his beast, David was pulling on the hackamore when the strong voice hailed again.

"You'll pull him under the canoe! Drop the rope! He'll swim out!"

"It is the Señor Hertzer," the *moso* whispered, and fear mingled so obviously with cringing respect in his tone that David looked up, startled, at the two men who were coming down a steep path to the landing.

It was easy to pick Hertzer. The big voice went

36

with his swinging stride, confident gait; was altogether foreign to his companion's precise, almost mincing step. Viewed from mid-stream, he appeared short, but the appearance was due to his stocky build, for he almost touched six feet. His face jibed with his voice. His large, coarse mouth told of appetites keen and brutal. Heavy brows overhung eyes vividly alive, but small and cold as bits of gray marble. Sliding suspiciously from under drooped lids, their glance indicated cruelty, which the strong grip he bestowed on David showed to be allied with passion. Summed, his face expressed his Austrian-Jew birth modified by American training, combining Slavonic heaviness with the thirsty acquisitiveness of the Jew, the whole toned by a dash of the reckless Yankee. Turned in at the collar, his white *camisa* revealed a hairy throat and chest; his rolled-up sleeves ringed arms equally hairy and bulging with muscles. The coarse body helped the coarse face in creating an impression of masculinity so intense that it would have been savage but for the grim humor that wrinkled his mouth. From these puckers a grin had spread out as he noted David's honorable but mistaken efforts on behalf of his horse, and a faint suggestion of it lingered to warm his greeting.

"Meagher's successor, eh? Glad to see you. Shake hands with Professor Phelps, here, your nearest neighbor. He's a Johnny Bull, but a good fellow, or would be if he could get the padding out of his system that he swallowed at Oxford. I don't know what the dickens he's doing here in the tropics, anyway. Ought to be nursing his professorship back in old England."

"That's only Hertzer's joke," Phelps demurred, as David addressed him by the title. "Over there we don't chuck dignities around as loosely as in your country; a professor with us is a 'varsity don. I did eat my commons at the temple—graduate in law, you'd call it. But everything's done to death over there—the bar, medicine, business—and when my governor acquired a controlling interest in Sol Suchia I was jolly glad to get the managership."

His "governor"! Parental influence, the force which scatters British fledglings broadcast from the Circle to the Equator, to fall like devouring locusts upon the world's high places. Everywhere one sees them, managing and mismanaging—mostly the latter —so exactly alike in leather puttees, riding-breeches, and exaggerated importance as though the product of a single father and tailor. Not that Phelps belonged to the worthless remittance type. His high, peaked forehead, sparkling eyes, indicated intellectual energies. But these merely emphasized his unfitness in that environment. The Indian boatman in his scanty cottons could not have appeared more foreign in a London drawing-room than he to the jungle. Of this, however, he was sublimely unconscious, and going up the path he exhaled egotism, manifesting his belief in himself as the centre of things by his domination of the conversation.

LA LUNA

"You came in by the La Plata trail?" he questioned David. "Then you must have met Hertzer's enganchars. What did you think of them? Looked ill? Well, I should say! We picked twenty out of the thirty to die within a month; didn't we, Hertzer?"

"And the others will never be worth a damn again," the Austrian answered.

With that decrepit procession still winding wearily through the chambers of his brain, David could not but wonder at the callousness implied by their indifference; but coming out on top just then his attention was drawn to the buildings—a dozen or so of *jacales*, which formed a small street at the beginning of a road that ran under lines of shading rubber from the river across the plantation.

The house—also a palm hut—stood farther back within the loop of the river, and so close to the bank that a stone could be dropped from the veranda to the water below. Rubber-trees shaded a path that led to the door through a garden, in which cabbages, onions, homely vegetables of the cold North, grew cheek by jowl with spiky pineapples, cocoa, vanilla, and other tropical plants. Roses, pinks, carnations shouldered vivid tropical flowers of a dozen orders for room about the house; a heavy perfume of orange blossoms stole across the gathering dusk from a thrifty grove.

"There isn't much left in *them*, either." Hertzer nodded toward a line of *enganchadores* in front of the nearest building.

39

THE PLANTER

Just in front of the field, haggard, worn, foul with the grime and sweat of the day's labor, they were, indeed, blood brothers to the scarecrows of the trail. With a gesture of irritable disgust, Hertzer ran on: "Rotten cattle! The money isn't in them. By-the-way" (he swung round on David), "you must have seen my Yaquis on the train, for I received a telegram yesterday from Tierra Blanca? You did? Then they'll be here in a couple of days, and I'll fire this bunch the minute they arrive. Better put your traps in the store for to-night." He suddenly switched subjects as the *moso* came staggering up with David's trunk. "Then you fellows can either go on to the house or wait till I see the gangs into the galera?"

"We'll wait." Phelps answered for both. "Yes, it's pretty," he replied to David's comment on the garden after Hertzer left them. "Trust your Dutchman to have his garden. While we fellows vegetate on tortillas and frijoles, leavened by a sprinkling of American canned goods, he wallows in fruit and vegetables—lives on the fat of the land. Really, he's the Sybarite of this howling wilderness. You wouldn't think it, to look at him," he added, "but he's positively luny on flowers. Scours the jungle for rare orchids, and will pay any old price for a fancy rose."

In view of what he had already seen the trait did seem remarkable to David, and the more he came to know the man, later, the more wonder it caused him. The æsthetic seemed so foreign to that harsh

face; was as grimly out of place as a flower which,
months afterward, he found growing out of the eye-
socket of a human skull. He had turned, curiously,
to glance after Hertzer, when his great voice boomed
out.

"Look at this fellow! Must have hid that sore
for a week! . . . Maggoty, by God!" followed a salvo
of Spanish oaths. And David was just in time to see
the offender, a wretched remnant of humanity, rolled
over by a vigorous cuff.

"He's curing the sick," Phelps said. "Come along,
if you'd like to see."

The tropics have no twilight, and that haggard line
showed as a dirty smudge in the dusk; but, drawing
nearer, David saw that all had rolled up pants to
the knee displaying sores and swellings which Hertzer
was treating with boracic powder, plastering it over
sweat and dirt.

"Granos," Phelps explained. "They're climatic.
We should have them just as badly if we didn't keep
clean."

"And that's what you call 'curing' them?"

Phelps replied by a shrug. "Primitive, I'll admit,
but you should have seen Meagher's practice. I saw
him one night treat calentura, a fistula, dysentery,
and rheumatism with the same dose of starch—ordinary cold starch. 'Ye'd be the better av a lick av
Christian Science ye'self, Phelps,' he answered my
chaff. ''Tis said that faith will move mountains,
an' health depends on mental attichudes, an' if an

enganchar don't know the difference, starch is the same to him as quinine an' a damn sight cheaper.'"

"Now, then! Andarle! Andarle! Off with you, every mother's whelp!" A second roar signalled the close of the function, and as chaff from a wind the miserable skeletons scattered — seemed to blow out and away from the booming voice.

"'The sheep know the voice of the shepherd,'" Phelps maliciously quoted. "Come on to the galera?"

Following the disappearing line, it brought them to the last and largest of the huts. Sixty feet long, thirty wide, it had yet been built in the cunning tropic fashion, without nail or scrap of iron. Bamboo rafters, braces, plates, all were bound in place with pliable *bejucas*. A couple of well-directed machete strokes would have let out the split-pole sides, but, guarding against this, a mesh of barb-wire covered them from end to end. Wire was also stretched over the rafters inside, forming a bristly ceiling that repelled all attempts on the palm thatch above. Fringed by a fence eighteen strands high, the *galera* was a huge cage—a cage within a cage.

Entering, David saw by the light of a few lanterns, which waged feeble war on the gloom, that a double tier of bunks ran down either side. In the lower a man could not sit uprightly; his head would have been torn on the wiry cobweb had he essayed it in the upper; and, to add to the discomfort, only a *petate* (straw mat) came between the occupants' bones and the angular palm-ribbed flooring. Though little larger than a modern drawing-room, fully fifty *enganchadores*—men, women, and children—were crowded into its dark maw, and in the tiers that stretched in the gloom beyond the lanterns there was room for as many more. As, passing in, the file paused at the iron kettles from which an overseer was serving rice and frijoles, the swinging lanterns afforded fitful glimpses of eyes sunken and fever-glazed, of faces livid beneath their dirt. In the five minutes required to serve the evening meal a sickening fetor loaded down the hot, dank air.

"But the women and children?" David said, as Hertzer locked the door. "You surely don't leave them in with the men?"

"Why not?"

"But they cannot have any privacy. Where do they wash?"

"Privacy?" Hertzer grunted, contemptuously. "They wouldn't thank you for it. As for washing, we march them down to the river Sunday afternoons. But let us go in. I'm hungry."

"That?" Phelps answered David's glance at a bell that hung in a tree-crotch hard by the door. "The velador (watchman), you know, rings it every half-hour through the night to show he's awake."

Dusk had now merged in night, close, oppressive as a nightmare, that shrouded the jungle across the river in inky blackness which was accentuated rather than relieved by the greenish incandescence of a myriad lantern - flies. Turning a corner, they suddenly came from thick darkness into a band of red light, and as Hertzer paused at a door to give an order, David obtained a glimpse of women, half-naked, kneeling beside the cooking-fires, who rubbed tortilla paste with heavy pins on stone *metates*. It flashed out a lurid picture in reddish bronze; then his stumblings continued till he stepped into lamplight that streamed between the house and outside kitchen.

Only that it could boast of a brick-tile flooring and had bedrooms cut off its length by partitions of matting, the house duplicated the *galera* in its inside features. Above the split-pole siding, the same serried rows of brown palm ribs curved up out of the lamplight into the gloom of the lofty apex. A few chairs, two lounges spread with native *zarapes*, a table and desk (the latter piled with Hertzer's papers and account - books), and a phonograph on a wooden stand summed the furnishings, which bore the earmarks of home carpentry. The table was set with iron-stone crockery, and from the chair that Hertzer placed for David he could see a woman and a girl at work in the outside kitchen over glowing charcoal braziers.

Even at that distance he could not but notice the vivid contrast between them and the *enganchadores* he had just seen in the *galera* cook-house. Instead of the dirty chocolate, the skin of the elder woman shone like beaten gold—had the rich hues that mark the pure Indian blood unmuddied by Spanish strains.

LA LUNA

A primal woman, round-armed, deep-breasted, her shapely amplitudes were such as Phidias dreamed of and tried to fix in marble. A loose white bodice clothed them, but was cut so short that her waist and bust showed whenever she raised her arms; a cotton cloth, blood red in color, clothed her limbs. Coming and going between kitchen and table, she moved with soft stealth on naked feet, carrying herself uprightly and with balanced ease. Though broad, her face was comely in outline, and vividly expressed that brooding motherhood, passion-of-animal tenderness peculiar to aboriginal woman. Her voice, answering a question of Hertzer's, had that soft refinement that had caused many a traveller in Mexico to glance out of his window expecting to see the best blood of Castile, only to find a couple of *criadas* (servant girls) exchanging the news of the town.

In color the girl was much lighter. Her skin rivalled cream in hue as well as texture, and when she bent to the light a yellow tide rippled through the brown of her hair. On a delicate scale, her features were Hertzer's: the nose less pronounced, eye passionate instead of cruel, mouth sensuous without his coarseness. Though slighter in figure than the Tehuana, she gave promise of the same voluptuous development, which fact caused David to set them down as mother and daughter.

"Hertzer's daughter," Phelps confirmed, when the Austrian went out to the kitchen. "The other's his woman."

THE PLANTER

"His wife?"

Phelps looked up in quick annoyance. "Look here, Mann, this isn't New England, you know. When a fellow has lived, like Hertzer, twenty years in the tropics, he's apt to follow the patriarchs a bit in the matter of wives. He's had so many, I doubt whether he could say which was Patricia's mother; but he doesn't need any one to tell him that he's her father. She's the apple of his eye. He had her educated at the Oaxaca Convent, so she has all the small accomplishments."

As aforesaid, David's youthful clay had been kneaded into some resemblance of his mother's pattern. Reared in a community which held a fiddler a suspicious character, and catalogued dancing among the deadly sins, it was perfectly natural that the looseness implied in Phelps's remarks should stick in his gorge. When the girl came in with Hertzer his bow verged on the imperceptible, his glasses gleamed coldly as lenses of ice.

"The prig!" Phelps thought. Then remembering certain beliefs and orthodoxies of his own that had frizzled under tropic heats until they resembled nothing so much as clinkered sins, he modified his harsh judgment. "Oh, well, he'll learn, and that, too, quickly."

The meal saw the partial fulfilment of his prophecy, for youth does not lend itself to bigoted condemnation, and the girl's refinement of speech and manner —bred of the convent— soon wore the edge off his first sharp judgment. As the meal progressed, more-over, he came more and more under the fascination of a nature that had been moulded by tropical environment out of all semblance to the average Northern girl, and as she could not open her lips without giving off a flash from some unexpected facet, she had for him all the charm and sparkle of a vividly new personality.

These feelings of his were, however, not unmixedly pleasant; they verged too often on surprise. For instance, he revolted when, springing up, she impaled a lantern-fly and pinned it in her hair, where it glowed, waxing and waning like some weird emerald; he chilled at her quiet comment on Phelps's grumblings over the laziness of his cook-house women — "Why don't you whip them?"—only to thrill and glow all over as she took a fledgling paroquet out of her bosom and showered caresses and endearments upon it with sensuous abandon.

"I found it to-day," she said, offering it for his inspection. "I shall teach it to talk."

Afterward he saw many native women thus nest fledgling chickens. One day his Tehuana cook produced eight which she was mothering until their rightful parent should have completed the conquest of a last refractory egg, and so he came to understand where the girl learned the practice and how common-place it must have appeared to herself. But now he blushed. Withal, he could not but feel her perfect innocence; and what with these lightning changes

of feeling, she impressed him very much as the orchids
of the jungle had that same morning—splendid, vivid,
flaming, yet so strange as to mingle revulsion with
admiration.

Having, on her part, but a limited experience in
white men, and none in the genus New England, she
found his staid quietness equally strange; but setting it to bashfulness, she was vastly surprised by his
blunt refusal to sit in to a game of poker at the close
of the meal. Pausing in shuffling the cards, she
turned arched brows upon him while she advanced
the only argument that seemed to her germane to re-
fusals. "We don't play large stakes. You couldn't
lose more than a hundred dollars."

A hundred dollars! Now, Northfield had its gam-
bler—a barber, in whose back parlor it was said as
much as five dollars of real money was won or lost
in a single evening. Three-card men, too, occasionally blew into town, but usually their shrift was short,
as they generally jumped from the fat of a private
mobbing into the fires of public justice. With certain other adventurous youths David had sometimes
played "seven-up" with beans, at an exchange rate
of five to the nickel, in view of which reckless experience imagine his surprise. Only a hundred
dollars!

It was a difficult situation—as difficult as callow
youth is called to face. Hertzer's glance of cold suspicion slid like a lance over the top of his cards;
Phelps was regarding him with dry amusement. A

touch of contempt was adding itself to the surprise in the girl's amber eyes. Yet, if he reddened, he returned a stout nod to the Englishman's question:

"Perhaps Mr. Mann's reasons are conscientious?"

Virtue had triumphed—not without wounds to the conqueror. Through a thick magazine, which he picked up from the lounge beside him, he felt the girl's curious glances. He could not stifle a feeling of meanness, and as later he noticed the absence of the wild excitement, greed for gain, which he had associated with the game, insidious doubts of the absoluteness of Northfield standards crept into his mind. Seated where he could overlook Hertzer's hand, he soon perceived that whereas he had thought the game to be one entirely of blind chance, it really required the constant exercise of skill and shrewd judgment. Twice he saw Hertzer lay down good hands, and, though the reasons lay beyond his inexperience, he felt they were governed by causes light as a wink. It was interesting, too, to note the difference in their playing. While Phelps rattled away, carrying on a lively conversation with the girl, Hertzer played a silent game, using signs to fill his hand, shoving the stakes to the centre without a word. Apparently indifferent, his gray glance took in everything; seemed, at each deal, to pierce down through the Englishman's dry imperturbability for the motives behind his play. As for the girl, she played like the eternal feminine the world over: flushed over her winnings, pouted over her losings; through all,

shed the glamour of her rich presence over the game.
If David had been invited to play an hour later,
Draconic virtue might have shed some of her laurels.
However, he was still looking on when, after a stage-
like clatter of approaching hoofs, two planters from
up-river dropped in, bringing with them a Missourian
rubber promoter.

Graduates of American universities, David was
drawn at once by the planters' frank breeding, but
he recoiled from the promoter, whose starey blue eyes
indicated a fulsome coarseness that cropped out in
his instant assumption of friendly familiarity, loud
laughter over his losings, pretence of nonchalance
at his winnings, his braggings about the blooded
games he had played "back in Saint Jo." The girl's
icy stare and Hertzer's swift frown checked his attempts at compliments; but neither Phelps's dry
sarcasm nor the planters' open jesting could kill his
mouthings. Continuing, they paved the way for his
downfall, which came when Hertzer, who was left in
with him on a jack-pot, paused to consider his hand.

Tired of looking on, David had returned to his magazine, but he heard the Missourian grumble: "Just
my luck. If this had been Saint Jo that pot would
have turned me something."

"Take your hand out of that!"

The imperative challenge brought David out of
the magazine in time to catch the Missourian's blank
surprise as, hand still out-stretched, he stared at
Hertzer across the table.

LA LUNA

After that considering glance at his cards Hertzer had dropped them, and now lightly drummed with his finger - tips, his impassivity contrasting strongly with the other's startled glare. Beside him his daughter sat, chin propped on both hands, red lips parted in the beginnings of a smile. The expressions of the others varied from bored disgust in Phelps to embarrassment in the planters.

"I—I—beg your pardon." Stuttering the apology, the Missourian withdrew his hand. "I thought every one was out."

"What was that you said about Saint Jo?"

Not to mention his neglect of the apology, Hertzer's tone was imperative to the verge of insult, and the fellow looked up quickly. It was, however, only a flash in the pan, and, shuffling uneasily, he replied, with a grin: "Only that we don't play no limit down there."

"That so?" Hertzer flipped a twenty-dollar bill to the centre. "Well, it's your call, and no limit but the roof. If that isn't high enough for your sporty blood, we'll go outside."

"Oh, I reckon it 'll hold me for a while." Laughing, the other glanced up into the brown gloom of the rafters, but his merriment was forced. "Twenty to play—raise you twenty more."

"Raise you a hundred," Hertzer came promptly back.

So far the Missourian had played from a pile at his elbow, but now he had to reach for his wallet, and as he unfolded it upon his knee David was in a position to see his fumbling fingers. "Come again!" he laughed, as he covered the bet, but returning from the centre his hand clutched the table.

So slight as to be almost imperceptible, the action was yet sufficient to account for Hertzer's sudden sparkle. "Hand me my check-book, Patricia," he said, and the grim puckers about his mouth spread in a smile as he noted that she had already taken it from the desk.

Several hundred dollars were already on the table— a large sum even for the reckless tropics—and while he was writing the others looked on in silence—silence so complete that David could hear the sputtering of the pen. Glancing around he saw that the girl was watching her father with glowing eyes. The planters masked excitement under a show of rolling cigarettes. If possible, Phelps had abated a little of his boredom. Sitting rigid, the Missourian looked on, while a greenish pallor crept up through his malarial sallowness.

"Raise you a thousand!"

Through another silence the Missourian stared at the check—stared while the *galera* bell troubled the hot night with its heavy tolling. One—two—three —at the tenth stroke flooding color washed out his pallor, and he burst out in whining protest: "Look a-here! I've four hundred in that pot already, an' a thousand's a large sum. I'm not doubting any one—" Stopping, he stared helplessly at Phelps, who was scrawling his name on the back of the check.

LA LUNA

"But I don't know you, either."

"You know me?" Taking the check, one of the planters scrawled his name beneath Phelps's signature.

"Yes, I know you are good for it, Mr. Ewing, but—" Wiping the perspiration from his forehead, he shuffled off on another tack. "I don't count it no shame to admit that I haven't that much about me. What's more, I don't reckon it good sport to jump a fellow above his limit in a friendly game. I'm a stranger—"

Hertzer had looked quietly on, and now he reached suddenly out and tore up the check. "How much have you?"

"About six hundred."

"Well, I'll write a check for five hundred." The puckers spread in a satirical smile. "That 'll leave you enough to gain home to Saint Jo."

But if pricked in his wind-bag, the boaster had by no means exhausted his shufflings. Blinking, he still stuck to his whining argument: "An' that's sure good of you, but I'm doubting my hand's worth it in the face of your stiff play. You see, I was allowing to call you this bet. Now if you let me copper your last for a—"

"Show-down?" Taking the word from his mouth, Hertzer shook his head. "It will cost you just four hundred."

Fading, the grin had left his face harsh and cold, so mercilessly cruel that its inexorableness penetrated even the other's thick hide. He threw his hand among the discards. "Well—it's yours. But you'll give me my revenge?"

"Sure!"

As Hertzer gathered the cards for a fresh deal, Ewing rose. "Leave me out. The moon's up, and I'm going for a breath of air. Will you come, Mr. Mann?"

David had looked on with an interest so absorbing that he started at the sound of his own name, and following down the garden path he saw every detail of the dramatic scene—Hertzer's fierce face, the girl's golden gaze, the promoter's craven grin — mirrored in splashes of moonlight beneath the rubber. His first remark, too, displayed curiosity more than the disgust that was to be expected from his training.

"Wasn't Mr. Hertzer a trifle hard on your friend?"

Ewing turned with a shrug. "He was looking for it, and Hertzer couldn't be expected to stand for all that brag. If he hadn't called his bluff, some one else would. He's no friend of mine," he added. "Brought letters to the plantation from our Chicago office, and of course we have to show him around."

He smiled at the artlessness of the next question. "Who had the best hand? Quien sabe? The Missourian was certainly bluffing or he'd have whacked up for a show-down. Hertzer may have been, but if he was no one will ever know it. No, we don't usually play so big," he laughingly explained away one more query. "I can readily see how, dropping in on a game like this, you might take us for dyed-in-the-wool gamblers, though it wouldn't matter if we were. What a fellow wins one night, he loses the next, and the luck strikes a fairly even balance at the end of the year. But come on, and we'll sit down on that tree."

From their seat they looked out over the river, whose double bow cut a huge initial — gigantic S— out of the sable jungle. The night-birds had stopped calling; even the *chacalahuas* (wild hens of the wilderness) had ceased their noisy cackle. So bright was the moonlight that each pebble showed like a black hole in the pale yellow of the sandy *playa* opposite, and, pointing at what appeared to be a gnarled limb, Ewing said: "Look at the 'gator."

"Where? That? Are you sure?"

"Just watch." Pulling his gun — a Colt's forty-five—he fired, and instantly a silvery spume, geyser of pearls, rose where the log had been, to fall and subside in lacey shimmerings. "Can't kill them," he commented, "unless you get the brain through the eye or the heart from behind the shoulder. However, the shot's not wasted. Teach him to keep clear of our bathing-grounds."

"You don't mean to say that you bathe there?" David asked.

"Of course; so will you to-morrow morning."

"But isn't it dangerous?" Afterward he learned that the saurians are as shy of man as any of the jungle children ; but before Ewing could answer

Hertzer's bass boomed out from the veranda: "Who's shooting? That you, Ewing? Quit it; you'll raise the camp."

"What a voice!" Ewing admiringly commented. "How do you like him? No," he admitted, "you haven't had time to judge, though I doubt whether longer acquaintance will help you. That Slav-Jew blood is a weird mixture. He's a puzzle. A perfect tiger with his enganchars, he's fond of animals, loves his horse next to his daughter, and, if rumor doesn't lie, killed an Indian who maltreated his dog. And he's a good neighbor—so long as it isn't business." Pausing to laugh over some memory that had instigated the qualification, he went on: "It may seem funny for me to speak like this, but, isolated as we are, we have to do a certain amount of trucking and trading with one another, and he's cinched us so often that we feel it a duty to put the stranger wise. So look out if you trade with him. Apart from that he's all right—hospitable and kind in his rough way. He nursed Meagher through yellow-fever—rather, he swore him out of it, for Meagher always said that he got well to spite him. And you can depend upon him in a pinch. Brave? He walked on his lonely into Carruthers' galera and took the machetes away from fifty mutineers. Then—you saw Carmen, the boatman? Did you notice his eye? Bad Injun, all through. He was stableman over at Las Glorias till he got drunk one day and laid siege to Phelps in his house. Now, it's no reflection on Phelps. I wouldn't

have budged myself while that drunken brute sat
by the door whetting his knife to a razor-edge. But
Hertzer, who happened along in the nick of time, kicked
him off the veranda without even troubling to pull
his gun." Pausing, he laughed again. "You bet it
was nerve, but right on top of it the Jew came crop-
ping out. While Phelps was still in his funk Hertzer
bought Carmen's store debt for a song, then ran him
eight hours ahead of his horse to the Jefe-Politico of
San Juan, and had him enganchared for debt to his
own plantation. Trust him to turn a penny out of
any old deal. But it was nervy, all right—nervy as
the deuce. Why, these woods are full of volunteers
—free Indians, you know; we call them that to distinguish them from the enganchars — whom he has
beaten or cheated. Yet he sits at night, lights blazing, windows wide open, and so far no one has taken
the dare. Yes, they'll get him yet," he admitted.
"Some dark night he'll step off his veranda, and—
plunk! a knife-handle will hit his ribs. In the mean
time he shears and drives them like sheep. But you
must be tired," he finished, rising. "I have to meet
the ranchero who butchers for the plantations here
to-morrow, so I stay all night. What do you say if
we turn in? No need to disturb Hertzer. He keeps
bunks rigged up for visitors in one of the out-houses."

Their way took them in among the huts which
loomed sere and black in the tender light, and, passing
the *galera*, the night wind brought them a whiff of its
fetor. A natural excitement over the evening's novel

experiences had abated in David the misgivings he had felt approaching La Luna, but issuing now on a huge sigh, the sleep breathing of the imprisoned laborers poisoned the night like an evil breath, transmuting the very moonlight into a sorrowful emanation.

At the house Phelps and the Missourian were quarrelling over a play, and just then Hertzer's boom drowned their wrangling: "Start up the music, Patricia!"

Came her laugh; but though earth knows nothing happier than girlish laughter issuing from lighted windows, it rang hollow in the shadow of that dark *galera*—sounded wicked, uncanny as merriment at a funeral. He could not but feel the dreadful contrast: laughter, light, good cheer — shouldering squalor, gloom, fetid despair; and driving it deeper arose the brassy blare of the phonograph, affronting the pale night with its prostitution of music.

He sighed his relief when the bunk-house door closed behind them. But he had not considered the bird-cage siding. The blatant strains filtered through, continuing until Phelps—who was also staying the night—came stumbling over the threshold. For hours thereafter he lay and stared up into the raftered gloom above a trickle of moonlight while the *galera* bell timed his tossings with melancholy tollings, and when finally he fell asleep it was to take his place in the miserable procession of the afternoon, to file with it through the land of dreams on an endless trail of sorrow.

V

IN WHICH THE SHEARLING FEELS THE WIND

THE crack of a rifle aroused David at daybreak, and, dressing quickly, he joined Phelps and Ewing on the bank outside just as a white belly flashed out of the water below. It showed only an instant, but that was sufficient; for a bronze body shot out from the bank and followed down, showing in the clear water foreshortened to the size of a frog. Then, out of a splash, Carmen, the boatman, emerged, upholding the fish in his hands.

"It isn't so much a trick as it looks," Ewing said. "You gauge your angle, and aim a few inches below to correct the deflection. Try your luck; there's a big fellow coming in to the bank. They're poor eating," he added, after the fish had scuttled away from the wide splash—"soft, like all warm-water fish, yet palatable enough after steady frijoles. Come on down for a dip."

Rising five minutes thereafter, the sun saw David dive from the identical spot whence the alligator had taken the water, and albeit he imagined the ugly beast tugging at his toes, he suffered no other damage.

THE PLANTER

Explosion best describes the sunrise, covering both the bursting of the orb from crimson mists that rolled like a conflagration over the silent jungle and the orgy of sound that followed. Parrots and macaws competed with the noisy *chacalahuas* in a chorus for which booming monkeys and piping wooddoves supplied the bass and alto; and in the midst of it the Tehuana's high, clear call announced the breakfast at which David ate with relish his first tortilla.

Patricia did not sit down with them, and toward the close of the meal a feeling so subtle as to be at first indefinable was beginning to assert itself as disappointment when she suddenly appeared in her bedroom door. Pausing to stretch in a languorous yawn, the sleeves of her kimono slid back, and David glimpsed polished arms, a mouth vividly red behind small teeth, loose hairs flying—an aura of gold about heavy brown masses. Falling into her figure, the loose folds added billowy voluptuousness to the sensuousness which exhales from a woman fresh from her sleep.

With a nod and a smile she passed out down the path to the river, and David did not see her again, for the *moso* had already brought his horse to the door. But the picture went and stayed with him. Always she appeared in his thought thereafter as he saw her that morning—luxurious, voluptuous, sensuously beautiful, yet vividly alive as a young tigress.

Ewing, whose plantation lay on the other side of

THE SHEARLING FEELS THE WIND

Verda, was to ride with him, but stayed at the stables to wrangle with the Mexican *ranchero*, who was cutting a beef carcass into rope-like strips to dry in the sun. So he rode out with Hertzer and Phelps, who were going to inspect some young rubber.

For half a mile the path led through clean rubber —beautiful trees, whose wand-like branches and rich tufted leaves drooped from the top, umbrella fashion. Passing through this planting, Hertzer constantly evidenced the trait that expressed itself in his garden. He seemed to know each tree—could recall at sight the cause which affected its growth for good or evil. There was something parental in his interest; the glance he turned on a sick sapling was tender as those he kept for his daughter—softer, in that it was devoid of animal love, the fierce, almost sexual, passion that coarsened his love for her. Carrying his saddle-machete unsheathed, he lopped useless limbs as he rode along, while his cold face kindled almost to kindliness as he talked theory and methods of rubber culture in the light of his own experience.

Here he had planted bananas, that the heavy shade might kill out the grass, deadliest enemy of young rubber. There he had sown melons and squash for the same purpose. Yonder he was experimenting with *cacao*, tapioca, and *yucca* for starch. But the hand of the practical Jew had bent each experiment to some present use: melons and squash would feed his pigs; bananas vary the diet of his *enganchadores;* the *cacao* served his own table, and brought thrice

61

the price of coffee on the market of Vera Cruz. Yet pride—the pride of work—dominated even that strong trait, governing his every gesture, rang in his tone as he reined in on an elevation and swept the prospect.

"There isn't a finer stand on the Isthmus."

The rubber certainly justified his boast. From their feet it ran off ruling thousands of acres without a break in the dark-green lines that drew to a point—narrow cape—where the huts rose, cones of gold, under the morning sun. Beyond and all around the jungle heaved and tossed its uneven masses, rolling in great waves off and away to break on the dim shores of a distant range. Here a scum of yellow palms flecked the green, there clump cedar thrust up like brown jagged roofs; underfoot a flame of flowers ran over the grass; and all was enclosed, hemmed in by an enormous cumuli—huge cloud pillars upholding a brazen sky.

Kindling to its magnificence, David asked: "Is Verda like this?"

"Well—not quite," Phelps dryly answered, and, turning, Hertzer rode on laughing.

A little dashed, David followed, but his enthusiasm would, in any case, have quickly died, for topping a second rise they came suddenly upon Hertzer's *enganchadores*.

Their line was strung for a quarter of a mile along the face of the *monte* (unclean rubber). Though, as Hertzer explained, this particular planting had been cleaned to the very dust six months ago, a dense tangle rose thrice the height of a man, swamping the young trees with its fecund life. Striking in against the cleared face, the tropical sun extracted its essences, heating the dank air till it respired like steam, in which frightful atmosphere the men worked shearing grass, shrub, and weeds close to the ground with heavy machetes. Barely eight o'clock, and their dirty cottons were already coated with a glistening scum of sweat. Their pantings could be heard at a hundred yards; yet if a man paused—be it only to straighten a weary back—a machete of one of the eight *cabos*, who oversaw the line, would drop flat across his shoulders. Exhausting labor in a cool climate, it was murder under the boiling sun; but Hertzer merely laughed as David remarked that no Northern farmer would work a horse in such heat.

"No more would I." Leaning over, Hertzer smashed a fly on the neck of his beast, an action singularly at variance with his answer. "For I'd own the horse, and there's the difference. I can only contract these fellows for six months by the law, but they can't leave till they're out of my debt; and what with the labor contratisto's fee, the railroad fares from the city of Mexico, and clothing that I supply them, that takes a year." With a frankness that almost sterilized his brutality, he added: "In that time I calculate to get everything out of them that is in. A man is never worth a damn again after I've finished with him."

THE PLANTER

"But is it necessary—" David was beginning, when Phelps interrupted.

"There's the point. It is. This may seem rotten bad from a humanitarian point of view, but ethics always did, and always will, give way to economic necessity, and with all its faults this is the only practical system. The world needs rubber, and needs it badly, for the wild supply is giving out. But you can't grow it without labor, for here the jungle grows eighteen feet in a single season—runs like a flood across the plantations. Of course, it's hard on the laborer; the enganchars die like flies in the rainy season. But, after all, it is only another and more modern form of the struggle for existence, and if they die, what of it? They are the thieves, drunks, and debtors of the Mexican cities—offal, you might say—and I really believe we do a service to mankind at large by transmuting their worthless lives into serviceable rubber. There's the point—the world must have rubber, and it is up to us to supply it, and you'll have to sink the humanities if you expect to do your share. Did you ever read Mr. Benjamin Kidd on *The Control of the Tropics*? Well, all this is foreshadowed—"

"Oh, damn Ben Kidd!" Hertzer broke in, impatiently, on the other's pedantries. "To hell with your evolutionary theories! All I know is that I've got to clean my rubber, and I'll do it if I kill the last peon in Mexico."

Afterward David came to understand their ineffable callousness; to recognize that constant exposure to suffering blunts sympathy, and that, inheriting the system from the Spaniards, the American planters had gradually passed from revulsion at its cruelties to blind acceptance as the only possible method. He himself was to feel the effects of usage. But at this first contact, while those fevered skeletons bent at their heavy toil under his eyes, he could accept neither the frank brutality of the one nor the dry sophistries of the other. Silent, he remained unconvinced, and just then Ewing rode up with the *moso* and pack-horses, and they proceeded on their journey.

"Remember that there's always an extra plate at my table!" Hertzer called after.

"And if you get stuck or need advice, I'm your nearest neighbor!" Phelps shouted. Then he turned, grinning. "What do you think of him?"

Hertzer shrugged. "A bit of a change after Meagher."

"I should say. Innocence itself. I think he was a bit shocked at your household arrangements."

"He was, eh? Wait till he sees your layout."

This time Phelps shrugged. "Rather—wait till he sees Andrea." And they both burst out laughing.

When, an hour later, David rode out of the jungle upon the said "layout," it proved to be a three-year-old boy and a girl of five with their mother, a shapely Tehuana, who gave them musical greeting from the door of Phelps's hut. The boy was almost as dark as she, but the girl, who rode at Ewing's saddle-bow across the plantation, combined Indian depth of eyes and hair with an almost Saxon fairness.

His remark, "Phelps's kid," fully explained the Englishman's testiness concerning Hertzer's patriarchal practice, and his further observations were equally illumining. "You'll see a good deal of this sort of thing down here, Mann, and I suppose that it is to be expected—at least, I don't feel qualified to judge, for I brought my wife down to keep me straight. But one thing is certain: you cannot throw healthy civilized men among savage women for long periods of time without detriment to the moralities as we know them at home. They are bound to take native wives, and if the practice ended there it wouldn't be so bad. The women are none the worse for it, because it fits in with their come-and-go ideas of marriage. But"—pausing, he patted the child's dark curls—"here's the hell of it—right here in Felice's small person. Of course, Phelps will do the right thing by her—as far as he can. Intends, at present, to have her educated as Hertzer did Patricia. But, to my thinking, that will only leave her in worse case. Sooner or later Phelps will go home—your upper-class Englishmen always do. Then what becomes of Felice? Without education, she would settle down in her natural sphere with some volunteer Indian; with it, there's nothing left for her but to become some white man's mistress."

THE SHEARLING FEELS THE WIND

Viewing the flower face, small, comely lines that protruded from her single garment, a wee white shirt, David found it impossible to conceive of desertion. "Surely he couldn't leave such a pretty tot?"

Setting her down, Ewing looked frowningly after her as she ran at full speed of her short legs back to her mother. "I have known a half-dozen who did. No, the best we can wish her is that Phelps gets out while she's still a baby."

Plunging again into the jungle, the trail dropped over a hundred-foot bank into a deep *arroyo*, first of a series that alternated with morasses in the stagnant gloom of palms and tall timber, and as, for another hour, the horses were either laboring, belly-deep, in sticky mud, or tobogganing down on bank on spread haunches to scramble like cats up another, conversation narrowed down to an occasional direction from Ewing.

At noon they emerged from dank, sticky shade, plunged into the bath of heat and fierce sunlight that drenched the Verda clearing, and looking over it from the *arroyo*, which formed the eastern boundary, David understood why Hertzer had laughed at Phelps' dry answer.

From low hills the land ran in hummocks and ridges to the river, which here wound through sand-flats. Around an unsightly jumble of huts, on a centre ridge, some fifty acres of year-old rubber reared its dark-green foliage from a litter of stumps, fire-scarred limbs, trunks of felled trees, beyond and around which small patch young jungle submerged the clearing. But of rubber, the vast and thrifty cultures of Mr. Osgood's pamphlet, David saw nothing.

"Used to be some—over there," Ewing answered his dismayed question. "Three hundred thousand trees?" Doubling in the saddle, he hooted and howled in derision as David quoted the pamphlet. "You might find ten—with a microscope. You see, the old company left Meagher without money for three years, and the jungle simply ran in and swamped the plantings. I went through it with him one day, and found perhaps fifteen hectares—forty or so acres, you know—that will pay for the clearing. But even that is badly set back. It would be better to let it all grow up for a second burning. Practically, you'll have to begin all over again."

"And he wants—my mother—to invest her entire fortune—in this!" David gasped.

Ewing was leading, and he whirled in the saddle. "Who? Osgood? He's the slim-fingered chap who came down to buy the plantation? Phew! Mann, telegraph her at once! You can send it out by the *moso* when he goes back to-morrow. And mind you pitch it strong. Why, if Verda was La Luna, with its fine showing, I'd advise just as strongly against the investment, for it has yet to be proved that the millions sunk in American rubber will ever come out again."

This was not all that he said. There was more, much more, and it was delivered with a heat that must have set many pairs of ears sizzling in circles of American high finance; but, as in his excitement he forgot a pregnant caution relative to the wire, it might all have been left unsaid so far as David was concerned. Had he warned him to have the Gringo operator charge it against the plantation, according to the custom on that river, the *moso* could never have yielded to the lure of five pesos intrusted to him for payment thereof. But as he did not, it may as well be stated here, as elsewhere, that the inquest held a week later by the Jefe-Politico of San Juan on such remains as came out of a drunken brawl with machetes, revealed not the slightest trace of either wire or pesos. As, however, all this was still of the future, the narrative goes on with Ewing's concluding remark:

"The work-folk are going in to dinner, I see. We'd better hurry, for we may have to break in on their rations."

Raising his eyes, David now saw just such another procession as that of the woods winding across the clearing. It seemed, indeed, that wherever he was to meet them the *enganchadores* resolved into files or lines, driblets of dirty humanity thinly streaming over the face of the land; but it had remained for this to break the back of his patience by the addition of a last cruel straw. For though they had bent for seven hours under the broiling sun at the toilsome machete work, each man was loaded down with a log that would have tried his freshest strength. Like a sick snake the line was wobbling in and out the stumps when the new master of Verda descended upon it and Maria Guadaloupe, the *mandador*, who walked behind.

Paced better describes the *mandador's* movement, for he swung in his gait like a leopard. Low-browed, broad-cheeked, his face was not unpleasing. His brown eye twinkled, and he laughed as a man stumbled; his voice, addressing the laggard, was low, almost caressing in tone. "Move a little faster, please?" A mother could not have spoken more gently to her child, but a tyrant imperiousness underlay the smiling surface; for when the man suddenly sank under his load a blaze burned out the twinkle, his mouth drew in a savage line, his machete flashed up and fell with a strident curse. Heedless of the dumb eyes, protesting quiverings of the worn-out body, he raised to strike again, but stopped as, with angry clatter of hoofs, David came at him as though to ride him down. But his advent was worthily described by the *mandador* for the benefit of Rafaela, his woman, at dinner an hour later:

"It is that he falls upon me like the winter norther, all blowing and blustrous, and talking so quickly that I who, as thou knowest, Rafaela, speak the Americano muy facile, comprende only the 'damns' until the Señor Ewing rides up to tell that this is the new manager in place of the Señor Meagher, and that I am to make the hombres cast off the wood—the wood, see you, that is needed to cook the meal! Was ever such a madness!"

THE SHEARLING FEELS THE WIND

Of such madnesses Maria was to see so many in the following weeks that his eyebrows took to roosting permanently under the eaves of his hair, where they now retired while he explained the cook-house need.

"Better let them take some of it," Ewing suggested; so after compromising on two men to a log, David rode on to make the acquaintance of Rafaela.

A shrill vituperation and thud of blows met them as they approached the cook-house, and, riding up to the door, David saw through a blue veil of smoke a woman, big and burly as a man, who was beating a thin slip of an *enganchada* with a stick as thick as her arm.

"She burned a tortilla, the hussy!" the virago grumbled, explaining to Ewing. "The beast fools too much time on her babe."

David's eyes had been drawn to the women who knelt at the *metates* and rubbed corn into paste with a movement very like, but infinitely harder, than that of a laundress upon a washboard. Outside the noon sun was dropping vertical rays upon the hut, adding its heat to that of the smoky fires; sweat rolled down naked breasts and shoulders as they slaved with the heavy stone pins, casting the while frightened glances up at the furious head woman. And now he saw three brown mites on piles of dirty rags over against the split-pole siding. Stark naked, they lay kicking feebly under the attacks of the *rodedores* (devouring flies), whose every bite brings blood. But whereas a single nip would have drawn a lusty howl from a child of civilization, the tiny creatures had already learned the lesson of that squalid life—to endure in silence. A writhing of their puny features represented their best at a cry; but though the mute woe of it would have brought a Northern mother rushing with tender cries, it produced only a glance of stealthy misery from the slaves of the *metates*.

"That's Rafaela." Ewing answered his question. "She's the mandador's wife, and bosses the cookhouse."

"Then tell her to give them time to look after their babies," David said, and so rode on with his sick heart toward the *jacale* which had been Meagher's house.

"Her daughter did Meagher's cooking," Ewing continued, following. "And you can't do better than keep her on, for she speaks a little English and makes a stagger at American cooking." Laughing, he added: "But you will have to look out that she doesn't put you in the same boat with Phelps and Hertzer. She's a raving beauty in her Indian way. There she is now, coming out of the outside kitchen. Ole! Andrea! Bring the key!"

At his shout the woman—girl, rather, for she could not have been older than twenty—disappeared, but came quickly out again and stood waiting, poised on a rich hip. As they approached she returned Ewing's nod, then took David in with a swift glance that embraced his personal assets from the brim of his hat to the tips of his shoes. The survey was apparently satisfactory, for her large black eyes, white teeth, red lips were equally implicated in flashing welcome.

"All that I have is yours, señor."

While she was fumbling the rusty padlock, David was able to add to his slower inventory a straight nose, broad forehead, clouding hair, skin fine as yellow satin, perfect arms and shoulders, and a figure that fluxed in soft moulds beneath her white chemise.

"Come into your house, señor?" she invited, throwing wide the door.

"It is just as Meagher left it," Ewing warned. "So be prepared for a bug or two." As two scorpions and a tarantula led a legion of fat cockroaches in a race for the palm thatch, he laughed. "You'll have to get used to them, for this is a country of insects. Muchos insectos, eh, Andrea?" And when she nodded, smiling, he ran merrily on: "To say nothing of roaches, which don't count, scorpions and tarantulas that do, there's pinilillas, rodedores, niguas, myllacuuillas, without mentioning ants and snakes. The first's a sucker, the second bites, third's a borer and carries his own corkscrew to insert himself in your tender places; the remainder—oh, well"—he burst into hearty laughter at David's grimace of repulsion— "it isn't half so bad as it sounds. If you turn your clothing inside out mornings, and empty the scorpions out of your boots, you ought not to average more than a bite or so a week."

THE PLANTER

Without insects the place was not too inviting. A small hut, it had the usual hard mud floor, split-pole siding, palm-leaf thatch. A rickety table, with dusty account-books piled between rusty pens and a dry ink-bottle, an equally rickety bench, a three-legged stool, and canvas *catre* summed the furnishing. And while David turned his disconsolate regard upon these relics of the late Meagher, Ewing rattled along with his merry chatter.

"It isn't exactly what you'd call luxury, is it? But just wait till we get our first rubber on the market. Teak floors, sir, and mahogany furniture — nothing too good for ours. And this will look more cheerful after your traps are scattered round and we get outside some grub. Now hurry, Andrea, and do your darndest. Afterward," he finished, as the girl disappeared, "we'll walk around and size up things."

When it appeared, the "darndest" proved to be a *chili-con-carne* of jerked beef, lean and stringy, tortillas and frijoles, helped out by a can of tomatoes, the last of Meagher's American stores. Hard enough fare after his mother's delicate catering, its stimulus combined with Ewing's gay clatter was yet sufficient to bring David out of his dumps. Romance, the errant damsel who had given him the slip in the jungle, returned to gild the squalid surroundings with her radiant effulgence. He noted the graceful curve of the roof to the high peak, and how nicely the serried rows of brown palm ribs harmonized with the pale yellows and greens of the siding. A sudden rubbing of his feet marked his endeavor to realize that the floor was really mud. His smile told of his delight in the fact that it was really he, David Mann, who was being served by an Indian girl in a tropical hut.

Be sure that Romance presently incarnated in the latter's ripe person. Leaning in the doorway, a hand on a rounded hip, she talked while they ate, drowning Ewing's questions in liquid floods of Spanish, yet, for all her volubility, she found time to observe David. Openly and by stealth did she study him —for she smiled if their eyes met without troubling to drop her own—and when afterward he and Ewing made a tour of the buildings, she watched them from the door of her kitchen; her glance flowed after, touching, enwrapping him with its question.

So busy was he picking up the threads of his new life that David did not see, nor would, in any case, have understood; but Ewing did, and the key to its dark puzzle inheres in a remark made as he paused, going home, to look back from the farther edge of the clearing. David had gone in to set his things in order, but Andrea sat in her kitchen door picking at a guitar, and as its melody throbbed through the clearing Ewing muttered:

"The tropics against New England! My money on the tropics!"

VI

NEW ENGLAND *VS.* THE TROPICS

NEW ENGLAND *versus* the tropics! How often has that battle been fought and — lost! For just as Nature here brought pause to the southward creep of giant glaciers in the young earth's time, so she has established her bounds against the invading blood of the Northman, reducing it with heated languors, lusts, and passions. South of Twenty, English, French, German, Spanish flux in a common irritable humanity that is distinguishable only by accent; even a Connecticut Yankee yields up his sterner individuality to the climate. All of which is merely preliminary leading up to the war waged by Mr. David Mann, of Northfield, Maine, against the Tropic of Cancer.

Accounts of the first round in that famous combat are by Maria Guadaloupe, who, albeit there unwillingly, was in Mr. David's corner and alone witnessed the fight. The fluctuations thereof had, as before prophesied, caused the *mandador's* eyebrows to retire within the purlieus of his hair, wherefore he needed only to raise hands to a corresponding altitude to express his unbounded astonishment to Ewing, who met him crossing Verda a few days later. His exclamation, "What is this they have sent us in place of the Señor Meagher!" must also be credited to wonder rather than inquiry, for without pause he proceeded with the iconoclasms of Mr. David.

First of the tale: he had caused water to be led by a ditch into a big trough by the *galera* door, besides which provision for morning ablutions Maria had standing orders to march all hands to the river for a swim at the close of each day. Next he had abolished that plantation institution, the Sabbath morning task; had lengthened the noon siesta by an hour; finally had brought confusion into the *mandador's* scheme of things by introducing piece-work—a hundred and fifty *metros*, lineal, of cleared *monte* to constitute a day's work. Lastly, he had set up a nursery, the women taking turns to care for the babies, and—here the *mandador's* expression of quizzical bewilderment testified to the cunning nature of the blow New England had placed in Cancer's midriff— a new *galera* was to be erected for the women.

Maria Guadaloupe's eyes bulged as he commented on this reform. "For why, señor? Was there not room and to spare in the men's galera?" But his eyebrows descended to participate in Ewing's grin.

"You think the mujeres won't thank him, Maria?"

"The señor will have his little joke." Sobering, he continued his complaint. "Then I am not to beat a man without permission—I, señor, who drove a hundred men in the Valle Nacional while this youth was nuzzling the breast of his mother. Carajo! how else shall one get the work out of them?"

"They seem to be moving lively enough," Ewing said, after a glance at the line.

"Si, señor, but for what? To make an end and gain back to the galera." Indicating a tall fellow who had slashed a lane into the *monte* ahead of his fellows, he snorted: "See Grande, there. The sun is still three hours high when he finishes yesterday; whereafter he takes his siesta in the shade, the pig, while I, his mandador, must needs stand in the sun and listen to his snoring. Is this proper, señor, for one who, as I say, has driven his men in the Valle?"

"Oh, a hundred and fifty a day isn't such a bad average, Maria. I doubt whether my fellows do it."

"But Grande would do two hundred, the beast, could I but lay the flat of the machete again on his back."

"He might—for one day," Ewing mused, as he rode on to the store where he found David immersed in an inventory of *chilis* and needles, maize, gay cottons, *aguardiente*, rice, and other stock inherited from Meagher.

"How do I like it?" he repeated, wiping the perspiration out of his eyes. "Oh, it wouldn't be so bad if it were a bit cooler. A hundred and seventeen in the shade this morning. Just fancy! That amount of heat would kill every egg in an incubator. If a fellow wanted to go into the chicken business here he'd have to raise them on ice. But what tickles me most is to see myself selling copas of aguardiente and cigarettes to the work-folks when they come in at night. Whiskey and cigarettes! Imagine the horror of the folks at home!"

His grin, while a little dubious, showed how far he had fallen below those difficult standards, and he laughed heartily at Ewing's account of the *mandador's* grumblings. "I suppose I do jar his notions, and, though he is too polite to say so, I'm sure he thinks the plantation is going to the bow-wows. But I couldn't stand for things as they were."

"Andrea?" Ewing asked, smiling at his earnestness.

"Oh, we're getting along fine. She's teaching me Spanish, and puts on such authoritative airs over the business that I'm quite carried back to my primer days and live in fear of a spanking."

"'I love, thou lovest, we love'? Of course she began with the conjugations?"

If David's merry peal had not been sufficient answer, it was corroborated by the girl herself, who came in just then for rice and peppers. Puzzle mingled with vexation in the glance she turned on David's unconscious back from the rear of the store, telling plainly as words that her golden opulence was not yet entered as an active ally on the side of the Tropic of Cancer. As she flowed with easy, flexuous movement out of the door, the calabash of rice splashed with blood-red peppers gracefully poised on her head,

Ewing broached the errand that had brought him out in the heat of the day.

"Hertzer's Yaquis came in the other day just after we left, and the canoemen who brought my maize up from San Juan this morning said there was trouble over there last night. They hadn't details; thought that the velador — night watchman, you know — was killed and that two Yaquis got away. I'm going over now, and you had better come along, for, if it is true, Hertzer will want us to watch the trails to-night."

The novel experiences of the last few days had left David small time for reflection, yet from between events the face of the girl of the train had peeped at him; nor had he found it possible to exclude her from the devoirs he paid at the shrine of disappointed love ere dropping asleep at night. Kate's face had acquired a disconcerting knack of merging in that of Consuela, and his sudden brightening could not now be regarded as a tribute to the former young lady. Too shy to ask if the señora and her daughter were still at La Luna, he made such a quick saddling that one hour brought them out of the jungle morasses upon Phelps, who was dismounting at his stable.

"I have just come from there," he told them. "Yes, Ilarian was killed. We don't know how, but suppose that he either went into the galera of his own accord after lock-up, or was enticed by a Yaqui woman. Anyway, his screech roused the camp, and when Hertzer got there he found Ilarian flopping around on the floor like a dying chicken, neck cleanly wrung, face staring up over his shoulder. You know, Hertzer sleeps like a cat, so only two escaped, a man and a woman, and he's certain that he winged one, for a cry followed the shot he sent after them through the fence. Hope he did. It would never do to have them get away; the others would be forever bolting. I was out all night on the river trail, and have to watch again to-night, so you fellows had better trot along, for I'm dying to sleep. Say, Mann," he called after them, "there's a girl over there who knows you —or was. I understand they were to leave to-day. If half of what mamma says is true, you appear to have been going it some. She's posting you as Sir Galahad—perfect, brave, and true. Look out, old man, or she'll be letting you in for a mother-in-law."

"Some people I met coming down," David answered Ewing's quizzical look. "I rendered them a small service. The remainder is all his fooling."

But if he was able to turn off Ewing with this fair show of indifference, his anxious colors instantly betrayed him to Patricia, who slid from a hammock under the veranda as they came up the garden path an hour later. She smiled as he glanced quickly at the screen door in passing, and an alloy of disdain mingled with her merry teasing.

"No, señor, she is not there. Oh, *what* a frown! Is it so bad as that? Now, if I had only known—I might have sent for you." Observing a mocking pause, she went on: "Would you really like to see her? Oh, look at the sun breaking through the clouds! For that you *shall*. Come here." Leading him to the edge of the veranda, she pointed down. "Now, look. Ola! Consuela!"

As before noted, the bank dropped from the veranda a hundred feet into the river, sheering so precipitously that one could easily have dropped a stone into a canoe that had just cast off from the landing. A big dugout it was, one of the slow fleet whose units crawl like alligators up the warm streams of the tropics to disgorge knives, machetes, gay cottons, and other contents of their wide stomachs at Indian villages and lonely plantations. Along its flat plank gunwales two Indian boatmen marched, bearing hard on long punt-poles, propelling the boat with the spurn of their feet.

"They brought up my corn," Ewing said. But David heard neither that nor Patricia's giggling comment that la senora had preferred the river to a pacing mule out of tenderness for her fat. It is doubtful whether he even saw that lady waving her pudgy brown fists in frantic greeting. His eyes drew at once to the face that turned up, startled, at Patricia's call.

"Como esta usted, señor?"

How went it with him? Alas, Andrea's lessons had not touched on salutations! Though a smile flashed up with the greeting, he could only wave and watch the clumsy craft speed with unexpected and lamentable swiftness down-stream; watch the face with its clouding mystery lessen and fade till only by bulk could he distinguish mother from daughter.

It was not his first experience in departures. But whereas the pain of others had been drowned in noise of bells, hiss of steam, rush and roar of speeding trains, there was something infinitely lonely in this silent drifting. It was like the passing out of a life. The parting blast of the boatman's conch-shell floated back from the bend, lugubriously mournful. And whether or no these unusual conditions intensified his mood, he was conscious of, even wondered at, a feeling of regret that was out of all proportion to their acquaintance.

"I shall never see her again," he had told himself, looking down on her from the train. Now disappointment caused him to add, "I wish I had not," and was itself wiped out the next moment by chagrin.

While he stood at gaze the amusement had faded out of Patricia's smile, leaving disdain in command of her mouth, and as the canoe now veered at the bend, she suddenly exclaimed: "She's kissing her hand! Answer! Quick, or you'll be too late!"

For all he knew it might very well be a custom of the country, and she afforded him no time to think. "Quick! Quick!" Then as, following his answer, the far figure turned with a gesture that even at the distance was eloquent of anger, she burst out laughing; laughed, bending and throwing up her hands in the uncontrollable merriment of a child or savage; laughed pointing, a slim finger at David, who did cut something of a ridiculous figure standing with hands out-stretched, as though to drag the canoe from behind the bend.

"Oh, why did you do that?" he flung round upon her. " She meant it for you."

But she merely laughed the more—laughed answering Ewing's questions. "What is it all about? You should have heard la señora tell—how by the fire of his eye Señor Don David did put to flight a burly rascal, the insulter of her daughter. It was equal to the best page of *Don Quixote*. And the pretty señorita? Though she frowned at mamma's flowery version, she plainly approved of Don David."

"And you must needs spoil their romance?" Ewing scolded. "Of course we know that these green temples are dedicated to your worship." He waved at the jungle. "But I wouldn't be so unblushing in putting out my signs."

"I? Jealous?" She bridled in mock anger. "I? Who just gained him a kiss? I am sure that Señor Mann will acquit me of the charge?"

But David was too sore to return aught but a serious face to her smile. "Was it necessary to make me act like a cad?"

A trifle nonplussed by his sternness, she regarded him uncertainly for a moment, then slipping back into the hammock, she swept her skirt about her ankles with a movement which, while modest and deftly feminine, somehow seemed to accentuate her natural sensuousness. "Do you feel so *very* badly?

Then I apologize. I'm sorry, very sorry, for my foolish prank. And, really, we would have sent for you only that father has had all of the cabos away with him in the jungle ever since the escape."

Leaning upon a white elbow, she smiled in his face. He could not but see the red lips parted in tender, if affected, contrition; but the Anglo-Saxon reserve caused him to shrink and stiffen against her glowing seductions. "She asked for me?" he coldly inquired, and replied, when she shook her head: "Then there was no reason for you to send."

While he looked stiffly out over the river, she turned arched brows on Ewing, who silently worked his lips. "Serves you right."

She made a face, then, after a half-minute's study of the straight back, she asked, in tones of hurt contrition: "Then I am not to be forgiven?"

"If you know the young lady's address you might write and ask it."

Again she looked at Ewing, who telegraphed: "Now, will you be good?"

"Watch me," she breathed. With pathetic seriousness that set Ewing off in a spluttering roar, she said: "I certainly shall. What would you have me say? That—that you intended it for mamma?"

If bent by training a bit toward the solemn, David was not devoid of humor, and now he joined Ewing's laugh. "Suppose we call it off. None of us are likely to see her again."

But if, with a laugh, the incident thus passed, it

left neither he nor Patricia in quite the same relation. He had obtained a second glimpse of the savagery that had manifested itself in the impalement of the lantern-fly, and the flash was the more vivid with himself in the part of the beetle. On her part, she could not but feel the small part her beauty had played in making him overlook her prank. For the first time since their full flowering her charms had failed of their natural purpose in the subjugation of man, and his contumacy excited her interest. Whereas she had noticed him before only to laugh at his spectacled sedateness, she now gave him stealthy attention up to the moment that Hertzer came in, hot and tired, from a fruitless hunt. And if her interest took more after that of a cat in a mouse than the healthy curiosity of a maid toward a possible husband. it was none the less intense.

VII

THOUGH Phelps had told them that Hertzer was angry enough to murder the runaways out of hand, disgust governed his action more than passion as he tossed his pistols and machete aside.

"I'm sick of this sort of thing," he grumbled. "Two days, and not a man at work in the fields. I'm going to send to New Orleans for a brace of bloodhounds. One pair would do for all the plantations on this river, and we can share the expense. No, didn't see a sign of them; but we'll get them sure tonight."

Now it had seemed to David that a man would be more completely lost in the labyrinthian jungle than a needle in the traditional hay-stack, but they all laughed when he stated his doubt. "You see," Ewing said, "the jungle is just a tangle away from the trails, a web of bejucas criss-crossing thick brush. Their only chance is to follow an arroyo down to the river and try to steal a canoe. But as they are sure to know that the canoes will be watched, they are more likely to try the trails."

87

THE PLANTER

"Of course they'll try to work around the plantations," Hertzer added; "but they can't make any headway without machetes. It's a cinch that they haven't more than passed Phelps's in the one direction or Carruthers' in the other. This is their second day without food, so if you fellows will take care of the trails between your places, we can't miss them."

"How do you like the idea of a man-hunt?" Ewing asked.

The question startled David, brought him excitement vivid as that which gripped him when, years ago, he had sat up and shivered from the dread interest of *Uncle Tom's Cabin* as much as the absence of the blankets which hid his night-light from his mother's careful eye. At first the romance of it dazzled him, and he listened eagerly while Hertzer and Ewing discussed probabilities in the light of other escapes. Thinking of the hunt, he lost sight of the hunted until a remark from Patricia stripped away the golden haze of romance, exposing the ugly truth.

"Will you flog them, padre? You remember, you said that if you ever caught a runaway who was strong enough to stand it, you would make an example of him that would last forever?"

"Will I?" Hertzer was sitting astride his chair, and now leaning on his crossed arms the position emphasized the peculiar forward angle, characteristically Jewish, at which his neck came out of his shoulders. Big head lowered and thrust out added a suggestion of thirsty cunning, animal baseness to

his naturally cold cruelty. "Will I? This chap is
the biggest Indian I ever saw. The others tell me
that he was a chief up in his own country, but that
won't save his hide. Chief or no chief, he'll have to
go the road."

"A chief in his own country?" Then it must be
the great Yaqui of the train. David recalled the
conductor's remark, "*The planter that gets him has
his hands full,*" and there came flashing into his mind
two pictures—the Indian in all his magnificent muscularity side by side with the woman who had dropped
by the trail, wretched remnant of contract slavery.
And to make of the former such a one as the latter
was the business to which he had just engaged.

If he had been asked just then to join the hunt he
would surely have declined. He intended, indeed,
to take the first opportunity to do so. But however
well endowed in the matter of jaw, youth is ever
doubtful of itself, and before an opening offered the
thought of his own fifty skeletons rose to paralyze
the righteous impulse. Who was he to cast stones?
A driver of *enganchadores* himself, forsooth, likely
to have runaways of his own. Still, if he did not act
on the reflection, it filled him with distaste. He
turned a reluctant ear to their further plannings.

Stretching his club-like arms, Hertzer rose, yawn-
ing, after half an hour's talk. "Now I must turn in
and get some sleep. It's too hot for you fellows to
start out just now. Better take a siesta here on the
veranda, and ride out to your stations after an early

supper—or if you feel like bed, the bunk-house is ready."

"Too stuffy," Ewing objected. "This is good enough for me."

As regards heat there was little to choose between house and veranda, for not a breath of air stirred beyond the brown shade of the eaves. So hot it was that a python skin which was curing on a board crackled as it shrank and pulled, one by one, the tacks along its fifteen feet of length. Stepping out to examine it, David experienced a shock as though he had plunged into a hot bath. Sunlight fierce and yellow as flame beat on and about him, drenched the plantation with heat heavy as a fever. The street between the buildings, paths, the road under the shading rubber, burned like throbbing arteries; save the low mutterings of the Yaquis prisoned in the *galera*, no sound broke the somnolent silence. Eminently suggestive of delirium, those uneasy mutterings rhymed with David's reflections and were not to be drowned by the heavy snoring which presently issued from Hertzer's room. After Ewing, too, had fallen asleep in his hammock—Patricia had followed her father inside—he walked over to the *galera* and peeped through the split-pole siding at dark, desperate figures pacing in the black shadow, restless, uneasy, as animals in a cage.

The sight was not calculated to soothe his troubled reflections, and returning to his chair on the veranda he looked out over the river at the jungle slumbering in tremulous heat. Other than the occasional splash of a fish, there was nothing to disturb his thought, distract his attention from the attacks of conscience; and as that article was of the robustious New England variety, it led him a lively dance up to the moment that Ewing woke up and looked at his watch.

"Five o'clock, bah Jove, as Phelps would say." After a glance through the screened window, he added: "And Rosa is setting the table for supper. We'd better go out and see that the horses get their maize. Likely as not Carmen's woman is already grinding it for her tortillas."

Returning, they passed the *galera* cook-house, and as they came opposite the door Ewing nudged David. Inside two women squatted with a dish of frijoles between them, from which they were eating, using bits of tortilla for spoons. The swart Zacateca who faced the door was Hertzer's head woman, but David would have passed without recognizing the other if a slight turn of the head had not revealed Patricia's profile. Having slid quietly out after her siesta, she still wore her kimono, a loose garment of a red so brilliant that it flamed in contrast with the duller crimson of the others' vestures. Down its fire her hair flowed to the mud floor, sweeping it, stirring the dust as she reached to the dish.

"Gee!" David breathed.

His wonder was not due to her presence there. She might be on some errand. But the squaw pose, animal habit of eating! Her dishevellment, evident

91

ease in the smoke and dirt of the hut! And he had caught her speech, even and rapid, the garrulous flow peculiar to the gossip of Indian cronies. Shedding manners, culture, all that she had learned in the convent, she had gone back a thousand years to her mother's people.

"Astonishing? Not a bit," Ewing said, as they walked on. "Train them, educate them to the limit, but you can't smother the savage. You ought to have seen Mrs. Dutton—white as you or I, played the piano, guitar, spoke three languages besides her native Spanish; yet as soon as Dutton went off to the fields she would slip off to the galera cook-house to squat on her hams and eat tortillas. Of course she was lonely. But our women don't do it, nor the pure-bred Spaniards. Did it because she liked it. And you ought to have seen her face. Naturally refined in type, her lips seemed to puff out, her eyes darkened, and from clean Spanish she would drop into the broad Indian locutions. You would hardly have recognized the woman who sat with us at table."

It was equally difficult to recognize the vivid barbarian of the cook-house in the demure girl who poured their tea half an hour later. While a soft dress of white toned her richness down to maiden simplicity, her solicitude for their wants was perfect in its quietness; the sisters of the Oaxaca Convent could not have improved upon it. Now, the most stupid of men could not but have marvelled at a nature which could thus put the habit of civilization on and off with its outer garments, and David, who was by no means stupid, greatly wondered. He caught himself searching amid the inflections of her speech for the taint of her recent garrulity, but failed to find it. In trying for physical revelations of her other savage self he was more successful—or thought that he was. Only that morning Ewing had told him that the eyes of snakes shone red in the dark, and he shivered when, looking back as they rode away, he saw the amber lights of her eyes resolve into filmy red, faintly luminous in the dusk of the eaves. It was weird, uncanny—gave him a feeling such as he had not experienced since the days of his childish belief in wizards and witches. He wondered if she could see in the dark.

Hertzer had not appeared at the meal, but he thrust his head, all shaggy and tousled, out of the door to bellow after them: "By-the-way, Mann, have your mandador stand watch and watch with your cabos over the canoes to-night."

"'Watch and watch'?" David commented, as they rode on. "One would think that he had been a sailor."

"He was," Ewing answered. "He was born in Trieste, the Austrian port on the Adriatic, where his father, a half-breed Jew, ran a sailors' boarding-house. Such places are never quite what you would call forcing-beds for virtue, and if one-half of what Hertzer tells about it be true, the place had 'Fisher's Boarding-house,' or Kipling's ballad, heavily discounted. From murder to plain ordinary crimping, everything went, but Hertzer proved too unruly even for those generous limitations, and his father shanghaied him at seventeen, sold him for twenty dollars to a vessel outward bound around Cape Horn. He—"

"His own son?" David interrupted.

"His own son; threw him in extra with a batch of drugged and drunken sailors. 'I never blamed the old chap, either,' Hertzer always says, telling the story. 'It was the only profit he ever made on me, and it takes a man of parts to sell the prunings of his family tree.'"

"But his *own* son?" David repeated.

Laughing at his shocked surprise, Ewing went on: "Anyway, he didn't prove much of a bargain. Both skipper and mate were of the old truculent school, but whereas the vessel was known previously for a 'hell-ship,' the brimstone began to bubble forward as well as aft when Hertzer regained his senses. The first day out he struck the mate, and though never a day passed thereafter without his being beaten to a blue jelly by one or other tyrant, he fought back like a cornered wharf-rat, kicked, bit, chewed, swallowing punishment like candy. And he was dangerous. Once he dropped a marlinspike from aloft and cracked the skipper's hard pate. His knife whizzed from black darkness one night and stuck in the cabin door close to the mate's ear. After that he supped on blows—breakfast, dinner, and tea. Indeed, from Cape Verde to Rio Janeiro you could have traced the ship by the continuous sound of cries and curses. Yet when the brace of bullies were stricken with yellow-fever, and the crew put the vessel in shore and deserted *en masse*, he stayed and nursed them through it.

"Why? God knows. Hadn't got his bellyful of fighting, I suppose. Says himself that he intended to kill them, and hated to have Yellow Jack beat him to the job. Anyway, if he was looking for fighting, he found it in plenty, for they made him second mate after they had worked the vessel back to Rio and had shipped a crew from the government jail.

"Think of it! That the men were not to be allowed to land on South American soil was the one stipulation of the Brazilian authorities, and fancy the two burly ruffians with that tigerish lad driving that gallows crew of thieves, bandits, assassins—landsmen all—driving them, too, with blows and curses. For pure desperation it beats the buccaneers. No one knows how many of them they killed, nor does it matter; they only robbed the gallows. The wonder is that they worked the vessel around the Horn to Valparaiso and back to New Orleans, where both Hertzer and the remnant of rascals unloaded themselves upon poor old Uncle Sam.

"The next year he spent in the States, engaging in occupations that ran from bar-tending in New Orleans to the smuggling of opium and Chinamen into San Francisco. He even ranched out West, but the plains could not hold him. At twenty-five he was back in the free-and-easy tropics running trading

ventures up the rivers from the Gulf, from which he
stepped naturally into the rubber business ten years
ago. In that time he has been with three different
companies; La Luna's the fourth. And—there's no
scandal in this, Mann, the facts are known to the
country—between cheating his enganchars and the
pickings of the wrecked companies, he's pretty well
off—so well off that he'll probably buy up La Luna
if she goes the way of the others."

David, who was riding ahead, checked his horse.
"You don't mean to say that—he cheats those poor
wretches?"

"Don't I? Well, you remember the batch that
you met coming in? I was there when he paid off.
Not a man received more than twenty per cent. of
his dues. Do you know what the beggar is doing at
the present moment? Sends out the others whose
time is nearly expired to work by themselves in the
field. Only this morning he was complaining to me
that they wouldn't run away."

"And Phelps?" David asked. "Does he—?"

Ewing nodded. "It's quite general. Enganchars
are fair game for everybody."

"And—you?"

Ewing laughed a little shamefacedly. "Well, you
see, as I told you before, I brought my wife down
with me, and her strict notions keep me from living
up to my opportunities. We'll never be rich. By-the-
way, she charged me to invite you to dinner next Sunday. You must come, for a fresh face is a godsend."

Whether or no he intended to change the subject, David did not renew his questions, and they rode on in silence up to the moment they met Phelps coming out from his own place. What with two Colt's forty-fives, a machete, and the Winchester carbine that swung at his saddle-bow, the Englishman was an arsenal in his own person, and he laughed, patting the carbine at Ewing's joke.

"Comes handy—either to pot jaguars or for a shot at a running man." Then, noting David's weapon-less condition, he exclaimed: "Mann, where *are* your guns? You *haven't any?* Good Lord, haven't you yet learned the first of the tropic commandments, 'Thou shalt not leave thy house unless well heeled'? To say nothing of wild animals, or a volunteer Indian with a knife, there's always the off chance of a mutiny among your enganchars. Here, take this of mine! And if his nibs falls to you and fails to throw up his hands, shoot as quick as the Lord will let you."

With this bit of pleasant advice, Phelps left them, but paused at fifty yards and called Ewing back to whisper. "Look at him! Handles it like a music-roll; and he's going after a man who cracks necks like peanuts. For Heaven's sake, Frank, show him the business end and have him let it off."

"It does look like a cannon—on him," Ewing chuckled.

It felt so to David at first, but he soon grew used to its thumpings, and uneasy tolerance presently merged in swollen pride when, under Ewing's direction, he succeeded in hitting a tree at a dozen yards. It was a large tree, and truth compels the statement that he did not repeat the feat, but he made a good deal of noise, and in the excitement attending the practice, he forgot its object, and had cess of the attacks of conscience until they reined in on the farther bank of an *arroyo* at dusk.

It was situated about half-way between Phelps's place and Verda, and it did not require a second glance to explain Ewing's meaning. "This place is as good as any." For everywhere the bejuca spread its spider web, tangling trees, palms, brush in a woven mat, beneath which the *arroyo* ran as through a tunnel.

Indicating a saber whose buttressing rocks formed a giant arm-chair, he continued: "Whether they come down this arroyo, or one nearer to Phelps, they must pass this way, so you had better camp here, close to the trail, for naked feet make little noise. Of course, it is possible that they have worked around Verda, in which case they'll fall to me. But if you do get them, remember—no fooling. Shove your gun into the man's stomach, and if he moves let drive. A shot will bring me or Phelps. We'll hear all right, for sound travels a dickens of a distance at night. Your horse would only give you away, so I'll take him along and leave him with mine at your stable, then walk on to my station. Pity you couldn't have Guadaloupe for company, but he'll have to watch the canoes. Anyway, it wouldn't be much gain, for these Indians are nervous at night; he'd keep you on edge all the time. And really there's nothing to be afraid of. Jaguars seldom attack a man, and other animals don't count." Despite this cheery assurance, he muttered to himself as he rode on through the falling shadows: "Hope he believes it. It's mighty nervous business, and I don't half like it."

Though his pride would not have admitted the fact, neither did David, yet he kept his nervousness well in hand, and turned a composed face to the dusk settling like a mist among the trees. The hour brought with it none of the cool peace of a Northern twilight. Sickly breath of luxurious vegetation oppressed the hot air, and there was at first much noise —booming of monkeys, chatter of parrots, clamor of macaws. Through a siren whistling of beetles, shrill, insistent, torturing to the ear, came a cry, strident though muffled, and instinct thrilled to the voice of a tiger. But silence came with darkness, mirk night that fell hot and stifling as a black fever, and he was left staring up at great palm-fronds which hung like curved scimitars in a web of *bejucas* against the sky.

Then it was that conscience spoke with a still small voice upon the hush, bringing a recurrence of doubt. On night's curtain the figure of the Yaqui flashed out; then, by association of ideas, he saw himself peering from the car door at Consuela and the starer, from the clash of which pictures an idea flew like a vivid spark—because the Yaqui had resented a smilar or worse insult to a woman of his tribe he,

THE PLANTER

David Mann, descendant of abolitionist fathers, was lying in wait to capture and return him to captivities that transcended the iniquities of Southern slavery!

Be sure the thought brought him upright on his feet. "I won't! I won't do it!" But the following reflection relaxed his strung muscles. "If Hertzer's man is to go free, why not the poor devils on my own plantation?"

Just then he was minded to go the lengths of his logic. He saw himself in a succeeding exaltation returning home to cast their price in Mr. Osgood's face. Ensued, however, the chilly thought: "He would engage others to serve under a harder master."

He sat down again.

But not in weakness. For as he sat thinking the stern cultures of his youth brought forth fruit, and he saw his duty plain toward the miserable creatures who had fallen into his wardship. But the Yaqui? Presently, however, he arrived at even this difficult solution—he would march him to Verda and hold him till Hertzer promised decent treatment.

The question of his own procedure thus determined, he had time to speculate on the probable action of the other party to the contract, and the gooseflesh rose all over his body as he remembered Phelps's description of the *velador's* death. "Hertzer found him flopping around the galera floor, neck cleanly wrung, face staring up over his shoulder." And somewhere in the jungle, perhaps just across the *arroyo*, the Yaqui was moving with the soft stealth of naked feet!

Bursting suddenly upon him, the thought brought quick panic, an impulse to rise and run, so urgent, strong, that he must have obeyed only that he felt if he once yielded pursuing terror would drive him insane. He shrank, instead, within the buttressing roots, clutched Phelps's pistol, and waited until pride again commanded his fears.

"He's only a man, unarmed at that," he murmured, and within five minutes his thought had returned to Consuela and the events of the morning.

With her he floated down the river, following its vast sinuosities by gleaming *playas* where huge saurians took their torrid siestas, always with the broidered screen of the jungle on either hand. And as lately he had always slid from thoughts of her into his sleep, habit presently asserted itself. He yawned, nodded, sat up blinking bravely, then drowsed, nodded again, and so slipped away.

And while he slept there came to pass things stranger even than dreams. Soft rustlings, low gruntings impinged on the silence, and a drove of coons brushed his feet going down to the water. Later a tapir swung leisurely along and stopped to browse around his tree, and other of the jungle children came curiously to see. Red-hot pinheads marked the eyes of a snake, bluish luminosities those of a deer; green slits in the night denoted the long-tooths. In silent procession they came, looked, then hopped, wriggled, or ran away as a pallor, mist of light, palpitated through the forest. Under its pale effulgence trees again stood out, black skeletons against the brightening sky; then all of a sudden a big copper moon sailed up and peeped at David over the edge of the forest. As though not satisfied with such cursory inspection, she pursued her course up and on, to drop, an hour later, a flood of light upon him through a gap in the leafy ceiling, and just then a wild pig raised its head from the water and scurried, grunting, away.

Had David been awake he also might have heard the low moaning that had startled the beast, would have seen a mass deepen in the shadow across the *arroyo* ere it resolved in the light of moonlit waters into a man bearing a burden. He could not have missed the whisper that stilled the moaning, the splash of water falling from a leaf twisted into a cup, labored breathing as the figure toiled with its burden up the hither bank. But he slept, slept on when, after stilling the moaning that had begun again, a man glared at him from the deep shadow on the crest of the bank.

For the space of three breaths he stood; then a dark convulsion marked his attempt to lay his burden down. But a moan followed—a low cry that pierced David's sleep and caused him to stir. But when, a minute later, he sat up and looked around, he saw only the lace of *bejucas* across the sky, a pale quivering where the moonlit waters emerged from the leafy tunnel.

VIII

—THE MAN

SO bright was the moonlight that David mistook it at first for the dawn which issued hours later like a warm sigh from the palpitant east. Ashamed of his faithless watch, he shook off sleep and trained his ear thereafter to every sound, but only the mutterings of an owl disturbed the early hours.

Leaving his post at daylight, he came out on the Verda clearing just as the sun fired its yellow roofs. It was the best hour of the day, and the cool peace of the morning conspired with relief from the night's strain to stimulate his spirits. The whistle that timed his brisk walk also celebrated the fact that the fugitives were still at large. He hoped that they might get away, and, under stimulation of the hot coffee and tortillas which Andrea had in waiting, hope waxed rosier, grew and grew till it had attained almost to certainty when, at the close of the meal, Hertzer, with Phelps and Carmen, clattered up to the door.

He stood in the doorway, a picture of blank surprise, staring at Phelps, who burst out: "Where are they? We didn't hear your shots. You see, the night wind set from us to you."

"Why—" David began.

But Phelps ran on: "Carmen picked up their tracks at the first arroyo beyond my place shortly after daybreak, and we followed them on to your tree. After that we just galloped on, for we knew that you had got them. Where's Ewing? Did you do it single-handed?"

David continued his blank stare under the volley of questions. "But—I didn't—" he began again; then, remembering his sleep, he stopped.

It was awkward. While Phelps was talking Hertzer looked on with thirsty eagerness, but now his expression suddenly reverted to its natural harsh suspicion. The Englishman seemed surprised. Even the Zacateco's brown glance betrayed his knowledge that something was wrong, and, to add to David's embarrassment, Andrea was standing in her kitchen doorway. Yet he blurted the difficult truth.

"I'm sorry, but I'm not used to night-watching and I fell asleep. If they passed me it must have been then."

"The hell you did!" Hertzer exploded, after a moment's consternation. "G—!" he began, then paused, biting his lips. But the check merely dammed his passion, for the next instant he broke out in violent profanity, streaming oaths in English, Spanish, German. Face writhing, convulsed with angry disappointment, he was, however, less ugly in his frank rage than Phelps in his cold innuendo.

"Oh, come! If Mann felt that way he had a right to slip off to his bed."

It was said in his superior way; but even his pedantic assurance shrivelled as David glanced from him to Carmen. "You are judging me by your own experience."

Now, though the accident of neighborship threw them a good deal together, Hertzer privately held the Englishman with his dogmatic precision in the contempt natural to his brutal nature. Also he had the primitive sense of humor which responds most quickly to some one's hurt. Wherefore the allusion to Phelps's unpleasant *contretemps* with the Zacateco was bound to draw his laugh.

"Poked you in the ribs that time," he grinned. Once more his cold self, he went on: "Well, the only thing left is to ride on and see if they got by Ewing. Come along—if you feel sufficiently rested. Take Carmen's horse. He can saddle yours and follow."

"Mira, señor! Mira! Mira!" Even as he turned to give the order in Spanish, the Zacateco pointed eagerly at hovering specks above the forest.

At his cry Andrea stepped out and stood gazing from under her hand. Phelps and Hertzer both were staring, and as David allowed his puzzled glance to wander from one to another, explanation presented itself. Since sunrise a solitary vulture had held vigil on the peak of the *galera*, and now spreading heavy wings he sailed away leading the leaden tribe that, a moment before, had been hopping among the buildings.

"He's right!" Hertzer exclaimed, with an oath. "There's carrion over yonder, and as the birds don't light it's a cinch that some one is keeping them away." Face quivering like molten metal, piercing eyes searching the distant blue, he ran on: "It's them, sure. The one I shot is dead—or dying; t'other's watching. Let me see—that will be about half-way between here and your place, Phelps, and about three miles back from the trail. The moon was up when you woke, Mann? Directly above? Then they saw you and turned into the arroyo. That 'll be our road. Here! Jump on Carmen's horse! Come on!"

With a word to the Indian he rowelled his beast and shot off at a gallop, setting a pace across the plantation and through the dry jungle beyond that tried out David's newly acquired horsemanship. Jolted, joggled, switched by trailing branches, he somehow managed to keep his saddle until the first of the morasses obliged slower going. With his returning breath came wonder at the impulse which had caused him to mount and follow, and he was still wondering when Carmen, who overtook them at the tree, led down the bank into the *arroyo's* green tunnel.

As aforesaid, the stream ran under rather than through the jungle, winding beneath vegetation se dense that light filtered in as a thick green haze. Rising twice the height of a man above them, the banks shut off the little air that moved above, so they moved in an atmosphere still and close, heavy as steam. At every yard the *bejuca* dropped its loops and snares to the water, forcing them to bend double as they slipped and tripped over water-worn bowlders. Alternating with mud, quicksands made it still heavier labor. After five minutes of it David's heart beat like a pile-driver against his ribs, while Phelps stooped every few yards to wash the acrid sweat out of his eyes. Both gasped their relief when Carmen would pause over the tracks of a pig or pugs of a tiger; but Hertzer, whose iron frame seemed to defy fatigue, motioned him always forward, nor permitted a rest until his keen eye picked a footprint from the mud of the bank after an hour of slavish toil.

Its evidence was hardly required, for a beating of wings, swish and swoop of vultures, had already informed them of the closeness of their quarry. Confirming Hertzer's judgment, that rhythmic pulsing killed nascent hope in David. Oppressed by the loom of trouble, he watched Carmen worming up the bank, yet for all his heaviness could not but thrill to a memory of a cat crawling upon a bird in his mother's garden. When, after a peep over the crest, Carmen turned to beckon them forward, he saw also the same savage exultance that had blazed in the beast's green eyes. With it mingled surprise, a touch of the wonder which he experienced himself a moment later; the wonder, but none of the pity that brought the tears to his eyes.

THE PLANTER

Wiping them with the back of his hand, he looked again. From the bank the land sloped to a shallow dell heavily shaded by tall timber, so blackly shadowed, indeed, that it was devoid of underbrush save where a stream of light broke down through the naked arms of a saber. Killed by lightning-stroke, the tree now bore, in lieu of leaves, a grisly crop of vultures. Hundreds crowded the limbs, branches, the very twigs. David had not imagined that the whole land held so many of the carrion creatures as perched on that single tree, yet other scores darkened the ground, and through the break in the forest roof he saw a winged cloud moving in swirls and eddies. Save when disturbed by some abrupt movement of the man who worked below, the vultures on the tree sat still and silent. Then the craning of livid necks, flutter of coffin plumage, was singularly like the movement of wind through the plumes of a hearse. Their dead eyes watched as he dug in the soft mould with a staff and his hands.

Rifting down through the saber, the light struck full upon him so that he stood out in the shadowy dell like a figure under a slant of light in some dim cathedral. Though Hertzer's description had convinced David of the fugitive's identity with his great Yaqui of the train, big men had not been so rare among the prisoners. But it did not require a second look to recognize the deep torso, lithe muscularity which conveyed the impression of liquid force. Turning to strike at a bird that had pecked at a huddle of

rags which lay to one side, he revealed the eagle profile, sombre eyes, stern mouth. Sleeplessness, star-
vation, the heavy travail with his burden—none of
these had been able to detract from the stoical dignity which wrapped him like a mantle.

After driving away the vultures he leaned for a
while on his staff looking down on the dead woman,
leaned and looked unconscious of alien observation.
There was something leonine in his pose; yet for all
his stern composure sadness radiated from him; grief,
keener, more poignant, than the wildest manifesta-
tions of sorrow. So standing, while heavy wings pulsed
through the heated silence, his ineffable loneliness
stabbed David with so sharp a pain that he turned
involuntarily to Phelps.

The Englishman, too, seemed affected. His lips
even formed the soundless phrase, "Poor devil!" But
the accompanying shake of the head robbed his sympathy, testifying to his continued adherence to the
standards of philosophical inevitability as laid down
by Mr. Kidd.

Turning at a rustle on his left, he saw Hertzer poised
on fingers and toes like a runner at scratch. The
attitude accentuated the peculiar angle of his neck,
his enormous animality. Head lowered and slightly
swinging, eyes blazing under shaggy brows, his bear-
like body hung for a moment in balance ere he
launched after Carmen over the bank. Springing
up to follow, David tripped on a *bejuca* and rolled
back to the very bottom of the bank, and when he

scrambled again to the top he saw Carmen leaping his last yards under a flapping cloud.

Paralyzed by a sick excitement, he stood looking on.

After yielding a start in tribute to surprise, the Yaqui had straightened, gripping hard on his staff, and through his chaos of feeling David sensed danger in that quiet waiting. Until Carmen was almost upon him he moved no muscle—quiet that deceived even the Zacateco. Thinking, perhaps, that the man was about to yield, he paused, machete raised— paused to his sorrow, for, with a movement subtle as that of a striking snake, the heavy staff rose and fell. So swift was the blow that David's eye could not follow. But he heard a sharp tinkle, caught the flash as the machete flew in pieces. Simultaneously the Yaqui's hands shot out, took Carmen by the head as a player catches a ball, and without arrest of his momentum sent him sprawling, with only a vicious wrench to account for his hideous screech.

In eighty yards the Indian had gained full twenty on Phelps and Hertzer, but quick as was his disposal, only a fraction of time intervened between Hertzer's bull rush. The Yaqui had stooped instantly for his staff, but to David, looking on, it seemed that nothing could save him from Hertzer's blow. But the stoop was merely a feint. Springing from his crouch, he came up inside the other's guard, arms wreathed about his waist. Even at that distance David could see biceps and flexors writhing under the brown skin, constricting like pythons into Hertzer's bulk. A sudden twist—which foiled Phelps, who was now dancing round them for a chance to put in a blow—showed him Hertzer's face all livid, mouth horribly gaped, eyes starting yet furious in their agony. During the seconds they swayed and swung his huge fists never ceased raining blows on the Yaqui's back —blows that resounded through the glade like the beating of a drum. But even his enormous strength, ferocious masculinity, was unequal to the crushing of his vitals, and just as Phelps's chance came he was lifted and thrown violently upon his head.

If the Englishman had used the edge, the business had ended there and then; but in obedience to Hertzer's previous instructions he struck with the flat, and, glancing, the blow fell harmlessly upon the shoulder. His hoarse cry as he went down with the Yaqui's hands at his throat broke up David's coma. All had occurred in a quarter-minute, and now pulling his pistol he ran shouting and firing, indifferent to the risk of hitting Phelps—ran thrilling with horror, conscious only of the brown hands fumbling the Englishman's throat. Flying wide, his bullets could never have saved him. Yet they served by attracting the Yaqui's attention—caused him to look up just as he had set himself for a wrench, a fleeting glance which still afforded time for Hertzer to seize his machete and topple him over with a heavy blow delivered from his knees.

"Oh, my God!" Springing up, Phelps clutched

David's arm. "Oh, my God, Mann! I felt him reach around my neck to my chin, and I couldn't stop him. Oh, my God! Another second—"

"Blast your neck!" Hertzer broke brutally in on his frenzy of agitation. "Look at Carmen over there, and my ribs are all stove in. Here, help to tie the brute. If he comes to we'll have the job all over."

Though he must have been suffering intensely, he did the tying himself, then led over to Carmen, who now lay quiet save for a low moaning. "Only a dislocation," he remarked, with the same brutal indifference. "The beast hadn't time to do a good job. You chaps sit on his back and legs while I take a haul on his head. Now, all together! Heigh-ho, away we go!" He laughed as the vertebræ cracked into place. "Now, Mann, if you'll just bring a hatful of water he'll eat from the hand in five minutes. I'm going to cut a few bejucas to put in pickle for our friend."

Laughing harshly again, he picked up his machete and moved a few steps toward the thick jungle. The passion of conflict had apparently passed; outwardly, at least, he was his usual cold, sardonic self. But his calmness was merely superficial. Coming on top of that long, vexatious hunt, his discomfiture at the Yaqui's hands had inflamed his savage temper; raised it to a pitch that was bound to force an outlet. And noticing that the prisoner's eyes had opened, he now deflected his course and stood looking down upon him. David had gone for water. Phelps still knelt by Carmen. So neither saw the answering look, the stubborn hatred, bitter triumph that touched off his rage.

Turning at his furious oath, David did see his heavy heel descend on the prisoner's face, the shower of kicks that followed. In his furious obsession, animal desire to crush and grind, he danced back and forth, driving his heel into body, ribs, stomach with the "heugh" of a woodman—so utterly possessed that he forgot even the machete in his hand until Phelps, whose nerve was completely gone, screamed aloud:

"Hertzer! Hertzer! You'll kill him!"

Thus reminded, he swung the blade on high, tiptoeing to strike while his roar boomed through the forest. "Kill him? Yes, by God! I will!"

Had it fallen the head would have been lopped like cabbage. But even in this, the climax of his passion, the acquisitive Jew whispered in the ear of the Bersark Slav, and he turned the blade so that it fell flat on the naked shoulders. "No, I'll work him to death by inches!"

Delivered with all of his weight, the blow fell with the thud of a shovel upon a grave, and a wale lifted spotted with red where the blood forced up through the pores. Through all the Yaqui had endured in silence, and even now his flesh yielded only a slow shiver to the torture; and as Hertzer raised to strike again, the weapon was suddenly snatched from his hand.

"You brute! Oh, you brute!" David's protest issued in choking sobs. "You beast! Coward! You dared not have done that if his hands had been untied."

For a moment Hertzer stared into the lad's white face, then he swung his open palm, struck out wildly, blindly, with such violence that David was lifted from his feet. "You pup! You mealy mouthed pup!" From its usual booming masculinity, his voice rose to a strident yell. "You dare to fool with me! I'll—"

But the blow had loosed in David — David, the meekly spectacled, of the Sabbath-school training— had loosed his father's soul from his mother's leash, the soul that had dominated the roaring bullies of a dozen lumber-camps. Before Hertzer could finish his threat he was up, and came like a bull-dog straight at his throat—came from a second fall and a third, fighting as if he liked it.

According to accepted traditions—traditions of fiction—he ought to have won, and he would if pluck were the only concomitant of a victory. But truth compels the statement that he received a thorough drubbing. He emerged, however, without damage to his spirit, for when, beaten to a pulp, he could no longer break from Phelps's restraining hands, he still continued to hurl defiances: "You brute! Coward! You brutal coward!"—continued them in the face of the Englishman's whispered warning:

"Hush, Mann! Hush! he'll kill you!"

—THE MAN

The struggle, however, had afforded the necessary outlet for Hertzer's passion, and he returned only a sarcastic grin to the lad's reproaches. Glasses gone, one eye closed, nose freely bleeding, it must be confessed that he did fall sufficiently short of the heroic to justify the smile, but as he never dreamed of his being heroic he suffered nothing on that account. He issued his defiances up to the moment that, having got the Yaqui to his feet, Hertzer drove him toward the *arroyo*, with Carmen following.

"Come on, Phelps;" he called, looking back from the crest of the bank.

"You, too, Mann," the Englishman urged. "You can't stay here." Noting the lad's look at the dead woman, he nodded up at the vultures. "They'll undertake it."

Instead of following, however, David stepped down into the shallow grave and began to dig with his machete.

Turning, Phelps raised eyebrows at Hertzer, who winked; then for a space both stood, staring. But with the passing of the Englishman's hysteria had returned his reverence for the proprieties, and he presently broke out: "Oh, look here, Mann, this will never do. No white man ever works in the tropics. It isn't good form, and if it gets around that you buried a dead enganchada you'll lose caste even with the natives. Come along, and I'll send out a peon."

"I'll wait till he comes."

"Oh, come on."

David went on digging.

Phelps gave up.

Glancing up as he walked away, David saw the Yaqui looking back at him from the crest of the bank. Throughout the struggle the man had displayed a sullen indifference. What to him if the white men chose to beat each other? But when David stepped into the grave, black hatred had given place to startled surprise. Now his stoicism emitted a flash—a look so poignantly human that it pi rced David's heart like a sword. Like a ray through a storm cloud it flashed out, and he was gone.

Now, David was only a lad—a lad raised in a tender atmosphere with sympathies unseared by suffering; so let him not be charged with maudlin sentiment because he sat down and cried. They came again, the tears, when in placing the woman in the grave half an hour later he disturbed her shawl, and so found himself looking into a face young and comely despite its darkness. What with the softness of the forest mould he had made a quick finish, so no eyes but those of the leaden watchers observed him upon his knees, no ear caught his murmured prayer. Rising, much comforted, he filled and smoothed the grave with his hands, and so left the poor slave to sleep in silence and solitude that was broken only by the muffled requiem of departing wings.

IX

A VISIT

MIDWAY of the same forenoon Andrea lounged in the cook-house doorway. One foot on either side of the sill and comely shoulders propped against the thill, her position made up in comfort what it lacked in elegance, and had other advantages in that it permitted her to keep an eye on the trail while training her ear to the gossip within. As the sun approached the meridian its vertical rays burned the dust beyond her outer foot, throwing so narrow a shadow that her smooth arm made a splash of gold beyond its edge as she stretched in a yawn. Above, the sere thatch rustled dryly to a stir of air with parched cracklings; the rich tufts of a rubber-tree near by had lost their gloss, hung limply as steamy rags. Under that fierce blaze, indeed, green things fried, dry things cracked or crumbled, live things—such as Rafaela's chickens and pigs—hugged the shadow under walls, and stood, beaks agape, tongues lolling. Andrea, however, seemed to enjoy the heat. Placid as a cow in a sunlit meadow, she took her ease, which seemed the more enjoyable by contrast with the perspirings of the *enganchada* women who formed a sort of chorus to the gossip.

In essence this did not differ so very widely from the tattle that may be heard at a Fifth Avenue table any day of the week. But whereas the admiring exclamations with which the chorus punctuated the head woman's discourse might easily have come from the lips of the satellites of some woman of fashion, they were the more excusable because Rafaela's heavy fist hung ready to punish the laggard in adulation. In subject and range of conversation the comparison may be carried still farther; for beginning with Hertzer's runaways, it had passed to Patricia; and after taking the usual liberties with her person and character, had moved on to Andrea's prospects. In setting forth these, moreover, no society woman on the trail of a husband would have been more enthusiastic than Rafaela; she differed only in her perfect frankness.

"It is for you pigs of the plateau to rub and scrub, with the machete-flat for pay and a worn-out enganchador for play," she told the chorus, with more of candor than politeness. "But Andrea, she can take her pick of the Gringos."

"Si, si!" The woman whom David had saved from the stick now made up for the humiliation then sustained through her by the head woman, in her vigorous show of belief. "Si, señora, and Don David the first of them. Only four days on the finca, and 'tis easy to see whose way the wind sets."

"Si, si!" the others echoed.

Encouraged by the dawn of a smile on the head woman's grim visage, the first woman ran on: "Of course he will take thee to the fiesta of San Juan next year, Andrea. And I am no judge of a man if there be not a dress of crimson velours to the fore, with embroidery so stiff that it stands of itself."

"And an American gold eagle to add to thy neck-chain," a second added.

"Si, she will ruffle it with the best of them," came in a third. "Lola, the woman of Señor Phelps, will not be nearly as fine."

"No, nor the Señorita Patricia." The first woman rose to the highest peak of flattery, and so achieved her reward.

"Go thou and suckle thy child, Casamira." The head woman graciously acceded to a request made an hour before. "But remember—not too long."

Thus stimulated, and under the urge of their own aching breasts, the other mothers fell to, each trying to be first in quality and quantity of her complimentary teasings; plied Andrea with jokes that would have caused David to burn could he have heard the mildest, and which were yet innocent enough judged by their standards. For a Zacateco marriage endures only so long as circumstances permit; a woman is at liberty to marry again when conditions break the tie; and as to keep the house of a Gringo is the dream of every Zacateco girl, there was nothing improper in their hints that Andrea's estate already bore the color of her hopes. Had there been, Rafaela's fist would have quickly corrected the lapse. As it was, she joined in the chaff which would have been broad enough in a congregation of young matrons poking fun at a newly married girl, led them to fresh attacks after Andrea's every denial.

"Nada, nada, señoras. No es!" Time and again she flung it over her shapely shoulder. But there are ways and *ways* of saying no, and the accompanying smile was twin to that of the young girl who, feeling pretty sure of her game, takes time by the forelock and whispers in her chum's ear: "But we don't want it known yet."

Whether or no she intended this interpretation, this much is certain: Casamira's allusion to the fiesta of San Juan fired Andrea's imagination, and for an hour thereafter she mused, returning only an abstracted "Nada, señoras," to the lively banter. Velvet eyes fixed on the far spot where the jungle trail debouched on the clearing, she dreamed of the fiesta, the greatest of the year, the fiesta where the womenkind, white and brown, for a hundred miles around would strut in glories of velours, lace, and linen. It was, to be sure, still months away, but in this short time Andrea had sized her man and knew him for no ordinary Gringo to be won by a smile in the dusk. His subjugation might require every day of the time. Still he was young, therefore presumably generous, and if properly handled— She was seeing herself outshining even Patricia at the fiesta when a dark figure impinged on the quivering waves of heat. The subject of her reflections rode into the clearing.

The speculation in her glance gave place to astonishment and dismay as he rode in among the buildings, and her cry, "Oh, señor!" brought her mother and the other women to the door.

What with the heat, emotional exhaustion, and the sleep which weighed heavily upon him, David had ridden the last miles in a sort of coma, dim dream through which fragments of the events of the morning floated disconnectedly. But now, remembering his bruises, he reddened and turned his face away from their curious stares. "It is nothing," he answered Andrea's voluble questions. But he was not to escape so easily. She ran after, and while unsaddling at the stables she drew from him, or, rather, he permitted her to create her own version of the story.

They had caught the runaways?

Yes.

And there had been a struggle?

Yes.

These wounds? Surely the devil of a runagate had not dared to lay hands on the sacred person of a Gringo?

Fortunately for David's sensitive conscience the latter question was really an exclamation, for without waiting for answer she ran on, cursing his assailant with a variety and quality of oath that would have raised David's hair had he understood. So tired, however, that her cursing seemed to come like a sough of a distant forest, he never even listened. It is doubtful whether he missed her when she suddenly left the stable or heard her come in as, later, he sat on the rickety bench in the house trying to make up his mind to wash his sore face. Dimly he was conscious of a calabash containing a green, succulent mess like pounded spinach, which she set on the table at his elbow; but before he could make up his mind whether or no this was for consumption, she suddenly plastered a handful over his eyes.

It felt so pleasantly cool that he cancelled a first impulse to struggle, contenting himself with a blush that almost cooked the plaster in protest at the intimacy of the treatment. But he was almost too sleepy for even this gentle shame. He yielded himself up in drowsy enjoyment; sat still even when a smooth arm touched his cheek as she reached around to smooth and massage his bruises; sat until, sinking back, his sleepy head brought up on a pillow that was soft and warm.

Uttering a quick apology, he straightened in stiff rigidity and would have broken away but for a feeling of ungraciousness. Her quiet answer, "Nada, señor, it is nothing," helped to soothe him. Another minute and he relaxed, felt only the comfort of the hands smoothing his aching flesh; was pleasantly conscious of light rifting in yellow bars through the split-pole siding, of motes dancing in bright beams, of the rich dusk of the brown roof above. Bearing more heavily upon him, deep sleep presently robbed his senses, and his head drooped to the girl's bosom as easily as it had ever gone to that of his mother.

"Hello! What the—"

Springing up, David saw Ewing grinning in the doorway.

"Sorry I butted in," he said; "but I had to come over for my horse, and I wanted to hear the news. It will keep another day."

"Here!" David stopped him as he made a show of retiring. Reddening, he stammered: "You—you surely—didn't think—"

"No, I didn't," Ewing dryly interrupted. "It doesn't pay—in these latitudes. What's the matter with your face? Looks like corned-beef and cabbage."

With angry bruises distributed among Andrea's poultices, his countenance undoubtedly bore a startling resemblance to that homely dish; but just then David's concern was all for his moral complexion, and he ran eagerly on: "Look here, Ewing. She insisted on treating my bruises, and I was so dog-tired that I fell asleep under her hands."

"'Sleeping Beauty,' masculine gender, eh? And she took base advantage of unconscious loveliness. Poor chap, how I pity you! Oh, come," he added, laughing, as David frowned, "don't get mad. I'm only joshing. But what about your face?"

"In a minute." David glanced at Andrea, who stood waiting, ready to resume her practice. "Now, will you get me something to eat?" he asked.

THE PLANTER

Nodding, she picked up her calabash, but, though she complied cheerfully enough, her glance at Ewing, passing out, could hardly be considered complimentary to his presence.

"She, at least, believes that two's company," he laughed. "Tha plaster is good dope, all right. I've seen it used before. But I'd advise personal applications after this if you wish to avoid matrimonial complications. Now, tell me all about it."

He nodded when David finished. "Hertzer's surely a bad man to cross. It's a wonder you came out so well. You ought to have seen the dose he handed to Meagher, and that over a simple deal in beans. The Irishman kept his bed for a week. But I'm keeping you from your rest. I slept all morning, so now I'll just ride on to La Luna and see what's doing. See you to-night."

David walked with him to the stable, where he exchanged the horse he was riding for that which he had left the night before. When he returned Andrea had just finished setting out his meal, which he ate in uncomfortable silence, omitting the lesson in Spanish which usually enlivened the meal. Though she waited upon him with quiet civility, he felt, or thought he felt, her reaching out to a secret, more intimate footing. Whenever she passed behind him he straightened involuntarily, and was furiously angry at the thrills which his flesh, the exultant unconquerable flesh, yielded to her proximity. Sitting very rigid, he avoided her eye, returned brusque

124

monosyllables to her questions, almost yelled his
refusal when, having cleared away, she brought in
her calabash for another dressing.

Afterward he did a thing that had never occurred
to him before. The door, a poor affair of split poles,
boasted a cross-bar, which he dropped into place
before he lay down to sleep, a precaution that drew
Ewing's smile when he returned that evening.

"Virtue intrenched," he muttered, smiling; but
went on with his recital of events without comment
after David had let him in.

"Well, I arrived just in time for the execution—"

"You don't mean to say they killed him?" David
burst in.

"Not exactly. Better if they had. When I got
there they had the poor devil stretched out, hands
and feet tied to two stakes driven into the ground,
and Hertzer and two cabos were whaling him at once
with slim bejucas. It isn't the first flogging I have
witnessed. I've paddled a few myself. But—ugh!
it was brutal, and, worst of all, Patricia saw it—
looked on from the house veranda. As it turned
out, it was well that she did. You see, Hertzer was
bound to degrade him in the eyes of his fellows
who were ranged up under the cabos' rifles. If he
had cried out, I really believe she would have seen
his heart cut out without a shiver. But he didn't;
and after ten minutes of it she came flying out, a
white flutter of garments, and fell on Hertzer like a
hawk on a dog.

"'You sha'n't touch him again!' she cried, and clung to his arm. He stared down at her just as you said he did at you this morning. Once he raised his free fist, but she gave him eyes as hard as his own, and he dropped it again with a laugh. 'He's yours—that is, what's left of him.'

"There really wasn't much. I thought he was dead, for he lay with a bubble of foam on his lips. But she had him carried to the house, and prepared vinegar and water herself to wash his bruises. A young wife could scarcely have shown more solicitude over an injured husband: yet when he was once more on his feet she ordered him back to the galera with an indifference that outdid even Hertzer's coldness.

"She even joked with her father. 'Don't forget that he's mine. I have always wanted a slave of my own, and now I've got one. If you need him, you'll have to buy him back.' And she laughed when he asked her price, answering: 'Oh, a couple of silk dresses and a trip to Ciudad Mexico.'"

"As though he were a dog!" David commented.

"Exactly. She would probably have raised as much fuss over a hound. As they spoke in Spanish, the Yaqui understood, and I tell you, Mann, if he had given my daughter the look he turned on her, I wouldn't dare to take a chance on his life. But though Hertzer saw it, he only laughed. He was glad the fellow's spirit remained unbroken, for he takes the same delight in breaking a man that you or I might in subduing a vicious horse. But now I must be going. I've hardly been home these three days."

Stepping with him to the door, David took a deep breath of the fresh night air. "Well, adding what you have just told me to the little I have seen of Mr. Hertzer, I'm not sorry that we quarrelled. We shall not see much of each other."

"Don't be so sure." Ewing looked up from the cinch he was tightening. "He has nothing against you. Seems rather to admire your pluck. He and Meagher were thick as thieves in less than a month after their squabble, so don't be surprised if he drops in on you."

"Well, he need not."

"Oh, look here," Ewing protested, "I don't take much stock in him myself, but on this river we are only a half-dozen white men against three thousand Indians. We can't afford quarrels."

Looking down from the saddle, he saw in the light from the doorway the ten generations of Puritan ancestors that looked out of David's eyes.

"I have no quarrel with him, but I cannot endure his methods, and so shall leave him alone."

"But you can't. You don't know Hertzer. With him there's no middle course; he's either your friend or your enemy, and in the latter case he'll do his best to do you up. Be advised. Treat him decently."

"Oh, I'll be civil. I wouldn't be other to his dog. But as for friendship—it is out of the question."

"Very well, so long as you don't antagonize him."

Ewing let it go at that. "Now, remember, you are to come over to dinner next Sunday."

"With this face?"

"Why, of course. Keep on with Andrea's dope, and there won't be much left. You couldn't have a better introduction to my wife. She's almost as rabid as you against the system," he added, laughing. "Really, I doubt it is a mistake to bring you together. I'm afraid you'll run me off the plantation."

By Sunday, indeed, the swelling had altogether subsided, and beyond a blueness under one eye David's countenance had resumed its usual pacific mildness. His glasses, to be sure, were gone—smashed irretrievably in the struggle; but, as before hinted, they were due to his mother's fears rather than a real weakness in his sight, and he was delighted to find how easily he got along without them. As Ewing had said, the bruise proved the best of introductions, not only to his pretty little wife, but also to the half-dozen planters who had drifted in from plantations fifty or a hundred miles away by trail or river to lazy a day upon her veranda, and forget their loneliness in the sweet feminine presence.

"You don't mean to say that he fought Hertzer?" these exclaimed, with incredulous whistles at Ewing's explanation of the discoloration, and his conduct in this respect cancelled the contempt excited by his heterodox opinions concerning the treatment of *enganchadores*. If they rallied him a bit, offering wet nurses for use in his *crèche*, they yet made him of their number, told him stories, and gave him sound advice about his rubber.

And Mrs. Ewing championed him against the good-natured raillery before them and in private. "What if the poor creatures are faithless and ungrateful?" she encouraged him. "That does not excuse cruelty in us. We owe it to ourselves to do the best we can for them. Keep on; you'll put them all in the wrong."

The visit went far toward reconciling the lad to his labors in other ways, injecting a spice of social intercourse into the tedium of the long hot days. "You can't have a piano in a climate that melts soap on the washstand," Ewing said, apologizing for his phonograph. "And this is the best we could get of its kind." So nocturnes, grand opera arias, band concerts floated out on the steamy dusk—music gone to brass, but good enough in default of better. It enlivened an hour, thickened it with crowding memories, sent him home the following day happier, more content.

"Oh, he'll come," Ewing said again, when, departing, David expressed a doubt as to Hertzer's proposed visit.

Judging by his own feelings, David found it hard to believe, and when Maria Guadaloupe reported one evening a week later that Hertzer had crossed the plantation that morning disbelief settled in conviction.

"That settles it," he thought; and dismissing the

matter from his mind, he proceeded to "despatch" the men who were drawn up in front of the store. Glass in one hand, a jug of *aguardiente* in the other, he followed the *mandador* down the line, supplementing the daily ration of *cigarros* with a *copa* of the fiery liquid, and had barely gained half-way before a snatch of song drifted in from the far edge of the clearing:

> "Nearer, my God, to Thee, nearer to Thee,
> E'en though it be a cross that raiseth me—"

"Ewing," he thought at first; but he noticed as the sound drew nearer that, besides being off key, the singer flatted his notes and was following his own time in and out the tune in a manner that would have been impossible for the planter, who sang a correct barytone. Turning at a titter behind him, he saw Andrea, who was waiting to draw the morrow's ration of corn, covering her mouth; the *mandador* and his two *cabos* were also hiding grins, while a wan smile lightened the sombre gravity of even the tired *enganchadores*.

"It is the Señor Hertzer," Maria Guadaloupe replied to his question. Then he remembered that Ewing had spo en of Hertzer's passion for music—how he kept his phonograph going in and out of season; would listen as long as any one would sing; of his preference for hymns because of their simpler melody.

One branch of the trail crossed the clearing a half

A VISIT

mile from the buildings, and he thought and hoped that Hertzer was upon it. But, drawing nearer, the raucous strains told that he had taken the turn which led to the house, and as David filled the *copa* for the last man Hertzer rode up, and tied his horse to a hitching-post.

Although his reformations toward cleanliness had already reduced his sick-list, there were still a few left-overs—*granos* (blood - poisonings), calenturas— from Meagher's dirty régime, and just acknowledging Hertzer's nod David turned to his medical practice.

Not one whit disconcerted, Hertzer leaned in the store doorway and looked on in silence. "Are you working those fellows?" he asked at last, and he shrugged his big shoulders as David shook his head. "A mistake. That fellow"—he pointed at a febrile tatterdemalion who was shaking with calentura— "will die in the teeth of you, so why not get out the little that's in him? You don't see why he should? Well, listen. Here, you! Veinte-dos!" He called the man's number in Spanish. "You are going to die, aren't you?"

"Si, señor!" The answer came with an alacrity that was almost cheerful.

"There you are," Hertzer went on, after he had translated his question. Dropping into a sort of confidential colloquial vein, he continued: "It's the funniest damn thing, but they seem to be able to die at will, and when the bug once gets into their heads you can't get it out—even by flogging. And it's infectious—will clean out a galera quicker than yellow-fever. So if you have a fairly healthy lot, you'd better drive them while you can. They'll go off like rotten sheep when the rains set in."

Without answering, David dosed the last calentura with quinine, then marched the others to the trough at the *galera* gate, and stood there superintending the washing. Lazily, Hertzer followed. While talking his manner had been entirely devoid of embarrassment, evidenced only a diabolical humor; now a grim twitching at the puckered corners of his mouth was all that he vouchsafed to David's silence. With a *sang-froid* that was even more remarkable, he said, as the last patient filed into the *galera:* "It is too late for me to make Phelps's for supper. If you will have your moso give my horse a feed of corn, I'll walk around with you and see what you've done while the girl cooks supper. I may be able to give you a few pointers."

And his cool assumption served. Had he attempted either explanation or apology, David's compelling candor would have undoubtedly caused another rupture. But he was helpless in the face of a calmness that took no more cognizance of the recent past than if it had been dead and gone these thousand years. So, though he had little stomach for Hertzer's company, he was bound by tropic tradition and ordinary politeness to extend his hospitality; and if he must spend time with the man, better to be out walking than cooped up together in the narrow house.

A VISIT

So, with Hertzer leading at a brisk pace, they started.

At first David bore himself stiffly; but once among the plantings and Hertzer talking, interest partly banished constraint. For now, as on the morning when they had ridden with Phelps over La Luna, Hertzer's one enthusiasm again possessed him. His harsh features lit up with an almost tender animation as he led here and there, pointing, suggesting.

"Now, look at that!" he said, pausing by a brush-heap, clearings which had been piled in the open between trees. "That will never do, though you will see the same thing on most plantations. You know, rubber roots close to the surface, and if you keep on clearing *away* from the trees instead of *toward* them, the soil is gradually scraped away and you leave a depression for the rains to collect. Rubber can't stand a sour wet bed. So have your men pile the monte around the trees. It makes a mulch in the dry season, runs off the water in wet."

Time and again, too, he unsheathed his machete to trim a tree, and passing through an uneven planting he advised restocking from a nursery, complementing his advice with the offer: "I have a couple of thousand thrifty plants that I don't need. You can have them cheap."

Apart from the flash of calculation which accompanied the offer, his manner all through displayed genuine interest, and the afterglow from his enthusiasm lent almost friendly color to a remark made as they walked back through falling dusk. "Ewing tells me that Osgood tried to get your mother to invest in *this* ?" He swept a contemptuous hand around. "You wired her? Good. Wrote, too, I suppose?"

Partly from lack of time, but principally because as yet opportunity had not served for the sending out of a letter, David had not written. Hertzer shook his head. "In this country wires are uncertain as lightning. They sometimes hit. It would have paid you to send out. Now, I'm going down to San Juan to-morrow, so you had better scribble a few lines after supper."

Now, if David had abated a little of his stiffness, his purpose remained untouched, and had he consulted only his inclination, he would surely have refused the favor. But just as though he divined his mental processes—indeed, with a sort of ironic intelligence—Hertzer hustled him along toward whatever end he had in view. For, after Andrea had cleared away after their meal, he lit his pipe and threw himself at length on David's *catre*.

"Now, I'm good for an hour. Fire away with your writing."

This was the time to refuse, but even David's stubbornness halted at the ungraciousness in the face of such good-humor, and, albeit unwillingly, he sat down to his writing. Such a thing as a twinkle was altogether foreign to Hertzer's cold eye, but, looking on from the bed, the lamplight showed him grimly smiling behind a blue veil of smoke, and if sarcastic pucker ever told a secret, he was pleased at his success in handling the refractory youth. His eye, now quiet and thoughtful, again piercingly sharp, told also of some end, and catching its vivid intelligence in a casual glance, David sustained a sudden recurrence of suspicion.

"What *is* he up to?" he wondered, as he bent again to his writing. "There's a string behind all this kindness."

There was, and it showed when the letter being duly sealed and his horse brought round, Hertzer rose to go. "By-the-way," he said, "I have a quotation on maize and frijoles from a Vera Cruz house that almost cuts San Juan prices in two, and I thought I would let you in on it. How many arrobas of each do you think you could use?"

The cat was out of the bag—such a measly cat, such a dirty bag. Murder, piracy, highway robbery, no one of these would have given David a tithe of the astonishment that he felt at this sordid motive. It seemed so exceedingly small, so miserably inadequate to such a violent scoundrel. Yet in the very moment of his wonder Ewing's warning flashed into his mind. "He's cheated every one of us. Look out if he trades with you."

Quick to understand, Hertzer trimmed sail to the cold wind. "Of course you don't need to give me an answer to-night. Look over your stores, compare my prices with San Juan. Any time will do in the next month."

THE PLANTER

He was too skilful a mariner; better that he had held on the same tack, for David was still in the first throes of his wonder. "So this is the heart of his kindness," he thought, and under the urge of his disgust he blurted his mind.

"Thank you, but I prefer to do my own trading."

For a pause Hertzer stared, while his heavy brows swept down and his big mouth drew into an iron line. Of the planters who knew and feared him no man would have dared such an unqualified refusal. But the very novelty of it amused him, and he suddenly burst out laughing.

"Oh, very well," he grinned, holding out his hand. "Good-night."

But David drew away, and so for a moment they stood, the lad stubbornly quiet, the man searching him with piercing, suspicious glances.

"No?" he questioned, at last. "But remember— it was you that refused your hand."

Following to the door, David listened to his departing hoof-beats. The man's quiet had shaken him where bluster would have failed. For the moment he felt very much the Pharisee, and was minded to call him back. But in the very moment of the thought Hertzer's harsh voice broke out in a discordant parody:

"Jesus, lover of my soul, let me to Thy bosom fly."

Going in, he shut the door.

THE TROPICS *VS.* NEW ENGLAND

A LAZY drone from the cook-house floated into the store, where David sat at his accounts. It was extremely hot — even there in the shade — for now at the close of the dry season each day seemed to be trying to outscorch its predecessor. Bursting at dawn from bloody mists, a flaming sun poured liquid fire upon a brazen earth, baked it to a crackle through the long hours, then left it to stew in darkness, and render night hideous with emanations of superabundant heat. The band that fell through the open door across the floor glowed like the aurora of a furnace. Motes sizzled like sparks from whitehot metal in the bars which rifted through the pole siding, and when in its slow crawl across the shadow one of these touched David's boot he moved his foot from the burning heat. Though he was wearing the thinnest of cambric *camisas* it showed wet in patches, and he paused often to mop his streaming face; but having granted his parboiled complexion to the heat, it required other explanation to account for a certain embarrassed look about his eyes.

"Confound it!" he muttered, between moppings. "Why didn't I come in the other way?"

The question referred to the path which led in from the smothered rubber that, in accordance with Hertzer's advice, was now cleared and burned off in readiness for a second planting at the coming of the rains. As it ran in the scorched open he had returned this morning by a longer way which followed the river through thick jungle, had been sauntering along in full enjoyment of the palm shade, when a turn of that treacherous path about a huge saber brought him plump upon Andrea at her ablutions.

Viewed in the abstract, here was really no cause of perturbation. He had already learned that in the *tierra caliente* moral issues are not concealed by clothes, that Virtue, where found, is likely to be going in her own golden skin. If startled when first he came on one of his *enganchadas* pounding her single chemisette on a river bowlder, he had grown to their innocent nudity and now passed it daily with that indifference which neither looks nor turns away. Why, then, his embarrassment? Standing, a bronze naiad by the water's edge, quiet and unconcerned, the girl had given him the usual "*Buenos-dias*" as she stooped for her chemisette. So far all was proper, in perfect accord with heated conventions, and had he walked on she would undoubtedly have continued her toilet with perfect indifference. But whether or no his paralysis was due to a sudden revelation that the *enganchadas*, gaunt and labor-worn, were not such as tempt the sin of the eye, he stood stock-still until, glancing up, she caught his red embarrassment. For a moment she stared, surprised, then, just as he turned to retreat, disappeared under a flash of white. And now in the pauses of his summing he groaned over that fatal hesitation, mixing regret with wonder that the morality of clothes should be so infectious.

"If you'd only gone on," he grinned, through set teeth, "she'd never have given you a second thought. But now — how the dickens am I to face her at lunch?"

Reading no answer in the cook-house drone, he returned to his column, only to leave it again as the figures merged in a vivid picture — a nude bronze, bediamonded with liquid jewels, rising from flashing waters beyond black palm shade. Time and again the persistent vision brought anarchy into his calculations, and something other than chagrin was responsible when next he groaned. It told that heat, insects, smothered rubber, and labor problems were dwindling into insignificance beside this new factor in his fight with Cancer.

"Ole! Don David!" A clear voice interrupted his next bout with the figures, and two letters floated one after the other down the band of sunshine. "They came up-river with our maize. Don't you think I am kind to bring them over this hot day?"

As she leaned over her horse's neck to peep in, the ripple in Patricia's hair flamed into burning gold; her rich face burst in like the sun on David's dark mood. "After you have left us alone for a whole month?" she went on, with mock complaint. "And even now you don't ask me to come in. I had intended to stay for lunch, but now I shall ride on to Ewing's."

He had waited only to pick up the letters, and the threat brought him hurrying out. "Oh, if you would?"

"What? Ride on?"

"No, no! Stay to lunch."

If a little surprised at his fervency, she had no way of connecting it with Andrea—who had come to her kitchen door—so gave it her own interpretation. "So you *are* human. I was beginning to doubt it," she added, as he lifted her down.

"As bad as that?" he laughed. Indeed, in his relief at escaping the impending *tête-à-tête* with Andrea, he bubbled over. "Oh, come! You know I have been very busy, and—"

"You quarrelled with father," she frankly supplied. "But that doesn't excuse your boycotting me. I think you are a bear."

"Better that than a bore. You see, if I had come—"

"I might have wished you away?" She looked him over, mockingly serious. "We—ll, perhaps."

His laugh carried back to Andrea, whose bronze took a deeper shade when he called for her to set an extra *platilla*. There was, however, no trace of anger in her quiet service an hour later. She returned glib thanks to Patricia's compliments upon her tortillas; accorded stealthy servility to condescensions so arrogant in their assumption of infinite superiority that they roused David's wonder while helping him to regain his lost control. His embarrassment faded in the face of her subserviency; he could eye her steadily before the end of the meal; was master of himself and the situation when Patricia rose to go.

"Your letters!" she cried, as they walked to the stable. "You never even looked at them."

"Your fault," he laughed. "One from my mother, too. It will keep till I see you away."

But with a vigorous shake of the head she sat down on a log at the stable door. "No, señor, you will read it now." And she looked out over the river till recalled by his whistle.

"Anything wrong?" He repeated her question. "Listen to this."

Opening with Kate Somers's approaching marriage, his mother followed up two pages of condolences with a vivid description of a pilgrimage she and Kate had taken in search of a house, nor seemed to have imagined apology necessary for comfort and countenance thus tended to those who had put a blight on her son's affections. Ensued six pages of church news—picnics, socials, the luck of a revival in adding Mr. Osgood to the roster. Then, after three pages of inquiries and cautions concerning David's health, the usual momentous postscript, which he read aloud:

"You remember you were to have wired me if the plantation did not come up to your expectations, and as you neither wired nor wrote, I felt perfectly safe in taking a special offer of Mr. Osgood's. I have bought five hundred shares of Verda stock."

"Five hundred shares!" Patricia gasped. "That is—"

"Fifty thousand — gold," David groaned. "The bulk of her fortune."

"But why didn't you wire her?"

"I did—sent it out by the moso who piloted me in."

"And of course you gave him money to pay for it? That accounts for it. You ought to have written as well."

He almost blurted out that he had, but stopped as he remembered the circumstances attending the writing, stricken by sudden doubt. "Well, it's done," he said, instead. "The other is from Osgood. Let's see what he has to say."

It was not much. In view of recent additions to the company's capital (David grunted) Mr. Osgood felt himself justified in giving Mr. David a "raise" of fifty dollars per *mensem*. In addition, the plantation working allowance would be substantially increased; with which larger funds at his disposal the company would expect larger results and good reports—especially the latter.

"It's a bribe!" David snorted. "I shall refuse it."

"I wouldn't," Patricia commented. "It's your

own money. I'd ask him for more. He wouldn't dare to refuse you—just yet."

"I *could* do more for the men," he mused. "Well, I'll think it over," and he turned again to the letter, which closed with an allusion to his mother's investment. Mr. David would be pleased to know that it had been made on a special plan which called for half-yearly dividends instead of the usual—

"Paid out of her own capital," the girl dryly interrupted. "Well"—as she paused, musing, there flashed upon her face the hard look of her father, a resemblance fleeting as the thought which called it into being—"well, you're the biggest stockholder, and, being here on hand, it will be your own fault if you don't get a little more than your own."

He glanced up quickly, but irritable disgust died under her frankly innocent look. She was not to blame for her moral obliquities, and he said, quietly: "If I ever get my own I shall have to recreate it."

She nodded, and while he brought out and bridled her horse she watched him with a curiosity that was at variance with her next remark. "I wouldn't take it to heart. Saddle up and come over to Ewing's with me."

Felt or no, he kindled to the spoken sympathy. "I'd love to, but I'm writing my first report to go down by canoe to-night. It will take most of the afternoon, but I'll be ready when you come back and ride with you part of the way home."

"Will you, really?" His eyes were on the bridle,

his thoughts on his letters, so he did not notice the sarcasm. As he arranged her stirrup, she went on: "Very well, señor. In just four hours I shall be yours." And not until she was beyond ear-shot in the jungle did she free her laughter. "He will go *part* of the way, Patricia! Only part!"

Meanwhile, back at the store, David had fallen again into frowning meditation. Capable of turning a brave face to the accidental stroke of fortune, this was the harder to bear because he knew it for the direct result of a double treachery. His letter might, of course, have miscarried. But though he tried to give Hertzer the benefit of the doubt, he felt him to be quite capable of its destruction, and was surprised only at the audacious refinement on his revenge when, a few days later, the letter was returned with an apology to the effect that it had just been found in a forgotten pocket. And Mr. Osgood's motive in sending him down to Verda now stood out as under a calcium spot — the clearer because disgust at Kate's engagement had killed the last vestige of the calf-love which had rendered him helpless as the animal itself in the hands of a butcher.

"I was a fool!" he raged—"a blind, puling, sentimental fool!" Nor would his anger permit him to advance in mitigation the conspiracy of events which had guided what must be conceded an exceedingly long shot, on the part of the financier, plump into the bull's-eye.

Snatching his pen he dashed off two letters, either

of which would, if delivered, have brought this story to a traditional end by securing his return to his native heath. The writing, however, opened an outlet for his anger, permitted cooler reflection. He had nothing to gain, either by frightening his mother or antagonizing the financier. "I'll stick by it till my time comes," he muttered, at last; and while the second letter to his mother was based on cheerful acceptance of the situation, the envelope to the financier contained only his formal report.

He had just sealed the latter when the clear call sounded again without the door. "Ole, Don David! Faithless! Already he has forgotten his promise to escort me *part* of the way."

Not to mention the premeditated mischief in her eye, the accent ought to have given him abundant warning, but his mind was still on his letters. His preoccupation went with him past the cook-house— where Patricia's character was undergoing thorough revision at Rafaela's able hands—through the blistering heat of the clearing into the dank shade of the first morass; and by the time he was able to shake it off, soft solicitude had replaced the lurking deviltry in her look.

In this dry time it was possible for two to ride abreast, and, reining in so that he could come alongside, she gave him the full benefit of big, dewy eyes at a range of a yard. "I was thinking of your misfortune all the time that I was away."

He flushed in his surprise, but gratefully answered:

"That was awfully kind. But please don't worry on my account. I'm almost glad of it."

"Why?"

Under stimulation of her pleased interest he told of his coddled youth, desire to make his own way, finishing: "I have always wanted to hoe my own row, but hoeing is tiresome, and if a fellow has too much money there's always the temptation to quit."

"But won't you find it dull here?" she asked again.

It is possible that he might have disarmed her with a significant "How could I?" But, deceived by her sympathy, he blurted instead a declaration of war against Cancer; talked improved labor conditions, regeneration of plantations, when he ought to have been admiring her eyes; held forth with such lengthy enthusiasm that they were a mile or two beyond Phelps's place before he finished where he ought to have begun.

"Then life here has its compensations."

"Yes?" she said, innocently. "For instance?"

"It is romantic. Instead of driving a prosaic quill in a law office, here I am riding through a tropical jungle with—"

"With?"

Her smile brought his gallantry from under eclipse "The most beautiful girl in Mexico."

"Including the Señorita Consuela?" she demanded laughing.

The girl of the train was a long way off, and youth

is faithful to fascinating memories only in tales. "Including the Señorita Consuela."

An orchid thrust a tongue of fire from the mould of a decaying tree, and, pointing, she said: "For that, señor, you shall fasten a flower in my hair."

His first essay in such delicate business, a little bungling was perfectly natural, and, squirming round under his hands, she laughed up in his face. "I'm sure it is wrong, and I have no glass. Oh, I know! Bend your head — closer — now I can see myself in your eyes."

What a position for sober David! Her breath fanned his cheek, the subtle perfume of her hair filled his nostrils. From a few inches his eyes looked into hers, which shone wide and clear as pools of translucent amber. Slightly parted, her red lips were raised invitingly. He was aware of her figure pulsing its vivid life through every swell and curvature. Then, as though the temptation were not enough, a movement of his beast crushed him against her. His hands were still trembling in her hair, but as the contact sent a flame through his veins they dropped to her waist. Stricken with sudden blindness, his lips went searching; then—her beast bounded under her spur and he was almost thrown to the ground.

"No, Davidito mia!" Her voice came out of a cloud of dust at the next turn. "You were to see me only *part* of the way, and this is the La Luna boundary."

Recovering his balance with a violent effort, David curbed his beast, which had started to run, wherein he violated a well-known tradition of Romance. Your hardy lover would have given the horse his head and have taken his kiss on the run, at the hazard of the damsel's neck—not to mention his own. But a chicken does not bring spurs and comb from the egg, and David had, metaphorically speaking, just stepped out of the incubator. So, while it is true that he felt the impulse, he just sat his beast and stared while his expression ran the gamut through surprise, anger, to grinning shame. *Davidito* (Little David)! It really was absurd!

"Well," he breathed, at last, "you were looking for it, and you got it." To which popular expression of mortification he added, as he rode slowly back toward Phelps's place: "You darned fool! If ever a puppy needed a hiding it is you."

Arrived at the Englishman's boundary he had choice of two trails, and whereas, yesterday, he would surely have taken the one around the clearing, he now rode on to the house; a small matter on the surface, yet significant in view of his thought—"I think you've been a bit of a prig"—and which all goes to prove that the discovery of a mote in one's own eye inclines to charitable measurement of the beam in that of our neighbor. In David's present mood said foreshortening went the length of acceptance when Phelps, who was taking the cool under his veranda, insisted on his putting in for supper.

"I had about concluded that you had put me on the black-list with Hertzer," the Englishman said as he led in-doors. "But better late than never; and I'm awfully glad you came, for I'm feeling blue to-night. No, not ill—just plain homesick. We all take it at times—except Hertzer, who never had a regret in his life or a longing that he couldn't satisfy —and in these latitudes you get it hard. Though you would think it ought to aggravate the disease, I have found a good jab-fest about old times to be the best cure; works on the same principle, I suppose, as the old recommendation to 'Take a hair of the dog that bit you.' Of course it's pretty hard on the listener, but"—he nodded, laughing, at the door— "your remedy is always in sight."

If there were any virtue in the prescription it should surely have worked his cure, for talk he did—of gray spires and nodding trees, the caw of rooks around hoary gables, green lanes and smiling fields of Merrie England. While his children played about the mud floor, and his Tehuana wife gravitated between the table and a glowing charcoal *brasero*, he harked back to ancient Oxford with its 'Varsity boat-races, proctors, and dons, interspersing lively narrations of rows between Town and Gown with reminiscences of smoky London. Old Drury, the Haymarket, the Empire, Irving and his Lyceum, roaring night life of the brilliant Strand; as the magic names ran off his tongue his eyes sparkled in the dusk of that tropical hut like fog-bound lights of the great city. Above the odor of garlic and stewing frijoles his dilated nostrils seemed to sniff the smoke of far-off Piccadilly.

"Man!" he exclaimed. "I can see it lying low in the parks on a winter's evening! What wouldn't I give for a single whiff!"

Running on as he did, without pause for question or comment, David was left free to watch the Tehuana, who on his entering had extended the usual musical welcome. Taller than Hertzer's woman, her features were finer cut without loss of the characteristic brooding maternity. Apparently absorbed in her cookery, he saw her deep eyes turn constantly to Phelps with sympathy and understanding. Ignorant of English, he felt that she intuitively sensed the invisible threads that pulled with the strength of cables, and when, picking up little Felice, she placed her on Phelps's knee, the unconscious pathos of the action caused him a stab of pain. Sensitized by weeks of loneliness, he realized that upon one side at least something other than passion underlay this primitive union; that it was sanctified by that sacrificial love which is the essence of marriage. He saw —and the vision came as a great temptation—that with all his homesickness Phelps would escape, that night, the dreary solitude that always entered with him into his own dark hut.

"Sorry you can't stay all night, old man," the Englishman said as David rose to go. "It's rather dark just now, but you'll have a good moon in another quarter of an hour. They tell me that you are doing fine over there," he went on while David was mounting. "Burned off all your smothered rubber?

Good work, and not a bit too soon. We can look any day for the rains."

His cheery good-night followed David in among the buildings, through whose bird-cage siding he caught the red glow of *braseros*. The *galera*, with its fetor and lanterns, made a blur on the dusk, then a smoky flare of many fires showed him Phelps's *enganchadas* still at work in the cook-house. The twang of a guitar from the *mandador's* quarters went with him into the jungle, where he rode in pitch darkness through an ocean of sound—whistle of beetles, scream of quarrelling birds, incessant buzz of insects. But these died when the moon rose, and as, thereafter, he rode from black shadow in and out of splashing moonlight, there came only an occasional strangled roar to set his horse a-tremble.

It is doubtful whether he heard it, so busy was he with his thoughts: the embarrassing rencounter with Andrea, his bad home news, Patricia's trick, the glimpse of Phelps's home life, each had its turn, and, travelling around the circle, the last brought him back to the first as he rode into the Verda clearing.

The plantation slept. Dark and silent, the conical roofs uprose like so many straw beehives gleaming faintly yellow in the tender light. His glance went first to his own house, and in vivid contrast to its solitary darkness there came flashing into his mind a picture of the Tehuana under the red light of her *brasero*, the warmth, love, passion of maternity in her soft eyes. Then it wandered to the kitchen

THE PLANTER

where Andrea not only cooked, but also lived, slept, and otherwise had her comely being. Then — up flashed the reverse of the picture. Once more he saw Phelps's eyes sparkling under his high, peaked forehead as he talked of home and country in complete forgetfulness of the girl-child in his arms.

With a vigorous shake of the head he rode on to the stable.

XI

CANCER SWINGS, AND—

A "NORTHER" brought the rains, a mighty wind
that bellowed among the palms and screamed
through the *bejuca* tangle, that uprooted trees, beat
and bullied the jungle till it roared with a thousand
voices. From a high knoll David overlooked its vast
torture, squirming life; watched it leap and toss, an
ocean of pain, with infinite writhings; saw the great
waves sweep from his feet around tall tree islands
to break on far reefs of brown cedars—watched till
his stunned ear refused further commerce with the
clamor, and silence came as a surprise with the pat-
tering rain.

A hundred inches' precipitation in three months
can hardly be termed a Scotch mist. By the time
one-quarter had fallen it seemed to David that the
Gulf must have joined hands with the Pacific across
the Tehuantepec isthmus. Instead of paths, canals
connected the lakes which flowed over the morasses.
A boil of yellow waters, the river ran outside its
banks, bearing a scum of dead wood, trees, drowned
cattle and pigs, acres of greenery — sweepings of a

THE PLANTER

hundred miles of jungle and many an Indian village.
Yet was there no cess of the rain. Day after day it
slanted in warm sheets upon the sweltering earth,
for behind its wet veil burned the July sun, and did
the clouds break for one minute the firmament instantly filled with steam that soft-cooked David and
his men at work replanting the burned acreage in
this the tropical seed-time.

It was tiresome as well as wet work. "Don't let
your men drop seed," Hertzer had warned him.
"They'll either miss holes or plant it too deep, and
though gaps *can* be filled from the nursery, the plants
are never as thrifty." So while the gangs punched
holes in the oozy soil, he dropped the seed, three to a
place, to be afterward thinned to a single plant.
For a month he hardly straightened his stiff back,
and what of the water that poured from his face and
neck off the end of his nose, that feature felt sore and
began to look like a worn cathedral gargoyle. And
from the streaming fields he came in at night to a hut
that was almost as wet from rain that had driven
through the pole siding. Could his mother have seen
these damp cloths he called his sheets!

If he had yearned for hardening experience, the
quantity supplied so far exceeded the specifications
that it is hardly a matter of wonder that his night
thoughts should sometimes turn enviously to Ewing
in his comfortable bungalow, to Phelps whose hut
boasted a mud fireplace. It required no more strain
of the imagination for him to see Ewing's pretty

little wife airing him a change of garments than to picture the Tehuana moving on similar errands for Phelps. Nor is it surprising that when contrasted with his own wet cheerlessness, the comfort of these Sybarites should appear as an attribute of the married state inseparable from the feminine presence; thoughts which explain his silent assent to the innovation when one evening he found that Andrea had set his supper out in her kitchen.

"It was so wet in the cabin, señor," she pleaded, when he looked in from the sloppy dusk between the huts—quite unnecessarily. Besides the inevitable *brasero*, the kitchen contained Meagher's old cooking-stove, and while changing his things for others only a shade less damp—their condition may be gauged by the fact that his cake of Pears' soap had melted on the stand—he could hear the stove's roaring welcome, catch a glint of crockery under the gold of the lamp, sniff a savory stew. To exclude the damp air Andrea had hung *zarapes* around the walls, with which bright background it required only herself in spotless chemisette, crimson skirt, to complete the picture of homely comfort.

He ate luxuriously that evening, and as, drawing thereafter into a corner by the stove, he watched her at her household duties, he absorbed other than the heat. His starved senses fed on the multitude of subtleties which go to make up the feminine atmosphere that men feel but do not recognize till removed from its sphere. His eyes followed the hand and smooth arm that went repeatedly to her hair. He watched the velvet lashes sweep down till they brushed the red health under her bronze; the easy flexures of her supple body. He bathed in her presence, an indulgence none the less dangerous because unconscious, and which was rendered still more so by a veneer of refinement that overlaid her vigorous animality, that courtesy of manner and tone native in all who speak the Spanish tongue. Simulating modesty, it put him at ease, left him free to laugh at the plantation gossip which she retailed with girlish humor. And if she gave him laughter for laughter, responding with a vivacity one would never have expected from the obsequious creature who had cringed to Patricia, she governed herself with such skill that he never noticed when she quietly rubbed out the line between master and servant.

The obliteration occurred after a correction of his Spanish. "Mi padre esta muerte," he said, telling her that his father was dead. Then he stared, rather shocked by her laughter, until she explained that his wrong usage of the verb implied that Mr. Mann, senior, was merely temporarily dead, and might be expected to resurrect at any moment.

The remark itself was intended to correct a misconception of hers that his father must be actively engaged in the company management, but she followed in through the opening to his home life with a question concerning his mother — "She is alive, señor?"

It was none of her business, but what with her deceptive courtesy, he not only answered, but presently found—rather to his own surprise—that he was telling her all about his home. "And the señorita?" she asked, when he suddenly paused.

"The señorita?" he repeated, puzzled. "I have no sister."

"No. She whom you love?"

"I!" he exclaimed, in his surprise. It was inconceivable that she could know anything of Kate, yet she shook her head when he began: "If you mean the Señorita Hertzer—"

"No. The Americano in your own land."

Once more Kate flashed into his mind—to be again ejected. Then, curious about her thought, he asked: "What makes you think that I am in love?"

"You are different from the others."

"The others? Whom?"

"The Señors Hertzer, Phelps—all the Americanos on this river."

"How?"

She paused, meditating, eyes turned down on the chemisette she was ironing for to-morrow's wear. Thud of an iron pressing hot linen under golden lamplight—here is the quintessence of housewifery; and while his eyes followed her easy flexures as her weight moved with the iron, subconsciousness took cognizance of the fact and added its force to her answer: "You have no woman."

As aforesaid, David's eyes had already opened to

157

her part in his problem. But whereas, hitherto, he had studied it through the big end of the telescope, which thrust her back into the distance, she had turned the glass for him and now loomed within reach of his hand. As modest as he was sober, there was no misreading the steady meditation in her glance; yet if it caused the blood to leap to his face his answer was firmly serious.

"No, I have no woman."

"Then you are in love?"

"Perhaps. Why not?" Yet, despite his smile, he winced at a sudden realization that he had unconsciously put it forward as a protection.

"What is her name?" Her question came steadily as the thud of her iron.

"Consuela." This time he was surprised that of all possible names this should most readily slide from his tongue, and his heightened color was not lost by Andrea's observant eye.

So far she had looked doubtful. Now she said: "Ah, you blush! Then you are really in love." She quickly added: "But Consuela is a Spanish name?"

"We use many Spanish names in my country," he answered, and changed the subject. "What's the Spanish for iron, Andrea?"

Yet no change of subject could alter the fact that from a negative abstraction in thought this part of his problem had evolved into a positive temptation. The knowledge went with him to his damp bed that night, accompanied him next day to the dripping fields, loomed always thereafter behind the veil of waters, ready to thrust in on the first moment of reflection, to demand an answer from his youth. And if it was not given at once the delay must be charged to the anxieties that suddenly filled his mind to the exclusion of all else.

For sickness came with the rains. Though he did his best by his men, providing extra clothing from his own salary to enable them to sleep dry at night, though he gave them better food, and care such as had never been known on the Isthmus, he could not rebuild broken constitutions, purify blood vitiated by the hoarded vices of twenty Spanish generations. They began to die on his hands.

First went Veinte-dos. One night he came in complaining. Morning saw him shaking with calentura. He died in a week, fulfilling his pledge to Hertzer. And so with others. "I shall die, señor! I shall die!" a man would cry, and despite quinine, special food, David's careful nursing, die he would, and another mound be added to the row in the forest. By ones, then twos, occasionally in threes, death swept them out of his hands until it seemed to him that return to their *pais* (country) alone could save the remnant. Yet this was impossible. The work had to go on; for while they were planting new rubber, the jungle had boiled in over the old — now swept, a green sea, over his best trees.

Its growth was unbelievable, miraculous. Slashing a wild *platina* one day, Maria Guadaloupe had David stand by while the succulent stalk put forth a fresh shoot. It grew half an inch in an hour—vivid type of the fecund life which sprang up and flowed after the gangs even as they swept it out of the plantings. Always it hung on their rear—creeping, crawling, a resistless tide that claimed at night the ground that day's labor had paid for in sweat and death. It got at last on his nerves—already worn by a touch of malaria—loomed in his imagination as a huge thug with itching fingers eternally stretched at the throat of his rubber; an obsession that, leaving the campus at night, would sometimes cause him to start, as though at a cry, and look back like a timid pedestrian up a dark street. Withal he fought it yard by yard, foot by foot, inch by inch; fought through fevers, calenturas, dysentery; fought it under the frown of Death himself, nor paused until the plantation was clean at the close of the rains.

Then, as a man from a nightmare, he awoke from his trance of labor and looked about him to count the cost. Having thoroughly weeded that fetid garden, Death had passed on, leaving seventeen graves in the jungle. Seventeen? David felt like a murderer—even when Phelps, who poled up-stream at the first slack-water, laughed in his serious face.

"Seventeen out of sixty, and your plantation clean as a pin!" the Englishman commented, as they walked together up from the landing. "Why, I lost twenty-three out of fifty, and my rubber is drowned. I shall have to touch my people for an extra appropriation. You got off cheaply, my dear fellow. Forget it. It's part of the price that has to be paid." Having thus testified before the "God of Things as They Are," the disciple of Kidd dropped into a tone more befitting the homesick Englishman of four months ago. "But say, old chap, you are looking awfully seedy. There's nothing left of you but jaw, and your eyes are all glazed over. Taking quinine with your coffee? That's right, but you need some one to look after you." Grinning, as David paused to unlock the store door, he added: "I had expected to find you settled down with Andrea to comfortable housekeeping."

Rightly understood, David's quick frown indicated misgivings of his own rather than irritation at Phelps. If intended to check the latter's freedom, it would have failed in any case. Always eager for argument, he sprang to pick up the gage of battle. "Why not? It would be perfectly natural and proper, as the conventions go here. Really, I should have thought you would have learned in your law course that instead of being fixed and arbitrary as people are accustomed to think of them, morals are variable as the wind, unstable as water—change from epoch to epoch, and are never the same in different countries. While Jacob, the father of Israel, had two wives, and Solomon, its king, a thousand, our custom restricts us to one, and a Roman priest is bound to celibacy." He was going on in his school-masterly fashion—"There can be only one test for morality: its effect on the sum of human happiness "—when David quietly interrupted.

"In all its consequences."

"You mean the children?" Phelps looked up from the soap-box on which he had just seated himself. Accepting the challenge, he ran on: "Socially, the mixing of blood is good for the race. Your Anglo-Saxon, biggest-brained and most warlike of all types, sprang from a heterogeneous mixture of Romans, Normans, Angles, Saxons, Celts—"

"Monogamists all." David registered a second quiet objection.

"By law," Phelps corrected, grinning. "As for their practice, read Roman history and study the life of our modern cities. A minute! I know what you are going to say. In spite of excesses, the monogamic law preserves the family and conserves the strength of the nation. It does — has done it for so long that its practice has become instinctive with the Anglo-Saxon. While your German, Frenchman, Dutchman intermarry with native women all over the world, your Anglo-Saxon—who lives as freely as any—refuses to darken his blood by legitimizing his colored children."

"And the children?"

Again Phelps accepted the challenge. "I was just coming to it. Take Patricia. Where could you find a healthier or handsomer girl? Some day she will marry a planter, and her legitimate children will be none the worse for a lick of the blood."

CANCER SWINGS, AND—

"And supposing he had gone away when she was small?"

"She'd have made a better Indian. No, Mann, frankly, I don't see where your theory lets you off, unless you believe it to be ordained. And even then, if Genesis doesn't lie, God saw that it was not good for man to be alone, and the commentators haven't been able to dig up anything about a preacher or license."

Now, though David's opportunities toward philosophy had been limited as his mother could make them —she would have enclosed him in a ring fence between Genesis and Revelations—he had found time for the surreptitious reading of several agnostics—had even dipped his immature beak in the polluted fountains of "the arch-fiend Ingersoll." And his answer not only surprised Phelps by its breadth, but was significant in that it set forth thoughts ripened in the fires of recent experience. "I recognize your logic," he said, slowly, "and almost all that you have said had occurred to me before. But I'm beginning to doubt whether logic has anything to do with questions of feeling. It seems to me that it is all a matter of temperament. You are born with certain instincts that are trained into what we call a disposition, and the quantities are so varying that no two act alike under the same conditions. Other things being equal, the whole question becomes one of personal viewpoint. What seems right to you may be wrong for me, and—"

THE PLANTER

"New England morality still stands the strain," Phelps laughed. "Every man a law unto himself, eh? Well, that's fairly broad doctrine—we'll let it go at that." Raising quizzical brows, he continued: "After all, there's no dogmatist like your Tolerant. Instead of leaving you in the quiet enjoyment of your uncomfortable morals, here I have heckled and pecked you until, out of sheer boredom, you are driven to take a complacent view of my own slack practice. To change the subject, have you seen or heard anything of Hertzer lately?"

"Haven't seen a white face for three months."

Phelps nodded. "Nor I, till I poled down to La Luna yesterday to try and borrow frijoles. Didn't get them, by-the-way, and if you can spare them I shall presently touch you for ten arrobas. Well, I found Hertzer in full enjoyment of a brand-new judicial appointment. Deputy-acting-assistant policeman and justice of the peace would about represent it in English, and, not to mention the dignity inherent in the title, he expects to make it turn a profit when the teak and mahogany begin to come down on the tail of the flood. You see, ridiculous as it appears, these thousands of square miles of heated jungle are the private property of powerful Mexican families. Of course the owners never did and probably never will set a foot on the land. But still it is privately owned, and when the Zacatecos, who have rafted timber down these rivers for the last two hundred years, come down this fall, Hertzer will hold them up till they prove ownership. If they can't—and that's a cinch—he'll confiscate the timber, and after deducting the rake-off for his superior, the Jefe-Politico of San Juan, he stands to make a couple of thousand, Mex. Did you ever hear of balder robbery?" However, a gleam of admiration chastened his reprehension, a touch of regret modified his tone as he finished: "There's another application of your theory, Mann. Though it were to make us instantly rich, neither you nor I could do it. To the devil with these limitations!"

"The Jew!" David commented. "What a Jew!"

"Yes, but the Jew militant. These Zacatecos are no joke. I wouldn't like to tackle the job."

"And how is he getting along with his Yaquis?" David asked.

"Pretty well. After a flogging or two they got down to work, and he nursed them like a father through the rains. Now, don't jump to conclusions! He hasn't been miraculously converted to your labor theories. It's easily explained. They are his for life—private property, like so many head of cattle, and he treats them accordingly. And now to business. What of the beans?"

"You can have them," David said, after a glance at his stock.

"Another of your limitations," Phelps laughed. "Though his store is stacked to the rafters, Hertzer wouldn't lend me a bean. Wanted to sell me at sixteen prices. You'll never be rich, Mann. Now, if you will please have some of your fellows carry them down to the canoe, I'll walk out with you and take a look at the rubber."

It was still early, and as the declension of the sun in Cancer had already lowered temperatures, it was, for the tropics, a cool day; though, measured by degree, the heat yet rivalled the Northern dog-days, the morning had for them all the flavor of cool October. The familiar cackling of Rafaela's hens helped the impression, and as they walked by the cook-house the clarion crow of her game rooster rang out as clearly as those which float with a whiff of wood smoke over autumn fields. From the surrounding woods, too, the *chacalahuas* (wild fowl) competed with the domestic clamor. But for these, and a far-off booming, melancholy call of monkeys, they might have fancied themselves at home.

As aforesaid, a fifty acres or so of rubber had been kept fairly clean, even in Meagher's careless time; and now what of the rains and David's careful husbandry it upstood in serried array, wand - like branches all tufted with leaves, rich and thick as green velvet. Even the new plantings had put forth stocky plants, and coming back through five hundred acres of it Phelps repeatedly expressed his admiration.

"It is fine, Mann—fine! I don't see how you did it. Verda used to be a joke on this river, but I see that we shall have to turn elsewhere for an awful example. Even Guadaloupe enthused over it when he met me at the landing—that is," he amended, "he enthused over the rubber. Seems to think you are making a fool of yourself with the men. What's this about your leaving the galera unlocked at night?"

His sudden look of suspicious concern drew David's smile. "Only an experiment. For the last two months the men have been coming in alone from the fields, one by one, each as he finished his stint. So far we have had no runaways, and I intend, if possible, to give them complete freedom. You see, if they could only hunt or fish a little after hours and on Sundays, they would be healthier as well as more contented. Indeed," he went on, after a modest pause, "I half believe that I have solved the problem of tropical labor."

Again Phelps raised quizzical brows. "Yes? And how?"

"By colonization. I have already given three men—who have wives and children to anchor them—a cabin apiece with land enough for their corn and frijoles. In return they are to keep two hectares of rubber thoroughly clean throughout the year, and I have figured that I can pay them a dollar for each day's actual labor, and still get the work done a hundred per cent. cheaper than by enganchars. What do you think of it?"

"What do I think of it?" Phelps had listened impatiently, and now he exploded. "I think it's all damned rot! Whoever saw a plateau Mexican who would settle down anywhere but in his pais? I see how it is, Mann"—his voice dropped to a mendicant whine: "'I'd love to stay with you all my life, señor, you are so kind and pleasant and nice!' They have been feeding you that sort of tommy-rot. As for coming in alone, did you expect them to run away with the river at flood and the jungle a bog? Wait till the water goes down." They were now back at the river, and, looking down on the canoe, Phelps finished: "I see it is loaded, and I'll have to go. But take my advice, Mann, and leave well alone."

"To-morrow," David called after him, as he went down the bank, "is the fifteenth of September, the Mexican Fourth of July. I'm giving them a whole holiday, with a barbecue during the day and a dance at night."

Phelps shrugged without looking round. "More lunacy. They won't thank you—are sure to take it as a confession of weakness. They will think you are afraid of them. Severity, I tell you, is the only thing. But I perceive you are hopeless. It's the New England virus at work in your veins. I can only commend you to the saint—whoever he is—that protects one from runaway enganchars."

Meeting Guadaloupe just then coming up from the canoe, he stopped and held him in talk for a minute. From above David could not hear what they said, but he caught the *mandador's* brown grin, and when, with mutual headshakes, each went on his way, he smiled, thinking that he understood.

Out of black night a bonfire played like a vivid fountain sending a red rain of sparks out to vie with the greenish twinklings of a myriad lantern-flies, splashing the store, *galera*, and cook-house with crimson spray of light.

The barbecue was over. Of three porkers, whose dying squeals had risen a reluctant pæan to Mexican independence, there remained only the savory odor which still clung about the pits, unless one add a still subtler essence, the greasy content on the faces of the *enganchadores* who were clustered about the platform David had had erected for dancing; and this was fast dissolving in thirsty expectation as they watched Maria Guadaloupe stir and taste a caldron of *tekala* punch.

In honor of the occasion they had donned clean cottons, which, brilliantly white under the firelight, intensified the black and bronze of eyes and faces, and formed a startling background for the gala crimson of Rafaela, Andrea, and other half-dozen Zacatecas from an Indian village across the river. These, free people, with their menfolk, in *charro* costume—skin-tight trousers, bolero jackets, silver or gold laced felt sombreros—occupied benches on either side of David's chair of honor, and no dame in the stalls of a theatre could have achieved superciliousness chillier than that in the glances they directed at the cookhouse women on the opposite side of the platform.

This was a rude affair. Scarcely half the size of a prize-ring, it had yet taken two men the best part of a week to whipsaw its boards and stringers out of the log, and because, perhaps, a perennial dearth of lumber has moulded the form of tropical dancing, its narrow limits sufficed for the eternal jig which had been going on for hours. Very like the Irish dance in its constant change of partners, its action was not nearly so violent and moved to a slower rhythm. Supposed to represent a wooing, it was in its simplicity analogous to the dancing of grouse that precedes spring mating. As, with crimson skirts outstretched, one of the Zacatecas glided right and left under the flash and play of the firelight, it were easy to imagine her a gorgeous bird; the posturing of the man advancing upon her were no more intricate than the struttings of a cock grouse; the tinkling accompaniment of guitars and high nasal chant of a single singer were surely less musical than the twitterings of birds.

The singing, as David soon found, had its own significance. As a girl climbed onto the platform one of the half-dozen instrumentalists would improvise a line in her honor, which would be instantly capped by a rival singer, and thus, line by line, her qualities would be celebrated, till one or other failed of a rhyme. Whereupon both would repair to celebrate success and drown failure in Guadaloupe's kettle.

Than that scene with its fire and action going on within the lit circle of conical palm huts there could be nothing more opposite to the cool quiet of a sober Northfield evening, yet David did not feel it strange or unfamiliar. In six months he had grown to the bronzed faces, heat and color of jungle life, fire of southern skies over dusks jewelled with amethyst flashes of flies—grown to it till the old life loomed as a dim dream very far away. And surely it was a far cry from the David of Northfield to the youthful patriarch who sat amid his big, brown family and smiled at practices that, aforetime, would have raised his hair in horror; who tested the *tequila* and raised his glass almost jovially in response to repeated toasts to his health, yet kept a careful eye on the kettle while delightedly watching the dancing of his enganchars.

At first the free people had seemed inclined to stand on their caste, but the steaming *tequila* had soon washed out the line. The singers, to be sure, substituted parodies for praises in accompanying the cook-house women. But so that the comparison were made in good dance time, neither Casamira, Panchita, nor any other seemed to take offence at the likening of their waists to a tub. Poor slaves of the *metates*, their labor-stiffened muscles did not lend themselves to grace. They moved with jerks, like marionettes, bobbed up and down, taking their pleasure seriously, without relaxing a facial line. Yet for all their stolidity they evidenced such enjoyment, sheer physical delight, that David gravitated between pleasure and pity. Until twelve he watched them foot it, and when he stood at the door while they filed into the *galeras*, their radiant "*Buenas-noches*" caused him to revert, with a smile, to Phelps's

discouraging words. Their smiles were the first he
had ever seen on the face of *enganchadores*. Snatches
of song followed him back to the fire, where the other
half of his problem lay in waiting.

Returning, he saw that Andrea—who took the
platform as he left—was dancing alone. At the distance her spread skirts flamed like scarlet wings,
and she seemed to be hovering over a vermilion confusion of men and women who came and went about
the platform. It was neither the first nor the fifth
time she had danced that evening, but even a careless eye might have discerned a difference, sensed a
purpose behind her continued glidings. Instead of
throwing her kerchief to her choice out of the dozen
men who were clapping hands and hissing to attract
her attention, she moved in the monotonous time
of the dance until David resumed his seat. Then,
as though that were her signal, she snapped her fingers at the musicians and broke into the step of a
lively fandango.

Arms swinging, fingers snapping, body swaying
languorously with the music, she circled and recircled
the platform in an abandon of luxurious motion.
The *tekala*, which burned like fire in her veins, had
melted her veneer of reserve, and every limb, line,
and curve expressed her vital animality. As, going
away, she swayed and looked back at David, her
short, loose tunic raised to the uplift of her arms,
revealing the nude waist and starting bust, redly
golden in the firelight, her pools of eyes caught the

glow and shone like ruby velvet; she exhaled sensuousness, and as her gaze caught and held his, David shivered, was affected as though by a powerful odor.

It was not the glimpse of nudity. They were now commonplaces of his life and had been in evidence all evening. But her every languorous movement seemed to call with a soft voice, to breathe an invitation, and he blushed with sudden shame—blushed, and in the act of blushing was aware that shame was merely the upper layer of feelings that were unanalyzable in that turgid moment. He glanced uneasily to right and left. But while the men were watching the play of her kerchief the singers stooped over their instruments; the women were beating the time with their hands.

As she came swinging and swaying from another turn her eyes again singled out David, and he ceased to breathe as she made to throw. It was, however, only a part of her coquetry. But if he gasped when the kerchief fluttered to the hand of a young Zacateco, relief was curiously mingled with another feeling— one which he immediately denied and thrust out of consciousness. Denied admittance to his thoughts, it still manifested itself in contrary impulses to retain and leave his seat. He wished to leave, but did not like to; and he sat on, watching the dance until he suddenly realized that by doing so he was countenancing the very feeling he was denying. Then he immediately rose and walked away to his hut, where he found the feeling strongly intrenched.

Moreover, it refused to be ousted. "Why didn't you stay?" it whispered. "Or you could have broken up the *baile*."

"Pish!" He snorted his scorn of the idea.

"Then why did you leave so suddenly?" Truthful conscience now took a hand in his cross-examination. "And why that backward glance from the door?"

"Well—" David began. Then being naturally as honest with himself as with others, he faced the issue squarely.

He was certainly not in love with Andrea—that is, as poets write of the passion. He made the necessary qualification; but what of the ugly feeling that had thrust through his shame when her kerchief fluttered by him? The Zacateco, a clean-limbed fellow, with straight, imperious brows and nose, had hovered about her all evening. When they were not dancing, his guitar had tinkled perpetually in her honor, continuing the court, and David was now sufficiently posted on Zacateco customs to know that, if sufficiently impressed, the girl would probably cross the river and set up housekeeping in his cabin that very night. If not in love, then her choice had violated a sense of physical ownership, and the realization of it caused him to pause aghast at this sudden glimpse into the abyss below consciousness where works the silent machinery of nature.

There was no getting away from it. While, in the pride of his robust morality, he had continually ejected her from the swept chambers of his thoughts, she had quietly crawled in again at the basement windows. The very act of rejection had created the surety of acceptance, and it had required only the touch of jealousy to bring knowledge of it up from nascent consciousness.

He acknowledged it. "I was surely jealous." Then out of his travail burst a bit of slang than which nothing could better have described his feeling: "My God! where am I at?"

In the flash of that frank confession he saw himself on the edge of a precipice, an abyss from which the huge hand of the cave man reached up to grasp the moiety that was left him in this disciple of a severe school, and he heard the howl of the original beast clamoring for his meal of golden flesh. And, as if this were not sufficient, a still small voice issued out of the dark — the logic of Phelps supporting their claims.

Between them he had a hard time of it. Let moralists uphold shocked hands, æsthetes wonder at his taste, the fact remains that in this, the hour of his discovered weakness, the poor lad called every canon of established morality before the bar of his awakened senses and found them more or less wanting, insufficient to the needs of the case. "Thou shalt not!" read their law; but when was a law effective without a policeman? And public opinion, the policeman of morals, here worked against the law. So he tossed and turned in a fever until shouts from across the river announced the departure of the

Zacatecos. Then he lay still as death, barely breathing, till a soft foot-fall and the click of Andrea's door started him into fresh ragings at himself for having listened.

"You'll have to get rid of her," he groaned, at last. "To-morrow she can move into her mother's cabin, and I'll do my own cooking."

Whereupon, and in the absence of anything better, conscience permitted him an hour or two of sleep.

XII

MR. DAVID GOES DOWN, AND—

DID he live up to that hardy resolution?
In the cool perspective of morning, midnight reflections are apt to lose some of their fever, and an early dip in the river cooled David so much that when Andrea served his breakfast, with her usual quiet stealth, he was inclined to set it all down as a nightmare, an opinion which strengthened as he ate his meal. In the face of delicately broiled fish, tortillas light as snowflakes, coffee hot and strong, it is hard to be severe, more especially when severity carries with it the penalty of being condemned to the horrors of one's own cooking. So, appeasing conscience with a promise to choose a more fitting opportunity, David went out to work.

Andrea's opinion may be best deduced from her replies to Rafaela as they watched him ride away from the door of the cook-house.

"I tell thee," Rafaela argued, "that he liked not thy dancing with Candelario. His face grew black as mine, and I caught the jealous flash of his eye. Laggard as he is, he felt the spur. One more such touch—" She snapped her fingers.

THE PLANTER

The girl's shoulders quivered like shimmering satin. "Ay, but now how shall one give it?"

Leaning her mighty brawn against the door-jamb, Rafaela laughed in scorn. "Ohe! the blood runs colder, the wit slower since my day. Ask for thy wage, and he will instantly see thee headed across river."

Andrea's dark brows rose. "But if he pay me?"

Rafaela expelled a huge breath. "Pouf! waste no more time. White meat is sweet to the tooth, but dark more filling to the belly. Candelario is a clever hunter, and the fish fight for a chance at his net."

"And I am to wash his camisas?" the girl questioned, scornfully. "Grind his tortillas, with stick for my pay when the liquor is in him?"

"'Tis the lot of us all," Rafaela grimly answered. "Only this morning thy father laid his machete across my back, as though I could help his calentura. It is to escape it that I give thee advice. For six months hast thou played this shy fish, with never a nibble until last night. If thou wouldst see him leap from the water, lift the bait—lift while the hunger is on him. 'Tis thy only chance—take it or not." With which she went in-doors, leaving the girl to muse on the threshold.

It was, of course, a chance! But the fiesta of San Juan was drawing near, and if she were to ruffle it there in silk and velvet something must soon be done. The more she thought it over the more she inclined to her mother's logic, and when she finally rose and went back to her own kitchen she had made up her mind to give David notice at lunch.

Unaware that he was to be thus hoisted with his own petard, David jogged along, meanwhile, in pleasant company with Conscience. "She is really a fine cook," he argued. "If her ambition would pause at that?" said Conscience. "Of course, of course!" David hastened. "If she steps over the line again—" "Fire her at once," Conscience finished, and so left him to his work. For he was to be very busy that morning inaugurating his colony.

Taking the three men, its nucleus, with him, he marked off land for their corn down by the river, measured its rental in hectares of rubber they were to keep clean, and had still time enough before lunch for another operation. Fifty acres of his oldest rubber was now tall and stout enough to stand the wear and tear of rubbing cattle. "Once in that stage," Phelps had said the day before, "a few cows are worth a batch of enganchars. They'll keep the monte pastured down to the ground, and turn you a few dollars on the side. Fence it, and turn some in. You can buy all you need from the Zacateco rancheros across the river." In accord with which advice he now divided contracts for the fence among his three retainers.

What of these interests, the stir and healthy action, he forgot Andrea and his midnight tossings, returned, as he thought, so closely to his normal that he laughed aloud when they did recur to memory as he rode in

to lunch. Jealous. indeed! What if she did go to her
Indian? Nor did he realize that his philosophizings
upon her going were based on the fact that she had
not gone until she touched off the petard as she
brought him his coffee.

He looked up, darkly flushing. "You want to
leave?"

"Si, señor." She gave him steady eyes.

She had blazed the way he had expected to hew for
himself, but as he waited, hesitant, his mind flashed out
and down it to a hut in the tropical forest. It was
difficult to find the philosopher of an hour before in
the stammering youth who gave answer. "Eh—you
don't mean—to-day?"

"At your convenience, señor," she staidly answered.

Equally difficult was it to discern the philosopher
when, lying at length on his *catre* a few minutes later,
he stared up into the brown gloom of the apex. He
was not thinking. He saw and heard Andrea carrying the dishes out to her kitchen, was conscious of
sunbeams that laid slender fingers of gold between
the siding, watched with some interest the travels
of a scorpion along a bamboo rafter; but while reg-
istering these externals his mind refused commerce
with the tumult of feeling beneath its dead calm.
Things of the past, plantation business, events of
the future it quietly considered. He remembered
that he was to cross the river that afternoon to look
at some cattle, and presently he heard himself telling
Andrea of his intention. Her queer, considering look

caused him to glance in his glass, but, though he
turned uneasily from the harassed eyes which stared
out of a red suffusion, he did not reflect on the cause
behind them.

That morning Guadaloupe had risen complaining,
and, though David now found him waiting outside
the store for a second dose of quinine, he stoutly repelled a suggestion to lay off; neither would he permit any other than himself to ferry him over the
river.

"V. esta infermo tambien?" he said, as he saddled
the dripping horse on the other side.

Replying that he was not sick, David mounted and
rode on into the jungle. Crossing the river he had
experienced a sensation of pleasure in the sheen of
the water, musical plunk of the pole, muscular energy of his swimming horse. Now he noticed the
graceful curve of great palm feathers, flame of orchids
in mossy shade, the flight of brilliant birds. Once
he reined in to admire a tree, large as a Northern
oak, which bore a bright orange bell at the end of
each twig in place of leaves. Also he watched the
rise and heavy flapping flight of a scarlet-crested
vulture, king of the leaden tribe, and when the path
suddenly debouched on a clearing wide enough to
be styled a plain he exclaimed his admiration.

Burned off, years ago, by a fire that spared only
the sturdy oaks, it had been kept clear of *monte* by
the cattle which spotted its vivid green with patches
of red and white. Knee-deep in verdant pasture

that rolled in sunlit waves around the dotting oaks, it looked more like some lordly English park than a clearing in the heart of the tropics. The village with its palm-roofed huts seemed sharply out of place as the brown *ranchero*, in *charro* suit and wide sombrero, who came riding out to meet him.

With the *ranchero* — the same with whom Ewing had wrangled the morning after David came to La Luna — he rode from band to band. But though he chose his beasts and reached an agreement as to price and time of delivery, though he acted all through like his usual reasonable self, he was curiously conscious of a dual personality — a David who saw, heard, bargained, and who looked forward with a dim shrinking to the moment when he would be compelled to give pause and reason with the other David who was held, blind and speechless, in the grip of a huge amorphous instinct.

After the bargain was closed it had to be sealed with a sip of *tekala* in the fashion of the country, and as they rode into the village the doorways filled with brown, curious women and girls whose smiles ran the gamut from bold to shy. One, a pretty baggage of eighteen, called after him. "She say will you have her to keep your house?" the *ranchero* translated, grinning broadly, and as, glancing back, David caught the challenging flash of dark eyes a vivid impulse leaped through his veins consuming his will, enslaving his senses. Thereafter he saw everything through a shimmering haze sensuous as yellow sunlight — the comely women, graceful girls; the children, small golden blots in the dust; the full-breasted mother suckling her babe in the *ranchero's* hut.

Riding homeward, too, that dominant instinct directed his senses. The love-calls of birds, the wood-dove's gentle piping, floated through dusk that was soft as a sigh. From the high trees came the domestic clamor of monkeys; everywhere the parrots winged in their pairs. In the jungle gloom palms leaned to each other softly caressing; *bejucas* writhed in a fierce embrace. Darkness itself settled like the quiet of satisfied love over a vast fecundity of which procreation was the only law.

It was quite dark when he reached the river. Across the stretch of livid waters the buildings loomed, a dim blur pierced here and there with yellow-and-red beams of lights and fires. Waiting for the canoe, he heard lively chatter in the cookhouse—Rafaela's harsh command, the wail of a child; then, clear as a bell, but with a throaty ululation in it like the coo of a wild pigeon, Andrea's laugh floated out on the warm night, and again a fierce excitement leaped in his throat.

He hardly noticed that it was Rafaela who ferried him across. Leaving her to stable and dry down his wet beast, he walked on to the house, where Andrea, clean and neat as a pin, waited to serve his supper. With a brusque " No quiero comer," he closed the door —almost in her face—and sat down to think. But think he could not. His whole power was concentrated on resistance, an effort real and sustained as though he were trying to hold down a man stronger than himself, and there was no iota left over for thought. Elbows on knees, hot face in his hands, he sat on the edge of his *catre* shivering or glowing to successive surges of feeling that strained at his resolution as a sea tugs at a ship's cable; and when, rising, he lit his lamp at last, the act was analogous to that of the mariner who cuts a dragging anchor to make a last desperate run for port.

He found no harbor of refuge in the account-book he first picked up. Throwing it aside, he opened a volume of Kipling, the property of Phelps, and idly turned the pages till his eye fell on M'Andrew's hymn:

" Lord, Thou hast made this world below the shadow of a
        dream."

The pomp and swing of that high-sounding line instantly riveted his attention, and every association of early training caused him to grasp at the name of Deity in this his moment of weakness. Dimly feeling that help had been vouchsafed him, he read on to where the old engineer cries out in anguish of spirit, ". . . How far, O Lord, from Thee?"

" How far, O Lord, from Thee?"

It thrilled him, that great cry; and had he stayed his reading there, he might have been strengthened for another day's resistance. But he read along— M'Andrew's lustful envy of couples "kittlin' in the dark behind the funnel stays," his raking of the ports in pride, down through the remorseful confession of surrender to the tropics. The "playhouse scenes," the "soft lasceevious stars" that "leered from velvet skies," the land-breeze "milk-warm wi' breath of spice an' bloom"—David saw, felt them: the soft stars even then shining down without, the wind that breathed its fragrance through the siding; saw, felt them as he read on in a heat to a line which brought a vivid picture flashing out on the page:

"But swells the ripenin' cocoanut an' ripes the woman's breast."

From silvery waters beyond the black palm shade uprose a nude bronze bejewelled with running diamonds. Once again he felt his head sink to the warm breast as on the day she massaged his bruises, and at the memory his flesh, the exultant unconquerable flesh which has defied the mortification of a thousand generations, cried out aloud.

Springing up, he snapped the book shut. It had no message for him. If Presbyterian dogmatism could not proof M'Andrew, the stiff Scotsman, against the slow sweet poison of the tropics, what hope was there for him?

Suffocating, he walked to the door and swung it wide, but closed it again as his lamp threw a nimbus around Andrea, who was sitting in her doorway. There was nothing unusual in that. Almost every evening she thrummed her guitar in the cool. But he felt that she had been watching, sensed knowledge of his travail in her quick considering glance—both knowledge and invitation, and he went back to his furious wrestlings.

"I must get rid of her," he told himself, and was conscious while saying it that her absence would not vitally affect his problem. His fight was with Cancer. If he discharged Andrea he would still have to deal with the women and girls of the village, who had traded at the store before the rains and would come again when the water fell at the ford, to fill his days with the flutter of garments, glint of golden flesh. Were it only for that night, a week, a month, he felt his ability to battle it out. But it would require five years, perhaps ten, to get his mother's money out of the plantation. Ten years! He paused, listening, for she had begun to sing:

> "Viva el sol, viva la luna,
> Viva quien sabe querer.
> Viva el que en el mundo tiene
> Pena por una mujer."

Her voice lacked even a trace of the nasality which characterized the singing of his men. But for the same throaty ululation that inhered in her laugh, she sang like a white woman, and David knew enough Spanish to interpret the refrain:

> "Long live the sun, long live the moon,
> Long live he who love has known.
> Long live the man who e'er has sought
> Woman's true heart to call his own."

MR. DAVID GOES DOWN, AND—

The sweat streamed down David's face. His lamp once lit he could be seen from without easily as though he were in a bird-cage, and suddenly feeling her eyes he turned and blew out the light. Then he stood spent, streaming perspiration, conscious only of the ease that followed the passing of resistance.

> " Nina, mine thou art,
>   My heart and soul art thou.
> Come, my love, my darling come,
> Why com'st thou not to me?"

Simple enough in themselves, the words absorbed the quivering passion of the accompaniment, one of those melodies of old Spain that rise and fall with the swing and surge of feeling, and breathe along with living passion something of the melancholy of sated love.

At the close of the verse she sat, still as death, pupils dilated, watching his door. A minute passed —two—three—then, as her strained ear caught the faint creak of his door, she rose. Her own light still burned, but as his shape took form in the opposite gloom, she slid inside, and he saw her face, a mask of gold, raised to blow it out. Darkness wiped her out. There was no moon, but the fire of stars showed her again in the doorway. He could make out her eyes wide pools of dusk, faint swell of her chemisette, the hand that presently trembled from the shadow into the starlight.

A peculiar tranquillity had descended upon him.

THE PLANTER

Only a trembling, sharp as an ague, told of the fires beneath the unnatural calm, of the senses vividly alive. His ear picked out of the hush a restless stir of sleepers, mutter of dreamers within the *galera*, rumble of talk in Guadaloupe's hut, a sigh from the opposite shadows. At that his foot rose, slowly, lifting against the lead of habit; but even as it crossed the threshold a yellow oblong split out of the dark mass of the huts, and a woman came running down a sudden stream of lamplight.

XIII

—TAKES THE COUNT—

COMPLETING the step, David was almost knocked down by the woman's headlong rush; but, recovering, he saw it was Rafaela.

"Oh, señor!" she gasped. "El vomito negro! El fiebre! It is not calentura! He has the yellow-fever! Un remedio, señor? Quinine—give me quinine!"

Even in that dim light he could see her huge brawn quivering like jelly, and her brown convulsed face helped his startled faculties to comprehension of the situation. "Yes, yes, I'll get him quinine at once!"

Glancing at Andrea's doorway, he saw to his relief that it was empty, a feeling that gave way to surprise as, uttering a sudden yell, Rafaela bolted inside. "No, señor, no!" Her strident protest came out of black darkness inside. "No, señor, it is muy infecto! Muy malo! Un remedio, señor? Un remedio?"

Still not understanding that she wanted the medicine for herself, he repeated: "Yes, yes. It is in the store. I'll get it as we go by."

"No, señor, I will not go."

189

"You—won't go?" he asked, unable to believe his ears. "To your sick husband?"

"No, señor." And she broke again into strenuous babblings that the fever was extremely infectious, begging him to bring her quinine.

Aghast at a selfishness which outdid that of the animals, David waited a minute in silence. He had to have help, but, though insurgent passion had sunk again in the deeps of consciousness, a hesitant shyness, touch of shame, made it difficult to call Andrea. When he conquered it she appeared at once in the door.

"You will come with me?"

"No, señor." Her answer was commonplace in its quietness. But not knowing as yet the slightness of tropical family ties, he stared his astonishment.

"You are afraid?"

"Si, señor." She admitted it just as calmly; and as he turned to walk away she called after: "And go not you. It is muy infecto."

Stopping, he looked back. She had moved out into the starlight which toned the blood-red of her skirt, bathed every soft flexure in softly sensuous light. But whereas his heart had leaped into his throat, choking him as his eyes fed on the wild beauty of her in the dusk, he now sustained a sudden revulsion. Her wide eyes held neither pity nor concern, only dark disappointment.

"*Won't* you come?"

The plea aimed at the justification of himself as

much as her. It was an attempt to prop a falling idol, re-establish the ideal of primitive womanhood, passionate, brave, free, that had conquered him that day. But the idol refused to be set up, and, turning again, he walked away, angry and disgusted, to fight the fever alone.

Of the disease and its treatment he knew only that Hertzer had pulled Meagher through the collapse which follows the nausea by stimulant mustard baths and liberal use of quinine. And having procured his materials he routed out Tadeo—the most intelligent of his three retainers—to heat water in the cook-house, where fire still glowed.

The proof of infection by mosquito-bites still lay a couple of years off in the womb of the future, and approaching the cabin David's flesh crept, he experienced a shrinking repugnance as though it centred in a cloud of germs. But the feeling vanished when he looked in at the door. Blazing at full on the table, the lamp showed him every rough appointment — *brasero* and *metate* in one corner, the cedar chest that held Rafaela's fiesta wear, the *mandador's* machete and pistols hanging from the post of the bunk on which he himself lay face turned up to the light. In one day his healthy bronze had faded to a ghastly yellow; the flicker of his eyelids expressed complete exhaustion; his whisper, faint as a rustle of dry leaves, barely carried across the cabin.

"Don't come in, señor. Es muy infecto." Old pirate that he was, slave-driver and murderer of *enganchars*, his one ideal still held him—the fealty to his employer he had learned in the Valle Nacional, the "valley of terrors, hell of the enganchars." And memories of his quizzical good-humor under reform, invariable politeness, sometime considerate kindness, flooded the last touch of repugnance out of David's mind.

"Lie still, you old scoundrel," he said. "Open your mouth once more, and I'll fill it with quinine."

Too weak for other protest, he took medicine like a lamb, submitted without a murmur to a bath that was hot as mustard could make it, essayed only one more whisper as David got him back to bed. "Lock the galera, señor!"

If politely, he had yet consistently opposed what he considered the señor's latest idiocy; and while David considered that a week's trial had approved his latest innovation, he humored him with a pretence of compliance. Going out, he sent Tadeo to bed, then returned with some idea of watching. He had failed, however, to reckon with his own exhaustion. He had no sooner stretched out on Rafaela's chest than he fell asleep.

He did not wake until the rising sun laid a bar of yellow across his eyes. Springing up then, startled, uneasy from a sense of neglected duty, he saw at a glance that his patient had failed through the night. His nostrils were pinched sharp and yellow as wax. But for his labored breathing there would have been no telling his stupor from the quiet of death. While pouring brandy between his teeth, David was conscious of unusual stillness, almost Sabbath calm, without. Stepping to the door later, he saw neither smoke at the cook-house nor heard any stir about the *galeras*.

"Lazy beggars," he thought, as he walked across the *galera* compound to rouse the laggards. "Guadaloupe would count this one to him." And though the sunlit silence did force some inkling of the truth upon him, he did not realize how much it favored that disciplinarian's labor theories until, from the *galera* door, he looked down a long line of empty bunks.

Across them fell a shadowy lace of poles and wire —the imprisoning wire he had tried to abolish. The harsh rustle of palm thatch on the eaves without accentuated the deadly stillness within. Still only half believing, he walked rapidly to the women's *galera*, from there to Tadeo's hut—all were empty, and a glance down at the landing showed that his small canoe and three dugouts were gone. Yet with the fact staring him in the face, his mind refused to accept it, and sitting down on the bank he gazed vacantly at the swift-running water.

Yesterday had seen him centred in an order that seemed fixed and permanent—hub of a wheel of life, director of its revolutions. Only twenty hours ago he had inaugurated plans that ran into the coming years. But while he slept the wheel had burst, scattering its units beyond his scheme of things, and he was left alone with a dying man in a deserted camp. Small wonder if it seemed incredible, or that, when perceived intellectually, he should still be haunted by a persistent belief that his people must be at work in the fields.

The hallucination did not, however, exclude a lively appreciation of immediate consequences. While not improvident in his management, humanity had caused him to extend more than the usual store credits, and as, given the opportunity, a peon is always in debt, the runagates owed him. The sum was not much. Deducting wages due them, a month's salary would probably square the deficit, and even at this early stage he resolved that the plantation should not lose through his foolish trust.

More serious was the loss of time. Holding its perpetual threat over the plantation, the jungle would now roll in and it would be hard to overtake its great green wave. Then there was the ridicule! News of his reforms had floated up and down, ascended every tributary, crossed to other rivers, until all the plantation houses were abuzz with tales of the young fellow who had started out to teach old hands the business. What a ripple of mirth would now go floating after! He could feel Ewing's good-natured pity, see Phelps's superior smile, Hertzer's cold sneer; and these were only premonitory of the vast laugh that would shake the Isthmus.

But, worst of all, harder to bear than failure, ridicule, ingratitude, was an illogical but persistent sense that he had drawn the calamity upon himself. When disaster crushes the human soul it turns naturally to introspection to find a moral cause, and, given David's early training, he could not but feel a casual connection between the present catastrophe and his last night's weakness.

"I guess I was tried in the balance and found wanting," he groaned at last; and there is no telling to what depths of self-abasement he might have sunk if just then a voice had not broken up his bitter broodings.

"Your breakfast is ready, señor."

Andrea's naked feet had brought her to his elbow, and now, bright and fresh from recent sleep, she stood smiling down upon him, the comely materialization of the temptation he had just abjured.

"You!" he cried, springing up.

In all consistency he ought to have majestically bidden her "Hence!" But when was human nature consistent? Her smile broke like sunshine upon his unhappiness, steadied his universe, which had been whirling darkly this last half-hour, gave him something to tie to. When every one else deserted him she had stayed! Temptation, her cowardice, were lost in the dazzling flash of her small white teeth; her smiling presence condoned all.

It would not have been difficult for her to complete his conquest just then, for his lonely unhappiness rendered him peculiarly susceptible. But he was protected against himself. Behind that pleasant smile her faculties sat in conclave resembling a coroner's inquest rather than a court of love. She drew back from his impulsive advance. Though he did not notice it, she kept the wind between them walking to the house. Instead of serving him as usual, she had placed everything necessary for the meal on the table at once, and she carried on conversation from the door.

"Si, señor." She nodded assent when he spoke of the desertion. "They have all run away. Guadaloupe always locked the galeras after you slept. Señor Phelps told him not to let you—"

"Yes?" he prompted, and she finished:

"—not to let you make the big fool of yourself."

Here was a revelation; but he had passed beyond astonishment, and it brought nothing but a grimace. "With such a start, I suppose it is no use trying to catch them?"

"No, señor," she promptly answered. "They are already forty miles down-river."

"And Rafaela?" he asked, after a pause. "Where is she?"

"Gone to her village, señor. She crossed the ford at daybreak."

He did wonder a little, both at the ease with which Rafaela had snapped every tie and Andrea's calm acceptance of the fact, for they bespoke individual independence, an almost animal detachment beyond his comprehension. But it was only a flicker of interest. His mind returned at once to the business on hand. If pursuit *were* impossible, new help could not be secured too soon. In any case he needed advice and assistance.

Her smile was sufficient answer when he suddenly asked if she would ride over to Las Glorias with a note to Ewing, and her delight dominated her fear so much that she went with him to the stable and stood by while he saddled his beast. The smile came again when his hand clasped her nude foot lifting her to the saddle, but her pleasure had issue from her vanity. She did not respond to the thrill that went up his arm, and if he could have seen her dismount and wash the foot at the first *arroyo* the sight would have chilled the warm sense of companionship which cheered him as he went back to the fever hut. As he did not see, she loomed in the background of consciousness all day as a warm and pleasant feeling, for his duties absorbed his active thought. What of wood-chopping, heating of water for mustard baths, his hands were full up to the moment that the weird blast of a conch-shell brought him out to find Ewing's dugout at the landing.

It was the first they had seen of each other since the rains, and the planter's face radiated friendliness as he gave David merry greeting. "Hello, Sir Galahad! You've been at it again! You'll excuse me if I don't land, but I have to think of my wife. Anyway, I don't see what right you have to go mixing it with yellow-fever. If it were one of ourselves it would be different, but, though Guadaloupe's a fine old chap, he has his own people to care for him."

He nodded at the tale of Rafaela's desertion. "They are not all like that. Either Phelps's Lola or Hertzer's Rosa would have stuck it out to the bitter end. It is not so bad with Andrea. You cannot expect much in the way of filial affection from children who are kicked out to do for themselves almost as soon as they can toddle. Now, about your men: with canoes and twelve hours' start you can bid them a long good-bye. The only thing to do is to wire a contratisto from San Juan and have a new lot expressed down — presto, pronto! If the trains are running through—and they ought by now —you'll have them inside a week. Shut up, now! It isn't a bit of trouble. I'm clean out of everything and had to go down to stock up."

After an isolation of four months the glimpse of a white face was to both like water in the mouth of a desert traveller, and after Ewing had undertaken several other business commissions, they still talked for the joy of it, chatted away, easing the strain that has caused many a lonely planter to saddle up and ride three days through the *tierra caliente* to have as many hours of speech with his neighbor—talked, indeed, till a slip of the bowman's pole threw the dugout again into the current.

"Your horse made heavy weather of it," Ewing called back as he floated away, "so don't expect your girl till to-morrow." With a wave of the hand he passed on around the bend, and not until David entered the cabin — where further encouragement awaited him—did it occur to him that the good fellow had never used so much as a single "I told you so."

Whereas his patient had tossed restlessly all day, he now lay quiet, and it did not require an experienced eye to detect the difference between this natural sleep and his previous stupors. He breathed easily, a dew of perspiration wet his brow. When he awoke late that evening his usual brown twinkle replaced the fever stare.

"Si, I am much better," he agreed, when David jubilated over his performance with some soup, and if he knew of the liability of a second attack his dominant politeness prevented him from throwing cold water on his nurse's hope. "Perhaps," he replied to a prediction that he would be up and out in a couple of days. "Quien sabe?"

Next morning showed still further improvement, for, though weak as a babe, he awoke in his usual voice, and cursed the runaways with a variety and fluency that he could hardly have surpassed in health. Taking his soup, he read his nurse a lesson on the treatment of *enganchars*, asserting that they were, one and all, ungrateful pigs, and what could one do with a pig but beat it and lock it up in a sty? In fact, he showed such remarkable convalescence that Andrea was able to read a full bulletin of the case from David's face when she rode into camp that afternoon.

THE PLANTER

"He is better, señor," she said; and though her smile was merely a reflection of his own, he took it for genuine feeling and was pleased—both with it and the concern for his comfort instanced by her next remark. "You *must* go to your own bed to-night."

He had not intended it, but when Guadaloupe also insisted, asserting that he himself would sleep till morning, David compromised by setting his alarm-clock to call him at midnight. And the clock lived up to its contract. Its brazen vibrations set the night pulsing, startled the jungle for a mile around, roused Andrea to a repetition of the choked coughing, retching of nausea. But she did not call David, who slept through it all.

As well that she did not. He could only have stood by, a helpless spectator of the grim fight the *mandador* put up against his old enemy, the death he had faced in many a mutiny, watched stalking through his fields. Coming in, refreshed and cheerful, the following morning, he saw only the brown peace of the face.

If startled, he had seen too much of death during the rains to hesitate. Within the hour they carried the old fellow out to his place at the head of his silent workers; for, very much to his surprise, Andrea volunteered to help. Ignorant of her superstition that infection ends with death, her present conduct wiped out the last vestige of the prejudice inspired by her former cowardice, and he was equally deceived by her sudden burst of sorrow when he began to shovel

200

in the grave. Primitive as the death-howling of dogs, snorting of cattle over their dead, it was instinctive as fear itself and would as quickly fade. But as he could only interpret it in terms of his own feeling, it greatly moved him, added the strong bonds of sympathy to her physical attraction. When they walked back to the deserted camp, a man and woman isolated as Adam and Eve in Eden, he was in greater danger than at the moment when Rafaela burst in between them.

That evening, of course, the shadow of death lay between them. Danger lay in the days to come— days of bright solitude when warmth wrapped the silent camp like brooding love, and sunlight appeared as a reflection of her golden skin; when her sleep breathing floated out on the night like an exhalation from her luxurious presence; when Northfield and the old life would recede to an infinite distance, its belief and prejudices be engulfed in the whirling vortex of the present; when the old cold ideals of chastity would dwindle under the splendor of tropical womanhood, free, passionate, warm.

A blast of the conch-shell announced Ewing's return next evening.

"Sorry he's gone," the planter commented on Guadaloupe's death. "He was the best mandador, bar none, on the Isthmus, and you'll find it hard to replace him. How are you feeling? Tired? That's natural; but be careful. Don't forget the quinine with your breakfast coffee—twenty grains won't hurt you for a while. If nothing happens in the next five days you are all right. But if you feel the least bit off, send the girl over at once for me.

"The chances for men looked bad at first," he went on, discussing business. "I wired contratisto after contratisto, but whether it was because the jails were all empty, or that the peons have joined the W. C. T. U., not one of them had a man in stock save the Señora Morales, and she was sick in bed. Wouldn't do business at all till I wired that I was acting for you. That fixed it. The trains are running again, and, dead or alive, she'll either bring or send them down within the week."

As the high water still made heavy poling upstream, he talked only while his men landed David's goods, finishing as they pushed off again: "I saw Hertzer going down, and he said that if he had known, he would have come over to lend you a hand. And Patricia sends remembrances—of your last ride, whatever that means; she wouldn't tell me—and bids you be in readiness to escort her over to our place as soon as the trails dry a little more."

Dusk was already falling over river and jungle, which resounded with the evening clamor of beasts and birds, and after the heavy canoe had drawn down to a blot on the livid waters David went back to his hut, lit a lamp, and sat down to write to his mother.

He did not, however, make much progress. Across

the alley, between house and kitchen, he could see Andrea at work under the lamplight, and when, presently, some reference to his early days on the plantation caused him to look up from his writing, he saw again, with the clarity of his first impression, the velvet eyes, red lips, skin of satin overlaying perfect arms and shoulders, the figure that fluxed into new moulds at every movement. The dazzle of white teeth, as she caught his eye, vividly recalled her first salutation, "All that I have is yours, señor."

Thereafter the letter dragged, and when, having finished her work, she moved out to the doorway, he dropped his pen, straddled his own door-sill, and they fell to talking just as they did during the long, wet nights of the rains — she of quaint Zacateco superstitions and customs, he of what, to her, was far stranger, the cold life of the North. Though she was quite offended when he doubted her account of the snake which slips into bed at night and puts the tip of his tail in the baby's mouth while it steals the mother's milk; though she vehemently asserted the existence of the demon ape who lies in wait at springs to kidnap handsome women, her own cooing laugh thrilled through the dusk at the unbelievable phenomena of ice and snow.

"Si, I am very foolish that you tell me this."

"But it is true," he asserted. "And what about that ape?"

"That also is true, señor. Did he not run after Rafaela, my mother?"

203

"Poor ape—if he had caught her," David said, with a lively recollection of Rafaela's brawn.

If she giggled she fought none the less for the truth of her story, and while she cited innumerable instances that could be sworn to in church David lapsed into silence. Talking or listening, he had felt a stir within him, a pulse of feeling that heralded the arousing of that other David who had slept through the exhausting worry of the last few days, and now it possessed, obsessed him. Preternaturally acute, his senses extended like nerves through the embrace of the palpitant dusk; he thrilled at her nearness. Thoughtless, feeling only, he sat until, for sheer lack of an answer to her chatter, she also relapsed into dangerous silence.

If her hand had stolen out as on that other night? But it did not, and, rising presently, she went in to bed.

Neither did she give him the material encouragement necessary to overcome his timidity on the next or any of the days that she had her golden being alone with him — days when sunlight and solitude, languor of dark glances alike fed his passion, sapped his resistance. Not that she was cold. Her manner displayed always enough tenderness to keep him at white-heat. Primitive woman that she was, she yet played him with a natural coquetry, unmasking undreamed - of batteries, bewildering him by the flash of unsuspected complexities. She could be arch, gay, saucy, and fall the next moment into a warm silence that was charged with electricity like a lull in a thunder-storm. Yet, drawing him on, she still held him at arm's-length, until accident abolished the distance on the fourth evening after the *mandador's* death.

They had been sitting as usual on their respective door-steps, and as she rose to go in, stretching magnificently in a yawn, she suddenly remembered that frijoles were required to put in soak for next day's stew, and after lighting her out to the store he looked on while she filled her calabash. Her flexures bending over the sack were supple as those of a white girl-child; and when, turning, she waited for him to lead out, he paused to admire the picture the full whites, deep reds of her dress made in the dusk of the store; paused until, stepping to go by him, she tripped on a loose end of rope.

Luckily he had set the lamp on the rough counter, and he easily caught her. His first impulse was to lift her back to her feet, but as the soft fulness of her crushed in against his breast his muscles tightened with a sudden reflex. He strained her in to him for one blind second, for, breaking his embrace the next, she darted out, uttering a frightened cry.

So violent was the reaction that thought stood still; he stood staring blankly at the empty doorway. And when, picking up the lamp, he went out and locked the door, the actions were purely reflexes of habit. His red, confused stare, passing Andrea's closed door, was also devoid of thought. But the moment he closed his own door the wheels began to turn, the slow wheels of the gods that move slowly but grind exceeding fine. To specify his thought would be wearisome as unnecessary. Sufficient that anger, shame, furious remorse, each had its turn, and after an hour of it he flung outside to cool his fever.

There he found a copper moon hanging like a lantern in the trees, and while he paced the bank it sailed up over the sere roofs, flooded the still camp with soft light, touched the river in a bar of silver. But the soft, warm peace was out of tune with his mood. It was too much in accord with the causes that had brought his present remorseful humiliation. The vast spread of those indigo skies, "lasceevious" twinkle of stars, warm sighs of the nights had helped the shimmering days to bring him to this plight. So the quiet had no ease for his aching soul, saw no cess of his endless pacings. He walked for hours—walked, walked, walked till his back and loins ached, as he thought, from the drag of his leaden legs, till a fire of thirst sent him down to the landing.

Instead of cooling, however, water seemed to feed his fever, and a sudden chill sent him back to his hut to alternately burn and shiver in bed. Rising for another drink in the early hours, he saw in the glass that his eyes were suffused with blood, his face yellowish pale. But not until he was taken with the "black vomit," an hour later, did he associate the symptom with anything else than mental distress. And even then a peculiar confusion, mild delirium, debarred him from all but the dimmest realization of the fact.

"This is the fifth day," he told himself, listlessly, "and I've got it." But he did not care.

In the same dreamy way he sensed the pale radiance that at dawn slid through the siding—because, perhaps, it hurt his inflamed eyes. Later he heard Andrea stir, but it never occurred to him to call her. His own door stood wide, and he saw when she came and looked in, yet he made no attempt to attract her attention. Curiosity had died with interest, and the cry with which she drew back closed his remembrances for that day.

Next morning he was able to lift a corner of the fever veil and see himself staggering from hut to hut in search of the dead *mandador*. But he never knew how he got back to bed. Connected memories begin again as, lying in the stage of remission, he listened to a buzz of voices without the door.

"If he be not dead, what matter?" It was Andrea speaking. "Go thou in and secure the key."

His glance wandered to the key of the store that hung on a nail by his bed.

"Nay, let us break in," a man's voice objected. "One stroke of my machete—"

"Si, and the Gringo pigs will see the broken lock! Thou wert ever a fool, Candelario. Thou knowest the devil Hertzer? The evil eyes of him would find us even in Tlacotalpan. No, if the thing be done in order there will be none to tell that he did not sell the goods to the folk of the village. See! I will dip my kerchief in his Lysol and wring it to bind thy mouth. Nor needst thou to breathe. It will be done in a second."

"Carajo! no!" The man's voice was tense with fear. "Not for all of his store!"

In the ensuing pause David could almost sense the struggle between cupidity and fear. Then Andrea burst out: "Coward! Then bind my mouth."

Perfectly clear now, David's mind grasped not only every detail of the situation, but flashed back over its causes. Andrea's first complaisance, subsequent shyness, late reluctance were all explained. If he had escaped the fever she would have settled down in his hut. As he had not, she was there to rob his death-bed of goods to stock another housekeeping. In the cold light of which facts the new ideal of tropical womanhood—splendid, free, passionate, warm—shrivelled and shrank to a selfish mummy.

Over the cloth that covered her nose and mouth her eyes looked at him as she came to his bed. But neither mercy nor shame inhered in her glance. It could not have fallen more indifferently upon a dying dog, and through the wave of anger, bitter disgust, that presently deprived David of consciousness, he felt wonder at its animal detachment. A tigress could not have been less concerned nosing round for prey in its dead mate's lair.

From him her gaze moved to his gun and watch,

but her cupidity took counsel with cautious fear. She was not minded to provoke pursuit. Taking the key only, she moved toward the door, and as he had relapsed again in a stupor, he did not see the bit of by-play, touch of superstition. Passing the table, her eye fell on the gilt crucifix emblazoned on the back of a Testament, his mother's gift, and, pausing, she crossed herself, then with a low courtesy passed on and out.

Neither did he hear the bustle as they loaded down Candelario's canoe with the best goods of his store— that, or her remark passing out, after she had replaced the key on its nail:

"He will surely die to-night."

XIV

—BUT COMES BACK SMILING

WITH his usual contumacy, however, David refused to die.

Not that Andrea should be altogether cast for a false prophet. Her prediction was based on constitutions that were the product of license implied by the bitter toast, "The tropics—flowers without scent, birds without song, women without virtue, men without honor!" and she was not to be blamed for that which she did not know of the stern vitality of New England. For David not only refused to die, but even indulged in a lively dream about the time a respectable native would have made a decent exit.

The vision—at first he thought that he was awake, a phenomenon not uncommon in dreams—began when, coming out of his stupor late that afternoon, he saw a trickle of black in the doorway. Thin in its beginnings, it widened in half an hour till it filled the jambs and poured through the interstices of the siding in a stream that soon hid the mud floor under a carpet of quivering jet.

It was not the first time David had seen army ants.

—BUT COMES BACK SMILING

He had once timed the flow across his plantation road of a stream of the voracious atoms. Five yards wide, it took their billions just twenty hours to cross, and he knew that if a house happened to lie in their path they ate up bugs, roaches, food-stuffs, cleaned it of animal matter, living or dead. In one of their talks Andrea had told him of bed-ridden people who had been caught and eaten alive. But, too weak and confused for any speculation that required memory or thought, he dully watched the tide mount stools and tables, flow up the pole siding, wreath palm ribs and bamboo rafters in shivering black.

As the legs of his *catre* were planted in tomato-cans of carbolized water, he was safe—for a time—and he displayed a faint interest in the rout of the vermin out of the thatch. Fat cockroaches, scorpions, tarantulas, even small snakes, swarmed down the poles, a grizzly retreat, or, letting go, flopped heavily upon the floor. Running out from under the *catre*, one big tarantula cut a streaky wake through the ants with his many legs, on his way to the door. An elongated scorpion clove them like a canoe to the centre, where a full dozen of his kind stood, apparently dazed, rounded up, a glistening *rodeo*. But not until, glancing up, he saw dribbles of black on the cords by which his mosquito-netting was swung from the thatch ribs, did he sense danger for himself.

Even then his paralysis of weakness excluded fear. His stare into the face of that crawling death evidenced about the same amount of interest a new-born babe displays in its hovering mother, yet was sufficient to keep him from hearing a buzz of voices outside, tramping of many feet. When a shadow suddenly fell in the doorway he did turn listless eyes —upon the girl of the train. Then it was that he knew it all for a dream, and, tired out by the mental strain required to realize that fact, he relapsed into another stupor.

Contrary to the usual practice in dreams, the figure remained in the doorway. Also for a phantom it was unusually active, for, after a startled glance, it rushed with a realistic flutter of skirts across the crawling tide and returned, having pulled the sheet over his face.

"Magdaleno! Maria! José!"

Sunk in his stupor, he neither heard her call the *cabos* who were marshalling a long file of *enganchadores* into the *galera*, her assurances that the señor was ill of a typhoid, nor felt when they snatched up his *catre* and carried him out to the store. He swallowed the liquor that later she poured between his teeth, but lay like a dead man under her anxious eyes during the hours that it took José and Maria to pole down to La Luna and bring back Hertzer. His next impression was of the stimulant warmth that caused him to open his eyes on the planter who, while sousing him in a mustard bath, cursed him with a furious energy that aroused his tired soul to languid anger. During the five minutes in which Hertzer mingled his sousing and cursing in equal parts, David was conscious of profound deliberations as to the proper course to pursue, and when Hertzer stooped to lift him back to his bed, he made an ineffectual dab at one of the many faces that wobbled about him in a nimbus of profanity. Then, exhausted by the effort, he grasped the tub with both hands, and sat, weaving a little, staring vacuously, an image of impotent defiance.

"You would, would you!" Hertzer's grim puckers spread in a grin. "You'll pull through all right. It was a week before Meagher could even sass me back. Now, into bed you go."

His awakening next morning was much more pleasant, for then the girl of the train sat by his bed. Half turned away and leaned forward with hands clasped around one crossed knee, her position gave him not only the remembered tracery of her delicate profile, but also what he had never seen before—a small foot and pretty ankle. And while his weakness reduced his appreciation of these desired personal assets down to a mild content, he was perfectly satisfied to lie and look until, glancing his way, she sprang up with a cry in Spanish:

"He is awake, Señor Hertzer! Now he may have the soup!"

Withal his satisfaction he slid into another sleep between spoonfuls of soup, and his disappointment when he awoke later and found that Hertzer had taken her place caused the latter a saturnine grin.

"She was up all night, and she's taking her sleep,"

he nevertheless explained. With the wink of a satyr, he added: "Nice little girl to take for a walk in the dark, eh?" Then he laughed as David choked on a spoonful of milk. "Now, don't get mad. You are not strong enough to lick me yet."

Feeling that he was, David tried to rise.

"Just weakness," Hertzer calmly commented, as his head fell back. "It will pass off—if you lie still and restrain your blood-thirsty desires. That oughtn't to be so hard," he added, with a still more hateful grin. "You'll have her every night. I'd take double your risk with the fever for one-half your luck." And, considering that poor David had not said a single word, he finished with immeasurable impudence: "Now, you mustn't talk any more."

To enforce the command he moved out to the door and sat puffing his pipe, a grim figure, sardonically inflexible, and, with the exception of time consumed by a mustard bath, he remained there until Consuela came out of Andrea's hut to take the night trick. Then he fired one parting shot.

"Here she comes. Now, mind that you behave."

Through some freakish law of nature mortality from yellow-fever in the tropics is exactly one hundred per cent. less than in cooler and more northern zones; with which two-to-one odds in his favor it is hardly to be wondered that a steady lad like David should have won out to a reasonable convalescence in one short week.

—BUT COMES BACK SMILING

If one were to sum the treatment in the case it would have to be set down as an alternation of irritants with sedatives, for while by day Hertzer teased and tormented him out of his torpors in ways similar to those above set forth, stimulated his temper into an activity that really made for his physical good, the girl's gentle ministrations at night prepared him for sound sleep. And it would be hard to say which did most toward his recovery.

"I'd quit if it hurt him," Hertzer replied, grinning, to the remonstrances of Ewing, who rode over almost every day; "but it doesn't, and I confess I like the job. When I get through he'll know a little more both of himself and the tropics." And surely nothing escaped his sharp tongue: David's schemes, his relations with Andrea, former gallantry to his pretty nurse—each had its turn.

"Fifty enganchars at seventy per," he would muse, aloud. "Or does la señora make a discount for services rendered? Anyway—say three thousand cold cash? Pretty stiff for an experiment! The others were all in your debt, and you could easily have held them another six months — acclimated, too; worth double their number of new men."

Another time: "Andrea gone on a visit to her mother? Hum! There'll be the dickens to pay when she comes back and finds another in your—I mean her bed. I reckon you never saw these Mexicans scrap? They're the devil. Better take to the woods when they start in."

THE PLANTER

It was a similar and even coarser remark that brought an iron-stone soup-bowl straight at his head at the end of the week. A quick dodge saved him his brains, but his irritating grin accompanied his quiet comment: "Couldn't have thrown it any harder myself. I perceive, young man, that you are about recovered. Mañana I go home." And go he did, after flashing a familiar facet in his patient's eyes.

If his feelings had been chafed to the raw, David could not but feel his obligation, and he expressed it saying good-bye. "I'm afraid that I've been a troublesome patient, but I'm deeply grateful."

Hertzer, who sat swinging one leg from the table, raised big shoulders. "More than I'd be. Anyway, I haven't done any more than you did for your mandador, and I've done as much before for a nigger. Besides," he carelessly added, "I'm well paid. Wait till you see my bill."

"Bill?" David echoed.

"For maize and frijoles. There wasn't a kernel of either in your store, and as the men couldn't very well browse on rubber, I had my fellows bring up twenty arrobas of each."

Not to mention the beans owed him by Phelps, David had counted five other sacks and seven of corn while holding the light for Andrea. "Why—" he began, then stopped. A feeling of shame had kept him silent upon the piracy that deepened the treachery of her desertion; to which item, already charged to experience, he had now to add Hertzer's audacious trading. Forty *arrobas?* Almost six tons. Provisions for a year. And he could not refuse—under the circumstances.

"It was awfully good of you," he said, turning a cheerful face to the inevitable. And, offering his hand, he went on: "But that doesn't cancel my personal debt. You undoubtedly saved my life."

A vivid sparkle, cold as the glint of ice, lit Hertzer's gray eyes. He sat, neither moving nor speaking, yet his posture expressed a cold and significant triumph. "I told you not to forget that it was you who refused your hand," he said, at last. "As for your life — we'll wipe that off the slate. It may be that I didn't want death to beat me to it—or I may have further use for you. Until then—good-bye."

He paused, however, as just then Consuela entered the hut. Of all his tormentings—and he knew it—David had chafed most at a calculated freedom, half insolent, half admiring, in his manner to her. Addressing her, he invariably used the *"tu"* which Spanish custom accords only to relatives and intimate friends. As now, saying good-bye, he always tried to look in her eyes.

To David it seemed that she hesitated before giving her hand. He could not mistake her flush, the jerk with which she pulled it away. But, with a laugh, Hertzer passed out, and a few minutes later his voice floated up from the river in a raucous attempt at "Coronation":

> " All hail the power of Jesus' name,
>   Let angels prostrate fall—"

THE PLANTER

Until the discordance died in the distance the girl busied herself with the soup she had brought in. When she turned, the fires of shame had given place to a pallor that intensified the storm in her eyes:

"Why did he do that?" And before he could answer: "Was it because I am Mexican? I have heard that the Americanos despise us."

"No, no! It was because of me."

In his haste to soothe her wounded pride he hardly bettered the case, for she coldly questioned: "Because of *you?* Why?"

He saw at once how easily she could construe his explanation into a second familiarity. She was looking steadily at him, and the slight resentment in her glance threw him into wild confusion. "Because—because"—his stammering tongue served him well by blurting out the truth—"because he knew that he couldn't hurt me more."

As she bent again over the soup he did not see her smile. "Why should he think that of you?—you who—"

She got no further. Apologies and explanations of the kiss he had sent after her down the river had burned the point of his tongue these three days, and he plunged at the opportunity. Translated literally, he made a sad mess of it, what of his boggling Spanish; but, after all, the function of language is to express feeling, and she could not mistake his earnest sincerity. If she let him blunder along, her next remark proves that it was because she liked it, and she cut him off with a merry laugh as soon as she sensed his real distress.

"It is nada, señor. Already the Señor Ewing told me of that wild's girl's trick. At first I was angry. But my mother said: 'Consuela thou art a fool!' And when I remembered—" She swept away with a pretty gesture the months that lay between them and the train. "But now you must take this—and go to sleep."

"If you also will go to your rest," he stipulated. "You must be worn out by so much night-watching."

Small hands and pretty shoulders alike repudiated the suggestion. "I took my sleep during the day. I shall sit in the doorway and sew till you sleep."

He would have much preferred to talk, but if her rest depended upon his, silence was obligatory. He made up for it, however, by studying from under lowered lids the rich face, dark lashes that swept its deep bloom as she bent over her sewing. With feelings that oscillated between pain and pleasure he watched her needle slip in and out, for after the ants' house-cleaning he had been brought back to his own hut, and he could not but remember that Andrea had sat in the same place not more than a week ago.

It is possible for a nature of natural fineness to realize the repentant disgust of sated license without having undergone the actual physical degradation, and the contrast between this girl's clean delicacy and the Zacateca's luxurious animality caused David some such feeling. He sickened at the memory of his weakness. In her pure presence the glamour faded from Phelps's logic, dissolved like gilt in acid, exposing the base metal beneath; and David stood, head hanging, convicted by her virtue, for that strenuous conscience of his would not admit him to plead in exculpation the accident that had saved him from physical guilt.

"I d have done it!" he groaned, inwardly. "I'd have done it!"

It was not the first time he had thus suffered. But whereas the mental confusion which attends the first stages of yellow-fever had previously reduced his impression to a vague mental distress, his mind worked to-night with its usual clearness. He wondered what she would think if she knew, and so looked up from the black depths which are reserved for young men in love to the lit pinnacles upon which she sat so quietly—looked, despaired, and, despairing, essayed the first step to climb the heights.

It occurred to him that he had never thanked her for bringing his men down.

"Not asleep?" She turned as he spoke, gave him the equivalent in Spanish for "one good turn deserves another," and, after a hesitation, went on: "It was the mercy of God that I did. And surely He directed me, caused me to change my first resolve."

"You thought you would not?" he asked, as she paused.

She nodded, bending again over her sewing, but continued, after a few stitches: "I have learned many things in the last year, señor—ugly things, greater wickedness than I had thought the whole world held."

Pausing again, she went on, turning her face so that he could not see its quivering earnestness: "I have sometimes wondered what you must think of a girl who could lend herself to the engancharing of ignorant peons. But I would have you to believe that up to a few months ago I did not know. In Ciudad Mexico our men are well fed and cared for— have to be, or we could not contract them—and you yourself have read the indentures—'in all things the enganchador shall receive from the administrator of the plantation the gentle treatment a father accords to his child.' I believed it, señor—believed it true of the thousands who went through our galera. I thought what happy employments these must be when none ever returned, and so honored my mother as an instrument of great good in providing work for the poor. I believed in it until, going from plantation to plantation last year, I saw the cruel labor, sickness, stripes—met, in miserable remnants, the living skeletons of our careless happy ones. After that the bread on my mother's table smelled of their blood and sweat. I could not, would not, eat it.

"What could I do? Ten years ago—nothing. Ciudad Mexico is a city of half a million, and with the coming of the Americano there has been great business, stores, markets, railways that give employment to girls of education. So while by day I served in a store, by night I studied English and book-keeping, as now do many Mexican girls. And soon I shall take a better position."

She would "take a better position"? Even in Spanish it sounded so commercial, was so utterly at variance with her rich beauty, that he had to repress a laugh. "Then you speak some English?"

"A little," she admitted, with the prettiest of accents, and though she had not been cut off, like himself, from all communication with her own tongue, her knowledge, as revealed in further conversation, proved almost equal to his of Spanish.

"But you thought you would not come down?" he said, returning from these divergences. "What made you alter your mind?"

She laughed, a merry peal strongly reminiscent of the damsel who had teased him so unmercifully upon the train. "Ah, señor, your fame has carried even to Ciudad Mexico. Every contratisto who has delivered men in the states of Chiapas, Oaxaca, or Vera Cruz in the last six months has brought back tales of your—"

"Follies?"

"Humanities," she quietly finished.

"Any name that pleases you," he said, a little bitterly. "The fact remains—they have put me in a pretty hole."

"Hole?" Her brows arched, and when he had explained the colloquialism she commented: "Ungrateful they were, but still more cowardly. Now, see! I waited until you were stronger to tell you this. Five of your old men are back in the galera, and I do not believe they would have ever run away if they had not been afraid of the fever."

"Five — of my old gang?" he repeated, incredulously.

Nodding, she told how she had picked them up, starving, at a station a hundred kilometres up the line. Already they had regretted their desertion, and with a little urging they had told all—how, roused by Rafaela's cry, they had fled, like her, as soon as David slept; the overcrowding that had driven them ashore at the railroad bridge; their belief that all would have come back if the canoes had not furnished the opportunity to stray too far. Great news for him, strong meat for a convalescent, but the glow it brought to his cheek was not of fever.

"And you knew fever was on this plantation?" he questioned, after a silence.

"Merely that the mandador was sick, but—"

"But?"

"I knew you, señor. And it proved as I thought."

She had come over to the bed, and he broke a second glowing pause by thrusting out his hand. "You are a brick!"

"'A brick'?" Her brows rose again in pretty puzzle. "It is with that you build the wall?" And the merry peal came again when, after five minutes of his best Spanish, plus her English, the compliment was finally charted.

"You said five?" he questioned, returning to her news.

THE PLANTER

"Five, and I believe more will come in."

"If I could believe that," he mused, "I think—I think—I could try again."

"You must, or—I shall be sorry that I brought them. And now you must go to sleep."

"Yes—I can sleep—now," he gratefully answered.

And sleep he did—and dream, with more or less success, of scaling the aforesaid pinnacle.

XV

CANCER SUSTAINS A REVERSE

STILL, two days later, David awoke from the sound sleep induced by his first attempt at exercise to find Ewing smiling in at the door.

"Lazy beggar," the planter said, as he tossed a bundle onto the bed. "When you have climbed into these clean togs I shall be proud to lend you my arm as far as the landing. Until then you will pardon me if I 'ware your germ-infested presence and stay outside. Hurry, as the hero says to the girl, for the canoe waits."

"Canoe?" David began. "But—"

"But me no 'buts,' sir. From the mouths of two women the edict hath gone forth and may not be gainsaid. You are to repair with me to Las Glorias, there to be petted, coddled, and otherwise made much of till you shall have attained your usual rude health. The Señor Magdaleno has volunteered to care for the plantation, with a guarantee from his mistress; and to relieve that expression of sudden doubt I will add that she is to accompany you as soon as she has arrayed herself in a change of Mrs. Ewing's clothes.

Ah, such an ingenuous blush! So soon? But I forget
—there *was* a previous acquaintance."

Dodging a boot, he poked in his head again to hurl
a stage defiance. "Sir-r-r-r! I shall await you at
the corner."

Just as David finished dressing, his whisper came
through the siding. "Here she comes! Hurry, Davy,
hurry! A vision! A dream! Peaches! Peaches
Lovely peaches! I thought that would bring you.'

As the girl approached from Tadeo's hut, where
she had gone to change, David's eyes paid like hom-
age. Declaring that nothing was good enough for
her to wear, Mrs. Ewing had sent her best white
dress, and besides framing and accentuating the
creams, deep blooms of the rich face, the pretty costume was a perfect fit—according to tropical ideals.
For no white woman can live among the Tehuanas,
watch them move under their loose draperies, with
the upright grace of a swinging palm, without losing
her taste for the bursting-tight over-corseted Eu-
ropean styles. Avoiding either extreme, the dress
effected a compromise which, graceful in line, yet
clung more closely than Consuela's usual wear. A
ready she had bestowed several doubtful glances
on the reflection in Tadeo's three inches of cracked
mirror. Now her frank eyes looked appealing from
under the lingerie hat that replaced her *mantill*
But she gained ease with a candid question.

"How do I look?"

"Immense."

CANCER SUSTAINS A REVERSE

It was Ewing who spoke, but David's glance expressed much more, and, touched in some spring of coquetry, she flashed at once from his grave and gentle nurse into the laughing torment of the train. Though she took his other arm, lent all her young strength to his support, she rallied him all the way down to the landing.

"Don David did not speak? Since the letter of yesterday he can see only the fair Americana he left at home in Gringoland. She was well, I hope—and happy?"

No longer at the mercy of an interpreter, David could make a better defence, and remembering his last experience he wisely stuck by the truth. "Very happy—with her husband."

"Married? The heartless! Poor Don David! No wonder he had such a disgusto."

David had really done some glooming over certain strictures of his mother's anent his lack of charity toward Mr. Osgood, his philanthropist and friend. But whereas six months ago he would have stated the strict truth, he now merely nodded. "Yes. You see, she has only been married two months, and the wound is still bleeding."

They had just taken their seats astern and, a little startled by his seriousness, she gave him a quick glance. Then, seeing his smile, she turned with a laugh at her own discomfiture to watch the boatmen, and was too busy thereafter for further badinage, noting and commenting with the fresh delight of a town-bred girl on the new vistas that opened at every bend.

While she exclaimed, clapping her hands, at the slow flappings of a great white heron, peered down at the fish lazily moving in warm limpidity, chattered gayly with Ewing, David looked quietly on. Was it not for him a dream come true—the waking dream that preceded sleep the night he had lain out in the jungle awaiting the runaway Yaqui. Under overhanging vegetation, past gleaming sand *playas* where alligators took their torrid nooning, with always the broidered screen of the jungle on either hand, he was floating with her. It is doubtful whether he spoke twice in the three hours required to make Ewing's landing.

Though the house stood half a mile away from the river, the wailing conch-shell had brought Mrs. Ewing down to meet them. About twenty-five, she possessed the unusual combination of golden hair with dark-brown eyes. Over the middle height of women, she was built proportionately, yet through her delicacy of feature conveyed an impression of slightness. As Ewing was wont to put it: you would think her a sylph till she stepped on the scales. And sylph she was in all else that goes into the conception—grace of manner and movement, sweet temper, modesty, the pleasant tact that accorded so well with her refined face and put the strange girl at once at her ease. Lacking even a trace of reserve, patronage, or the effusiveness with which many a well-meaning woman would have damned the occasion, her manner dis-played that frank impulse toward friendship which, natural with men, is so rare in the greetings of women. Not that she omitted the swift feminine glance that pierces beautiful clothes and smiling surfaces to the core of the soul beneath. But, satisfied, she put her all into welcome.

"I'm dying to gossip, so you men had better walk on ahead," she said, slipping an arm about the girl.

And gossip she did, a perfect ripple of talk—not alone, if one judge by the silver of answering laughter which caused Ewing to smile at David. "They seem to be hitting it off first rate."

The oldest and biggest of the plantations on the Amarilla, the cleared acreage of Las Glorias was so great that it looked like a section of rolling prairie. It was hard to believe that the jungle, which loomed miles away as a low green wall, had ever come down to the river. Fully a thousand acres rolled in green pasture dotted with the darker verdure of oaks, great sabers, palms which Ewing had spared in the clearing, out of which rose the golden roofs of the house and work buildings—a perfect village. With cattle wandering at will over its checker of sunshine and cloud shadow, it were easy to imagine it some great Northern estate enriched with tropical flora.

"It ought to look fine," Ewing answered David's exclamation. "We have sunk half a million gold in it already, and for want of anything else to do will go on sinking as long as the faith of the instalment stockholder hangs out. It all depends on him. And really. Davy, he's the miracle of the ages. Just pause and think! During seven hot months the plantations are littered with monte a foot deep, refuse so dry as to be almost explosive. A cigarette - stub thrown carelessly aside, and — pouf! half a million gone up in smoke. But though we are at the mercy of any volunteer possessed of a match and a grouch, though the jungle would roll back to the river if we ceased operations for six months, come drought, come flood, come fire, the stockholder goes on pingling up his driblets."

Shrugging impatiently, he continued: "The thought of it makes me mad. For it's the sublimation of idiocy; the poor devil can never get back his own. When Uncle Sam investigated us after the Rubero fraud, the consul-general stayed here a day, and he told me that he had not found one plantation but was over-capitalized. Putting it coldly, we hadn't the goods to show for the money. And he told no lie. Take these miles of open land. They were once planted. We only put on the cattle after the grass killed off the rubber. Yet every acre represents an investment, and ought to be carrying four hundred six-year-old trees. Of growing rubber we haven't enough to cover a quarter of our issued stock."

"But—that sounds queer?" David questioned. "You don't mean to say—"

"No, it wasn't premeditated. Intentional rascality has been the exception. The fault lies here:

230

starting out, we all underestimated expenses of clearing, maintenance, and no allowance was charged against probable loss. Coming down to bed-rock" (in almost the same words he repeated the verdict the conductor had cast against the business on the train), "the business is individual as corn or cotton raising, and requires the economical care of a planter-owner. In the long run it will come down to that—after we have all gone into the hands of the receiver. In the mean time we have got to do the best we can, and trust that not too many widows and orphans show up at our funeral. Rubero was simply awful. Against a capitalization of two million, gold, they could only set seventy thousand, Mex, in assets, and their stockholders were mostly women, small store-keepers, and country school-ma'ams. Gives me a cold sweat every time I think of it."

"But how *can* they be so blind? I thought a stockholders' committee visited the plantation every year?"

Ewing laughed. "Oh, the inspectors? Yes, they come down with the manager, and what of wine-parties, tiger-shoots, and other junketings, it is hard to get them out to the plantations long enough to be snap-shotted under our largest tree. As for their reports—I'll let you read the last. Even the manager had to hide his blushes." As they turned in under an avenue of palms that led up to the house, he finished: "There's nothing picayune about our office. It knows how to treat people."

THE PLANTER

In appearance and appointments the house testified to the same lavish expenditure. A wide frame bungalow, its palm thatch and spreading eaves kept it in touch with the prospect which ran uninterruptedly down to the river. Tropical fashion, the bedrooms opened out on the spacious veranda, wire-screened throughout its length. The big living-room took up all one end, and was well furnished with a massive table and sideboard, a desk, chairs, lounges—all of rare tropical hard-woods made up by a cabinet-maker whom Ewing had retrieved from among his *enganchars*. Its walls were covered with trophies—a big alligator-skin hung over the sideboard opposite a twenty-foot python, the brown and yellows of which shone out from a scarlet mount. Jaguar-skins served for mats, and the bright zarapes on the lounges pleasantly relieved the sombre tints of floor and walls; lying on one of which David could see flowers, trees, a vista of flashing river, through any of the half-dozen casement windows.

"My house is yours." Entering, Mrs. Ewing gave them the usual Spanish welcome. With a spice of mischief she added: "You can settle on a division while I go out and see about dinner."

"Armadillo! Armadillo!" she came back chanting. "Did you ever taste it, David? It is delicious. And the armor makes a beautiful body for a mandolin. I've ordered the cook to scrape it for you, Consuela."

It had been a hard day—for David. But, if tired,

he performed creditably at dinner, his first well-cooked meal since his last visit before the rains. Not to mention the armadillo—which proved toothsome as the sucking-pig it resembled—a soup, roast beef, and real potatoes, he could have dined royally on the home-made bread. There was joy, too, luxuriously æsthetic, in the glass, silver, china, quiet service of the two Tehuanas in chemisettes and starched shirts whom Mrs. Ewing had trained for the table. What of the pleasant comfort of it all, he fell asleep over his coffee.

"Tired little boys must go to bed." Mrs. Ewing laughed at his apology. "Take him away, Frank. . . . And you?" She turned to Consuela as the men went out. "You must be dreadfully tired. I'm going to make you retire early to-night. Come, I'll show you your room."

To the good-night at the door she added: "We can never thank you enough for what you have done for our friend. . . . No, we have not known him long. Only since he came down." Then she gave the wife's best reason for a liking. "But Frank swears by him. Thinks he's the finest boy he ever knew—so good and kind."

Consuela had paused, a hand on the door, and both stood for a few moments smiling, reluctant to part. Then she threw the door wide. "Won't you come in?"

"I'd love to." And with her warm acceptance, the seal of the bedroom chat was placed on their growing intimacy.

Emerging a long hour later with a soft good-night,
Mrs. Ewing steered straight for a blue haze in the
dusk at the other end of the veranda. "And oh,
Frank," she said, as she slid to his knee, "you should
see her hair. A perfect cloud! So fine and long!"

"I'd like to. If you think she wouldn't mind—"

Having pulled his ears she continued: "Did you
notice her Spanish? Pure Castilian, with the lisp and
sound of the double *l*. I wondered how it was possible for that brown old woman to be her mother,
and it seems she's not. Her father married twice,
and because his people treated him shabbily—I suppose because of the second mesalliance—she stayed
with her step-mother after his death. And now she
earns her own living—sells opals, lace, and leather-
work to horrid American tourists in one of those
stores on Calle San Francisco."

"Don't go back on your countrymen, my dear,"
Ewing warned.

"Well, they are horrid. She told me just now
that the men snap-shoot her to her face, and one
woman took hold of her hair and asked if it was all
her own. What do you think of that?"

"Merely confirms a previous belief that all tourists
should be shot at the frontier," he laughed. "Like
you, I couldn't help feeling the girl's breeding, and
I'm glad, for Davy's sake, that the old lady isn't her
mother."

"What? You don't surely think—"

"I do," he interrupted, a little dryly. "But **why**

that touch of apprehension? I thought you liked her?"

"I do. She's just as dear and sweet, but—on a question of marriage! Don't look so cross, Frank. I can't help my feelings. It may be only racial prejudice—"

"Haven't you lived here long enough, Nell, to forget the vulgar American conception of Mexico— a knife, heat, sand, guitars, and garlic? Than Mexican good society, there's nothing finer in the world. Did I ever tell you what happened to Hale? He was a classmate of mine—nice fellow and well-bred, as it goes with us. When he came down to take the sub-consulship in Vera Cruz he brought letters to some Mexican families, and they let him into their circle—for a while. And he never did quite know why they eventually threw him out. Whether he pressed a girl a shade too closely dancing, or committed some other slight barbarism, he was dropped; and here's where I come to my point. Instead of firing him point-blank, with no end of smoke, in our unpleasant fashion, it was done quietly, by such imperceptible degrees that he never realized it till he found himself out in the cold world beyond their social pale. Little by little the invitations dwindled, till they came not at all. Though the men fraternized with him on the street, he was never again invited to meet their women. Now, that sort of thing is a cut above us—the delicate consideration. It's the product of a thousand years of Spanish culture. And coming back to Davy: if you once grant this girl's birth and breeding, he'll be mighty lucky to get her. But come on to bed. I can safely leave her to finish your conquest."

"It's done already," she acknowledged, taking his arm. "One question, Frank. What is a Mexican? I have only the haziest of ideas."

"Spanish grafted on Aztec—and don't forget that the Aztecs had evolved a high civilization while our woad-stained ancestors were still chasing one another with clubs through the forests of ancient Britain. Their society was graded in castes that never commingled. The highest was made up of priests and rulers, and I'll wager that Consuela's ancestry leads back through many a fine old don to the Montezumas."

It was very comfortable on the lounge. A pleasant breeze swept through the long room on its way to rattle the palms outside. The whirl of Mrs. Ewing's sewing-machine had died to an insect drone in David's sleepy ears, and if the muzzle of a Winchester Twenty-Two had not suddenly poked in between his ribs, another minute would have seen him fast asleep.

"Young man, you are having altogether too good a time." Ewing grinned in his startled face. "A week's steady loaf ought to satisfy even your lazy soul. Get out and earn your bread. This is Friday, and fail ye to shoot fish enough for dinner we shall banish you to Verda. Better take the Forty-Four, too, on the off-chance of a 'gator; and out of respect for a decrepitude that looks unequal to the weight of two guns, I hereby depute Mistress Consuela to help and take care of you."

"I'll go, too, if you like?"

But as Mrs. Ewing made to put up her sewing, Consuela shook her head with a smile that bespoke her appreciation of the thought behind the offer. "No, you want to finish that to-day."

"Then you must wear my khaki and leggings."

"I thought she might not like to go unchaperoned," she explained, when Ewing rallied her for a "gooseberry" after the two had gone off. "Mexican girls never go out with men alone."

"Case of can't, I guess," Ewing laughed, "judging by present cases. She takes to freedom like a duck to water. And did you see her fight for the heavy rifle? Got it, too. And that reminds me—I forgot to tell them Joachim is waiting at the river. But they can't miss him."

Nor did they. Taking the Forty-Four from Consuela, the Indian—a volunteer, hook-nosed, brilliantly eyed as a bird, but singularly small and withered for a Zacateco—turned on to a path that paralleled the river, a wonderful path which covered in a single mile every variety of jungle scenery. From inextricable *bejuca* tangles, it led across an *arroyo*, around a dank morass, under tall timber in greenish shade incandescent with a fire of orchids, to plunge through sunlit glades aboil with flowers beneath, effervescent above with a variegation of insect life, rainbow butter-flies, great dusky moths, dragon-flies as large as birds.

At first both man and maid were rather silent. Never much of a talker, David reflected a quiet that was unusual as its cause. When a girl has been taught to blush, if by chance her feet escape the boundaries of a flowing skirt her feelings on finding eight inches of shapely ankle exposed to the gaze of the world can only be measured by those of the débutante who appears at her first ball shorn of a foot of accustomed clothing at the other extreme. The said world being limited in this instance to diffident David, whose eyes never ventured below her waist, she quickly grew to the khaki skirt, and began to chatter in English, which, according to a recent compact, he answered in Spanish; and as seriousness, much less silence, was impossible in the face of each other's mistakes, her low laugh was soon replying to his rather solemn chuckle.

As regards the matter of their conversation, it would, if detailed, prove no more interesting than that of any young couple under like conditions, yet has significance in that it revealed to him more of her personality. Unspoiled by artificial culture, she astonished him by the play of vivid perceptions allied with a lively intelligence to interpret the feeling excited by things; and she had in full measure that feminine passion for wee flowers, tiny birds, small creatures which takes out from the mother love. She could find and point out paroquets, canaries, in the tops of the tallest trees. The tinier the lizard, the quicker her sight. Pouncing on a flower, mere spark in the grass, she would make him look closely, and — lo! in miniature, he saw through her eyes the blush of sunsets, spread of indigo skies, a world of delicate color, and was filled with sudden shame for his own dull vision. And she displayed such joy in it all, thirst to touch, taste, absorb the life and light about her—joy that was almost pathetic in its intensity when, in the very act of reaching out, she would pause and sigh at her inability to grasp it all, premonition of satiety. The action which began when an iguana suddenly burst from the grass under their feet came almost as a relief.

Even as the girl gave a startled cry, the great lizard flashed out on a sand *playa* which here lay between the path and the river, and was going like the wind for the water when headed by the Indian. Headed again by David, it crouched, hissing, spines erected along five feet of tail and backbone, snake head with its rows of saw teeth swinging in menace.

His first view of the beast at close quarters, David was drawing closer, but the Indian pulled him back. "Take care, señor! With one blow of the tail he breaks the leg of a dog." So from a safer distance he and the girl watched the flow of palpitant color through silver, green, to red as its breathing altered the play of light. And if she covered her eyes while he fired, she excused the murder.

"The flesh is good for food. The Indians love it."

THE PLANTER

When, farther on, they spied the first alligator through a break in the greenery, her excitement equalled his. While he made ready with the Forty-Four, she crawled up beside him, whispering: "Be sure you kill him. He eats the Indians' babies and the pretty deer when they come to drink at dark."

It was not a long shot. The beast was quietly sleeping within a hundred yards. He really ought to have split the brain in equal halves. But—she lay so close that he could feel her against his shoulder. Her breath fanned his neck. After staring at the splash of sand ten yards wide, the Indian walked on, and something in his grin set a reflection of David's fiery shame on the girl's cheek. They did not look at each other up to the moment that Joachim paused again on the edge of a morass that showed the tracks of deer.

Motioning them to crouch, he breathed between forefinger and thumb into his loose fist, producing a note thin as the whistle of a toy balloon, emitted at intervals with spells of listening between; and when a stick presently snapped in the forest he looked back at David with a nod at the Forty-Four. Uncertain what to expect, he cocked the rifle. But when, after a troubled note that imitated to perfection the bleat of a suckling deer, the timid mother threw away discretion and came with a bounding rush into the open, he rose, almost swearing.

"We don't shoot does up home, and I'm blamed if

CANCER SUSTAINS A REVERSE

I'll begin here. Vaminos, Joachim, nosotros tirare-mos los pescados."

Though he had spoken the English rapidly, her glowing sympathy told that she had understood. "It would have been wicked to kill the sweet mother. Yes, let us shoot fish."

The poor fish! For his cold-bloodedness, utter detachment from things sentimental, it has been decreed that he shall have no friend. Looking down from the high bank, she lent eager eyes to the search which would have been fishless had they depended on her untrained sight. She stared her incredulity when the Indian suddenly pointed.

"Mira! mira! señor. Look! Over there! Un pescado grande! A big fish, and he swims this way."

Neither, at first, could David see. But having gained experience of the microscopic Zacateco sight while shooting fish with Maria Guadaloupe, he waited until a patch of limpid brown resolved from the shining waters. "There!" he whispered, pointing over her shoulder. "Close to that snag."

"That!" she exclaimed, aloud. "It is too small. Oh, it is gone! I frightened it away."

Laughing at her startled repentance, David assured her that another would soon come in, and when it did she stood, petrified, till a splash and flounder of white followed his shot. A quick dash before it could slide out of the shallows, and Joachim had the fish out on the bank—not the minnow it had appeared, viewed through the deceptive water, but a speckled beauty over two feet long.

"Now, your turn." David handed her the rifle.

"I? But I cannot shoot."

Her eyes, however, told of her willingness, and having been instructed in angles of deflection she achieved beginner's luck and shot her fish. Her pleased flushings, shy enthusiasm, brilliant smiles at the trophy when hung by the gills from a crotched stick, would have melted an inveterate misogynist, and, kindling at her pleasure, David overdid it—kept on his feet a full hour too long while she attempted to repeat the feat.

It was in the midst of her jubilations over a second success that she noticed and cried out at his pallor. "Little pig that I am! I was to look after you, and see—I have walked you to death. Now you must lie down—here in the shade—and I shall fold my jacket for your head. So! Now rest while I get you a drink."

Twisting a cup from a large leaf, a trick she had just learned from Joachim, she brought water from the river, then sat down on the root of a saber, knees gathered in her arms—in what was now, to him, her familiar fashion—and looked out over the bright swirl beyond the overhang of the trees. The Indian had gone on with the Forty-Four to look for another alligator, and thinking, perhaps, that he might sleep she sat still, quietly musing, while, reverting to a habit of his sickness, he watched her with half-closed eyes.

CANCER SUSTAINS A REVERSE

The finely chiselled nostrils, ear pink and delicate as the whorl of a shell, rounded slenderness of figure, perfect symmetry of chin and throat, he saw all transfigured by clean young love, the love that worships with awe seeing flesh only as spirit. Ay, he looked, looked and worshipped until a cloud seemed to settle over her quiet musing and her bosom rose to a small sigh.

"What are you thinking of?"

"I thought you were asleep." And, answering his question: "I was thinking how happy your American girls ought to be."

"In what particular—"

"Their freedom to come and go. At home I could not do this. From the cradle our girls are jealously guarded. They go not even to church unescorted, see a lover only from behind the window-bars, are never alone with him until after marriage. It is slavery, degradation."

"You also—" he began, and she went on from his diffident pause.

"A girl who works gains more freedom, yet my mother always sent Magdaleno to take me back and forth through the streets."

"Yet she allowed you to come down here?"

"With him—who is almost a second father—in payment of a debt. But if she could see me?" She laughed, a musical gurgle rippling with the delight of that unaccustomed freedom. "Yes, your girls are much to be envied."

243

THE PLANTER

"And they don't even know it," he mused. "And, not knowing it, find other things to be miserable about."

"But they feel it. Have I not seen them walking on Calle San Francisco, upright, careless, self-sufficient, better protected by their honor than we by our iron bars? And in a few days I shall see them again."

Startled, he leaned upon his elbow. It was not the passion of revolt, regret in her tone, though these struck a vibrant chord. Had he been asked at any time in the last two weeks whether he were in love, he would probably have answered in the negative, no matter how much subsequent reflection might have modified the denial. She had, to be sure, lingered long in his memory, and the glimpse passing down the river had renewed the impression. Yet it had almost faded at the time she suddenly appeared at his door. But the ground had been well broken for love's seed. And now? Coming like a flash out of a cloud upon him in the summer of his quiet enjoyment, the hint of departure not only opened his eyes to the nature of a sudden unhappiness, but set the knowledge in them for her to read.

Perhaps because she feared he might express it, she jumped up, shook out her skirt, and fell to smoothing the wrinkles. He thought, too, that he sensed relief when she suddenly exclaimed: "Here comes Joachim! We must go if the fish are to be cooked for dinner."

Rising, he led back to the path, and, compared with his silence going back, his quiet coming out takes on the values of a boiler factory. Blind to the glances, half-amused, half-sympathetic, she levelled at his back, he stalked ahead, replying only in monosyllables to her remarks. He undoubtedly sulked—behaved very badly all the way to the house.

"Hullo, Mann!" a hearty voice hailed as they approached the veranda. "Glad to see you round again! Come up here! I have news for you!"

It was Carruthers, the planter from down-river, whom David had rarely seen since his first night at La Luna. But isolation breeds quick friendships. Having made his bow, and seen Consuela seated, he dragged David down into a chair beside him, and whether he believed them or not, a fine spirit dictated his regretful expressions at the lad's hard luck.

"Now, if it had happened to me or Hertzer, I would say all right. We are looking for it. But it was hard lines on you, the one man who has tried to be decent with his men. But I bring you a grain of comfort. On the way up I put in at the Zacateco village to see Don Julian about some beef, and the first man I met was your Mr. Tadeo. Yes, Tadeo," he answered David's look of surprise. "He, Seraphim with Maria, their families, and three other of your enganchars. I don't think the Zacatecos had fed them very well. They all looked a bit on the weazened, and were dead anxious for another go at your flesh-pots.

"'It was the fever, señor,' Tadeo said, almost

blubbering. 'For we love Don David. But now he will never take us back.'

"For the good of their souls I let on to believe it. Nevertheless, I lost no time in loading the outfit into my canoe, and the last I saw of them, men, women, and children, were heading out for your monte with a machete apiece. Never saw such thirst for work."

Now, if David had sulked, his pettishness was, after all, largely a product of his sickness, and at this confirmation of her prophecy he turned, glowing, to Consuela. But she was already up, clapping her hands. "Viva! viva! Five and six is eleven! Viva!" And she ran in to tell Mrs. Ewing.

Ewing, whom the outcry brought out of his office, expressed his satisfaction in more masculine fashion. "That's good for a nip all round. We're obliged to you, Carrie—having a wife who curtails our libations. Brandy for you, Davy — doctor's orders. Anisette, Carrie? That's peon's drink. How did you get the habit?"

"How did I get it, you blooming Sybarite? My company's poor. Bet I run our ranch on your kitchen allowance. Unless our stockholders pingle up a bit more freely, I'm likely to come down to aguardiente. Here's to the colony, Mann!"

"Tadeo and the little Tads," Ewing added. "May his quiver be full of 'em."

"No, makes too long a day," Carruthers said, when Ewing asked if he had come from home that morning. "I stayed with Hertzer all night. By-the-way,

CANCER SUSTAINS A REVERSE

Frank, you always said that some volunteer would get him some day. Well, it was tried the other night. You know he sometimes reads in bed—"

"Flower almanacs and rubber news."

Carruthers nodded. "Well, he dozed off with the lamp at full blaze, and while he slept some one let drive at him through the siding with a machete that had been filed to a stiletto point. Luckily the bed stood three feet out from the wall, and just as the point broke his skin the fellow's hand came with a thump against the siding. You can bet it wasn't an hour before Hertzer was up and out, but the jungle comes up to the house on that side, and he didn't get him.

"However, the weapon was there, and you know Hertzer's cold logic. 'A machete is forged to cut,' he said, showing it to me. 'Consequently the fellow who filed that point knew my habits, and the error in distance proves that he made his calculation from outside observations. Go around and look through the crack and you'll find that the bed seems to stand close to the wall.' And with only that and a kick to go on, he'd been sweating Carmen from early morning. Had him in the living-room where he could see the machete on the table, but hadn't asked him a single question—didn't through the long evening we sat at cards.

"In all that time the poor devil had neither eaten nor drank. His lips had dried till they cracked. He sat hunched like a frightened rat, eyes glued to

247

Hertzer's back up to the moment that Patricia retired. Then they drifted to her, and if such a thing
were possible his glance would have pulled her back.
I saw then that his grit was all in, and when I also
rose to go out to the bunk-house, he threw forward
upon his face howling for mercy—he, the man who
once sat at Phelps's door and whetted his knife all
day.

"I was sure Hertzer would kill him," he went on,
after a pause. "But the beggar never does do the
expected. He just kicked him up and out along the
path into the galera, and this morning the Señor
Carmen went out to the field. That's not all. Who
do you think he put in his place?"

"My Yaqui?" David felt it.

"Good guess! And would you believe it, walking
down to the landing with me this morning, he sent
him back to get his guns. After that flogging! 'I
wanted to see if he'd take a dare,' he said, buckling
on the belt. And he went off to the campus with
that big brute stalking along behind."

"Ph—ew!" Ewing's low whistle broke a short
silence. "Do you think he has tamed him?"

Carruthers shook his head. "Neither would you
if you'd seen his face. You see, he was under my
guns, and I never batted a wink while he was coming
down the path. No sir; if Hertzer does much more
of that sort of thing, there'll be an orphan around
his ranch. And that reminds me"—he turned to
Mrs. Ewing, who just then stepped out—"Patricia

said that she was coming over to-morrow to renew her acquaintance with Miss Morales."

"Too late. She leaves to-morrow."

"*To-morrow!*"

"Yes." She turned to hide her amusement at David's face of dismay. "How selfish sickness makes us! Did you expect we could keep her forever?"

"Davy would like to," Ewing chuckled. "I see his salary eaten up by pasears to Ciudad Mexico. Better apply for a rate, Davy." With a glance that indicated secret knowledge modified by slight puzzle, he asked: "But isn't this a bit sudden?"

"She intended to go sometime this week. The letter Carrie brought contained news of her mother's sickness. And you can prepare for bachelorhood, Frank. I'm going, too—for a change, and to do some shopping."

After a second amused glance at David she passed along the veranda into Consuela's bedroom. "Just look at his face!" she whispered, drawing the girl to the window. "Talk of funeral gloom. And all your doing."

One glance, and pity flooded the laughter out of the girl's soft eyes. "Poor fellow, I must tell him. *Do* let me?"

But Mrs. Ewing shook a stern head. "No, he deserves to suffer for his crossness."

"You surely don't intend to desert a poor widower?"

THE PLANTER

Ewing's protest was drawn by the appearance at breakfast of David in his khaki, which had come back from that primitive laundry—the stones of the river.

"Besides being base, it is unnecessary. Miss Morales says that you may have Magdaleno as long as you need him. Better stay till you are good and strong."

If David had been a trifle undecided, one glimpse of Consuela would have been sufficient to send him home to try and lose himself in the rush of duty. While she had resumed her usual black and wore her *reboza* draped over her shoulders, Mrs. Ewing was breakfasting in hat and travelling-dress—than which nothing more strongly conveys the premonition of loneliness attendant on departures. But as indecision was never of his faults, he rejected arguments, laughed at mock reproaches, and at the proper time took his place next Mrs. Ewing in the stern of Carruthers' boat.

Now, last night's sun had set on a mutinous David, a youth who reviled Fate to its face and would not down. But after wrestling through the dark hours —which, as every one knows, make sins of intent look blacker than crimes of commission—he had risen sorely chastened, oppressed with a lively sense of his own demerits, resolved to carry his cross to such Calvary as duty might appoint, a humble and contrite spirit which, however, was not equal to the strain of seeing Consuela in the bow with Carruthers. Three minutes after they cast off, the mutineer was again in the saddle. David, the bellicose, glared at the pair across the boat with feelings none the less injured because the arrangement had been purely accidental.

To do the planter justice, he would readily have consented to the alternative arrangement. It was never a penance to sit with Mrs. Ewing. But, ignorant of the thorns he was planting in David's bosom, he lived up to the charming opportunity and did his best to be agreeable.

Neither could an unbiassed mind have misinterpreted the girl's glance, the little *moue* which said plainly as words, "I'd rather be back there." But when was love unbiassed? He turned coldly away, and, offended, she engaged the planter in what, to David's inflamed vision, loomed as an outrageous flirtation. Even then she gave him an occasional tentative glance. But whereas a smile or other evidence of contrition would have brought her instantly upon good behavior, he added fuel to these fires of his own lighting by displaying an interest in Mrs. Ewing that would have been disconcerting if she had not found it so amusing.

But if, all the way down to Verda, they flirted grimly against each other from either end of the boat, all was forgiven when she offered her hand in goodbye after he had written a check in payment for his men. Magdaleno having carried a private grin back to his work in the fields, they were alone in the store when he returned blundering thanks for her kindness. But howsoever it may lack words, sincere feeling never fails to express itself. She smiled softly while he halted and stammered, nor made any effort to withdraw her hand until Carruthers hailed from the river.

"Hurry, you folks! I must make La Luna in time to head off Patricia!"

"And I may call on you in Mexico?" he asked, going down the bank.

"Surely." She turned to hide a mischievous sparkle which did not die until quenched by a sudden humidity as presently she looked back at his lonely figure. Then: "It was wicked," she said to Mrs. Ewing. "I wish I had."

As for him, once again he watched her go out on the silent river, the slow drifting so infinitely quiet and mournful. At the bend the conch-shell sent back a trail of hollow echoes. As before she rose while the canoe swung on the turn, and—he doubted his eyes—surely she was kissing her hand!

XVI

DAVID CASTS HIS BREAD UPON THE WATERS

"WHY are you looking so savage?"

Reaching from his perch on the store counter, Phelps, who had brought letters from San Juan, took the pamphlet which David extended with a fling of disgust.

"'Report of Verda Rubber and Improvement Company for fiscal half-year, April–September,'" he quoted. Reading on, his smile broadened into an unvarnished grin, and he finished with a laugh. "I needn't ask if you wrote it. The pen was dipped too deeply in wells of optimism to have come from your fist."

"Me?" David ungrammatically exploded. "I recognize only two paragraphs, and even those have been tinkered up."

"'How doth the busy Osgood improve Davy's gloomy periods,'" Phelps satirically misquoted. "With a wizard's touch he transmutes the black night of your reports into the sunshine beloved of stockholders, and still you are not grateful? I'd like to see your answer. Written already? May I?"

He glanced quickly through the letter that David had dashed off while he had carried mail on to Ewing. "Hum! You didn't exactly *call* him a liar. Frankly, my dear fellow, I wouldn't send this. The martyr-to-principle business reads fine in books, but isn't livable. I have always had my doubts whether the old saints would have made those little vaudeville plays if they had lacked an audience, and with the exception of myself there isn't a soul to watch you perform, and I shall only laugh. So why quarrel with your bread-and-butter—even if it is a bit rancid?" As David stamped the letter with a bang he jumped from the counter. "Wilful will have his way. I suppose that an investment of fifty thousand, gold, does carry its privileges. Let me have it and I'll send it on to Carrie's to-night. He has a man going down to-morrow."

Besides disgust at the flamboyant expansion of his own modest statements, David had felt that the exaggerations would work him real injury. While as yet Mr. Osgood had successfully headed off projected stockholders' invasions, it was not possible to do it forever, and in the event of inspection the properties must fall so exceedingly below expectation that he, David, would receive blame instead of praise for the work really accomplished.

"But let him be," he muttered, as he filed the revised version away with a copy of his own report, after Phelps had gone. "It was a good thing that I made these out in duplicate. Let him be. A rascal will hang himself quicker than a fool if you give him rope enough."

What of sickness, absence, and time used up in getting the new force down to routine, he was delinquent in his book-keeping, but he had no more than returned to his accounts before there came a fresh interruption.

"Favor de V. Señor? Una quartilla de arroz."

Looking up, he saw, framed by the open window, the laughingly mischievous face of the girl who had called after him as he rode through the Zacateco village. Besides the rice, she purchased a *medio* of hog fat, a needle, a *quartilla* of green chilis, and having taken a fine bunch of bananas in payment for this various order, David threw a handful of *galletas* (sweet knick-knacks) for her smile, and returned to his books.

"Desea V. una servienta, señor? (Did he require a servant?)

He looked up with a frown that evaporated under her smile. Shapely arms propped on the sill, face gathered in small brown hands, she went on to argue against his headshake. "I would not rob thee like Andrea did. Ask Don Julian, the ranchero, or Lola, my sister, who is the woman of Señor Phelps. They will tell that I am honest, and have never lived with a man."

Her statement of the last qualification was so commonplace in its innocent artlessness that David forgot to blush. And did it, all said, differ greatly from the "characters," written or verbal, that are handed around with servants among Anglo-Saxon peoples? "Jane is honest, an excellent worker, her morals beyond reproach." It sounds familiar. Anyway, he replied, with gravity befitting her earnestness, that if he *had* required a servant he would have taken her word in all the premises.

Curious as to her knowledge of the robbery, he asked: "Who told thee?"

"She came to the village, señor, with a canoe loaded to the water. Such a housekeeping!" The little hands, shapely arms went up with a gesture eloquent as graceful. "She said it was all of her wage; but we knew her for a liar, and the village would have none of her. So they went down-river, she and Candelario, to Tlacotalpan — the Gulf." Spread palms testified to the vastness of that world of waters. "You will never see her more, señor, and is it not that I shall take her place?"

As it happened David had already selected a cook from among the new women, and, entering just then to get some supply, she displayed a combination of age and ugliness rarely seen even among *enganchars*.

"She cooks for thee?" the girl repeated, wonderingly. "*She!*" And with a shrug that expressed unutterable things concerning his taste, she poised her calabash on top of her head and swung gracefully away, a flutter of crimson and gold.

Unsettled by these interruptions, David locked the store and walked out to inspect the fence which Tadeo,

DAVID'S BREAD UPON THE WATERS

Maria, and Seraphim were throwing around the old rubber.

It was, in any case, too pleasant a morning to spend in-doors. After a three-day norther, which had set the camp in a shiver, though the mercury never fell below eighty, the clouds had burst, spilling sunshine over a singing jungle. Whistles, twitterings, cut the clear air, which was shotten with an iridescence of insects. In the absence of haze he spied from an eminence that which he had never seen before—the *jacales* of La Luna, diminished as through the small end of a telescope, spots of gold in the jungle green; and he caught a faint belling, distant bay of the blood-hounds Hertzer had imported from the States. Though really warm as July in the North, the day—in comparison with past temperatures—had all the feel of spring, its stimulating freshness, and as David followed the path through his thrifty plantings he forgot Osgood, sickness, his recent troubles in plannings for the future.

Nor was his optimism without foundation. With material from the new draft, he had already begun to build around the nucleus of his colony. Of eight women, four—who possessed husbands—would presently occupy huts that were being erected by Zacateco volunteers. Three others, unmarried (at least lacking visible male attachments), would embrace the opportunity along with partners as soon as they could decide on a bewildering choice that comprised the whole draft. Even his housekeeper, solitary re-

mainder of this matrimonial sum, did not despair.
"Wait you; wait you, señor," she had assured him
that morning. "Wait you till the pretty ones are all
gone. House and land will not go begging for lack
of a few teeth." Withal, he was going slowly, exercising discretion born of his late mistakes. Like
the old *galera*, the new huts stood within a wire compound, outside of which families would not be allowed
at night until habit had bound them to the soil. And
he had hired a *velador* from the village.

Apart from such necessary restrictions, he aimed
at full liberty in play and work. At night he would
go into the *galera* and lend the incentive of his presence to songs and dancing. In the field piece-work
had proved itself with the new men even as it had
with the old. Pausing to exchange a word in passing
with Magdaleno, he saw two stout fellows at rest in
the shade. While he watched, three others joined
them, and the remainder were slashing on to a quick
finish.

The fence, when he reached it, proved well forward,
and sitting under a palm he looked on while Tadeo
trimmed, with deft machete, the rails that were
brought by his woman and three small toddlers.
Away on the other side he could hear Maria and
Seraphim. The clip, clip of distant axes told of
Zacatecos cutting bamboo rafters and palm-leaves
for his thatch. About him the rubber upstood, full
thirty feet, straight, well-branched, richly tufted;
he could look down its clean lines for a long half-

mile. And as nothing furnishes sweeter cud for meditation—unless it be the reveries of love—than the contemplation of the first fruits of creative labor, small wonder if he indulged in pleasant brooding, building, planning, always observed by the rich face which peeped from the windows of each airy castle.

"Mira V. señor! Mira! Mira!"

While he mused the distant belling had waxed and waned. Loud or soft, sometimes almost dying, it had drawn steadily nearer, and rose to a sudden furious baying as Tadeo called. The tall rubber all lay to the right, and, looking across the new plantings, David was just in time to see a man run into the clearing, then stop and face the hounds, which came loping out of the jungle with a horseman hard on their heels.

Hertzer! A runaway! The Yaqui!

Quick almost as the flash of ideas, the distant drama played itself out while David ran. A machete gleamed twice in the sun—once as the first dog sprang, again as Hertzer rode, roaring, down upon his man. Then David dipped into the trough of an earth roll; saw no more till he breasted the opposite rise and came suddenly on Hertzer.

Dismounted, he stood staring down on the great body that lay beside a headless hound, venting its magnificent life through a gash in the throat. At twenty yards David sensed the thought in the planter's pose, the gravity which manifested still more strongly when he turned and spoke.

"You saw it? No, you couldn't; you were down in the valley. Man, it was great!" His bleak eyes lit with a sudden blaze. "You see that I have my guns. Well, I gave him his chance, the chance he had earned—went at it steel for steel. And he'd have got me if it hadn't been for Bet, here." Stooping, he patted the hound. "For my horse shied. But she pinioned from behind, and I dropped him the very next stroke.

"Got away this morning," he went on, in the same absent way. "The coolest you ever heard. We were picking squash for the hogs. You know my patch—not twenty feet from the road. But it needs cleaning badly, and when I stooped to trim a vine he vanished—went from under my nose. No use," he finished, as David bent to examine the wound. "I got the jugular. He's all in. Needs only a grave, and he'll be ready for it by the time I can get out a cabo with a couple of men."

As yet David had not spoken. Without a word, even a glance, he slid to his knees and began to tear strips from the man's shirt to bind his rolled handkerchief over the wound.

Until the rough pad was adjusted Hertzer looked on. Then, with a recurrence of his usual sarcasm, he said: "I forgot. You don't hold with my methods. It wasn't for nothing the beggar headed for your place." Mounting, he added: "If you have time to waste on dead men, go right ahead. Only remember that the funeral is now up to you. Come, Bet."

DAVID'S BREAD UPON THE WATERS

With a careless "Adios" he rode off, more indifferent than the hound which did turn, howling, to look back at its dead mate. And if he paused within the screen of the jungle, it was only to grin as Tadeo, Maria, Seraphim came running at David's call.

"It's a cinch that he dies, but good luck to you. I know where to find him if I *should* be mistaken."

And mistaken he was. Exposed to view, the jugular was yet not cut. Weak life betrayed itself by the flicker of an eyelid as they laid him on the *catre* in Andrea's old kitchen. When, moreover, Ewing came shooting down-river in response to a hurry call, he found David, a trifle pale, washing his hands after an operation of eight stitches with a common sewing-needle and thread sterilized by passage through flame.

"Good for you, Doctor Davy," he whispered, as they both stood looking down on the man in his stupor of weakness. "Barring blood-poisoning, he'll be round in a week. Though I don't know whether it wouldn't have been more merciful to let him die. He'll have to go back to Hertzer."

"Will he?"

It was fine to see the sparkle in David's eye, but Ewing was too good a fellow to allow his friend to kick uselessly against the pricks. "What could you do? Hertzer has the law behind him."

"The law?" Besides tinting his pallor a healthy

261

bronze, the open life had filled out and straightened David. As he now swelled in his indignation, he loomed a full three sizes larger than the law clerk of Northfield. "The law? Is it ever invoked here except in defence of some iniquity? Will it take no cognizance of brutal murder?"

Ewing shrugged in comical protest. "I didn't make it, Davy; but, as a fact, it won't. Have you read any Mexican history? Well, you couldn't find a better way to improve your Spanish — though it doesn't give the inside of this Yaqui business any more than our American histories tell the truth of the Indian wars. The facts will never be known till some Carlisle graduate writes *The Conquest of the Americas* from the Indian point of view; but you can glimpse something of what it must have been and is from the behavior of some of our countrymen who come down here. There appears to be no good reason why a man who comports himself like a decent citizen at home should not behave abroad. Yet I have seen men—not only tourists, but others who have lived long enough in the country to know better—I've seen them thrust rude hands into the bosom of an Indian girl. Then if her brother, husband, or lover rises up to kill, the Northern papers all scarehead the atrocious murder, and egg our government on to revenge. I tell you the Gringo is the worst beast of them all when he loses himself. But, coming back to the point, did you ever hear of 'El Machetero'? My God! Look there!"

DAVID'S BREAD UPON THE WATERS

They were still standing, one on either side of the *catre*, and, looking quickly down, David was just in time to see the Yaqui's eyelids flicker. A single flash, and intelligence faded like light out of an evening sky, leaving the distended pupils vacant. Then the eyes closed once more.

"Did you ever see anything like that?" Ewing asked, as they crossed from kitchen to house. "He knows him." Seated on David's *catre*, he continued: "Every Mexican child can tell you of 'El Machetero' (the man with the machete). He's a Mexican general, one of the old fellows who fought through all the revolutions. He got his name from an exploit in the French war, a dare-devil achievement that discounts even the pirate stories I used to read in my youth. With less than two hundred of a force, he waylaid a French command of two thousand which was convoying treasure from Mazatlan on the west coast over the mountains to Mexico City. The revolution against Maximilian was just at its height, and as the arrival of money and men would have been sufficient to turn the scale in the Emperor's favor, 'El Machetero' waited till the French were far in the mountains. Then one evening he walked on his lonely into their camp, button-holed the colonel, drew him aside under pretext of having information for his private ear, and—cut his throat within call of his men. Immediately after, he had the jacales in which the tired soldiers were sleeping fired by flaming arrows, and poured in such a fire as they came rushing out that the entire command yielded. If all his men had stayed by him it would have been a difficult position. But made up as they were of cut-throats, brigands, assassins, the majority deserted with the treasure, leaving forty patriots to guard two thousand prisoners. He knew that he couldn't hold them after daylight revealed his numbers. To let them go would be the end of the revolution. To cut the story—I tell it only to reveal the man—he marched them out in twenties and cut their throats in the jungle—killed, killed till both he and his men grew sick of the slaughter, till their arms tired, continued killing till the morning sun dawned on less than three hundred survivors. Now, that's history, and you can imagine what it means when I say that this man was made governor of the Yaqui country.

"How he used his power is common news through the republic; but we'll let that go till your man is strong enough to tell it himself. But I must tell you of a little talk I had with Machetero in Mexico City. You know I have a political acquaintance up there, and I met him one day at the Legation, a fine-looking old fellow, round-faced, with a grizzle over the temples and a humorous twinkle—almost the perfect type of a well-to-do business man. I never could have believed one-twentieth of what I had heard of him if I hadn't seen the twinkle die as I mentioned a report of a truce with the Yaquis.

"'Truce'? he repeated after me. 'Señor, the Yaquis hold lands that are rich in minerals and have fine valleys well watered with pleasant rivers. They wish to hold them, for which I do not blame them. Were I a Yaqui, I would kill every Mexican that set foot over my borders. But'—here he gave a little shrug, sinister in its threat—'those lands are needed for our national development. Truce? There will be no truce, can be no truce, till the last Yaqui is killed or expatriated.'" After a slight pause, Ewing finished, "And that is the law to which you just appealed, Davy."

But David would not down. "But the man *is* expatriated," he argued. "Living now under the law, cannot he claim its protection?"

"Of whom? The Jefe-Politico of San Juan? He's thick as thieves with Hertzer. If you wish to get hurt, just try and buck that combination. Did you hear what happened to Johnny Miller?"

"Only that he killed a Zacateco and had to skip the country—like Meagher."

"But, unlike Meagher, he didn't skip in time. Well, the fellow tried to investigate Johnny's case with a knife, had him chased three times around the house before he gained lead enough to bolt in and get action with a gun. Of course it was self-defence under assault with a deadly weapon, but when Johnny was brought up, the Jefe ruled that the machete was an agricultural implement used in the cultivation of cane and corn. So Johnny was hawked back to jail, and about every other morning he received a note from the Jefe along with his breakfast roll and chocolate: 'My dear Señor Miller, I have a debt that troubles me mucho. It must be paid to-day. Can you lend me a hundred pesos?' And Johnny lent—all that he had, all that we had, all that his friends at home could scrape up, and he'd have been shot in the end if our ambassador hadn't got busy with Diaz. It was a squeak even at that; such a close shave that Johnny took the first train from the carcel, and shook all the way up to Chicago like twenty calenturas."

"But if he's such an extortioner," David still argued, "wouldn't he be glad of a chance at Hertzer? Couldn't his greed be made, for once, to subserve justice?"

"With an average man, yes. Your average will scrap for his wife, scrap for his life, but he won't take much of a chance for his money. But Hertzer isn't average. He'll scrap for a dollar as hard as you for your life, and next to a dollar he loves a fight. He'd be tickled to death to try it out with the Jefe, and the old rascal knows it—knows that all the rurales in Chiapas and Vera Cruz couldn't save him if Hertzer once started out to get him. So he prefers to hunt in couples—as they are doing now in the confiscation of floating timber. All of which leads up to this—as Hertzer is sure to come for his man, you'd better make a virtue of necessity and rob his triumph by sending him back yourself."

"I never will," he added. "You wouldn't yourself, Frank."

"Indeed, I would. I don't live on your high peaks
—wish I did."

"Well, I won't."

The hard glint, sudden set of his jaw convinced
Ewing of the uselessness of further argument, but
if he turned the conversation to other subjects, he
felt it incumbent upon himself to issue a last warning, departing next morning—for he stayed the night.
"Better yield gracefully, Davy," he said, going down
to the landing. "There! there! if you are going to
spring your principles again, I quit. Have it your
own stubborn way. And, say," he added, leaving,
"I am going down to meet my wife next week, and
I shall drop in and stay the night. By that time
your man ought to be well enough to talk. I've
heard so much about this Yaqui business from outside parties that I'd like to see how it looks from an
inside view."

For three days a "norther" had roared in the jungle,
but on the night that Ewing came again the wind
died down; only occasional puffs rustled the sere
thatch, stirred the palms of the clearing to dry rat-
tlings. Slanting between enormous violet cumuli,
the setting sun weirdly lit the jungle. An uncanny
glow streamed through the kitchen doorway staining
the white men's faces, restoring the red to the Yaqui's
colorless bronze.

In one week his wound had healed so healthily that
it now required only a daily dressing. But though

he was up, able to sit on a *catre*, he was still weak from loss of blood. His great frame displayed angles where the plating muscles still hung flaccid; the eyes that turned on Ewing burned in deep sockets.

"Surely I will tell of it, señor," he said, in good Spanish. "But where would you have me to begin— with the hap that sent me to the tierra caliente, or at the time when El Cocodrilo first began to press the Yaquis?"

"President Diaz," Ewing answered David's questioning look. "They call him 'The Crocodile,' because, while he is said to cry over every warrant which calls for the death of a man, he never forgets to sign them." He added, in Spanish: "We want all of it—from the beginning."

While they talked the sun had set, and as the tropics have no twilight the glow died at once, and the Yaqui's voice issued from warm dusk. Already David had noticed its difference in pitch and quality from that of Tadeo and other peons. His "Si, señor," answering a question, lacked the servility with which they endowed it; and while, as aforesaid, his Spanish was good, it lacked the music, ran in a monotonous Indian cadence.

"Then I will begin with the coming of Reuben, the Gringo, into our country when my head still lacked an inch of my mother's shoulder—at the night that he walked, unbidden and unafraid, into our camp among great rocks of the gods, the rocks that bear the snake-and-water sign of the old men in the far time before the Yaquis.

"With us it had always been a favorite camp. An open space within a confusion of tall sentinel rocks, one man could have held it against a thousand, for it was approachable only by the stream that ran out of a cave down a steep canyon. After a long trail, I was very tired that night. When my head dropped to my mother's lap my teeth gripped on the piece of meat she had just thrust in my mouth, and it was still there when I awoke under her sudden clutch and saw the man come striding out of the cave, down the water that ran blood-red under the firelight.

"Upstanding very tall, and of a great breadth, he seemed to my smallness to tower as the rocks. Because of his whiteness I thought he must be sick, and in the midst of his pallor blue eyes flickered and flared with the fire of famine, a wildness of look that assuredly saved him from instant death. For among our three families were Luis Bute, who had killed the three Mexicans who killed my father, Luis Matos, and others that had helped him account for a whole company of El Cocodrilo's soldiers. But what with that, and a doubt whether he might not be one of the old gods come out from his sleep under the cliffs, they held cocked guns and watched until, reaching the fire, he fished meat from a pot and sat down to eat.

"At that they all returned, and, peeping from behind my mother, I saw Luis Bute spear piece after piece of meat and hand them to the stranger, a service which did not prevent him from advising his quick killing in the talk that went on. 'For he is a Gringo,' he said—'first of a race countless as the pines of the mountains, greedy as wolves of the plains, fiercer than the tigerino of the jungles. As the Spaniard did to the Aztec, so did he to the Spaniard, setting his foot upon his neck, wresting away his lands. And as he did to the Spaniard, so will he do to you if this one be let go to carry the tale of the minas of gold and silver. First by twos, threes, then by their scores and thousands, they will overflow the land till not a man be left of us save such as work under the yoke. He must die.'

"In the same manner spoke Luis Matos, yet though the talk was made in Spanish, so that he could understand, the Gringo ate quietly, careless, unconcerned save when his glance fell on my mother. Then the blue sparkle died, his eyes grew mild and pleasant as summer skies, so gentle that I wondered she should tremble under my hand. And when he spoke, after Matos ended, his manner was quiet as his speech.

"'As ye say, I am a Gringo, and, as ye say, the tale of a mina will draw a Gringo even from overseas. As ye say, they will come, first like dribbling sand, then like sand in the wind until the land is theirs and none left of you except such as work under the yoke—and the yoke will be heavy, the labor hard, those that labor greatly despised. Yet listen! The tale of your minas may never go forth by me, for I have killed a man of my tribe, and the avenger of blood sits by my door. Neither may I take part with El Cocodrilo, for I was capitan along the Rio Grande in the border-fighting, and have killed more of his men than ye. But I can take your part against him. Give me that woman '—he pointed out my mother— 'and I shall be Yaqui as ye.'

"On that the men divided. Luis Bute still held for death, swearing that a Gringo always returned to his pais. But the man's careless bravery had won Matos, and when, after a long wrangle, the knives flashed out for the count, only Bute's was turned against him. Put out of my mother's blankets for the first time that night, I wished that the knives had all stuck in the ground.

"But my hate lasted only the night. When, next morning, he took one of the pistols he had let me clean, and brought down with a single shot a prong-horn buck from the rocks a hundred feet above, even I, the boy, knew that if the knives had gone against him the death-wail would have rung in the hills for some of ours; and that day I fought with the son of Luis Bute for a jest cast at my new father, and thought myself paid for a stone in the face when he himself bound the ragged wound.

"'We shall be amigos, little one,' he said, patting my head, and surely natural father had never more faithful son. Like his shadow I followed him—even into the fight when, with the two Luis, he wiped out a second company of soldiers sent against us by El

THE PLANTER

Flojo, the Lazy One, who had the governorship before Machetero. And as, after that, we were let alone, we hunted, Reuben and I, through years of slow peace north to California, south to where earth splits five miles wide and the mountains sink into the great Barranca de Cobre. Together we descended into its fevered bowels under the eyes of the cowardly Gentilos, perched like vultures on the crags above. With him I visited the gentle Tarahumaris, the first Yaqui to eat their salt. Sitting at night by our fire with Celsa, who was born that first year, between his knees, he taught me of his wisdom, what to look for, and what to ware in men, or told me tales of his own land and people, leaving out only the deed of blood that had driven him forth. Up to the time, sixteen years later, that he took Celsa, a woman grown, to the convent of Bocaina, he had never mentioned that.

"'That she may learn knowledge in books and give good counsel after we are gone,' he said, when Luis Bute asked what good she would have of it. And there was something of prophecy in the answer, for he never came back from that trail.

"'Gone north of the Rio Grande.' Now grizzled and beaked like an old eagle, Luis Bute repeated his old saying, 'A Gringo must return to his pais.' But he had travelled to a farther country; for six months later we found his bones in the mountains with those of three rurales in a circle around him—an evil day, not only by loss of his wisdom, but because Machetero was come at last to his place.

DAVID'S BREAD UPON THE WATERS

"To understand what follows, you must know, señors, that the Yaquis were always rancheros. Even during the wars they would snatch time to till a crop in some secret place in the mountains, and during the long peace they had built a hundred villages in as many fertile valleys. Now filling the hills with soldiers, Machetero would come on a village by night marches, fire the jacales, and shoot down the people as they rushed from the flames—old men, women with child, young girls — leaving not one soul to spread the alarm. Nor paused he with their total destruction. At all times peaceful Yaquis had brought produce into the Mexican towns, but now they were shot, without word or warning, and left to the dogs on the street. Neither respected he his own truce. Withdrawing his force, he would wait till some foolish family crawled back to a burned farm, then fall on again like a half-fed lion. Again he sent for the chiefs to come in for a peace-talk, promising safe conduct to go and return; but of the six who went, only Luis Bute returned, to die of the bullet that outraced his horse. So for three years he teased, harassed us, tempting us on to fight and be killed, just as a boy tempts a trapped panther to strike to its hurt, and all that time Celsa. my sister, was growing in body and wisdom in the convent of Bocaina.

"Twice or thrice a year I would go to see her, carrying always a buck or other meat present to the nuns, though I was a marked man, now that I stood in

Bute's place, and the country swarmed with soldiers. And always she met me the same. 'They think to make a nun of me—of me, thy sister! But they will see—only another year; there is still much to learn.' And how she learned! Of books, the sisters, priests, people, and soldiers with whom she talked concerning El Cocodrilo's intent toward us! Then one night she stole out and away with me to my camp.

"Nor did she come too soon. At this time we numbered over five thousand, of whom Machetero was rapidly killing out the rash and foolish, and now those that had not listened to Bute, would not listen to me, opened wide ears to her. She it was who warned them not to molest the Gringo mineros who, as Reuben had foretold, were dribbling over the border. 'For the little finger of their presidente,' she told them, 'is thicker than the loin of Crocodilo. Give *him* a cause against us, and we shall needs pray for the return of Machetero.' And in order that the Gringo should not join hands against us, we protected their minas against the rurales whom Machetero sent against them under Indian guise.

"Also she warned us of the storm brewing behind the summer of a six months' peace which followed a proclamation that there should be no more killing. 'Killing? Better that than their present intent. By ones, twos, threes, by hundreds, or thousands, as many as can be got into the trap, ye are to be haltered like cattle and sold to sweat out your lives on the rubber and tobacco fincas of the tierra caliente.' All of which she had picked out of the gossip of the fondas, for being almost as light of skin as Reuben, she could slip in and out of the towns passing for Spanish. Hermosillo, Oposura, Ures, Cruces, she visited them in turn at long intervals so that her face should not become known, and through her Machetero was foiled so often in the next two years that he raged against her continually, and offered a free pardon with a thousand pesos, silver, to any Yaqui who would bring her in, dead or alive.

"Ten times the sum would not have gotten him a single hair of her head, and with her help and espionage, we held him in check still another year. But to the wisest comes a moment of weakness, and hers, at least, was blameless, for it came not till she grew heavy with the grandson of Luis Matos. 'Take care! Take care!' She sent out the warning when Machetero withdrew his detachments from the hill forts into Chihuahua. 'Take care! it is only that he makes ready for a bigger hunting.' But this time our people did not listen. Success had turned their heads, and, feeding one another tales of how Machetero was beaten at last, they descended by hundreds from the hills and rebuilt the burned villages in their valleys.

"In six months all were at work sowing the seed maize, too busy for strict watching, and as Celsa was now close to her labor there was none to report the troops that were occupying the northern passes by stealth. With Luis, her man, I was spying on the force — the greatest ever sent against us — that was being thrown in a chain, every link a company, across country to the south. Even when it began to move north we had no great fear. By scores our young men slid through the mesh at night to turn and harass the movement with incessant sharp-shooting; the families thought to escape by the passes to the plains on either hand. But this they could not do, and when, after sweeping up a narrowing plateau between guarded mountains, the ends of the chain drew round together, it held eight hundred Yaquis—men, women, and children—helpless as rabbits in the coil of a python—with them, Celsa and her week-old babe.

"Surrounded, with machine-guns trained on their women and children, the men could only accept the promise of good treatment if they surrendered. Si, while they were disarming the promises flew thick and fast; but, the last knife gone, fathers were torn from daughters, sisters from brothers—no two of a family were left together. Babes were dragged from the breast and thrown to the ground, while their shrieking mothers were loaded into the tren that was to carry them to sweat out their lives in the tierra caliente. Of them all but one lad was freed to carry Machetero's word to me and Luis.

"'Come in, and I will make a treaty for you and yours to work at peace on your farms. Stay out but one day after this reaches you, and I will send you the head of Celsa.'

"'Us he will surely kill,' Luis said, as we rode; 'but with that he may spare her and the babe.'

DAVID'S BREAD UPON THE WATERS

"But he had no such mercy in mind—for us. The company of rurales to which we surrendered hurried us out to the railroad into the tren with the others, who told us of Celsa's fate.

"Even as the messenger left the camp she was brought with a firing-party in front of Machetero's tent and given one minute to pray. Alone, she would never have faltered, for the soul of Reuben was strong within her. But as the rifles rose she tore loose her bosom, revealing the pouting breasts of a mother, and she called out that they would also kill her child, pleaded, prayed for only six months of life to give it suck. And, less cruel than Machetero, the soldiers lowered their rifles. Three times they raised and lowered. Twice the officer pointed his own pistol, and as he turned away, Machetero rushed out, wildly cursing, and shot—the mother between the breasts, the babe, the officer, and emptied his pistol at his own men."

While he was talking dusk had merged in night, and the terrible climax fell on black silence. At first the recurrent glow of Ewing's cigar had limned his face in red obscurity, but while the even voice flowed on he had ceased smoking, and as he and David sat silently thinking, occupied by the same thought, only the open doorway showed as a paler darkness.

Three thousand and odd miles northward eager crowds were hurrying through streets aflame with electroliers, arc - lights, huge incandescences, to theatres ablaze with light. Around half a million

quiet hearths fathers smoked over the evening paper
while mothers sewed or knitted for the children who
were conning the morrow's lesson—the morrow that
would send the lawyer to his office, the merchant
to his store, the farmer to his plough, the mechanic
to his mill; and of those teeming millions scattering
to a thousand peaceful avocations not one could fall
to the ground without knowledge of the law. To
them romance was dead—or lived only in books
where tales such as this were read with a shudder
of thankfulness that the world had grown wiser,
more humane, beyond such things. Yet—and it
seemed horrible to David sitting in darkness palpitant with sorrow—these iniquities had been done in
their name. That their cities should be increased
in gold and silver, swollen fat with produce of earth's
outlying lands, this woman had been slain, this man
sold into a slavery that would coin his sweat and blood
into a second profit. The spinning wheels of the
automobiles then carrying luxurious women on errands of pleasure, the rain-coats and rubbers that
protected shapely shoulders, dainty feet, from the
wet, each and all of a thousand articles, down to the
nipple in the mouth of an innocent babe, the water-
bag in the hands of the merciful nurse, were splashed
with the blood of the Yaqui.

"Y la mujer?" Though he spoke very quietly,
Ewing's voice evidenced strain. "She who died in
the monte of Hertzer's bullet?"

"And who took her burial at the kind hands of

the señor, here," the level voice supplied. "She was sister to Luis Matos and my woman. When chance threw us into the same tren, neither spoke the other lest we be separated again. So we came together to the one galera."

"And Luis?"

"I know not, señor—save only that he was sent to the Valle Nacional."

Sister, friends, wife, dead or scattered! His tribe broken! He who had had his being under the shadow of eagles on sunlit mountains—a slave! They could tender only the sympathy of silence, and Ewing was rising when David plucked his sleeve.

Under the cold stars and out of hearing, he broke out: "I knew it was black business, but—my God!" After a pause he went on: "You know I took social science at Princeton, and, like most young fellows who are cutting their teeth on evolution, I was swept from my feet by its swing and scope. I made a god of Gravitation, worshipped Natural Selection. In those days I could have written you a beautiful essay proving the necessity of all this, but it is painful to watch the process. What futilities we are, Davy! Blind beetles crawling on the loom of fate till we get in the way and are crushed. Lust of gold, lust of women, and power—the old man's lust—govern us as they always did. To gratify but one of them we would extirpate a race. It's horrible. Let's sit down here in the fresh air till we get the taste out of our mouths.

"And do you know," he continued, after they had found a log to sit on, "that I have heard bits of his story before? A classmate of mine is manager of a group of mines in western Sonora that always employs Yaquis. Last time I saw him in Mexico City he told me they were the finest kind of workers, and would give no trouble if the government would only respect their just claims. At the last outbreak his Yaqui mandador escorted him out of the country, and when he came back, months later, not even a tool was missing.

"He spoke, too, about the killing of that woman—only he had it that she was a teacher trained by the nuns for service among the Indians—and he said that even the Mexicans of the border towns threw up their hands in horror at the treatment of Yaqui prisoners."

"Did you notice how modestly he spoke?" David asked. "Never a word of himself."

"Yes, and if he's the man the papers were full of these last years, he has dozens of victories to his credit. In some of the big fights the Yaquis wiped out whole regiments of soldiers."

"And you still counsel me to return him to Hertzer?" David asked.

Ewing's face showed grave under the starlight. "If you don't he'll take him—with all sorts of unpleasant consequences to you."

"Look here, Frank." Rising, David faced him. "Do you mean to tell me that you would give him up—after that story?"

"Well, you see—"

"Come, now—don't shuffle."

Looking into the honest eyes, earnest face, Ewing felt mean. He wished to say the wise thing for his friend, but the story was still on his nerves, and he exclaimed, with sudden vehemence: "No, I'm damned if I would! And I'll stand by you, Davy."

Ewing's canoe lay at the landing all ready to put off, and though they had spent an evening and night together, David had failed to communicate a matter that had lain at his tongue's tip all the time. Nor did he broach it until the other had actually taken his place.

"By-the-way, Frank, there's one other thing I wanted to mention. Miss Morales—eh—the señorita, you know—I was thinking—stop grinning, you ape!" With a desperate dash, he went on: "It's a rotten shame to have a fine girl like that earning her living in a tourist store. She's been learning book-keeping, and as you were kicking the other day about being so backward with your accounts, and as I'm pretty busy myself, it wouldn't be a bad idea to—"

"Go halves and hire her? Oh, Davy, Davy, what a specious excuse! How long would it be before I should be back at my own books? And—really, you know, she mightn't like to live here—without a chaperone?"

"Oh, shut up, you fool!" David ruffled, grew red

as a turkey-cock. "Of course I meant that she would live with you."

"You did, eh?" Ewing teased. "And what about my wife? She might not like to have a young lady of such superlative attractions in my—there!—I'll quit! Don't heave that clod; it's big enough to sink the boat." More soberly, but with a twinkle that had issued from some secret amusement, he added: "Well, I'll talk it over with Nell. Better slip in and come on home with us when we come back."

"Can't. Too busy."

"Bet you do," Ewing muttered, as the water widened between them.

XVII

A JUNGLE path is always ephemeral; continues, indeed, only by grace of the unwritten law that all who travel thereon shall unsheath the saddle machete and slash vigorously as they ride along. The rivers form the highways for the dugouts which carry to-day wild rubber and tobacco, to-morrow a crimson freight of chattering women fiesta bound, next week a corpse on its way to Christian burial in the cemetery of San Juan. But whatever the occasion—feasting, freight, or death—arrival and passage are announced by the same lugubrious conchshell.

Carrying across the plantation three days later, Ewing's returning blast recalled David from a pleasant dream. Having just seen the last of a dozen cows frisk heels as she was turned in through the new fence, he had sat his horse and mused of the time when Verda should be one great forest with herds of beeves browsing beneath its stately rubber. A *cafetal* and *cacao* plantation to furnish coffee and chocolate for both breakfast and market, with orange and banana groves, loomed quite near in the future. His order for California navels was already placed in Los Angeles, and that very morning Tadeo & Company had begun to brush out a piece of timbered jungle for *cacao* nurseries and the *cafetal*. And as he now rode back through the young plantings, the serried stand, deep, healthy gloss legitimized the larger dream.

His pace among the stumps of the clearing drew from Ewing, who was talking with Magdaleno in front of the store, a warning that eloquently testifies to his physical change. "Is your neck insured, young man? You'll do that once too often. Nell is up at the house—raving with hunger. If you don't wish to be bitten, hurry up and see what you have in the store."

Investigation disclosed canned tomatoes, sausage, sardines, and, despite Ewing's reassurances, David's confusion at their insufficiency prevented him from observing his twinkle and Magdaleno's grin. A duplicate of the twinkle sparkled in Mrs. Ewing's eye as she stepped outside to meet him, and what with his mixed confusion and pleasure he did not see any one else until a quiet voice broke in on his welcomes.

"Don David has forgotten me."

One glance into the friendly brown eyes, and Hamburger sausage, tomatoes, sardines cataracted to the ground, while David grabbed the small hand as though he intended to keep it for life. Indeed, he did not let go until Mrs. Ewing interposed a laughing remon-

strance. "Really, Davy, she may need it. And we
are all *so* hungry! Open those cans, and perhaps she
will let you take it again."

Red delight showing through mock sternness, he
turned upon her. "So this is why Magdaleno gave
me a 'nada, nada' whenever I mentioned a new mandador? I wondered why he was so contented. Explain? What does it all mean?"

"Only that we anticipated your lovely scheme,"
she answered, laughing. "Oh, cunning Davy! Frank
told us all about it. And did you think I would let
her go for good—and I so lonely? Why, it was all
arranged before we left, only I wouldn't let her tell
you because you had been so cross. And now aren't
you glad I did not? But come, pick up those things
and come in. I routed out your old woman, and the
tortillas are almost ready."

The cans opened, she took him quietly by the shoulders and forced him down on the *catre* beside Ewing,
then continued her merry rattle while helping Consuela to set the table. "And oh, Davy, we had such
a lovely time! They have a new soprano at the
Teatro Nacional, an Italienne—Tetrazzini. She sings
divinely, and her colorature is perfect. From here
she goes to San Francisco, then New York. Of course,
they will claim her discovery, but Ciudad Mexico did
it, with the assistance of Consuela and me. You
should hear her Lucia! We went every night that
she sang, unescorted, to the great scandal of la señora,
who threw up her hands in horror, but gave us up

after a few feeble protests. After she had made up
her mind to the parting, nothing would suit her but
that Consuela should be rebuilt on the Americana plan.
So every day we went shopping—oh, Frank, when you
see my bill!—and we helped each other choose our
things. Behold the result!"

Though David could not have told the colors of the
pretty travelling-dress and becoming hat if he had
been called upon to turn his back, his first glance had
impressed him with a difference. He felt as men feel,
without analysis, the taste in cut and material, the
style that added distinction to her natural charms;
but if he admired as well as felt it, the feeling was
not unalloyed. A touch of disappointment may have
inhered in the fact that he had felt closer to her
while she wore the *reboza* and plain black. A feeling
of racial superiority, so slight as to be unconscious,
still offset his tendency to self-depreciation. The
pretty clothes brought her up to his plane, yet set
her further apart. Just when he was having trouble
enough to rise from the mire of recent temptation,
sloughs of self-doubt, to climb the peaks on which,
as aforesaid, his fancy had enthroned her, presto!
she was removed to further heights.

This feeling colored his comment. "It's immense;
but I loved the reboza." An answer which gained him
an undeserved credit; for be a woman never so happy
in new clothes, she loves to think herself valued just
as highly in the old.

Deserved or not, Consuela's kindling smile brought

her again within his range, filled him with one of those absurd happinesses which are provided under the law of compensation to balance the pains of love. Thereafter he was content to watch the soft contours of throat and chin shift as she moved around the table, the long lashes that swept down to the health-blush as they sat at the meal, luxuriating the while in a sense of her nearness. Her presence filled the hut like sunshine; was to him as warm, palpitant, real as a delicate aroma. And as Mrs. Ewing shouldered the burden of conversation, there was nothing to interfere with his silent enjoyment.

It was near the close of the meal that she asked about the Yaqui. "Frank told us all about it. How is he?"

"So well," David answered, "that I lent him my rifle to go out and try for a 'gator who has been haunting our bathing playa. I thought the exercise would do him good."

"The dickens you did!" Ewing exclaimed. "Your rifle, too? Do you ever expect to see him again?"

"Oh yes, he'll come back," he added. "I rather wish he wouldn't."

"By Jove, that's so!" Ewing admitted. "That might be the best way out of it. Though even then Hertzer would be pretty sure to sick the Jefe on you for damages."

"What a complete scoundrel he is!" his wife put in. "At home we would as soon think of placing a Bowery thug on our visiting-list. Like trouble, the tropios give one strange bedfellows. We *have* to know each other. And, do you know, with all his brutality I find myself harboring a sneaking admiration. He is so thorough in it all, and has such fine streaks running through his coarseness. His love for—"

"Hush!" Whispering, her husband added: "Speak of the devil!" And the next moment Hertzer's bulk filled the doorway.

As before mentioned, a *jacale* offers no more opposition than a bird-cage to the passage of sound, and whether he had heard his name while tying his beast at the store, or judged by the sudden silence, he hesitated and slid a suspicious glance from under drooped eyelids. He entered at once, however, on David's invitation, and distributed nonchalant greetings all round.

"Patricia told me that you had gone by without stopping," he said to Ewing, "so I felt pretty sure you were straining to make here for lunch and home by dark. Glad to see you back, ma'am. Any dry-goods left in Mexico? Patricia was trying to persuade me to go up on a little pasear, but I told her she'd better wait till the stores had a chance to restock. Como esta V. señorita? Thanks, Mann, but I had a bite with Phelps. I *will* take a cup of coffee."

Seated, his glance returned to Consuela, without, however, any of the familiarity that had enraged David during his sickness. Expressing admiration mingled with a touch of wonder, it left her the instant she caught his eye. And when Mrs. Ewing explained the situation his comment was neither under nor over done.

"That will be nice, ma'am, for you and Patricia—all of us. There are too few white women on this river."

All the while he had been fumbling the knots of a handkerchief he had placed on the table, and now stretching the wings of a gorgeous butterfly, with a delicacy wonderful in his strong hands, he placed it for comparison beside a fresh-picked orchid.

"Got them both as I came along," he said. "Mistook, first, the plant for the fly, then the fly for the plant. Wonderful, isn't it?"

In the beautiful variegation of gold, umber, and carmine, correspondence of pistils with antennæ, down to minute markings, each exactly resembled the other. The plant might have been the insect spreading for flight, the insect the plant aflame in warm shade.

"I've seen this sort of thing before," he said, as they admired, exclaimed, "but never so perfect in detail." And thus launched on his favorite subject, he ran on to tell of curious biological coincidences he had observed in his wide travel.

As usual, when possessed by his one enthusiasm, his face lit up as he talked. The heavy features seemed to flow into lighter mould; his eyelids raised, abolishing the suspicion in the eyes, which softened almost to liquidity. And he spoke well, accompanying pithy descriptions of plants with circumstances or events attending their finding. Sometimes humorous, occasionally tragic, always grim or grotesque, these were vividly alive as the seamy side of the tropical life they displayed. Mrs. Ewing's healthy pallor soon paid tribute of rose to their interest; Consuela's riper colors took on a richer glow; even David forgot his speculations on the intent of this visit. Unconsciously they entered into one of those hours, all too rare when company, mood, and occasion combine to drug the sense of flying time. Presently Ewing was stimulated to contributory recollections. With delight his wife would pounce on some fact connected with her own experience. From a life utterly alien to theirs, Consuela drew happenings, strange or quaint. And David—he watched her; not alone, for despite his interest Hertzer's glance returned to her again and again, always with the same mixture of puzzle and admiration. Yet this interest was subservient to his subject; from which he never once strayed up to the moment that, looking at David, he disrupted their pleasant mood with the explosion of his purpose.

"But this isn't business. I'm wasting your time as well as my own. I came to get my man. It was mighty good of you to look after him, but I suppose you went on the principle that one good turn deserves another. Still, gratitude has its limits, and as I understand that he is able to be up and around, I won't have you bothered any longer."

The cold effrontery of it made Ewing gasp. Until he remembered its accidental beginnings he was inclined to think that the man's conversation this past

A SURPRISE

hour had aimed to create a feeling favorable to himself; and even after he rejected the thought as preposterous, he saw that, if accidental, Hertzer fully realized the advantage. Effrontery! After taking advantage of David's sickness to extort a scoundrelly profit, he was now trying to bind him with the memory of that cancelled service, silence him with the gag of gratitude.

It was a difficult situation; but where a more subtle man might have felt bound, David's plain honesty burst the false bonds. Very steadily he answered that the man was no trouble.

Negatively the reply amounted to a refusal to yield the Yaqui, yet it lacked the resistance of a positive statement, and for a second Hertzer hesitated. Then he took the bull by the horns. "Kind of you to say so, but I brought a led horse with me, and I'll take him along."

"No, you won't."

This time there was nothing left for doubt. At the blunt answer Ewing looked at Hertzer in quick alarm, nerving himself for an outburst. Less informed, the women yet straightened instinctively in their seats. But as Phelps always said of Hertzer, "you never can tell what he will do till he's done the opposite." He began to tie up the orchid with a multitude of small pats, deft touches, nor looked up till it was done to his satisfaction. Then, crossing his arms, he looked at David over the table.

"Why?"

THE PLANTER

Irresponsible as the glare of a tiger, and more cruel by reason of the thought which governed its leaping lights, cold sparkle, that hard gaze expressed his record, the vindictive will, indifference to consequences, contempt of life—his own or others. Yet David did not flinch. Rather he leaned farther over the table, chin thrust out in a way that raised a sudden memory in Consuela.

And he spoke very quietly. "Let me tell you something, Hertzer—a left-over from our last quarrel. The night I waited for this man in the jungle I had made up my mind not to return him to you until you promised decent treatment. Now that I know you to be incapable of it—"

"Nonsense!" Hertzer shrugged. "This is no question of enganchars. If it was, you could only claim that I manage to get a bit more out of them than the average planter. The Yaquis are my personal property, and I care for them accordingly—as if they were my horses or dogs. This man in particular has no cause of complaint—"

"You flogged him—almost to death."

"After he had killed my velador and run away. His own life is forfeit by that murder. I can at any moment take him down to San Juan for execution. Instead, I made him my moso—"

"The better to torment him, bruise his spirit."

"Perhaps." This time Hertzer grinned. "Until he knuckles under. But the fact remains—he abused a roustabout's privilege to move freely round the

292

camp by running away. For that I'll flog him again."

"When you get him."

Again Ewing nerved himself. But whatever influenced him—contempt for David's callowness, respect for his courage, the women's presence, or a combination of all—Hertzer only laughed. "As you say—when I get him." With an invitation for Consuela and Mrs. Ewing to come over and see Patricia, he went out, but turned to look back at Ewing. "As you have just come up, I suppose you have no errands for San Juan? I'm going down to-morrow."

"None, thank you."

Making the offer, his glance had touched David ever so lightly, and as his departing hoof-beats died, Ewing explained its threat. "He's going to sick the Jefe on you, Davy. The thing that astonishes me is that he should think you worth the trouble. I fully expected him to break the pair of us over his knee, then go sailing away with his man. It isn't a very flattering theory, but, really, I believe you amuse him."

"Takes me for some new sort of a joke, eh?" David asked, smiling. "Well, I must say that I prefer his contempt to his fist."

"And we must go, too." Mrs. Ewing rose. "We won't make home as it is until after dark. You are coming with us, Davy?"

With a regretful glance at Consuela, he shook his head. "Can't. We began clearing for cacao this

morning, and I cannot leave for a couple of days. I
will ride over the day after to-morrow."

But he went down with them to the landing.

While he and Hertzer had sat at gaze Consuela had
remained perfectly still, the glow of her eyes alone
revealing her tense interest. She was very quiet,
parting, but the colors of excitement were still flying
under the wide brim of the new hat after the boat had
shoved off, and just before they took the bend she
turned to Mrs. Ewing, speaking in Spanish, as she
always did to express complex thought.

"I know now what you meant when you said that
sometimes you almost liked the Señor Hertzer—it
is the strength, confidence, power behind the cold
fire."

"Funny that it should appeal so strongly to wom-
en," Ewing commented, on his wife's assent; "but it
always does."

"Why not, sonny?" Leaning, she gently tapped
his cheek. "It is the complement of our weakness.
We must have something to lean on. I don't think
that I am naturally more vicious than the average
woman, yet if I had to choose between wicked
strength and righteous weakness, good-bye my hopes
of heaven. It is an instinct, a survival, I suppose,
from the bad old times of the earth. But it is there,
and you ought to be thankful that we have progressed
sufficiently to prefer strength allied with goodness."
Indicating David's distant figure, she finished: "And
there you have the combination."

A SURPRISE

"Si," Consuela musingly agreed. "Don David is very good."

Though delivered with gentle gravity, some subtle accent caused Mrs. Ewing to look up quickly, and the results of her observation came out in a bedroom chat that night.

"Davy isn't going to have such easy sailing," she said, while combing her hair. "Oh yes, she likes him, but liking isn't love. It is very lamentable, and I know that we ought to be ashamed of ourselves, but the best of us like a touch of deviltry in a man. And Davy is so *very* steady."

"If he were to get drunk, or kill some one, do you think that would satisfy your criminal instincts?" Ewing asked, laughing.

"Don't be silly, Frank. You know what I mean. That girl has to be conquered."

"Well, you just give Davy his chance. A lad who has sand enough to defy Hertzer is not going to take a simple 'no' from any girl."

XVIII

—ITS SEQUEL

WAS there ever woman who could refrain from lending Señor Dan Cupid a helping hand? If so, her name was not Elinor Ewing.

While dressing on the morning that David was expected, she put down a small foot—which was none the less heavy because clad in its own delicate integument—upon a plan which Ewing had just evolved. "Dynamite fish, indeed?" she said, with a pretty sniff. "Do you suppose he's hankering for *fish?* Have you forgotten your own love-making—so soon?" And even when she had been gathered in and petted until the horrible doubt vanished, she still continued to play football with his plan. "No, sir, it is all arranged. Joaquin's woman has made me some Indian lace, and Davy is going with Consuela to get it."

Thus it was, that midway of the forenoon, the pair came to be following a jungle path which now flowed like a stream of sunshine between rank green hedges, again plunged through dank tunnels overlaced with *bejuca* tangles, and so by alternations led on to a tiny clearing at the lip of the singing river. Rich in its

sere colors as a straw beehive, Joaquin's *jacale* rose
by a shallow strand where lazily swung his canoe,
and, turning the corner, they saw the cause of the
laughter that had floated out to meet them, and were
carried back ten thousand years to Eden's ancient
garden. Two golden children, boy and girl, were dash-
ing water over a golden mother whose white teeth
flashed as each shower spread a wet veil over her
comely amplitudes. Just so might Eve have frol-
icked with her younglings in Pison eastward of the
Garden; and, innocent as Eve, the woman gave them
smiling greeting ere she began her toilet.

Though now well broken to such innocent nudity,
David blushed for his companion — embarrassment
that deepened into shame for itself as he noted her
unconcern. For while he stood, regretting once again
a training which had laid such stress on clothes, she
walked on to the water's edge and talked to the children till the mother dressed.

"Are they not lovely?" she asked, coming back,
and her fearless eyes, clear and thoughtless as those
of a deer, sharpened his shame while banishing his
confusion. Never did enthusiastic defender of the
nude in art feel more keenly that indecency resides
in the seeing eye. Withal, he was thankful for the
interval which permitted him to school his colors,
and he breathed easier when, the lace in hand, they
back-trailed on the path.

To the equatorial eye a northern courtship drags
its slow progressions with Cupid in the part of a herd

goading reluctant maids and tardy swains on to frozen consummations. In the tropics he flies like a hurdler, taking in his stride all the steps which appear necessary to temperate imaginations, and whether or no David's staid tradition had suffered by the climate, his wooing, going back, proceeded at unparalleled speed.

It had not, for the matter of that, gone so very slowly coming out. An hour together over his books—which he had brought over for that purpose—had worn the edge off his bashfulness, and when, starting out, she had demanded an opinion on a walking-skirt, sombrero, and the smallest pair of high-laced boots that were to be had in the city of Mexico, he had risen greatly to the occasion.

"Look like an Americana? Yes, only—nicer."

"Than *she*?" she had pursued, head tilted at a quizzical slant.

"Humph! Please don't!"

Some fleeting memory of a large foot which had once escaped from Kate's carefully trained skirts was responsible for his vehemence, but if it gained him a smile, her curiosity was also whetted. "Tell me about her—all?" she had commanded, as they began to walk.

He might have lied without violation of the conventions, but with rare sense he refrained from insulting the vivacious intelligence behind the smiling eyes. Describing Kate, he could not but wonder at the meagre details memory supplied—a bouncing girl with a fine figure, unlimited appetites for pleasure and

admiration, and small scruples as to how they were
fed, was about all he could remember. During some
dearth of her usual masculine aliment she had given
him full benefit of fine eyes, and he had succumbed
(from sheer inexperience, he put it), and after hearing all the symptoms Consuela had accepted the diag-
nosis.

"No," she agreed, shaking her head, "that was not
love."

At this point in an emotional investigation, whose
scope he would fain have widened, she had swooped
with her sombrero after a butterfly, and, having dropped upon it with the soft flexures of a child, she made
him stoop to examine the variegation of color and
markings. And thereafter her attention was entirely engrossed by external objects. He had to study
insects, climb trees after orchids, pick flowers—labors
that were not without their compensations. Over
one wee blossom they drew so closely that her breath
warmed his hand, her hair brushed his cheek as she
glanced up to speak, and before the guarding lashes
wiped him out, he saw himself for a delirious moment
dancing in her eyes. He had been still thrilling when
the path debouched on the clearing.

Now, and very much to his satisfaction, she seemed
less active, more thoughtful. As she walked ahead,
quietly musing, he was able to observe without fear
of offence the rich contours of cheek and neck round
into the shadowy glow under her chin, the straight
young back uprising columnwise from rounded hips,

lithe limbs that moved with the easy glide peculiarly Latin. And he was taking all the advantages of the position when she suddenly turned, indicating a saber by the river's brink.

"Let us sit down."

"Barkis was willin'." And while she cuddled into the chair-like roots, he selected a higher boll which permitted him to continue his pleasant study as, leaning cheek on hand, she looked out over the river. Her pensiveness accentuated that peculiar charm, certain elusive mystery, which had baffled his analysis often as he had thought of it. In it was no taint of the occult, nothing esoteric; nor did it take out from a morbid or twisted psychology. A healthy girl, lively and intelligent, she had yet all of woman's experience before her—love, marriage, child-bearing, of which vast continent of experience the expression was a reflection. Equally inexperienced, he could not know this, but simply felt its tantalizing suggestion of feeling untouched and unexplored.

So wrapped was she in her thought, he hesitated to intrude with a question calculated to renew the aforesaid emotional investigation until her lips trembled to a small smile. Then he said:

"You were thinking—of him?"

Looking up in quick surprise, she looked as quickly down to hide a mischievous sparkle. "How *did* you know?"

"Guessed. You must tell—even as you made me tell you. Did you—"

"Love him?" She vigorously nodded. "Yes, there could be no mistake in my case. I adored, idolized him—was never happy out of his presence." Stealthily peeping at his unhappy face, she added: "I always cried when he left me."

She peeped again at him darkly, staring over the river. After a miserable silence, he asked: "Then why didn't you—"

"Marry him? I—I couldn't. He—he left me."

"The brute!" he exclaimed, touched even in his misery by her apparent emotion. Then, with a good deal of thankfulness, he went on: "How could he?"

She shook her bowed head, and, looking down, he saw her shoulders were shaking, so he tempered the bitterness of his next remark with sympathy. "Then you still love him?"

"I always shall, señor. You see, he came very early into my life. And he was *so* handsome—tall, slim, nose aquiline, hair very soft, lovely and white—"

"*White!*"

She gave him wide, innocent eyes. "To be sure; I am speaking of my father."

He felt too much relief to join her laugh, and there was still room for catastrophe. "Was there — no other?"

The sun shone again, when she shook her head, with a chastened light as she went on to give the lonely reason. She was very young when her father died; afterward the convent school; and if her own taste had not revolted against the rough men of her stepmother's circle they could never have passed a guard zealous as that of the fiery dragon of fable. "She was very jealous for me," she finished her simple annals, "but always kind. How she cried when I came away!"

Of that David had heard from Mrs. Ewing that morning. "I am unfit!" the big brown woman had cried. "A rough woman in a rougher trade! I did my best to keep the child from evil, but now she is grown she will have no more good of me. So take her, señora—take her where she may be good and free." Then, like a prophet of old, she had wrapped her head in her mantle, refusing sustenance.

Now the girl increased his knowledge with many a tale of generous kindness, finishing: "But she knew as well as I that some day I must leave her."

From her past the pendulum swung naturally to his, and as its narration entailed some description of a life to which she was unfamiliar, he was drawn on to talk of the United States as a whole—of its mills, mines, factories, huge railway systems, great cities, the teeming millions whose each unit meshes harmoniously in the complex machinery of that greatest of social organisms. To her the tale might well have seemed incredulous, but, if her brows arched occasionally, her quick intelligence not only grasped its magnitude, but also proved its truth by a quick remark:

"It must be so. How else could the Americanos

who came to Mexico be so rich? It must be made out of some one."

The naïve comment reminded him so strongly of a socialist orator whom he had heard expounding the Marxian theory at a street corner in New York that he almost laughed. A quick glance showed her innocently serious of propaganda, and he was moved to inquire into the coincidence.

"In Mexico the hacendados enrich themselves by the labor of their peons," she answered. "Can an Americano become rich save by the labor of others? What of the peons of La Luna, Verda, Las Glorias, whose sweat is being coined into American gold?"

It was one more surprise to add to the many she had given him—the last required to wreck the flashing-black-eyes, rose-in-the-hair, cigarro-in-the-patio conception of the Mexican señorita he had gained from American fiction. In its place arose a new ideal of woman, tender, loving, devoted, a mother in embryo, the same the world over in all but externals.

"You were never in Mexico or other of our towns?" she went on. "Then you do not know the peon. At home he works one day to eat for three, and with a few extra centavos to celebrate the fiestas he is happy as can be. So you may know what slavery to him is this of the plantations. It makes me sad to see them trailing in and out of the fields. Of course the Señor Ewing is kind. But he leaves all to his mandador. And the others—of them all, you alone have any heart. I wish I could help you. It would"

—she lowered almost to a whisper — "might make amends, help me to forget—the bread that I have eaten—that chokes me whenever I remember it was earned in this shameful trade."

"You did not know," he comforted. "It could not be held against you. And you are going to help me. By taking the books off my hands you leave me more time to plan and work for them."

"But I want to do more," she said, brightening withal. "If you would tell me your plans I could help you with counsel, for I know the peon—what he can and what he will not do."

"Of course I will," he enthusiastically agreed. "I'd love to."

"Very well," she said, with a satisfied sigh, and so returned to the original subject behind this long digression. "But you were telling me about your father?"

Adhering strictly to his personal history, it did not take long to bring it up to that most momentous of dates, the day which saw their meeting; whereafter they fell naturally to the exchange of first impressions. Of course, he said that he had thought her very beautiful; of course, her vigorous denials drew him on to give reasons for his belief; of course, her opinions of him were delivered according to feminine fashion, in a sort of acrostic which may be understood either of two ways; of course, it would appear all very ridiculous to the young person who rants, raves, or splits hairs through the six hundred pages of the ad-

vanced woman novelist with the manifest intention
of showing her contempt for sex relations. Yet was
it exceedingly interesting to them, and it did differ
in its termination from the million and odd incipient
courtships.

As she rose to move on—Davy had taken root on
his boll—he saw her shoe-lace flapping loosely, and
not until he had dropped to his knees did he realize
that an ordinary service in America might loom as a
scandalous proceeding in Mexico. It speaks for his
wit that, if quivering with apprehension, he boldly
grasped the lacing; as much for hers that she submitted without a quiver to what must have appeared
in her experience as a capital operation; and if he
had not looked up, or she down, the business would
probably have come to the traditional conclusion.
But look up and down they did, and—great is Cupid,
who can with one touch transmute a dry New-Eng-
lander into a poet—reading one implication of his
position from her glance of mischievous intelligence,
he turned jest to earnest by bowing his head.

During the space she continued to look down upon
him, surprise wiped the mischief from her eyes and
then gave place to concern. Once her two hands
went out, and a warm flush told of the motherly impulse to take the bowed head to her breast. But
she checked in time, and as she stood biting her lips
her expression plainly ran: "Consuela, see what you
have done!"

But David could see none of this. A sudden re-

305

membrance of her devotion during his sickness, the terrible risks she had run, had combined under the warm spell of the moment to prompt his action. Already conscious of its precipitancy, he waited in an agony of expectation until, after what seemed a very great while, she spoke with gentle pity.

"No, no, amigo—not yet."

Through an immense anger at himself, he felt the delicacy that spared him; and though he would fain have argued the point, he rose at once and led off in silence. And just as he had taken the rights of the position it now fell her turn for private study. While he stalked ahead she took note of the frame, straightened and filled out with useful muscle, his independent carriage, the congregation of sunburned features which were now at one with the commanding jaw—noting all from the new view-point of a matrimonial declaration, and not unfavorably.

Unaware of this silent measurement, he plunged along, his mind revolving around various plans to bridge the chasm between them and the old friendly relation. And — again great is Cupid! — he found means in a simple flower, an orchid whose dusky flame burned safe from the winds in a hollow tree. Emblematic of love, its colors sealed his recent offer while asking for its pardon.

And she took it in that spirit. Her smiling murmur, "How beautiful!" as she touched it to her lips, referred to his act more than the flower.

"Yes, Don David's taste is excellent."

Both jumped, and as they turned, startled, Patricia Hertzer stepped out from behind a tree. "I arrived just after you left," she said, "and have been drumming my heels on the veranda ever since. You were gone so long that Mrs. Ewing sent me out with a gentle reminder that they eat at least once a day. I meant to spring out on you, but—" She laughed, indicating the flower. Then, after a survey of David's confusion from under lowered lids, she added: "It would look lovely in your hair. Let Don David arrange it—he does it beautifully."

Even a dull girl would have caught the significance, and Consuela missed neither David's blush nor Patricia's meaning smile. But either because she was too fair to note a past gallantry, or in rebuke of that small treachery, she bared her head.

"If he will?"

And the smile which accompanied the request put him in such heart that he felt equal to a comment as he stepped back to view his work. "I'm afraid I've made an awful bungle."

"Which you have, brother." But as Patricia stepped forward, hands raised, Consuela drew back. "Gracias, but I am pleased!" Nor as she led on was it possible to tell from her expression that she knew the blossom was dangling ungracefully behind her ear.

Following, Patricia left David to bring up the rear, a position which, however unwelcome, forced under his notice certain subtle changes in herself. The contrast with Consuela's delicacy most undoubtedly ac-

307

centuated his impression, but, allowing for that, it seemed to him that she had gained in the past months toward her voluptuous promise. Though still shapely, the threat of flesh made itself evident in the fuller lines of hips and shoulders. When she looked back to laugh her smooth throat creased under the chin. Her face appeared broader, mouth more vividly scarlet; a heavy languor deepened her amber eyes.

On her part she did not fail to catalogue the changes which had been the subject of Consuela's recent study, and they undoubtedly added a fleshly interest to the sheer pleasure she took in tormenting him. Crossing a single log that bridged a narrow *arroyo*, she clung to his hand longer than was necessary, then jerked away, and did all so skilfully that he felt sure Consuela must think the lingering originated with him. And she teased him unmercifully — spoke of their few rides together, as though they had been of daily occurrence, with more than one allusion to the attempted rape of a kiss.

"Take care, chiquita," she laughingly cautioned Consuela, "Don David is a caballero muy valiante— a great conqueror of ladies. Only by flight may one attain safety from his advances."

In view of all which it is small wonder if he sighed his relief when the path led out at last in front of the house, or that, even at a distance, his harassed look should draw a comment from Ewing, who sat with his wife on the veranda. "Just look at him, Nell! Taking his pasear between the two prettiest

girls in all Mexico, and you would think he had been
to a funeral."

"A superfluity of beauty is sometimes worse than
none," she laughed. "I'll wager Patricia has been
at her tricks."

He nodded. "She won't tamely submit to any
poaching on what she considers her preserves. But
I guess a little interference won't hurt Davy's stock.
Competition is the life of love as much as trade."

"What a beautiful animal it is!" she continued, in
a lower tone, as the three drew nearer. "And what
a pity she is white! Why? Well, she is absolutely
soulless—just a bundle of vanities and passions done
up in a splendid skin. I cannot conceive of her bringing content to any white man, and I have seen Indians for whom she would have been a perfect mate.
But white she is, therefore destined to make some one
miserable."

"Masculine gender, plural," he corrected, with a
low laugh. "She's handsome enough to put half a
dozen to the bad before marriage—even if that draws
her sting. But she'll find Davy's shell impervious.
He isn't a little bit flirtatious."

"Which won't prevent her from teasing him to
death. However, I shall save him this once by
placing him next Consuela at table."

"Umph!" he sniffed. "Do you imagine a mere
table can keep her off her prey. She'll go over it at
a bound. . . . Hello! you folks, actually back? Lunch
is an hour late, and the cook is howling for blood."

"And I'm hungry enough to eat him alive," David laughed. "Just bring him on."

Judging by the general performance with the first course, he had no monopoly of that best of sauces. Indeed, conversation languished until the dessert of sweet lemons—shredded Mexican fashion down to the separate granules—was well advanced. Busy as a healthy appetite kept her, however, Patricia's glance wandered frequently across the table, and, noting its tentative deviltry, Ewing yielded to an impish impulse.

"Where did you find them, Patrick?"

"*Where did I find them?*" Laying down her spoon, she leaned on her elbows, a position which brought into full view the fine curves of her arms and shoulders. With a glance of bright malice at David, she went on: "Under the big saber in a most romantic attitude. Don David had just presented a flower, and another minute would have seen him upon his knees—the Gringo before the Greaser? What a theme for a one-act play!" With a little laugh that fell hollowly on a sudden silence, she returned to her dessert.

Through acceptance and usage by the Americans themselves, the word "Gringo" has lost its original contempt in Mexico; but though "Greaser" has no such warrant, her skilful coupling of the terms crippled open resentment. Inwardly damning himself for his mercurial humor, Ewing first tried to carry it off with a laugh, then damned himself for laughing as he noted Consuela's sudden flush. His wife's

"Patricia! Patricia!" was better taken. But it remained for David to save the day. Without looking he was conscious of the pallor which drained away the flush, and the tail of his eyes gave him her eyes, wide and black in her face's whiteness. His own rising color marked the leap of his mind to a purpose high and worthy of the old chivalry.

"On the contrary, you came five minutes too late."

In a cold moment the declaration might have seemed absurd, but delivered in heat under a generous impulse to offset the insult, it lacked even a taint of melodrama. Mrs. Ewing's smile of quick sympathy attested her admiration. Her husband, who possessed in full the usual masculine horror of heroics, mentally ejaculated a "Bravo, Davy!" Surprise but no laughter mingled with the spite in Patricia's quick look.

"What? Really?" she asked. "Then let me be the first with my con—"

"Thanks," he dryly interrupted. "Only I can't use them. You see, she refused me."

While he was speaking a soft suffusion had drowned out Consuela's pallor, and at this second crucifixion of self before her altars, she gently touched his arm. "No, Dawid. I said 'not yet.'"

It is too bad that the age of dragons and giants is past. For at this, her first use of his name, valiance swelled within him so that nothing but the doing of some great emprise could have reduced it to livable proportions. If he could have just gone out and

311

slaughtered a giant! Instead, he sat very silent, and as it is difficult to descend again to the commonplace from exalted moments, it was Patricia's laugh that broke a glowing pause.

"So I was only a little early, after all? Then please put my wishes in cold storage until the proper time."

She had, however, too large a share in her father to quietly accept defeat. As she bent once more to her dessert, the amber of her eyes deepened to a black sparkle beneath the lowered lids. They were still ominously dark when she looked up again. "By-the-way, Señor Mann, what has become of Andrea?" To Consuela she went on without pause: "You know, Don David's housekeeper is the most beautiful Tehuana on the Isthmus." Her glance flashed back to David. "When is she coming back? Or did you—tire of her?"

Alluding on the surface to Andrea's service, the question lent itself so readily to another interpretation that Ewing looked up quickly. Real or assumed, her expression of innocent inquiry baffled his scrutiny, and as his glance shifted across to David he broke again into mental ejaculations. "What the dickens! Surely—why doesn't he say something?"

He could not. Having, as aforesaid, measured up his dealings with Andrea by the rigid standard of Christ ("Whosoever looketh upon a woman to lust after her hath already committed adultery in his heart"), he could only sit and listen to the tremendous scriptural warning ringing through the chambers of

his brain: "Behold, thy sin hath found thee out!"
Conscious of Patricia's sly triumph, Ewing's call to
speak, the wonder dawning in the face of the girl at
his side, his own bursting colors, he lived agonies in
the short pause before Mrs. Ewing spoke.

"She was a daughter of David's mandador who
died. She and her mother deserted them in their
fever, and have not been heard of since."

With enormous relief he heard Ewing's proposal to
have coffee served on the veranda, and her rejoinder
that they would come out after Patricia had seen her
lace. He felt himself moving toward the door like
a man in a dream. Came a second spasm of relief as
Ewing called out: "After all, I don't care for coffee.
I want to show Davy my bananas, and we'll just have
time before he goes." But he did not really emerge
from his trance of shame till they were well away
from the house.

"Now," Ewing then said, "tell me all about it."

His pleasant friendliness of tone and manner brought
it pouring out of David in a passion of misery—the
temptations which had dogged him waking and sleeping during the lonely months when the old ideals
seemed to have been drowned out by the rains, and
Andrea's luxuriousness loomed always behind their
wet veil; when, what with tire, trouble, and disappointment, life had resolved into a question of physical
pleasure. And Ewing listened with quiet sympathy
—even if he laughed at the conclusion.

"My goodness, man, if you cut up like this over the

things you haven't done, what is to become of the rest of us? Now, look here." He threw an affectionate arm across David's shoulder. "I don't want to belittle your personal ideals—the brand is too scarce around here. Yet I do believe, to reset an old proverb, that 'One touch of sin makes the whole world kin,' and you'll be none the worse company for having felt the truth of it in your own person. You were inhuman before, Davy, so inhumanly good that we had to strain to keep up.

"And you have no real cause for contrition. Desire is as natural as hunger. and many a promising lad has delivered himself up to the flesh and the devil for a quarter the price she offered. Candidly, I thought Andrea would bag you in less than a month. If I had any religious beliefs, I should be inclined to think that there had been a special interposition on your behalf. Having none, I reserve my right to criticise a Providence which is said to damn men and women for the exercise of passions of its own creation. Now don't run away with the idea that I am defending license. There's a reason behind moral law— even if you don't find it in Revelation. To all animals but man nature has appointed their seasons, He alone can misuse his passions, and as he has not advanced, in the bulk, to the point where he can distinguish between freedom and license, society does it for him. 'Behave, confound you,' it says, 'or I will send you to Coventry and restrain you from my virtuous daughters.' And it will continue to impose a practical if uncomfortable morality until the millennium arrives and intelligence balances passion—at least, that's the theory, one of 'em; there are a dozen others, from free-love, which would send us all to wallow in the swine-troughs, to the celibacy, which would wipe out race and problem at one fell whack. But I'm wandering. Returning to the point, you cannot be blamed for feeling desire, and ought to be thankful to have escaped on any terms. And now for a scolding: Why did you let that little beast bluff you? Your blush would have damned St. Anthony."

A little more at ease, if not entirely satisfied, David had now room to regret his supersensitiveness. "I suppose it was silly," he groaned. "But I've told you how I looked on it—and she sprung it so suddenly —and—when a fellow is in love—you know!"

Ewing looked his sympathy. "Yes, it brings him a bit closer to the angels than he ever was before—or will be again. I used to lie awake at nights to enumerate my sins, and they kept me busy counting. But I've lived straight—since."

They walked some distance in silence before David asked: "Do you think she meant it—that way?"

"Patricia? It was subtle and vicious enough to have come from a jealous married woman; but she has hung around Hertzer's cook-house enough to have eaten of the tree of knowledge. I wouldn't put it past her."

"And I suppose it is up to me to escort her home?" David asked, with another groan.

"No, she came by canoe. And, by-the-way, it wouldn't be a bad idea for you to go now. I should then be free to have a talk with Nell, and you may depend upon her to settle Miss Patricia."

David agreeing, they walked back to the stables. "Remember that you are to come early on Christmas Day," Ewing said as he mounted. "By Jove, that's the day after to-morrow! I'd forgotten. Phelps, Carrie, and a couple of planters from the next river are coming with their wives, and we expect to have no end of a time."

Though Ewing intended to speak to his wife at once, the fuss and bustle of Christmas preparation kept her so busy that evening fell before he found her alone in her bedroom.

"So you see," he said, in conclusion, "our Davy has a germ or two of original sin, after all, in his stiff composition."

"The poor boy!" she exclaimed. Thoughtfully she added: "But one might have known it. Good works don't come out of cold saints, nor generous impulses proceed from anything but passion."

"And you'll explain to Consuela?"

"Don't need to, dearie. She came to me all aglow with indignation as soon as Patricia left. She didn't believe it. If she had, I'm sure her generous anger at the treachery would have made her overlook it—not to mention his consideration for her at the table. Wasn't he great?"

"Fine boy," Ewing agreed. "In these cynical days it takes a big soul to do a thing like that—which reminds me, did you scold Patricia?"

"Didn't get the chance." She laughed heartily at the remembrance. "It was positively funny, Frank. Just as soon as you went out she turned to Consuela and said, with an expression of most beautiful regret: 'You must think me very rude, but you know I'm half Mexican myself or I wouldn't have dared to call you a Greaser.'"

Ewing burst out laughing. "She isn't, either. She's Indian. The little cat! Hertzer all over. Did you ever hear of such consummate cheek? And Consuela?"

"Turned her down with a quiet 'No importa, señorita.'"

"Ah, ha! There's your blood! But about Davy, Nell? It would be too bad to let him suffer the next two days."

"Nor shall he. Consuela and I both need exercise. We'll gallop over there some time to-morrow."

XIX

THE BREAD FLOATS OUT

MORNING brought a slight change in Mrs. Ewing's plan. "A third person is always de trop," she said, while dressing. "They will get along better without me. But I must have some excuse to send Consuela alone. Let me see . . . Oh yes, we need brandy for the pudding. I saw a bottle on Davy's shelf; and don't forget that you haven't a drop in stock when I mention it at breakfast."

"Mightn't she feel a bit embarrassed," Ewing doubted, "after yesterday?"

She shook her head. "Too honest. I never knew a girl so pellucidly sincere. False shame can have no part in her, for her thoughts are clear as her eyes and her actions flow out from her feelings. It isn't the transparency of simplicity, either, to be muddied by a sediment of knowledge. A good brain resides in that pretty head."

And surely it takes one woman to read another. Riding through the jungle a couple of hours later, the girl's expression flickered with her thought between the extremes of humor and sadness, but lacked

318

even a taint of the embarrassment that would have been natural in a coarser nature. When, issuing upon the Verda clearing, she spied David on the opposite trail, her call rang out free and unconscious as the cry of a bird.

Clear, high, virginal in its purity, it thrilled David's distant ears, penetrating several strata of misery which had formed over his feeling during the night. And though—oblivious of the fact that the brute has, and will have, its proper share in man until over-refinement brings death to the race—he had assured himself only fifteen seconds ago that he was a beast, unfit to look in her face, he now reined his horse round on strung haunches and shot across the clearing, taking logs, stumps, and a wide *arroyo* in his stride.

"Santa Maria Marissimi!" she gasped, as he rode up. "Such madness!" But though this was only the beginning of a scolding, she could not altogether repress a glint of admiration; he would have doubled the risk for half her smile.

Accompanying the pressure of a soft hand, the smile conveyed other things, sympathy and understanding, and, just as the sun licks up night fogs, its warmth dissipated his miserable clouds. Shining through a joyful suffusion, his answering smile may only be compared to the luminary bursting at dawn through scarlet mists; and with these silent expressions of trust and thanks, yesterday passed harmlessly out of their lives.

"So anxious to be rid of me?" Her eyes danced

under arched brows when he said that he would get the brandy at once. "I had intended—but no, now I shall go back."

"No, you won't," he contradicted, with boldness inspired by the aforesaid smile. "I'm going to hold you to your contract. How can you help me if you don't know the place? First, we shall ride around and look at the improvements—which will take until lunch. Afterward, you are to inspect the buildings and advise me on my plans. Lastly, I shall see you home?"

Delivered with a rising inflection, his Spanish sentences were transmuted from commands to requests, a subtlety which earned him a glance of soft approval. "Very well, señor," she laughingly acceded. "Lead on."

He in the lead, they came in five minutes to the new fence where they caught, down long vistas of silver trunks, flashes of red and white—the cattle peacefully grazing. Yesterday their census had been increased by one small stranger which stood with its mother close to the bars. Its fawn muzzle, mild eyes, ineffectual knees instantly drew Consuela's sympathies; nor would she consent to move on till she had watched with tender curiosity its boisterous assault upon the patient mother.

A longer ride put them into Tadeo's nurseries, where a checker of golden light was already rifting through the thinned woods upon a wild confusion of stumps, branches, felled trees; and here it was that

THE BREAD FLOATS OUT

Mrs. Ewing's judgment of Consuela's wit was proved by a bit of wise counsel. Tadeo, who with Maria and Seraphine was rapidly trimming the tangle, left his labors as they approached to unburden himself of a plan. In Ciudad Mexico, it seemed, two brothers and several cousins, all men of family, were wasting for an opportunity to enter the beneficent service of the Señor Don David Mann. Railroad fares, with a few odd pesos thrown in for expenses, would assuredly bring them down, and if he, Don David, would intrust him, Tadeo, with the necessary moneys— While with multitudinous bows and scrapings he thus delivered himself, Consuela had listened quietly, but here she interposed a quick objection in English.

"No, señor, he would never return." Reading David's disappointment, she ran on: "What would you? It is not that he is insincere or dislikes your service, but you have yet to learn that these are children, to be guided away from temptation. He is a peon, therefore changeable, irresolute, well-meaning, but variable as water under a wind. His familia? That would not hold him, for they are easy to come by on the plateau. Give him a hundred pesos, and you will never see him again. But, see, this does not mean that you shall reject his plan. You can take the names and addresses to-night, and I shall forward them with the money to my mother, who will find and send them down under care of a cabo."

"Bully!" he exclaimed, brightening. "Bully plan!"

"'Bull-ee?'" she repeated. "I must see what is that!" And, much amused, he looked on while she pulled a vest-pocket dictionary out of her white blouse. "'Bull-ee—One who abuses, torments, or otherwise persecutes his fellow.' Then it is that I—"

It was hard to maintain his gravity in the face of her quizzical wonder, still he managed to nod without smiling.

"How, señor?"

"By refusing to marry me."

Her laughter was proportioned by her previous mystification, and her answer came out of a smile. "But I did not."

"Then you will?" he eagerly asked.

Head slanted, eyes very merry under considering brows, she measured him teasingly before making provoking answer. "Who knows?"

"Consuela—" he began, pleadingly. Then—perhaps because she found it hard to deny his honest eyes—she whirled her beast, and though he instantly drove in the spurs, he gained for the next five minutes only a view of the supple back, lithe figure undulating to their mad gallop. Through the woods and far out on the open she headed him, nor paused until a sudden turn brought them upon Magdaleno and his men. Then reining in, she looked back with something of the triumph and invitation which mix in the gaze of a doe that has outraced its pursuing mate.

"And you scolded me!" he gasped, coming up. "What kind of a pace do you call that?"

THE BREAD FLOATS OUT

"But this was on a path," she innocently returned. Reading his own interpretation from the race, Magdaleno had bristled like some old brown hound; but at her laugh his hand dropped from his pistol-butt while he muttered in his throat: "Old fool! He is not of that sort." And like a faithful hound he stood, eyes fixed on his young mistress all the time she enthused over David's young rubber.

"Si," she agreed. "Only the other night it is that José, the mandador of Señor Phelps, tells it to me that La Luna itself cannot show a finer stand. It is two years' growth in a single season."

"And not a man sick in the galera," David proudly added. "Last year I had to do the best I could with Meagher's leavings. But with this clean start I hope to bring these fellows safely through the heat and rains. Hello! What is it?"

A man had detached himself from the line and stood, sombrero in hand, a few paces away. "Only to speak with the señorita," he answered, bowing and scraping. "That she may send the word to la señora in Ciudad Mexico—it is a good service."

Looking at Consuela, David saw the warm tide flood her face and neck as she answered: "And that will I. Isidro Labre, is it not?"

As, bobbing assent, the fellow retired, a second came forward, then a third, fourth—indeed, her passage down the line, which paralleled the path, resolved into a function, for no one of the simple children would miss the smile that had paid the first for his thanks. To his respects, the last added a request spoken so rapidly that David understood only a reference to a letter.

He caught Consuela's low question: "What is her name?" And she explained as they rode on: "I am to write to his sweetheart, for it is that Benito, who writes for those who cannot, is given to rude jesting and might offend the girl."

"But what will you say?" he asked, amused and puzzled.

"What I would say if—I were in love myself," she answered, with grave hesitation.

"Oh, of course!" he concurred, a little dashed, for she was riding ahead again and he could not see her smile. But the afterglow from that exhibition was too strong to be cooled by momentary pique, and presently he broke out: "Wasn't it fine to have them do that?"

"Especially for me." Her voice trembled, and, glancing quickly as she looked back, he saw to his surprise that the light had died from her face. With a slight shudder she went on: "At Las Glorias are some who came through our galera, and their looks as I passed them in the field this morning! . . . And their servitude is kind beside that of the thousands we sold into the tobacco slavery of the Valle Nacional."

"Oh, come, come!" he remonstrated, pained by her pain. "You, at least, were innocent. It cannot be charged against you."

"'The sins of the father shall be visited upon the

children even to the fourth generation,'" she quoted. "When I used to hear the priest read that gospel at the convent, I never dreamed it could apply to me."

Young as he was, David had yet lived long enough to note the swing and scope of that iron law, to see the drunkenness, incapacity, immorality of parents react upon innocent children and ruin their every chance in life. Moreover, he had recognized its use in the economy of nature to cut the weak and vicious from off the face of the earth. But neither philosophy, Scripture, nor his own feeling would permit him to bring a step-child within its scope.

She took, however, little comfort from the suggestion. "But to think, señor, that my very flesh is a product of that slavery! If I could only tear it from my bones—like the clothing earned by that shame!"

She had turned again, but he could see her shoulders shaking, and the pain of that silent distress enabled him to rise to a sudden inspiration. "Oh, I know!" And as she gave him dark, humid eyes. "Give it to me?"

At first she looked surprised, then angry, but this faded as she caught the sympathy behind his smile. Obliged to return it, she asked, with a touch of pathos: "What would you do with it—my poor flesh?"

"'Protect, care for it, cherish it till death did us two part.'" He paraphrased on the simple language of the Episcopalian service.

"I believe you would." She thrust out an impulsive hand, adding, as he rode forward to take it:

"We are going to be good friends, Señor Mann."
And though the "friends" was hardly to his liking,
he had to let it go, for just then they rode in among
the buildings.

"Oh, look at the niñas!" she exclaimed, passing the
compound which now enclosed the married quarters;
and as soon as the stable *moso* had taken her horse,
she swept down like a mother hen upon the dozen tots
who ran or rolled in the sunlit dust. Of them all,
only three small girls could boast a single chemisette.
But though these honorable attempts toward clothing
had shrunk through repeated washings to the dimen-
sions of a generous collarette, she gathered in as many
as both arms would hold, and sat down to fondle them
on Tadeo's doorstep.

Standing above her, David looked smilingly on.
At home he had often seen young girls make much
of children—sometimes with an eye upon masculine
watchers—but nothing to equal her complete abandonment. Her remark, made without looking up, "I
love children," was purely unconscious, and, making
it, her lips trembled with the passion of tenderness
that glowed in her big brown eyes. The drooping
figure, yearning of the head forward upon the slender
neck, expressed that dominant maternity than which
nothing more powerfully affects a man.

"If I could do something for these," she said, a
little mournfully, "I might then forget."

"So you can," he began. "After awhile—"

But just then she sprang up, scattering her small

brood. "Viva! Viva! I have it! La escuela! A school! I shall gather them in your jacale! Teach them to read, write, and sew! Come, let us speak to the mothers!"

It was hardly necessary; David's command would have been sufficient. But, infected by her enthusiasm, he followed from hut to hut, and listened, smiling, while each brown mother declaimed that her particular bratlings were not even worthy of the señorita's notice. Nevertheless, they were pleased as she, and, leaving them to mutual felicitations upon the lustres that education would presently confer upon their respective households, David led her away to lunch.

It is to be feared that she did not fare very well. How *could* one eat when plans of such magnificence were toward? She would do this, that, the other! She prattled until the very beans and *tortillas* acquired an academic flavor. Indeed, her plans for the mental uplift of his people ran as far into the years as his for their social welfare, and were closely interwoven.

"For, you see, señor," she said, at the end of the meal, "you will need administradores, storekeepers, clerks to care for your growing trade. Did you notice Tadeo's Anita, the sharp little face? She is to be my prize scholar, and will keep your books when—"

"We are married," he quietly finished, not sorry for the opportunity to give her chatter a personal twist.

"—I am too old for work, and so ugly that I frighten

327

the trade away," she made her own finish, demurely dimpling.

"You? Pouf!" He blew the very idea into thin air. Then, while she listened, head daintily inclined, he sketched her as an old lady—eyes of deep brown looking out from under snowy hair—

"Wrinkles," she supplied, drawing them in with a slim finger.

"No. The face reflects the spirit—yours will always be young. Figure just—"

"I shall be fat, a horror."

"Couldn't if you tried—too nervous."

"Don't make me thin," she pleaded. "Thin ones are always sour."

"Comfortably plump," he went on. "Just a nice, sweet old lady whose sons will tell her that she is more beautiful than their sweethearts."

"Sons? But, señor, I am to be an old maid."

"The idea!" he sneered.

"I am twenty-two, and in Mexico girls marry at sixteen. Already some of my school-mates have great niñas. I am pasado."

"Pasado, indeed! You are going to marry me."

Laughing at his calm confidence, she mimicked Patricia with a perfection of tone and accent that surprised while it filled him with chagrin. "'Don David is a caballero muy valiante. Only by flight may one gain safety from his advances.' Señor, you have convinced me of her truth. Bring out my horse."

THE BREAD FLOATS OUT

Her dimples, which had come and gone like rain-drops on a silent pool, had faded, and he needed to look closely to see the mischief peeping from under lowered lashes. "Spare me—" he began; but stopped as her glance went by him to the Yaqui, who had silently approached the door.

It was the first time she had seen him; and while he busied himself untying a bundle he carried under his arm, she looked eagerly on. Though it was only a week since he had left his bed, rest and the open had recolored his bronze, set the black sparkle again in his eye. As he stooped to spread a jaguar-skin over the sill, joints and muscles fell and flowed with the old, flexuous ease. When he rose, her eyes paid tribute to his bulk, which, stripped as it was of superfluous flesh, still filled the doorway.

"What a peach of a skin!" David exclaimed.

Stepping back, the Yaqui allowed a band of sunlight to fall upon it. Six feet from snout to tail-tip, its vivid spots burned amid the tawny fires of back and belly, which lit the doorway with a resplendent glow. Murmuring a "Magnifico!" Consuela joined David, who was upon his knees before it, and ran her hand with childish delight over and through the fur.

"I wonder where he got it?" she said, after a minute of admiring comment. "Why—he's gone!"

"To the cook-house," he said, glancing outside. "He's always like that: comes and goes without a word. Magdaleno seems to be the only person with

329

whom he will talk. It was from him that he learned
I was crazy for trophies, so now he brings me something every day. Yesterday it was a twelve-foot
'gator; day before, the biggest python I ever saw.
I'll have enough to stock a museum in a couple of
weeks."

"Two weeks?" She raised her brows. "Then you
think that Señor Hertzer will not—"

He shrugged. "Quien sabe?"

"If he doesn't?"

"Now you've got me." He shrugged again helplessly. "Of course, I can't keep him here; sooner or
later Hertzer would get him. If I turn him loose he
certainly can't walk back to his own people through
two thousand miles of hostile country. I did plan
to smuggle him down - river to the Gulf, only it is
doubtful whether he could adapt himself to an employment. Any way you look at it, his future is a
puzzle."

Had he known it, the first cause in a sequence that
would bring the solution was even then on the plantation; would appear as soon as Carruthers had seen
the stable *moso* give his hungry beast a feed of maize.
"What a beauty!" he commented, stepping over the
skin five· minutes later. "Your bag, Davy? The
Yaqui, eh? He's proving worth while." After greetings were over, he went on, with a doubtful glance
at Consuela: "By - the - way, it's he I want to see
you about—if Miss Morales will excuse us a minute?
She knows everything? In that case I'll sit down

and eat as I talk, for I've ridden six hours on cold tortillas and coffee."

"No, you won't," David contradicted. "Open your mouth, except to put grub in it, for the next twenty minutes, and I'll throw something at you." And it must be conceded that the planter found little difficulty in obeying.

"It is legitimate," he said, when David commented on his tired look as he shoved back from the table. "Night before last I played poker with Hertzer and the Jefe-Politico in San Juan till four o'clock in the morning—caught the old rip cheating, by-the-way: filled a lovely hand from the discards. Yesterday I rode all day, and, not to mention this morning, I must make back home before Hertzer passes on his way up to-night.

"It isn't that I am afraid of him," he answered David's look. "But so long as we have to do a certain amount of neighboring, what he doesn't know won't hurt him. He means mischief, Davy, for two of the Jefe's rurales are coming up with him, and you'll have them here sure to-morrow. However, there's still time for a checkmate if you chuck his man into a canoe and rustle him down to La Luna before they arrive." He added: "It's simple as pie."

"Simple enough, Carrie." Looking from one to the other, Consuela saw David's expression settle into a familiar obstinacy that would have been mulish but for its rightful purpose. "I'm awfully obliged for your trouble, but—I can't do it."

331

"Oh, nonsense!" Carruthers protested. "Do be sensible. Ewing told me how you felt about it when he passed the other day, but—"

"Did he tell you the man's story?"

"Yes, and it's tough. Still, when all's said, Davy, he's only an Indian, and if he persists in bucking a losing game I don't see why you should take it on yourself to pay his losses."

"And I wouldn't if he had wilfully taken it up with fate. But when he was forced in, compelled to throw with loaded dice, I can't see my way to give him up."

"But, man, you have duties—to yourself, the plantation!"

"To follow the right as nearly as I can."

"But what's the use?" Carruthers fumed and fretted. "With or without your leave, they'll get him, only without it you yourself will be landed in San Juan jail. Ugh!"

Had David known nothing of the filth and fleas of the Jefe's *carcel*, Carruthers' expression of disgust would have been sufficiently enlightening. The tail of his eye gave him Consuela's sympathetic shudder, and a glance showed her leaning forward, lips slightly parted, expectant, apprehensive. Her eyes were fixed on him, but he could not read their eloquent glow. Still, neither the doubt nor the squalid prospect could shake his resolution.

"As you say," he began, slowly, "I may go to jail, but it doesn't follow that they'll capture him. Over a week ago I spoke to—"

THE BREAD FLOATS OUT

Carruthers jumped, hand out-stretched. "No, no; don't tell me! I might be tempted to protect you against yourself. And now I'll have to go." Turning to shake hands with Consuela, he finished: "Now it is your turn. I leave him to you."

"Yes," she said, as David went out with him, "it is my turn."

Something peculiar in her accent stuck in David's consciousness, but he did not understand until, on his return, he saw her glowing face. Then its sympathy, faith, encouragement filled him with shame for the hesitation that had caused him to pace a few turns before coming back in.

"Well?" she asked.

"There's only one thing—the river."

Taking some Mexican bank-notes from his trunk, he called the Yaqui, who, as before, stood in silence while he explained the new turn in the situation. "So thou seest," he finished, "there is no longer safe harborage here. Take, then, these notes to Don Julian, the ranchero in the Zacateco village over the ford, and he will furnish a canoe with which thou mayest gain down-river to the coastwise cities where employments be many."

The jaguar-skin still blazed in the doorway, and as the man studied it all the time he was talking, David could not see the sudden change which centred on his eyes. Now looking up, his face was blank. His thanks and *adios*, as he took the notes and walked away, were so wooden, flatly stolid, that David winced.

333

Heavily disappointed, he stood looking after till a gentle hand pulled his arm.

"Never mind. You did your part."

She was standing very close, and, turning quickly, he saw himself, as on that other day, trembling amid brown liquid lights; and this time she allowed his hurt to heal before she wiped him out.

"Oh, well." He laughed as she did it. "Now for the consequences. Put on your hat. I must go over at once and make arrangements with Frank to look after the place if Hertzer spirits me away."

The hands that had reached up to the pins dropped again to her side. "Oh no, I shall do that—come over and live here till you return." Flushing, she ran eagerly on: "And that will not be long. See you, I shall write to my uncle, who is judge in Mexico city, to speak with Diaz; for though the Presidente is inflexible in purpose, and has done great wickedness, it was always to obtain a greater good. If he but know, not only will he succor thee, but also put out his strong hand to stay the waste of life on the plantations." All in a glow, she finished: "And if it be that you do go to the carcel, when you return—perhaps—I will."

It came so suddenly that he just stood and stared. Then, as his face lit up, she stepped back from his reaching hands, the old mischief leaping in the warmth of her eyes. "The carcel—first," she warned.

"To-morrow!" he exclaimed, happily, the first man who was ever made drunk by the prospect of prison.

THE BREAD FLOATS OUT

She was now tiptoeing to his glass, and she glanced sidewise under the arm that was raised to her hat. "What if I leave you there?"

"You won't. And don't forget—you promised."

"I said—perhaps."

But he was content, for she gave him her hand as they went out; nor took it back until both his were required to lift her to the saddle. The happiest man in the two Americas rode with her into the jungle.

A little less absorbed, and David might have glimpsed the Yaqui as they passed the store on their way to the stable. Instead of going down to the river-path to the ford, he had turned around the buildings on to the plantation road, and just as David and Consuela rode out of the clearing at one end, he paused to speak with Magdaleno at the other. He did not stop long, perhaps less than a minute; but all the while the *mandador's* tongue clucked sympathetic commiseration, and when he moved on, Magdaleno looked after, shaking his head.

From Verda to the *arroyo* where David had spent the night was an easy hour for a horse, but water still lay in the morasses. What with many détours, the sun was in the tree-tops before the Yaqui plunged down the bank and turned in under the leafy tunnel. It sank as he climbed out, an hour later, to the lonely grave in the glade.

Save that the kindly rains had spread it with a counterpane of flowers, all remained unchanged.

THE PLANTER

From its circumference heavy foliage arched up, a great veined roof, to the apex where light drifted like a thin mist down through the dead saber. Falling lengthways of the grave, one huge limb had lent its decay to the profusion of orchids, white, waxen blooms that loomed in the dusk like ghosts of flowers. Rising out of a green confusion of blossoming creepers, they wreathed the grave of the dead slave girl with magnificence of florage beyond the reach of an emperor; and as, throwing his *zarape* shawl-wise over his head, the Yaqui sank in a huddled heap, the glade might have been some dim chapel, himself a cowled figure of grief at the foot of a queenly sarcophagus.

For he remained stiller than marble while the mist of light faded; did not move when night blotted out its pallor; had not when, hours later, the moon slid down a pale finger through the saber. He took no note of a sudden stir of night life, whisper of leaves, rheumatic complaint of trees, movement of silent creatures in the black darkness outside his blanket; for, under it, great Sonoma deserts blazed like heated brass within the environing purple of mountains. He saw again the blue gulf of the Barranca de Cobre flame into rainbow color at the touch of the morning sun; once more his camp-fire flared among the carven rocks; beyond that a brighter glare, the flames of a hundred villages. Within those sun-bright limits he made again the pilgrimage to the shrine of Bocaina with her who lay beneath. While the barbaric Indian fifes, flat thud of drums, mingled with the thud

THE BREAD FLOATS OUT

of the great church organ, they marched on bleeding knees across the sharp stones of the square, up the steps, the long length of the dim shrine to the feet of the bleeding Christ, the God whom alone they had accepted of the Spaniards. On dusk richly lit by the glare of cooking-fires floated the laughter of young girls grinding corn at the *metates*, wild and sweet as the cooing of pigeons, and he felt again the happy unease of the wooing before the peace of marriage. Through the long night he lived it over and over—the hunting, fighting, loving—always to the same end: the gloom of Hertzer's *galera*.

Its fetor was strong in his nostrils when at dawn he rose and cast away his blanket.

XX

A CHECK, AND—

COMING home late, David rose early Christmas morning—so early, indeed, that he had almost finished writing out a schedule of instructions for Consuela's guidance when dawn transmuted the golden glow of his lamp into a smoky pallor.

"Why not do it here?" Ewing had argued the preceding evening. "Hertzer will never dare to take you out of the midst of his friends and neighbors. Stay all night and make sure of your Christmas." But as his presence was necessary at the inauguration of certain festivities for his people, he had refused—a decision which he had almost regretted stepping outside an hour ago.

A breeze had then moaned out in the jungle, and, viewed in that chill dusk which at once shrouds the death of night and swaddles the birth of day, principles shrink while cold facts enlarge beyond all proportion. Seen through its medium, Consuela and Las Glorias had receded inversely as the gray walls of the San Juan *carcel* drew near, and, stripped of every illusion, integuments of love and friendship, his spirit had shivered in a dank, dark world where strife, struggle, death seemed the only relations. Depressed, he had gone in to his writing, and yet—the question is raised as to the thermal relations of heat and heroism—when he now went out to watch the sunrise, doubt vanished with the mists, his mind turned cheerfully to his plans.

Besides a barbecue and dance, these aimed at full liberty to hunt, fish, or swim for his married colonists; and even the *enganchars* were to be free of camp and river under limited supervision. And the fun began early. Scrape of feet, bits of song, laughter, a hum of cheerful talk drifted into the *jacale* as he sat down to his *tortillas*, bacon, and coffee. When, later, he passed with Magdaleno to and fro among the huts, the brown smiles, glad faces, cheery salutations put him in great heart. In his own person he experienced the sensations of a feudal baron in the midst of a contented peasantry, and found them so pleasant that the morning was well on before he recollected Ewing's last warning.

"At least don't let him catch you napping. Come over for breakfast."

With it came the correlative thought: "If he does find me here I won't see Consuela again." And under its urge he gave Magdaleno last hasty directions while the stable *moso* was bringing out his horse. Mounting, he rode rapidly across the clearing, but paused on its edge to look back—too late, however, to see a horse and rider gallop in among the huts. Warning came with the muffled rhythm of pounding hoofs.

His impulse was to run, but the peat soil had deadened sound; and as he realized that the pursuit was almost upon him, his obstinate dignity asserted itself. He was sitting very straight and stiff when Patricia galloped out from behind a palm thicket.

"Merry Christmas!" she called. "Isn't it a beautiful day?"

After the first relief he did not know whether he would not have preferred it the other way. And if he found grace to answer, she had yet seen his quick glance into the jungle beyond, the relief flash and fade on his face, and she undoubtedly read his mind.

"Señor Carruthers was to have escorted me," she said, hiding a smile as they rode on, "but I waited and waited and waited till I was tired. Then I thought to catch Señor Phelps, but he had gone up by river. 'But if at first you don't succeed, try, try,' and you will get something better," she finished, with a brilliant smile. "How do you like my new saddle and habit? Presents from Santa Claus."

There could be only one opinion. Crusted and worked from horn to bucket-stirrups with silver, the saddle was as fine a piece of leather-work as ever came from the craft of Orizaba; the habit proclaimed an expensive tailor. A rich tan cord, it lay like fur to her figure, raising in David that recurrent impression of a young tigress, sleek, luxurious, sensuous, yet vividly alive.

Without waiting for a reply, she ran on: "The padre got my measure from my dressmaker in Ciudad

Mexico and sent it on to New York. He wouldn't tell what the saddle cost, but I managed a peep at the bills. The two came to almost a thousand dollars. Isn't he good?"

It was a large sum—even in Mexican currency—but David had ceased to wonder at Hertzer. And, after all, this lavish expenditure was strictly in accord with his nature, sprang from the same instinct which causes a Jew pawnbroker to load down his womenkind with ostrich plumes and diamonds.

"He is coming later," she said, after he had expressed himself on their price and beauty. With a sly glance from under drooped lids, she added: "Perhaps you would have preferred his company?"

In view of her malicious teasing of the other day, it was certainly hard to be thus drafted for her service, to ride in her train like a willing captive of her bow and spear. But, turning a good face to necessity, he laughed as he answered: "Well, hardly."

"Consuela, then? Ah, now he is silent! Is it that she is so much more beautiful?"

"She could hardly be that," he truthfully ventured, for a painter would have raptured over the torso's swelling magnificence, sweep of shapely limb, face blooming amid the shadows of a soft sombrero. Excluding expression, which is the odor of beauty, most men would have yielded the palm to her riper charms.

"Another 'hardly'?" she laughed. "How touching is your allegiance! The happy Consuela!" With an affectation of frankness so perfect that he was completely deceived, she added: "But, there! I do not blame you. She is as good as she is lovely."

If it be urged that he ought to have been more suspicious, it should be remembered that he had seen her in all less than a dozen times, always at intervals long enough for him to forget her tricks. Even the innuendo of the other day was merely a matter of suspicion, and its memory was purged by this sudden warmth. He gave her a look of glowing thanks in return for her false coin, and thereafter chatted pleasantly as they rode along; nor suspected her of meditating further breaches of his peace until they emerged on the Las Glorias clearing, and even then he was too occupied with the scene to notice. Always beautiful from any viewpoint, the excitement of anticipation accentuated his appreciation of the warmth and sunlight, peace of Indian summer which brooded over the clean grass-land, timbered ridges, tall palm islands around the house and huts. He was gazing his fill, and trying to make out Consuela's figure in a confusion of people upon the veranda, when Patricia spoke.

"I want to christen my new saddle. I'll race you from here to the house."

The suggestion did not lie with his humor. Obsessed by his passion to lead in all things, Hertzer kept the best horses in the country, and David was not minded to come tagging in at her heels. He had, however, no chance of refusal, for, shooting by to the

lead, she leaned over and cut his mare on the flank.
A nervous, nettlesome beast, which he had bought
from Don Julian along with his cows, she reared,
almost unseating him, then, as she shot out from
strung haunches, he reversed a first impulse and gave
her loose rein.

Before them the path ran in the straight for half a
mile toward the house ere it swung on a wide loop
to the bridge which crossed the *arroyo* in front of the
huts, and, though it was flying beneath him like a
whirling belt, David had time to see and think. As
they drew nearer he could see people running to the
veranda edge, and he set his teeth in vexation. Bad
enough to have fallen into this unwelcome cavalier-
ship, it was worse to have been tricked into a ridiculous race, worst of all to be beaten, as he surely
would; for though the little mare was living up to the
ranchero's selling boast—"You can match her against
the best in Señor Hertzer's stable"—he could not
lessen Patricia's lead by a yard. Vexed, as aforesaid,
to the soul, he swore with a force and fluency that
would have raised the hair of the David of old, and
perhaps it was this easement that cleared his brain
so that it leaped to a sudden chance.

From the bow of the trail a smaller path led on to
a foot-log that spanned the *arroyo* directly in front
of the house. Having crossed it time and again,
David knew that the banks were firm and trodden
clear of brush. About fifteen feet across, a Northern
hunter would have taken it in a canter, but his mare

was untrained. If she failed—or balked? Of the two he prayed for the former, with contingent broken limbs, as he swung her into the path. Only a few yards from the take-off, it whirled over a hog's back, but, though she was going like the wind, he felt only a heave like that of a boat rising over a sea. Followed her quick crouch, then, as though thrown up by powerful springs, she took the *arroyo* in bird-flight, and the next moment he was tugging furiously to prevent her from driving head on to the veranda.

It seemed so probable that the women guests scattered with small screams; but Ewing jumped to help, whispering as he caught the bridle: "Bully for you, Davy! Here she comes! Off with you and help her down!"

Looking backward over her shoulder, Patricia came tearing down the road. She had not seen David turn off, did not recognize his standing horse, nor see him till he stepped out from behind it to her own beast's head. Surprised beyond control, she then sat, eyes burning savagely down upon him from under her frown, till Ewing burst out laughing.

"Got you that time, Patrick!"

Though she joined the ripple of laughter that now travelled along the veranda, her eyes and mouth remained sulky, and as David reached up to lift her down he saw the knuckles gleaming white on the hand that held her quirt; her body, when she yielded it to his hands, felt like a coiled spring, and without even a "Thank you" she passed on and in.

A CHECK, AND—

The leap, brief fight with his mare, Patricia's discomfiture had all crowded into a few seconds, yet through the rush David had caught the anxiety and soft approbation in Consuela's face as she leaned eagerly over the veranda rail. He now saw that she had taken a seat by herself, and, though his heart jumped at the tacit invitation, he could not avail himself of it. Besides bidden guests, a half-dozen bachelors had ridden in from plantations far up and down the river, and what with greetings from old acquaintances, introductions to new, and the anxiety of all to learn the results of his experiments in colonist labor, an hour passed before he worked through to her chair; and even then he had to listen for another half-hour to the stale first impressions of a young American wife who, in the mean time, had seated herself by Consuela. A pretty and pleasant girl, he yet sighed his relief when she went in-doors and he was free to answer the question in the girl's eyes.

"I don't know," he replied, when she spoke of Hertzer. "I left late—late enough for Patricia to catch me. If he had intended—"

"Ah, yes," she interrupted, with a sternness that was belied by the softness of her eyes. "How comes my cavalier to be engaged in another service?"

"Now, now," he pleaded. "She overtook me, and I couldn't be unmannerly."

She surveyed him, head held delicately awry. "But was it necessary to race?" But she nodded as he explained how Patricia had struck his beast.

"Yes, yes, I know; she was bound to make of you a fool again. I cried out when you turned into the foot-path, but if you had not—I would never have spoken to you again. But her father?" Anxiety once more wiped out the flush of feeling, and nodding toward Boulton, a lanky Westerner from down-river below Carruthers: "The señor there saw rurales at La Luna as he came by last night. The señorita? She did not mention—"

"Only that he was coming on here later. I couldn't very well ask her."

She nodded acquiescence. "We were talking about it just before you came. They think you are right, but foolish."

"Funny combination," he laughed.

"And from the feeling they showed," she continued, smiling, "I feel sure they would defend you."

"Wherein they refute themselves. 'One fool makes many,' says the proverb. However, they won't be infected with my follies this time, for, if I'm not mistaken, there he comes now, alone."

As he also spied the distant figure, Boulton, the lanky, cried out, "Here comes Hertzer!" and with the exclamation laughter and chatter ceased, only for a moment. Realizing the constraint of sudden silence, one and all hid apprehension under a fresh irruption of talk. It was, however, forced; grew nervously jerky as Hertzer drew near; could not be hidden from his supernal suspicion by the volley of "Merry Christmases" which met him mounting the steps. Drawing into its characteristic puckers, his big mouth betrayed a half-humorous, half-cynical comprehension of the situation.

Quite at his ease, he gave and returned greetings with equal nonchalance. "Phelps, you devil, why didn't you wait for me? Came by river, eh?... Hello, Boulton, old horse!" To the newly married planter: "Murray, why haven't you been to see me? Your lady? Pleased to meet you, ma'am. Make him bring you over." His friendly smile at Consuela simmered down to a grin at David. "How are you, Mann? Your place looked like a Sunday picnic when I passed." But the observation was not made unpleasantly, and the grin plainly grew out of amused thought. And, as usually happens when a man is master of himself, his unconcern placed him in command of the situation. Five minutes saw him centred in a lively group whose membership counted some who had not hesitated to pronounce him a fit subject for lynching little more than an hour ago.

Despite, however, the fire of chaff, anecdote, repartee, that was going on around him, Hertzer still found time to observe both David and Consuela. Touching her, his gray glance lost its sharp sparkle, his smile, catching her eyes, was almost kindly; and though his expression resolved into amused contempt looking at David, he threw him more than one pleasant observation. "Your rubber looks fine, Mann," he said once. Again: "That's a nice lot of cows you had of Don Julian." And: "You have really done wonders with the place. I shall have to look to my laurels." Indeed, he was at such pains to please that apprehension quickly died; every symptom of strain vanished long before Ewing came out of his bedroom with an armful of towels.

"Who's for a dip before dinner?" he called. "It isn't everywhere that you can bathe in the open on Christmas Day. Come along, you fellows, Boulton, Davy, Phelps—you, too, Hertzer, it will sharpen your appetite for the pudding."

But Hertzer shook his head. "Not for me. To-morrow is my mandador's saint's day, and he's going downriver to-night to celebrate it in San Juan. I just rode over to give you a greeting, and I'm going back as soon as I've had a chat with your wife." And as they trooped down the steps he added: "Adios, and look out for 'gators. A little one, only a baby, opened a four-inch gash on one of my fellows the other day."

Instead of going in, however, he took David's chair. Whether or not she was still sulking over her discomfiture, Patricia had not reappeared, and as the other American women now rose and went in to help Mrs. Ewing—who had not been able to spare more than a nod and word to her guests—he had Consuela all to himself. Courtesy forbade her from following, and a slight embarrassment passed as he began to talk friendly commonplaces.

"How do you like an American Christmas?" Nodding at the palms, timber, sweep of sunlit meadow, he commented on her answer. " 'Tis a little early to ask—anyway, this isn't the real thing. Up North at this very minute sleigh-bells are ringing out on frozen roads while folks make merry in snow-bound houses; and here—look at it, warm and broody as an Italian summer." Offering an old envelope for her inspection, he went on: "Here's something I thought you would like to see."

To her it appeared a crumpled leaf, dry as any other bit of forest mould, but, while she watched, legs, body, and head resolved from its folds—a spring, and it was gone. "A beetle," he explained. "One of the fellows that kick up such a row at night. Would you believe that fearful whistling could be produced by the vibration of that fellow's wings?"

It was difficult of belief, but he had proved it by observation, and as, enlarging upon the subject, he went on to dissect into its component cries the volume of sound then drifting in from the distant jungle, the appeal to her own passion for nature caused her to forget a first vivid repulsion.

"It probably took that bug a million years to breed himself into perfect likeness to the leaves he feeds on," he said, returning from a lengthy digression. "But it isn't so wonderful when you consider how much even a man can change in a single lifetime. Take these university fellows—Phelps, Ewing, Carruthers. The last two were suckled, as you may say, on the Declaration of Independence, but down here they take to slavery as easily as Spaniards. All of them—"

"Except Don David," she put in.

He started at her quickness, but continued, smiling: "Except friend David, they all—"

"*Friend?*" Looking quickly, he caught the sudden resolution flashing out of her bright anger. "Why do you call him '*friend*'—*you* who even now have rurales in your house waiting to arrest him?"

Flushed, tingling with generous feeling, she sustained his stare—even when amusement displaced surprise. "You are mistaken," he slowly answered. "There are no rurales in my house."

It was difficult to challenge such deliberation, but she did. "Señor, they were seen—last night."

"You said 'now.'"

"Then they are at Verda—waiting for him?"

Again he shook his head, still smiling in secret amusement.

Not to be put off, she began: "Do you mean to say—"

"They went back to San Juan this morning."

This was still more difficult of comprehension; and while she sat looking at him, thoroughly mystified, an alloy of calculation interjected itself into his smile. Behind it his keen wits were working. "It isn't a case of intention," he interrupted, as she began to speak. Then, with a swift glance that belied his apparent frankness, he added: "You see, my Yaqui came back this morning."

"*Came back!—this morning!* But David set him free—gave him money with instructions to—" She caught herself in time to save the *ranchero* from betrayal.

"Yes, I know; he left the money with Magdaleno. Of course, I need not have told you this. It would have been quite easy to swear that I caught him in the jungle."

Whatever his motive—whether the Indian's sacrifice had really touched him in his own reckless bravery, or he was merely glad to have escaped the odium of David's imprisonment—his frankness served him equally well, for in her glowing surprise she failed to notice its calculation.

"I am so glad!" she burst out. After a diffident pause, she added: "We were all afraid—would you mind if I told? It would make such a happier Christmas."

"Of course not. Go right ahead."

Real or assumed, his heartiness gave him a second lift in her estimation, emboldened her to ask: "And the Yaqui? Now you won't—"

"Flog him?" He relieved her of the remainder, and, replying, his face lit with a gleam of genuine feeling. "No, it would be useless. 'Not till I can take my people,' he answered, when I asked him if he would run away again—and he meant it. So, being a bit puzzled as to what else to do with him, I've made him a cabo."

"A cabo?" she echoed.

"Yes; put him in charge of ten men. When I came out he was perched on a stump, large as life, overlooking his gang. Of course it is a bit of a risk, but I save the hire of a Zacateco, and they will do more work for him. But now I must go in and say good-bye to Mrs. Ewing."

Now, if character came only in those assorted shades of black and white which romanticist writers sell by the bolt, the generations would promptly knock their bad men on the head and life resolve into the simplest of equations. But when—not to mention the varying blues, grays, reds of moods and passions which occur in the most respectable of human formulas—your villain suddenly develops white streaks, it plays the dickens with the problem by the introduction of unsuspected sympathies. Had Hertzer, for instance, continued to pursue his ruthless course *à la* traditional bad man, Consuela would never have overcome that first feeling of repulsion. As it was, the touch of chivalry evidenced in his treatment of the runaway strengthened the good impression made by his frank avowal of defeat. She not only went in with him, but came out and stood looking curiously after as he rode away—attentions she would have altogether omitted could she have guessed one tithe of his reflections, either then or at any time during the past week, for she had been more or less in his thought ever since he had seen her on the day of her return in David's *jacale*.

Not that his thoughts were offensive. Though twenty years past the age when love's iridescence contains no red of passion, her delicate bloom had made its first appeal to the strain of æstheticism in his queer nature, the strain that, in fuller measure, gave old Israel its singing prophets, poet kings. He had set her apart from the voluptuous Tehuanas who had hitherto filled his life. But this granted—that she blossomed in his fancy like some rare dark flower— the fact of her womanhood was bound to bring her within the scope of passions that had never diminished under the check of restraint. Without these his intense selfishness, natural acquisitiveness, would have been sufficient to urge him to transplant her for his private enjoyment as he did the jungle orchids. In addition, David's rivalry fused all into a furious obsession.

Informed by Patricia of the scene at Ewing's table, he gave his own interpretation of Consuela's answer, "Not yet," as he rode around the Verda clearing. "Not yet!" he girned through set teeth. "Not yet!" frowning at the distant buildings. "Not yet!" as he plunged into the jungle on the other side. And as he rode slowly on every power of his cunning mind was bent toward its translation into "Never."

Coming out on Phelps's clearing, he was, indeed, so lost in thought that he neither saw the Englishman's children scuttle out of his path nor heard the greeting the graceful mother called after him from the door. Eyes fixed on his saddle-horn, he rode on. With their old sparkle hidden, his face was heavily Slavonic, coldly brutal. None could have dreamed of the thought burning behind its harsh mask, and he gave no sign until, at sunset, he emerged on his own clearing.

Then he broke out in a sudden laugh. "Why didn't I think of that before? Old Slim-Fingers, to be sure! He wouldn't listen to me when he was down here. Reckoned he'd make it on straight rubber, but he's had time to learn by now. I'll write him to-night."

Five minutes more riding brought him upon his men. Their line ran at right angles across his path, but, shining into his eyes from a low horizon, the setting sun allowed him to see only one figure—that of the Yaqui. Standing upon a stump in direct line with the sun, blackly silhouetted against the great red disk, he appeared to be lifted above the shadowy earth—loomed a figure mysterious, sombre, portentous as that of the last man overlooking the red doom of a world. And some ray of awe must have pierced down through Hertzer's gross materiality, for, reining in, he watched till the orb smouldered out, till quick dusk transmuted the lonely figure into a statue, gray as grief, looking down on the dim shapes of a fallen people. Perhaps he felt something of this also. Riding forward, his order to Tomas was given very quietly.

XXI

—HERTZER TRIES FOR "MATE"

FROM Hertzer, writing steadily in his *jacale* that evening, it is a far cry to the office of Osgood & Short in Northfield, Maine. It requires three days for even the blizzard to sweep down the Atlantic coast before, stripped of its snows, it hurls across the Gulf of Mexico upon Tehuantepec and Yucatan as a blustrous "norther." Ten days of slower travel would see the delivery of Hertzer's letter, but, swifter than the subtle wireless, the story flies forward to the morning of its receipt in the temple of high finance.

A glance around the office reveals the fact that its furnishings faithfully reflect the increased importance of the firm. Replacing gimcrack veneers of ash or elm, a mission table and chairs of solid oak lend their solidity to its reputation, for suggestions of fraud, bankruptcy, and other financial horrors are impossible in presence of their massive front. The walls have also been done over in tasteful burlap and carry a few good pictures. Axminster and Persian rugs add a costly tone and assist a grate fire to mitigate the chills of a polished floor. Only the partners

355

—who are warming themselves before it—remain unchanged, for these accessories of cheer and taste have not modified the frosty manner of one or the hopeless vulgarity of the other. If anything, Mr. Osgood's fires of hair and face are more at variance with his mien; Short's grossness was never more pronounced than when he now flings David's last monthly report upon the glowing coals.

"The pup!" he snarled. "I'd break his back if I had him here! Calls us everything but scoundrelly liars, and hints at that. You'll have to write it all over again. Why don't we fire him? There's nothing more to be got out of the old woman."

According to his custom at unnecessary mention of the unmentionable, Mr. Osgood raised surprised brows as he handed over a second letter without comment. "Read this. Rather a coincidence that they should arrive together, don't you think?"

"Who is this man?" After five minutes of steady reading Short looked up at his partner, who sat, lips drawn tightly, fingers weaving in the old uncanny manner, a financial shroud for some one.

"Manager of La Luna, and no man's fool. I met him when I went down to buy the plantation."

"Fool?" Short vented a savage laugh. "I guess not. What a scheme! Let me look over it again and make sure of the detail. . . . Hum! . . . The three of us are to organize the Amarilla Labor and Improvement Company for the purpose of working La Luna, Verda, and as many other plantations as can be induced to abandon their present ineffectual methods. In return for one-third stock, he puts in eighty Yaqui slaves, while we furnish capital to buy more and keep the thing going till returns come in. Sounds pretty good; but let's see." With a grin he went on: "As the executive officers of Verda rubber, Osgood & Short would naturally have the letting of contracts to Osgood & Short, the labor contractors, and could so be depended upon not to screw the price too tight. And as the cost of producing rubber exceeds our first estimates by about—"

"Five hundred per cent."

"And will eventually bankrupt the plantation company, Osgood & Short, the planters, will merely have to make an assignment in favor of Osgood & Short, the contractors, who will thereby acquire the whole works. Do I grasp the idea?"

"In all but one thing." While his thin fingers knit still more rapidly upon the shroud of Verda rubber, Mr. Osgood went on: "Osgood & Short will not actually appear as interested in either company. In the Amarilla we shall be silent partners. As regards Verda—to tell you the truth, J., I no longer own a single share. Now, all that remains is to dispose of yours—a little at a time, as the agents bring in new buyers, so as not to arouse suspicion. Three months will do it, and—"

He stopped, frowning, as Short burst into a howl of laughter. "That's the best ever!" he roared, holding his gross sides. "Oh, my golly! There's sure a pair of us, Osgood! I haven't owned a share this five months." Sobering presently, he sat up wiping his eyes. "But look a-here! I was depending on you to hold control, like you were on me, and this other thing's no good if we lose the executive power."

Mr. Osgood, however, waived the objection. "We sha'n't. You see, it was never necessary to vote our stock at board elections. The next one comes in two weeks, and all we have to do is to stand pat and let them elect us as heretofore."

"My Lordy!" Short broke a silence during which he had regarded his partner with unfeigned admiration. "You surely beat the devil, Osgood. Why didn't we think of this before?"

Shuffling a little under the compliment, Mr. Osgood answered: "I did. Hertzer mentioned the plan when I was down there. But I hadn't got to the inside of rubber then."

Short broke a second considering silence. "And friend Mann? This lets him out, of course. But won't he try to queer us?"

"Might — if he were here. But you read what Hertzer says about his being in love with some Mexican girl, and if I know anything of the young man, he'll stay down there—probably try for employment on some other plantation. Anyway, we'll have the thing organized and the contracts let to ourselves before we fire him."

"But what about mamma? You know she owns almost a third of the stock?"

"A full third, if not a little more." A ghost of a smile writhed Mr. Osgood's tight lips. "And all the better for us. There's the yellow-fever! Lucky that Hertzer mentioned it. If any opposition should turn up we'll tell her, and she'll be so crazy to get him home that she'll vote her stock according to orders. It's a cinch, J."

"A lead-pipe cinch!" Mr. Short reinforced the financier's unusual use of slang. Then, leaning back in his chair, he shook again with coarse mirth. "And —oh, my golly, fancy using his own stock, as you may say, to vote him out of his job! And a girl to keep him down there! Oh, my golly! Get busy, Osgood, and write Hertzer to get out the articles and send them up at once."

XXII

A MOVE IN ANOTHER GAME

THROUGH a chink in the back of his *jacale*, David peeped at teacher and pupils assembled in school. In this, the fourth week of its dedication to educational uses, the cabin looked quite the academy. Out of the platform which had served for the Christmas *baile*, Magdaleno had knocked up benches and tables of a size suitable for short, plump legs and tubby bodies. A broad plank, smooth-planed and painted, formed the black-board that bore a chalked line in English and Spanish — "A bad boy — a good girl," which unfair classification of the sexes was being assiduously copied by a dozen bronze midgets.

David almost laughed as he noticed that protrusion of small red tongue which has been found such an invaluable aid in writing by scholars the world over. Also the sidelong glances at Consuela—who moved among them, helping here, correcting there, with dignity quite matronly — were quite familiar. But these universalities having been granted, it must be admitted that the divergences from the civilized model were wider than the likenesses. Though the sartorial resources of four families had been strained to supply the respectable average of a garment apiece during the first week, usage had brought slacker practice. Deference once paid to the educational proprieties, clothing had decreased day by day till it reached the normal of three chemisettes worn by the elder girls. The remainder wrought in the comfortable nudity which, after all, was much more appropriate in view of the increasing heat.

"A bad-da boy-ee! A good-da ga-al!"

When, presently, they began to translate in singsong chorus, David had to turn away and gag himself with his handkerchief. It was not the childish treble or soft accentuation of the harsh English words, but the fact that in these days the assertion of vice and virtue in the aforesaid boy and girl was meeting him at every turn. Proud mothers told one another about it from the doorways of their respective *jacales*. In the cook-house it went as a kind of chant, timing the motion of vigorous elbows. He once overheard Maria and Seraphine drawing the shameful comparison out in the jungle; even Magdaleno's grizzled mustachios had been seen vibrating above the muttered phrase. In truth, the whole plantation seemed to be in the race for linguistic honors, and whatever his doubts as to the lengths the enthusiasm would carry, David could not but look forward to the time when an enlargement of the vocabulary would lend variety to the general performance.

Peeping again, he saw that one small girl had begun to nod to the sleepy cadence. Nod—nod—nod—with little forward plunges. But just when it seemed that she must fall, Consuela—who had been out of his line of vision—came in with a quick flutter of skirts and carried her off to her own chair. Sitting there she gathered the plump, wee body closer in to her bosom, then—and David thrilled—she lifted the child's hand and pressed it against her own neck. Time and again had he seen mothers do that, and, blushing furiously for his spying upon the unconscious revelation, he walked away pursued by a vision of a clear-cut face with yearning eyes above a small, dark head. And he moved none too soon, for he had barely achieved a respectable distance before a cessation of the drone and sudden irruption of speech announced the letting out of school.

A wistful tenderness still lingered in the droop of the red mouth when she joined him at the stables. But it vanished as he inquired how education had gone that day while lifting her up to her saddle. "Finely, señor," she answered, brightly. "Anita can say her English alphabet."

"Ah, my future book-keeper!" he laughed, as they rode away. "When will she be ready to begin? Next week?"

"Next week!" she exclaimed, with surprise that was belied by the merriment in her eyes, for she knew at what he was aiming. "Next week? Ten years, at least."

"*Ten years!*" Then, with business-like conviction, "I shall have to hire a stranger in the mean time."

If she chose to walk through the door he thus opened, be sure that it was in full confidence of her ability to slip out before he could close it. "Hire a *stranger*, señor? Then it is that you are dissatisfied with me? You intend to—"

"Fire you—yes." Nodding firmly, he went on to enlighten the puzzle in her arched brows. "Discharge you, you know—right away, too."

"Oh, the discharge; I see." Observing him with tentative demureness, "But—why?"

"I expect to be married next month."

"But, señor, you would not wish your wife to keep the books? You will still need me—"

"Yes, I'll need you, all right — but not to keep books."

"And the lady?" she went on, ignoring the last remark. "It is Patricia—or the pretty sister who is come down to keep the Señor Boulton's house? No? Will you not see that I am dying of curiosity to know her name?"

"Consuela."

"The same as mine! Tell me—is she beautiful—and nice?"

"Both," he strongly affirmed. Then being invited to describe her, he did it with such strong and tender feeling that her merriment gradually died. If he had snapped the door shut just then? But sweeping down to the red dusk of her cheek, the long lashes safeguarded her tremulous happiness, and he was gazing straight ahead as though he saw the beautiful ideal of his description flitting down the shadowy jungle vistas. When, finally, he looked again her way, mischief had repossessed her.

"And what, señor, might be this paragon's other name?"

"Morales—Consuela Morales."

Very alertly she made her retreat. "Ah, then you have made a mistake. You remember—she was to be your book-keeper until she grew so old and ugly that your customers were frightened away. From what you have just told me, she ought to wear another year. And I am sure that she could never be persuaded to leave her school."

"Couldn't you do that if we were married?"

"I?" She looked up with pretended surprise. "We were talking of your future wife."

The last month had seen a good deal of this innocent fooling. For reasons of her own — which will presently appear—she seemed to delight in drawing him on to hold him off. But whereas he usually allowed her to turn his love-making into laughter without protest, he now spoke with seriousness so intense that it simulated anger. "Stop joking, dear. I began it, I know, and it was wrong to approach you in a flippant spirit. But see, dear—I love you—will you be my wife?"

So it was out at last, in all seriousness, given with a gravity that precluded further trifling. Broadening as it crossed a dry marsh, the path here permitted them to ride abreast, and he had pressed in—so closely that he heard her small sigh, could see down through her eyes, those clear brown windows, the irresolution that issued from the conflict between inclination and some obscure contrariness. As a man stares into the quivering amber of a sunlit pool, he glimpsed her sudden impulse, thrust of feeling toward him. Then, just as a ruffle of wind leaves only a broken reflection, it was gone; he saw only her face framed in twinkling lights. But the glimpse was enough to raise up passion in aid of love, banish his timidity. A sudden bend gave him her lips, the moist red lips that made no attempt at avoidance. But as his arms went about the relaxed figure, she suddenly straightened and drew away as a shout rose behind them.

"Hello, you folks! They told me at the finca that you had just gone, and I've been riding hard to catch up."

Of all places in the world, the heart of a tropical forest might surely be considered the very safest for love-making; but it was just David's luck, and he cursed it beneath his breath, looking back at Phelps. As, reining in, they waited, Consuela's eyes telegraphed, "Do you think he saw?" But the confusion attendant on the doubt was not sufficient to prevent her from whispering: "It will be best for you to go back. He will see me home." And, answering his pleading look, "Mañana, I shall surely come."

While his coarser masculine fibre prevented David

from realizing her motive, the embarrassment natural in the presence of a lover only half-declared, the soft look which accompanied the promise almost reconciled him to the dismissal; he yielded to her wish with grace that brought its reward. For as, after a few minutes' talk, they rode on, Phelps in the lead, she turned, threw him a kiss from delicate finger-tips, and so left him to ride slowly home through an enchanted jungle, a country transmuted into fairy-land by the seeing eyes of love.

Meanwhile she was journeying through the light and color of the same magical country, though in the opposite direction. If Phelps had not seen the kiss, he might almost have divined it from her quiet brooding, soft silence that might have been less pronounced if she had liked him more. Academic to the bottom of his small, dry soul in all things outside the scope of his passions, his manner with her had always been tinged with that lofty patronage which Englishmen display to the alien, the consciousness of superiority which, based on the dead past, is left undiminished by the miserable accomplishment of the living present. It showed in his indulgent listening whenever she spoke, as much as in his laughter at the least of the flashes of wit, naïve humor that enlivened her conversation—the uproarious laughter one accords to the accidental cleverness of a child— was most offensive in his evident admiration, whose expression always ran, "You are very pretty—for a little savage." In view of all which, it is small wonder

366

that she now returned only monosyllables to his remarks, or looked up with quick offence when he began to speak in his patronizing way of her school.

"By-the-way," he said, concluding what was intended for a eulogy, "you have gained a convert. Hertzer was telling me yesterday that he would open a school at La Luna—if he could hire as pretty a teacher."

"Yes?" she asked, without a smile; and having thus killed his bald compliment, she added: "Then it is for you to apply? I am told that you taught in England?"

Now, between the graduate master of a great English boarding-school, say Harrow or Rugby, and the common or garden variety of board-school teacher, exists a gulf wide as that said to have been fixed between Dives and Lazarus—at least in the opinion of the master. Reddening, Phelps glanced quickly to see if the thrust were intentional, but, deceived by her calm innocence, he was going on to explain the existence and extent of the said gulf, when she touched him again in his weak pride.

"I should think it would pay better than rubber-planting."

Again he looked quickly, for the notorious poverty of his company was as a thorn in the side of his self-importance. But her inscrutable innocence preserved the secrets of bedroom gossip. Suspicious, however, as well as nettled, he withdrew to safer ground, venturing only commonplaces during the half-hour required to carry them into Las Glorias. But, if more careful, his temper did not improve under restraint. If more of respect there was less liking in the glances that travelled her way—then, at dinner, and when, thereafter, they carried their coffee out to the veranda. And after she and Mrs. Ewing went in-doors at dark, spite had about an equal share with his dominant egotism in shaping his talk with Ewing.

It is trite to exclaim at the triviality of causes which have sometimes brought about grave results. A hundred instances, light as the cackle of the goose that saved Rome, bring weariness to the mind, but the fact remains — if, out of the consideration so natural to her, Mrs. Ewing had not compelled Consuela to occupy the bedroom which had previously been her own, the girl would not have overheard the aforesaid conversation. Tired from teaching and the long ride, she retired early, leaving Mrs. Ewing to write home letters; and as her room possessed the only inside entrance and modesty constrained her from lighting her lamp, there was no warning for the men. Usually the dry rattle of palms would have been sufficient to drown their voices, and in no case would Ewing have imagined they could be heard the length of the veranda; but, aiding the conspiracy of small causes, a soundless night converted it into a whispering gallery with her window for its focus.

Had she even gone at once to the sleep her weariness had earned, the event would have addled in the egg, for time passed before the talk narrowed from plan-

tation affairs down to personal gossip. But what girl
ever went from a proposal straight to her sleep? In
this, the first moment of quiet, she sat on the edge of
her bed, dreaming soft dreams till Phelps's dry tones
pierced her reverie.

"Davy seems to be heavily smitten with your little
Mexican."

"You mean Miss Morales?"

If Phelps noticed the emphasis, it merely irritated
his self-importance, urged him to fresh offensiveness,
for he went on: "I thought it was all on his side when
I saw them Christmas Day, but this afternoon I caught
them kissing. Wouldn't it be a howling josh if he
married her?"

Following his thin chuckle, Ewing's cold answer
came out of the gloom. "No doubt I'm a little dense
to-night, but I fail to see it."

Through his colossal egotism Phelps felt the check.
"Oh, of course, she's all right," he said, hastily. Then
he continued with that apologetic warmth which re-
asserts the thing it verbally denies: "She's a nice girl,
mighty pretty and all that sort of thing, you know.
But, after all, old man"—here he became wisely paternal—"she is Mex, and it would never do. What
would his people say?"

"Hum! I thought that by precept and example
you taught the philosophy of mixed races?"

"Only socially." Phelps passed, if he felt, the sarcasm. "What is good for the race is sometimes hell
for the individual. As for my example—I'm not mar-

ried. But you don't mean to say, old man"—he dropped again into the wisely paternal—"that you are in favor of such a mésalliance?"

"Since you put it that way—I am." With explosive force he added, "What's more, I think he'll be damned lucky to get her."

"Then that ends the argument." Darkness covered Phelps's shrug, and only the quickened glow of his cigar betrayed his nervous irritation. When the uneasy gleam had become more regular he asked, "And what about Hertzer?"

"What's he got to do with it?"

"Only that he is in love with her, too. And if you know—"

"You, also?" Ewing interrupted. "Nell said the same yesterday, and I laughed at her."

"Laugh all you want, but it is so. I was joshing him a bit yesterday and he fired up like a boy in his calf-love. Seems to me that every one is going crazy —or I am."

"Now I begin to see," Ewing said, musingly. "So that is why he took the Yaqui's return so pleasantly. The old fox! Of course, it is perfectly absurd. Not to mention his age—forty-five, isn't he?—there's his record. Rosa is the last of twenty—"

"And that is the funniest ever!" Phelps chuckled. "He has sent her away."

"What!"

"He has. Set her up with a house and a sewing-machine in San Juan along with his other mistresses.

A MOVE IN ANOTHER GAME

There's quite a colony of them there. Indeed, when Carrie was down the other day, the old Jefe was asking about Hertzer's new girl, and he threw up his hands in horror at the idea of the damage his marriage would do to the census."

"Well, he needn't be afraid," Ewing commented, grimly. "Hertzer has carried things with a high hand, but, if I know anything, his face is now set toward his Waterloo."

Consuela did not hear that, or any of the references to Hertzer—better if she had; the knowledge would have served her well in the near future. Face buried in her pillow, she lay mute as a stricken deer while love and pride fought over the phrases that rang in her ears. "After all, she is Mex. . . . What would his people say? . . . You don't mean to say that you are in favor of such a mésalliance?" The distressful iteration prevented her from taking cognizance of other sounds. She heard neither the scrape of chairs, tramp of departing feet, nor the cuckoo-clock that cried off the miserable hours in the dining-room outside her door. Her reflections — will keep till she tells them herself. It is enough to know that certain intuitions had sprung from subconsciousness into the state of living facts; that she rose at daybreak, heavy-eyed from staring them in the face.

Five miles away as the crow flies, seven by the jungle path, David was also rising after a wakeful night. Heavy eyes, however, cannot be an invari-

able product of sleeplessness, for daylight showed a
fine sparkle in his. Perhaps he had never looked,
certainly had never felt better than he did when,
after breakfast, he rode out like a knight of old to
meet his lady in the forest. Indeed, his radiance
betrayed him to Phelps, who met him half-way between the plantations.

"Sorry it's me, old man," he grinned. "But just
keep right on and you'll meet her."

Though aching to punch his head, David nevertheless obeyed, putting his horse at a gallop the moment
he was out of hearing, and so in half an hour burst
into a sunlit glade along which she was riding slowly.
All night he had thought and dreamed, wreathing their
meeting with many a loveliness, delicate fancy, and
now his hands shot out—to drop again as he noticed
the sad eyes in their setting of purple.

"Why—Consuela!" he cried out, sharply. "What
is it?"

She also had done a little rehearsing—as is the fashion with maids who have made up their minds that
duty requires a "nay"—but the apprehension, anticipation of pain in his face, banished the kindly
preparation. "Oh, why did he overtake us yesterday?" she burst out against fate. "Then I should
have said 'yes,' nor ever have heard their talk. But
there! It is that I am wicked again, for just now it
was that I told myself: 'I am glad that he is saved
from the misery.' Yes, I am glad—for you."

In proof of her extreme gladness she tried to smile,

but her quivering lips refused the traitorous office, dropped instead into soft woe. "The Señor Phelps," she replied to his anxious demand. "He and Señor Ewing talked last night outside my window," she added, and so went on to describe the conversation. Finishing, she trembled so violently—this maid who, under the sting of injured pride, had promised herself to inform him haughtily that she could never marry an alien—that, fearing she would fall, he leaped down and lifted her from the saddle. Greater shame for that stern maid! She did not try to cast off the arms that remained about her.

"Nonsense!" he snorted, a little reassured by her complaisance. "Who cares for the opinion of that stiff-backed Englishman? Why didn't I know this before I met him!" He shook a valiant fist. "Well, I'll see him again—"

"No, no!" She pulled his arm down. "He must never know that I heard."

"As for my people," he went on, "I have only my mother, and she will love you."

"Your mother?" Shaking her head, she said, with simple wisdom: "If it were your father—he might. But your mother? A woman? Never! She would hate me for spoiling your life. And see, David"—he thrilled at his name—"this is not the first time. You remember Patricia—"

"The little cat!" he hotly interrupted.

"Yet she took her contempt out of the mouths of the Americanos who come to La Luna. And I have heard of the pride of your nation. No, David, it cannot be."

Her delivery of the ultimatum was almost up to the stern standards of the maid of the trail, but she weakened at his sorrowful answer. "Then you don't love me, Consuela."

"I do! Oh, I do! Not at first, perhaps, though I always liked you. It came so gradually—first liking, then respect for your strength and goodness, and I did not realize, fully, until last night I felt your love slipping away. Then I knew — that it was not coquetry that made me hold you off, but the desire to hear you tell it again, again, and again, the love of which a woman can never hear enough. It was instinct, the instinct which bids one make the most of the sweet time that comes but once in life. And now it is ended."

"No, just begun." He drew her closer. "Only just begun, dear."

"But—"

"If you love me, that's all there's to it," he said, logically, if with slang, and he cut off a second "but" in the most effectual of ways.

And for a while she submitted — lay in his arms, the mischievous beauty who had come between him and so much of his sleep, lay relaxed, almost swooning, while he took a sweet revenge for her small coquetries — lay till the resentful girl of the trail again awoke and covered her lips with her hand. In default of the lips, he kept on kissing the hand even while it gently forced his head away.

"There," she said, unlocking his fingers one at a time from her waist. "I let you—once"—the count was generous, a hundred being closer the mark—"because you are never to do it again. . . . *Never*," she repeated, as he tried to dodge the hand; then, as he succeeded, "Señor!" with such piercing sweetness that he drew back abashed—for a moment, only a moment, for the next he seized and lifted her, almost with violence, into her saddle.

"What are you going to do?" she asked, half afraid of the straight-browed, hard-lipped, iron-jawed man who had ousted the diffident youth from her courtship.

"Take you over to my place, put you into a canoe, and run you down-river to the priest in San Juan. You'll be a married woman this time to-morrow."

He meant it, and she knew that he meant it; yet from some obscure corner of her nature the moiety derived from some far cave girl asserted its approval of his masterly wooing. A gleam of admiration lightened the fear in her eyes, played there until the fear gave place to wistful amusement.

"He would never marry us without my consent."

He had not got so far as that, but if it brought consternation into his thought, he held sternly on without looking back.

"And from San Juan one may easily take passage back to Ciudad Mexico."

When, now, he did look back, the desperation in his glance caused her to relent. "If you do not make it too hard for me, there is still a duty for me here." With the slightest touch of the old mischief, she added, "But perhaps you would rather I went—"

"Back to that store? No, no! There, I'll behave —till you alter your foolish little mind." He added the saving clause.

"Very well, señor—"

"David," he corrected, unwilling to lose any ground.

"Señor David—"

"David!"

"David—let go my bridle-rein."

He had an idea that she intended to bolt, but the suspicion died when she rode quietly forward, and as, presently, she began to talk of her school, his plans— which she well knew stood next to herself in his heart —and very much to his own surprise he soon found that he was talking back quite freely. Awakening to the fact, he attempted a relapse to the status of the heart-broken lover. But the mood did not last. However unwilling to yield a jot of his unhappiness, he was too honest for such self-deception. He was soon talking again; had almost arrived at the normal when he left her to call in school, even laughed at her mischievous remark:

"So you will not need to hire a book-keeper, after all."

"Quien sabe?" he questioned, riding away.

That morning, moreover, it fell luckily that he had

A MOVE IN ANOTHER GAME

to allot gardens and measure off task-work, for the three families, Tadeo's relatives, arrived from Ciudad Mexico the preceding day; and engrossed in the work, he successfully tided over a second relapse and met her quite cheerfully coming out of school. Riding back through the jungle, optimism made further gains as he contrasted his present status with that of yesterday. At least she had confessed her love, besides —he thrilled at the thought—paying its sweet toll in kisses. As for marrying—time would bring that. And just before he turned back—she would only allow him to go half-way—he beguiled her into a cunning trap.

"And you won't marry me?" he asked, saying good-bye.

"No—David."

"But you won't marry any one else?"

She returned a still more vigorous "No."

"Neither will I," he affirmed, stoutly, if incorrectly. "Now, look here: if you won't marry any one but me, and I won't marry any one but you, we are engaged, aren't we?"

She did not attempt to refute this negative logic; and if silence gives consent, as said, then was he justified in reading her smile as assent. In any case it lit his homeward path, transmuting the jungle into the fairy-land of yesterday.

"Marry me? Yes, miss"—he concluded a pleasant reverie as he emerged on the Verda clearing—"if I have to bring mother down to make you."

THE PLANTER

A low afternoon sun was flooding the clearing with fluid gold that flowed in quivering waves over the small palm city, dark environing rubber, and through its warmth floated a busy hum, snatches of talk, shrill treble of children, laughter of women preparing the evening meal for the men who sang as they came in by twos and threes from the field. As, reining in, David drank it all in, there flashed up in his mind the reverse of the picture, the line of wretched workers that used to dribble at sundown over the hot face of the land in sullen silence. Out of that dark travail he had brought this sunny content. The thought was sweet in his mouth. The joy of accomplishment still shone on his face, when, riding up to the stable, he found Hertzer sitting on a box beside the door.

A certain lowering curiosity with which Hertzer had watched him approach gave place to his usual cold imperturbability as he uttered a casual greeting. "Pretty warm to-day? The heat is right on us again. I noticed coming out that my new clearing is almost dry enough to burn. I've been here nearly an hour," he went on, answering David's question. "But the time wasn't wasted. I was walking around looking at things. The Zacatecos did a good job on those new jacales. Here's a letter for you that came under cover to me."

Under his nonchalance, however, strong feeling made itself felt, a suggestion of the suppressed triumph that forced expression in a cold grin as David began to read.

A MOVE IN ANOTHER GAME

The grin vanished as David looked suddenly up. "I think you have made a mistake."

"Let me see. That's so. I gave you my letter. Here's yours." Though he spoke carelessly enough he could not altogether hide a feeling of discomfiture, and while David opened and read his own letter, Hertzer studied him with harsh suspicion.

The letter was not very long. Stripped of hypocritical expressions of esteem, its contents could have been squeezed into a couple of sentences. Owing to the dissatisfaction in his, Mr. David's, reports concerning labor and other problems involved in the cultivation of rubber, the company had decided to sublet its work and management to the Amarilla Labor and Improvement Company, of which Mr. Ludwig Hertzer was active manager. "On receipt of this," Mr. Osgood closed, "you will please hand over everything to him, taking a month's salary, with our compliments, in lieu of the usual notice."

Discharged!

Aware of the sunset's deeper gold, the bustle of life around him, David stood staring down at the letter, thought suspended, smothered beneath a sense of ruin utter and complete.

XXIII

THE MOVE

"AND how likest thou the service?"

Casamira, the wife of Seraphine, gave greeting to Tadeo's kinsman as she passed on her way to the river. In common with the other volunteer women, she had moulted the sad blacks of the plateau in favor of the gorgeous Tehuana reds, and as she tripped by, a flutter of crimson, water *olla* poised gracefully on her head, one would never have recognized the thin slave whom David once saved from Rafaela's stick. Her coquettish smile at the man also promised a new order of trouble in the Verda cosmos when a little more ease and good feeding should have restored the dominance of her flesh.

Breaking in on David's red confusion, her remark brought pause to his consternation. "This is rather sudden," he said, looking up. "And unnecessary— from my point of view. If they had exercised a little patience, I would have made the plantation self-supporting in a very few years. However, there's no use talking. I only want to ask one question. What will you do with the labor already on the place?"

THE MOVE

Hertzer's harsh brows lifted again while undoubted relief dictated his ready answer: "Take over your enganchars and credit their unexpired time to the Verda company upon our books. After they leave we shall use only Yaqui labor."

"And my volunteers?"

"They can take their choice — enganchar with us or leave. We can't bother with independent labor."

Again the sense of ruin rolled over David. Travelling helplessly around the camp, his glance took in the children at play in the compound, the men who ate supper out in the cool, the wives sitting to gossip in their doorways, the rumble of pleasant talk from the big *galera*. It was all to be destroyed, this content of his creation, and he was powerless to save it! The thought brought agony vivid as physical pain; sweat started from every pore; and in that moment he realized not only that his plans for his people had been born out of himself with travail real as the birth-labor of women, but also how, in a larger sense, he was meshed in the golden net of the tropics. Splendor of suns moving to crimson consummations over singing jungles, magnificence of teeming life, blaze of white stars in languorous skies, splash of great rains and silence of brazen heat, roar of the "norther," scented kiss of the night wind, these had passed like an insidious poison into his blood, gripped hold of his very being.

How much they had taught him, the tropics, of

his other unsuspected self? But his development in sense and reason had shown nothing so startling as the sudden lust to kill which now obsessed him, the intense desire to quench the sparkle, cold as the effervescence of soda, in the eyes of this man who was about to wreak irreparable damage upon his helpless people. All that he himself had seen, every act of his hard record, seemed concentrated in that moment, and David's fingers itched for the bull throat, itched to squeeze, sink in, till life and supernal wickedness oozed out together. Ay, he could have killed — easily, for them! But the desire passed with a sense of its own futility. With some dim idea of not provoking the power to break and scatter, he constrained himself to quiet speech.

"You wish to take charge now?" When Hertzer nodded he said, "The books are at Las Glorias. I am going there now, however, and I will bring them back to-morrow."

"Or we can go over them there," Hertzer answered. "I want to see Ewing to-morrow."

"Very well. You don't mind if I leave my things here for a few days?"

"As long as you choose."

He had spoken absently, under quiet strain, and as, mounting again, he rode slowly away, speculative curiosity returned to Hertzer's eyes. "So badly rattled he doesn't know what he's doing. Went off without a word to his mandador, which is just as well. . . . Better leave things as they are till I've had a talk with

the girl. . . . Wonder how much he read of my letter?
. . . Hello, he's woke up at last!"

From a slow walk David had spurred his beast to a
gallop, and, if Hertzer had only known it, the thought
behind the impulse was identical with that in his own
mind. For, groping through his stupor of misery for
çauses behind it all, he remembered, first, that Hertzer's letter was in Mr. Osgood's writing; then a sentence blazed out in sudden significance:

"Better keep our partnership quiet for a while."

"My God!" he cried aloud, as the concatenation of
lying pamphlets, doctored reports, and other small
rascalities flashed up to fuse in one idea. "It's a
conspiracy! They've gone in together to wreck the
company!" And, laying on both quirt and spurs, he
tore across dry morasses, took the *arroyos* in long
heaves, swept with swish and crackle of broken
branches through overgrowths, careless of thorns—
put the little mare at speed that brought him into
Las Glorias within the hour.

"What *is* the matter?" Ewing jumped up as he
burst in upon them at dinner.

"And your face!" his wife cried. "It is running
blood."

Touching it, he looked his surprise, for he had not
felt the thorns which had criss - crossed it into the
semblance of a creased flank steak. After one glance
Consuela ran into her bedroom, to emerge as quickly with a towel and bottle. "It is nothing—"
he began. But, exercising a pretty authority, she

383

made him sit down, wiped away the blood, then while he talked she bathed the cuts with witch-hazel. And while the small, wet hand moved softly over his face he would not have counted the pleasure purchased too dearly if the flesh had been stripped to the bone.

"Why, it's Rubero over again!" Ewing exclaimed at the tale. "Rubero in its early stages, for they formed subsidiary company after company, each letting contracts to the others at enormous profits, and when the thing finally went to smash it was impossible to fix the responsibility for the graft. And I don't doubt that's where Hertzer got the idea. As regards the other two scoundrels — if it wasn't for your big stake in the plantation, I'd say stand aside and leave their punishment to him. He'd clean them out to the last cent, leave them bare as dry-plucked chickens. But we can't do that. Now let's see. . . . The first thing is to get you reinstated. I think you told me once that your mother owned nearly a third of the Verda stock? More than a third? Better still, it ought not to be difficult to get a majority to oust that pair of rascals.

"Of course it will have to be done quietly. You won't dare to show your nose in Northfield till you have your *coup* all ready to spring. So I'm going to give you a letter to my uncle in New York, who will give you all the advice and help that you need. For he's not only rich, but he made it all in stocks, and what he doesn't know about them can never be

384

learned. What's more, he is especially interested in rubber, and I have already mentioned your labor experiments to him in my letters. 'If your friend solves the problem of tropical labor,' he wrote me the other day, 'he will do not only the rubber business, but the world at large, an incalculable service, for labor is the crux of every tropical problem. Keep me informed of his progress.' So you go to him well recommended, and if I know anything of the dear old chap he'll move heaven and earth to help you." Rising, he added: "But there's no time to lose. We can talk details going down the river. I'm going now to rout out Joachim. If we can get away in an hour you can just catch the morning train."

"And you must have some clean things." Mrs. Ewing jumped up as her husband went out. "How lucky that you and Frank are about the same size! Consuela, dear, I can do it alone. Just keep on with his poor face."

In the matter of clean things, David displayed masculine indifference, but he blessed the consideration that gave him a half-hour alone with Consuela. To a casual eye it might have appeared that he made poor use of the time, for he hardly spoke for twenty minutes. But love's silences were ever more eloquent than words. She understood her share in his quiet dejection, expressed sympathy through the petting of wet, cool hands, was not offended that his first words should relate to his people.

On the contrary, she offered quiet comfort. "You

have done your part," she told him, as once before. "And, see! you will soon return triumphant and reinstated."

"But it will take a month," he groaned. "In that time he can break and scatter them all over the Isthmus."

"No, for I shall gather and care for them till your return."

"You are a dear," he burst out, and so fell to kissing her fingers whenever they approached his mouth.

Doubtless because of his sore trouble she permitted it, nor made more than a flutter of resistance when, suddenly catching her wrists, he pulled her down till her cheek came against his over his shoulder. More shame for that stern girl of the morning trail! When he pleaded for a last kiss she laid her soft lips on his of her own volition.

"Because you are going away," she excused herself, and so straightened quickly as a tentative cough announced the return of Mrs. Ewing.

Good woman that she was in her sympathetic insight into the needs of lovers, she had brought cloaks for herself and Consuela. "As if we would let you go out on that cold, dark river without a soul to bid you good-bye!" she exclaimed. And the measure of his gratitude ran over when, all being ready, she led off with Ewing, leaving him to bring Consuela.

If anything, the lantern that a *moso* carried ahead served to emphasize rather than lighten the darkness, and David found it quite easy to slip an arm beneath the cloak. "You know we are engaged," he whispered as a little hand seized his. But instead of casting off his arm according to expectation, she drew it closer about her. Because of which he was emboldened to ask a question that had lain at his tongue's tip this hour. "Dear—if my mother asks it —will you?"

She did not answer at once—nor at all, in words. For some time the fluttering hand betrayed her agitation, but—just before the lantern picked the canoe out of swift, black waters—its pulsing ceased and he felt a reassuring squeeze.

"No time for good-byes." Ewing's voice broke like the knell of fate upon his intoxication. "Kiss 'em all round, Davy, and jump in." So, albeit under sanction of Mrs. Ewing's hearty example, the mute promise was sealed by a kiss.

Quick as ever to understand, Mrs. Ewing snatched the lantern as the canoe floated out and held it close to Consuela's face—so close that David could easily see the eloquent smile, the love glow in the warm, brown eyes. It bloomed like a flower in the rich night, the delicate face with its rare coloring, and when it had drawn down to the size of a petal her call still drifted across the dark waters—

"Buena ventura!"   (Happy fortune.)

XXIV

IN the nature of things the pain of a departure
strikes harder upon those left behind, for besides
having neither new scenes nor people to distract from
brooding, familiar objects recall the absent at every
turn. As next morning Consuela gently rocked on
the veranda, her wistful eyes, mouth drooped almost
to tears, told their lonely tale. Though the land-
scape blazed outside with a brilliance of green, luxury of foliage unseared as yet by the waxing sun, her
gaze passed over its beauty, glued to the distant
river down whose black reaches she was travelling in
thought with David. San Juan, gray and squalid in
the cold dawn, the bubbling fecundity of the *tierra
caliente*, the brown, teeming life of the thousand palm
villages which dot its steaming jungles, these passed
in remembered procession ere fancy climbed with the
panting engine, crazy, jolting cars, out of the blue,
misty canyons of Orizaba to Ciudad Mexico, on the
plateau. There, at the bounds of experience, fancy
halted; not that she could not or did not imagine
David speeding northward by faster trains into the

heart of a land densely peopled and heavily forested with the skyscrapers of the picture-postals. A sudden blush even marked a thought of herself accompanying him in the capacity he most desired; but the idea was ousted as soon as conceived.

"No, no," she murmured. "His mother will never consent—or if she does? Still are there others. No, Consuela, it was wicked of thee to lend encouragement."

In direct contradiction of this pessimism, her happy colors persisted, added their glow to the suffusion of light that strained down upon her through a reed *petate*, drenching with fluid gold the loosely coiled hair which framed the delicate tracery of her features, dyeing her white morning wrapper with tints rich as the creams and rose-dusk of her face and neck. Sitting there as under the soft radiance of a stained window, she made a picture, fresh, virginal, rare as the illusive ideal which sets the artist raging at the limitations of brush and canvas—a picture that drew a gasp from Mrs. Ewing, another woman, when she presently stole to the door camera in hand.

"Oh, you beauty!" she mentally exclaimed. "You little beauty! If Davy could only see you now! If you were the least bit inclined toward frivolity—what a time he would have! Let me see! . . . with that light . . . an eighth of a second should do."

Click! click! click! six times repeated as fast as she could turn up the films, caught a Consuela quietly pensive, archly surprised, appealingly protestant for just one moment to arrange her hair, sweetly vexed at the refusal, lastly exhibiting small, white teeth in consenting laughter; a series beautiful in their soft lighting as well as subject, and which were to cause David's heart to leap in his throat some two weeks later.

"He whispered me to do it while kissing me good-bye," Mrs. Ewing laughed. "There, don't look so jealous, dear! He only used me as a road to you."

"Jealous—of *you?*" How Mrs. Ewing longed for another film to catch the wide eyes under high protesting brows! "You, who have been so good and kind? See, he is my most precious, yet would I give him to thee—if I could."

"The saving clause." Mrs. Ewing laughed merrily again. "I think I see you! Anyway, you won't be put to the test. One man is trouble enough—at times." Pausing, she looked across the clearing. "Some one is coming—over there—across the foot-bridge."

"It is the Señor Hertzer. David said he would come this day to inspect the books."

"Yes, it is he." While the laughter died in her eyes she went on: "I must say that I don't feel like receiving him. It is all very well for Frank to talk of keeping the peace among neighbors, but one must draw a line somewhere, and this time he has surely overstepped it. Of what use is friendship if we are not loyal? I shall tell him exactly what I think of his conduct—"

"No, no!" Consuela broke in. "For, see, he has the

power now over the Verda people, power to break and scatter. Rather it is that we should be pleasant, manage him till David comes again."

"That will be something of a contract, dear, he is so acutely suspicious," Mrs. Ewing mused. Then, while seriousness settled in meditative mischief, she added: "But it would be lots of fun. Only we shall have to go slowly — simulate coldness and leave him to conquer our reserve. Here he comes! I've just time to run in for a bit of sewing. It is an invaluable aid— good as a man's cigar—in conversation; leaves you free to raise and lower your eyes."

She had just time to slip into a rocker before Hertzer rounded the work-buildings, and at the sight of them, quietly sewing, he was filled with sudden misgivings. "Ready to jump me," he put it. And he— the man who had frozen with cold laughter the furious passion of his cast-off Tehuana wife as he took away her knife—shrank under the ice of their tempered greetings. Not knowing whether or not to dismount, he shuffled uneasily in the saddle while asking for Ewing.

"He took David down-river to the train," Mrs. Ewing coldly answered. Withal, she took care to leave an opening for explanations. "The poor boy is dreadfully hurt at the manner in which his company has treated him, and is going North to demand explanations. What is this company that is to work Verda, Mr. Hertzer? He seemed to have only the vaguest understanding himself."

As she expected, and very gladly, he jumped at the
lead. "One that I have organized with American
capital, ma'am, to work not only Verda, but also La
Luna and other plantations, for we expect eventually
to get them all on this river. You see, things can be
done so much more economically on a large scale,
they'll just naturally have to come in. There's no
sense in keeping up a dozen different gangs of enganchars when half the number, properly managed,
would do better work. Take Las Glorias, for instance.
Though you employ about seventy enganchars all
the year round, your rubber is never more than half
clean, for, by the time the gang has worked through to
one end, there's a six-foot growth at the other. But
under our system we should throw in men enough
to clean it down to the gravel in a couple of weeks,
then it would be off your hands for months. At the
most, three cleanings a year would keep it in the finest
trim."

"And we shouldn't need to keep enganchars at all?"
Mrs. Ewing looked up from her sewing with a beautiful pretence of interest.

"No, ma'am, only a stable moso and your house
servants. And think of the saving in book-keeping,
oversight, and so on! It would lighten Frank's work
fully two-thirds."

"Why, how nice!" she cried. "Don't you think
so, Consuela?" With equally well-acted pensiveness
she continued: "But poor Davy! And he worked *so*
hard on his colony scheme!"

"Got results, too. Verda's in fine shape." His keen glance noted a further thaw, and more at his ease he went on with assumed regret: "But old methods have to give way to the new. After all, it is rubber we are raising—not natives."

"That is so," Mrs. Ewing sighed. Looking down again at her sewing, she demurely added: "At first we were inclined to take up the cudgels for David, but I suppose it is only right that his company should look first to its interest." She sighed again. "Of course, that doesn't lessen our regrets for him, merely alters our point of view. And his volunteers! I suppose they will have to go?"

"And my school?" Consuela burst in. "Oh, my poor little children!"

Here was no acting, and the genuine feeling in her cry drew his glance to herself from Mrs. Ewing. "That is one of the things I came over to talk about —if you can spare me a few minutes." It was not necessary to add "alone," for Mrs. Ewing rose at once.

"Of course she can. I have to go in now, but I shall see you again at lunch. You *must* stay—it will take some time to go over the books. You had better bring them out here, Consuela dear. It is so stuffy inside."

While the talk was going on Hertzer had stolen repeated glances at the serene face, the graceful head that rose like a dark tulip from the billowy white of her dress, and, as she now followed in-doors, his eyes went after, drinking thirstily, greedily, of her youthful freshness. He made slow business tying his horse, and in its midst a sudden gray blaze, quick clinch of his hard fists, marked a vision of her moving about his *jacale* in that same way. But by the time she had returned with the books he had pulled down the blaze to quiet interest.

"We won't bother with them now." He laid a huge fist on the books. "None but a fool would question David's honesty — or accuracy, for matter of that. Plenty of time when he returns—if he ever does."

The serene countenance returned only mild curiosity to his quick look. "You think he will not?"

"Can't say, but I'd think he'd be very likely to take a disgusto and stay up home when his mission fails—as it surely must. If he should, we'll just transfer his enganchar accounts to my books at the end of the month, giving Verda credit for the value of their unexpired time."

"And the volunteers?" she questioned.

"I was coming to that." Smiling at her eagerness, he went on in a strain that indicated both knowledge and understanding of her passion of self-reproach, desire to make amends, repay the unconscious profit she had had out of La Señora's business. "I know what an interest you took in his colony scheme, and, while I'm not going to deny that he'd have made good you know just as well as I do that no other man could. The patience, perseverance, sense of duty required for the job are not to be found in the average gringo—at least, in the variety that flourishes about here." Calculated, or issuing naturally from his hardy indifference to consequences, the frank praise served him equally well, and in either case he did not fail to note her sudden accession of interest. "I haven't got them," he ran on, "never had and never will have, for I'm too old and hard in the mouth to be broken to such gentle tricks. But it doesn't follow that I don't recognize the value of the scheme now that it is working. I do. What's more, I mean to keep it going—if I can find some one to undertake the management."

"You mean—me?" Though his tentative look invited the question, she hesitated to believe the fates so kind.

But his nod affirmed the look. "Yes, in preference to any one—partly because I need Magdaleno and can't get him without you"—he hurried to cover the ulterior motive with a show of bluntness—"and because you understand and can manage the people. Of course, there'll be a few changes. All labor comes under my contract, and they will have to figure on the books as regular enganchars. But they will be free to come and go, cultivate their holdings, and receive the same pay for work performed as before. Now, what do you think of it?"

It was a big question to decide off-hand, but hesitation had vanished with doubt, and she answered at once, "I would do anything that did not interfere with my school."

"It won't. Now here's my proposition. You are getting eighty a month, Mex, to keep the Verda and Las Glorias books? Then I'll give you a hundred to keep mine and manage the volunteers, and the work won't be so heavy but that you'll have plenty of time for your school. Of course, you will have to live at Verda—"

"With Magdaleno," she said. "That will be nice."

"And the sooner you go the better." He grinned as he added: "I suspect that Magdaleno doesn't altogether like to see me pottering around there. You know I stayed all night, and this morning he sniffed and growled around my heels like a sulky bull-dog; wouldn't go out to work till I left."

"Yes, he was always faithful," she smiled. "How would it be if I went back with you after lunch?"

"Fine!" he ejaculated, slapping his thigh.

"Then, if you will excuse me, I will go and get ready."

As she rose and went in-doors he watched her as before, and if Mrs. Ewing could have seen his quiet triumph she would have abated something of her joy at the report the girl gave in the seclusion of her bedroom. "What luck!" she breathed, for Hertzer sat not far from the open window. "What luck! He has played right into our hands. Who would have expected it of such suspicion! But Frank always said that suspicion was born of credulity, and now I believe it. He's been so easy that I doubt whether I'll be able to keep a straight face at lunch."

THE GIRL PLAYS THE MAN'S GAME

In the face of such success it was difficult to maintain the tempered reserve she had marked out for herself. But if Hertzer noticed her cheerful lapses, occasional mischievous smile, they served to blind him the more, for, as a man is his own measure of others, he could only view them in the light of his own contempt toward David. "Out of sight, out of mind," he thought, listening to Consuela's laughter at some secret sally. "She'll soon forget—if she ever cared."

Watching them ride away after lunch, however, Mrs. Ewing did have her doubts, and gave them musing expression. "I don't altogether like it. . . . But she will be perfectly safe with Magdaleno, . . . and I shall make Frank ride over every few days."

On her part, Consuela was presently exercising herself on another score; for, as they passed from the blazing heat of the open into the cool of timbered jungle, there burst from the crude husk of Hertzer, the slave-driving, acquisitive, dominant Jew, a new person of open laughter and kindly glances—one who, while kindling with enthusiasm over newly hatched plans, displayed an embarrassed deference toward her almost boyish.

Even if she had sensed the motive behind it all, she must still have been touched, for one and all of his plans aimed at her own comfort or pleasure. As it was effectually screened by his age, the twenty years between them, she credited it to kindness and was moved to contrition for her double-dealing—contrition that grew and deepened when, with a certain bitterness, he began to speak of himself.

"I don't doubt that it seems queer to you that I should talk this way. I know that I'm counted a hard man on this river—not without reason. But if some of those who raise their hands at me had had my beginnings, . . . well, to put it lightly, they'd be just as far from the priesthood."

With hot feeling that sprang from a sudden realization—by contrast with her delicacy—of the cruel handicap imposed on his birth by fate, he went on to tell of those beginnings—the hard knocks of his loveless youth in the wicked squalor of the Trieste boarding-house, brutalities of the following years at sea, misguidance of the easy-living tropics—and as he ran on, picking from that seething riot of life that which was fit for her ears, sympathy strengthened contrition. She was feeling dreadfully wicked when he came back at last to his plans.

"But I'm sick of it all and I'm going to make a change—show them that Hertzer can make men as well as money. I intend to build a big camp for my Yaquis—have already selected the site, a sort of plateau, high and dry in the rains, with a fine view and handy to the river. It will be laid out on sanitary lines—drainage, running water in the wash-rooms, big, roomy *galeras* and separate huts for families, all inside a compound half a mile square. I'm even planning for a doctor; either some young surgeon with a taste for the tropics or one of the other kind—the outcasts, clever enough chaps—whom drink drives out from the competition of the cities. Such a one would be plenty good enough for me, and with a small salary and a little practice among the plantations he could do pretty well."

This was not all—a hospital, amusements, holidays, everything that would make for content of body and mind figured in his talk, which lasted from Las Glorias to the Verda clearing; and, however chimerical it may all appear in view of his past performance, he was not necessarily insincere. The mood is the man—for the moment. To the most wicked comes a time when, if only through satiety, evil palls and the spirit leaps to a vision of better things; and while the girl's soft eyes beamed approval it was easy to turn to the good. Sincere or not, the talk produced a reaction with her in his favor, and she gave immediate assent when he proposed to open a school at La Luna.

"Without counting the Yaquis," he said, "old Tomas has four children, and we could rake up five or six more among the cabos."

"Oh, the Yaquis!" she exclaimed. "The poor little slaves! I should love to teach them best."

With a smile almost soft enough to be a reflection of her tender pity, he went on: "There's one, a girl of fifteen, whom you can have for a servant. And we'll fix up a hut for you close to the house, where you can teach—and sleep when you don't feel up to the ride back to Verda. She can take care of it."

This last proposal brought them to the forks of

399

David's trail, and whether or no he had purposely delayed it, he continued, without giving her time to answer: "And now I must leave you, for La Luna hasn't seen me for two days, and I rather expect to find my big Yaqui running the place. In any case it isn't a bad idea to let you explain things to Magdaleno; he'll take it better from you. See you again to-morrow, or next day at the latest."

With a pleasant "*adios*" he passed on along the outer trail, leaving her to ride forward and unbosom herself of compunctions and explanations to Magdaleno, whom she met coming out of the store. The old fellow's grizzled mustachios bristled above puffed lips as she told of the plot against David. He smiled grimly at Mrs. Ewing's clever play, and frowned at the aforesaid compunctions while giving quick answer.

"What sense in thy distress? Once a tigerino, always a tigerino. If it be that the Señor Hertzer make this great business, it is not of goodness, but for his own profit. But Don David? Pleasant, kind, the big heart of him turned so to the good of men that I, who was in this service of enganchadores from my youth, have to learn from him in my age that great works proceed only out of mercy. There is a man— child! Think only of him, and go forward without flinching in the face of this other, that we may keep the people together against the return."

"Only I would not like it that he should be turned from the good through me," she was beginning, when he sternly interrupted.

THE GIRL PLAYS THE MAN'S GAME

"If the good be there, it will out. If not, of what avail thy effort? Come, give me the horse, then we will have the old woman make ready the cabin."

A little comforted, she would have been still more at ease could she have divined Hertzer's reflections riding homeward. Turning onto a side-path after he passed Phelps's place, he came out in a few minutes upon the plateau, the site of his future camp. The height of land thereabout, it gave him a glimpse of La Luna and, down-river, a cloud of smoke above a clearing that Carruthers had burned off that morning. Up-river, Phelps's house and buildings rose like pointed rocks from the yellow-green scum of a banana-patch. Beyond, the Verda roofs glinted in the sun, and still farther he picked a dark patch the size of his hand from the brighter green of the jungle—two thousand acres of Ewing's rubber. And as he took it all in, the gray blaze lit again to a sudden vision —of people coming and going between serried rows of *jacales*, roomy *galeras*, mushrooms of fancy that sprang up all over the wide plateau. A dry rattle of palms in the jungle was as the stir of wind in their sere thatch, and through the murmur of insects he heard the hoarse commands of *cabo* and *mandador*, the hum and bustle of a great camp, the half-thousand Yaquis that were some day to do the work of that river.

Nor halted fancy there. While his gaze wandered from plantation to plantation his thought kept pace with his eyes. "Carruthers's people? ... poor as crows.

THE PLANTER

... Phelps's company is tottering. ... Verda? ... as good as mine. ... Three years should finish Las Glorias. ... The man who is here then, ... with money to buy, labor to work them! ... There's a million in it for him. A million! a million! a million!" With each exclamation his strong hands shot out, convulsively grasping, while the gray blaze waxed and waned in recurrent glow. Then as he recalled the clearing, burning, planting, long years of toil and travail in tropical heat and sweltering rains, the free spending of life and treasure that had gone into the making of it all, he burst out in laughter, loud and prolonged, utterly unlike his usual dry chuckle. "To think ... that they were doing it all for me?"

For some time thereafter he sat his horse, hotly musing. After the gaining, the spending, and down a vista of golden years, he saw, red-litten by tropic sunsets, the chrome walls of a great *hacienda* with its entourage of bronzed servitors, men and maids, thronging flower-grown *patios*, pillared *corredors*. Also a town house in the Colonia Roma or other fashionable quarter of Ciudad Mexico; and as the woman follows the work, Consuela presently moved and had her flower - like being in both demesnes. Parisian dresses, jewels, equipages, he surrounded her with every luxury that wealth can feed to the whims of a woman, and—significant fact!—not till he had ransacked the world for her pleasure did his fancy pass on to Patricia. She ... should marry an *hidalgo*, into one of the old Mexican families. Her children would then enter official life, . . . have a say in the government, . . . mayhap breed a president among them! And so, mounting flight on flight, he saw flowing out of his own loins—his, the brat of the sailor's boarding-house—a family great as those of the feudal baronies, minor kingdoms of his native Austria.

Sweet as was the thought, his mind soon reverted to the events of the day, and as, retracing them step by step, he saw Consuela again upon the veranda, a vision of white in a golden mist, he straightened to his full height, and like an explosion it came out of him: "Once at La Luna, God himself can't take her from me!"

Hands clutching at the stretch of his great arms, coarse mouth working, eyes one gray glare, he was not pretty to look upon, but it passed in a flash, settling in a sheepish grin. "Hell! you're ranting like a kid. Off home with you." Withal, the purpose behind the explosion remained unchanged. "Patricia must go over with an invitation to-morrow," he muttered, riding away. "I'll tell her to-night."

He did not, however; for as he dismounted at his stable, Carruthers and Boulton hailed him from the store: "Come over here, old Hunks, and treat. We've had a pay-day, and intend to give you some action on your wad." And, as they lived up to the promise, it was three o'clock in the morning before he got to bed.

All through that long evening he studied the girl at her play with furtive unease over the top of his cards. Still more significant! When—after the manner of girls who are not loath to be handled—she snatched Boulton's winnings and got herself thoroughly tousled in the following struggle, Hertzer looked on with grim tolerance, almost approval, where once he would have thrust between with a fierce reprimand. And as usually happens when intensified by long waiting, his unease developed into actual nervousness by the time—the planters having departed—he was able to broach the subject at lunch next day.

"Ask her to visit me?" she repeated. "Why? I don't like her."

"But I do."

His black brows had lowered in expectation of an outburst, but she answered, with bitter carelessness: "Oh, that's the tattle of every cook-house on this river! You needn't frown. I'm not to be frightened like Rosa. Besides, I'll go — to please myself. I have a score to settle with Mr. David, and I couldn't have found a better way. But don't deceive yourself. You are not going to get anything out of it. She's no Tehuana, to be bought with a tin of sardines." And flinging a command for him to order her horse, she whisked into her bedroom to get ready.

It chanced that his stable *moso* had not yet returned from an errand to the Zacateco village, but, stepping outside, Hertzer saw the Yaqui eating his rice and tortillas in company with the other *cabos*, in the shade under the cook-house wall; and, after ordering him to bring out the horse, he sat down on the veranda to watch Patricia away. Pleased with his success, he merely grinned as she switched the heads off some favorite flowers walking down the path; but even he gaped when, leaning back, she cut the Yaqui across the face as she galloped away.

"The little devil!" he muttered. "Grows more like me every day."

The other *cabos* were laughing hoarsely, and, always curious in matters of violence, Hertzer turned his intent gaze on the Yaqui. Even at that distance he could see the welt through his bronze. But without sign that he had felt, or notice of his jeering fellows, he moved back to his place and went on eating.

Calling him after the meal was finished, Hertzer set him to work clearing implements and stores out of a hut that stood a few paces back from the house; and as he carried in with his own hands and arranged a *catre* and bedding, washstand, chairs, the hard speculation in his glance dissolved in brooding almost tender.

THE GIRL PLAYS THE MAN'S GAME

XXV

THE SHEARLING DEVELOPS HORNS

AND while Hertzer ransacked his house and store for furs, trophies, *zarapes*, fixing and fussing with care almost womanish, David was hurrying northward.

Needs not to detail his transition from the Stygian blackness of the Amarilla to the electric glare of a New York night. Two days of slow jolting on the execrable tropical road, twelve hours in Mexico City —whose cathedral and shrines, *plazas* and *patios*, almost beguiled him of his anxieties—two other days of swifter travel on the Central Mejicano to El Paso, with fifty hours of luxury on a crack American road, brought him through in just one week:

Of his sensations at the change from the heated silence of the tropics to the furious bustle of that giant bedlam, a chapter could also be written. As next morning he set out to find Ewing's uncle, the thunder of elevated and roar of surface trains, bells, whistles, clatter and clangor of vehicles and cars, deafened and stunned him. Walking the canyons between skyscrapers, he paused often to observe the hurrying crowds with something of wonder and not a little disgust. By contrast with the brown smiles of his own people, the hard, tight mouths, avid eyes in ash-pale faces, seemed like the fitful fancies of an evil dream; and he sighed his relief escaping from the mad race into the comparative quiet of a tenth-floor office which bore the name "Ewing & Crowther" in gold on its windows.

Large, roomy, and well-lighted, the offices were identical in furnishings with any of the hundreds within a stone's-throw; but to David, a country lad before his rustication upon the plantation, the type-writers and messengers, large force of busy clerks, appeared with the prestige of the unknown, and he stood very quietly among the customers who thronged the counters till it pleased a lordly young person in buttons to throw him a card.

"Write your name and business."

Resisting a desire to reach over and shake off every last button, David complied, and had no more than scribbled his name before Buttons relapsed into depths of obsequiousness. "Oh, Mr. Mann! Mr. Ewing is expecting you. This way, sir."

"Expecting *me?*" David wondered, but the solution awaited him in the richly furnished inner office.

"So here you are, my boy! Glad to see you." As he entered, a hale old gentleman met him with hearty greetings. "Frank wired me all about it," he continued, laughing—a deep, rich laugh that belonged with the kindly red of his face. "A fifty-dollar cable, if you please—'collect,' of course. I don't mind the expense, but I do wish the young villain had taken time to weed out his 'buts' and 'ands.' If I'd been as careless of my pennies when I made my start—Well, well, this is a careless generation, and in these days of big things thrift doesn't count like it did. Sit down, sit down, my boy, and tell me all about it."

His own chair paid tribute of respectful creakings to his massive build, and while talking, David took admiring note of his bearing, upright almost to stiffness despite his sixty years, the grizzle of thick hair, sagacious eyes set wide of his thick, strong nose. Probity, intelligence, fearlessness, dwelt in his level glance. It was a face to inspire confidence, and as he listened, nodding at each count in the tale, David felt his anxiety decrease.

"And now for your plans?" he said, when David finished.

"They are very much in the rough, sir. I intend to call the shareholders together and contrast the plantation, as advertised in Osgood's lying pamphlets, with its condition as I found it, expose his revision of my reports, tell what I have done, and so let them draw their own conclusions—they can only form one." Very modestly he added, "I studied law for a couple of years, and it seems to me that the evidence justifies an indictment for fraud."

"So you read law, eh?" The old gentleman nodded approval. "A good thing to do—if it's only to make one shy at litigation." Frowning dubiously, he continued: "Now, as regards an indictment, I don't doubt that you are legally right, but conviction is another thing! It might prove deucedly expensive, and I don't suppose that many of your shareholders are people of wealth. . . . Storekeepers, farmers, and school-ma'ams, eh? the usual country company. That lets out litigation, and perhaps it is just as well. You see, even if Osgood & Short appear openly as partners in the charter of the labor company, it would still be impossible to make an alien company, doing business in a foreign land, produce its papers in an American court. Frank told you that I was interested in rubber. . . . Well, I had my lawyers look into the Rubero fraud—I owned a few shares in that, you know—and if there'd been just a fighting chance to convict the scoundrels I'd have spent a hundred thousand to do it. But for that very reason there wasn't. Now, with your rascals, the case is slightly different. I have done business with them in the past—investments, and so forth; and as I understand it, they run a country banking business a little bit on the Shylock, but respectable as such things go; and, what's more to our point, very profitable. Like every one else, they went into rubber as a legitimate speculation, but now intend to kill the goose to get at the egg. If they were New-Yorkers we might as well quit; they'd put the thing through on their gall. But a certain amount of reputation is necessary for your country Shylock, and their action depends altogether upon whether the expected profit would exceed the damage accruing from exposure. Coming to the point, we have simply to get in and beat them at the good old American game of bluff."

"*We?*" David questioned. "You surely don't imagine that I expect you to waste valuable time on my affairs?" He was going on with thanks for the kindly advice, when the old fellow burst in:

"There's your New Englander, just as unwilling to take as to give something for nothing! *Your* affairs, indeed! And this to me, who was losing good money in rubber while you were still at school! The whole problem, my dear boy, centres on this little experiment of yours in labor, and do you think that I am going to stand by and see it fail for lack of help— or money, if it should be needed? Besides, I am not nearly so disinterested as you think. After the exposure Verda stock is bound to take an awful slump, and if it goes down to my price I shall buy in some for Frank. You see, my brother left only about enough to finish the lad's education; but while I've always had it in mind to do something for him, I want to do it in such a way that he'll have to go on and finish the job himself. You know him—frank, lovable, kind, a good head for business, but not much push. You, on the other hand—pardon me, but it shows at a glance—need some one to apply the brakes; wherefore, to my thinking, you would make ideal running-mates. How does it strike you?"

How did it strike him? Despite his absorption in his work, David had had his full share of desolately lonely hours. With Ewing's pleasant companionship to look forward to, he would not have exchanged places with the greatest potentate on earth, but in the midst of his expressions of thanks came a sudden doubt.

"But can he leave Las Glorias?"

"He will have to, pretty soon, in any case, for the company is going downhill fast. I hold some of its stock—a flea-bite, twenty thousand or so—and I have thought seriously at times of applying for a receiver—would have, only that I might be suspected of an ulterior motive. Of course I don't wish to trade on others' misfortunes, but since the world began one man's loss has usually meant another's gain. And when it does go some one will buy it in cheap, and why not us? With Verda for a starter, the three of us could form one company, you and Frank and I, to try rubber out to a final conclusion. What do you say?"

What could he say? During those weary days on the train despair had dogged him closely; he had lost hope as he viewed and reviewed his case, till little was left him but a set purpose to damage the rascally promoters to the extent of his means. But now not only reassurance but fortune glimmered before him, affecting him so that he could hardly stammer his thanks.

"Phut!" The old gentleman blew them away.

"I intend to make money off you. Now to business. Thanks to Frank's cable, I was able to fix things to leave. In one hour a train leaves that will land us in Northfield after dark, a proper hour for conspirators. We have just time to lunch, and we can do our planning on the train."

When the night train delivered the two at Northfield, a cracked bell was calling to week-night prayer-meeting, and thus it came to pass that David actually brushed elbows with Mr. Osgood going up-town from the station on the narrow board-walk. It would, however, have required daylight for the financier to recognize the pale, stooped student whom he had shipped off to the plantations in the erect, sunburned young fellow under the Stetson sombrero. Though he did turn, it was Mr. Ewing's silk hat and metropolitan style which drew his attention, and, as darkness covered their entry at the widow's gate, he passed on without suspicion to his place in church.

"If he saw you, the cat's out of the bag," Mr. Ewing commented, as they passed up the walk. "But I don't think he did. When I glanced back he was looking at me."

Again, if Mr. Short—travelling, in a double sense, in a direction that led away from the place of prayer —had passed five minutes sooner, he could not have missed the mother's exclamation, "Why, *David!*" at the sight of her son in the doorway. But here luck served once more, for drawn blinds and shut door hid both greetings and ensuing explanations from his roving eye.

In her natural joy Mrs. Mann was disposed to prolong the one at the expense of the other, and it was Mr. Ewing who brought pause to her flow of question and comment. "Come, come, little mother, you are to have him for a whole week. We must get down at once to work. I suppose you know a good many stockholders?"

Content so long as she could sit with David's arm about her, she ran off a string of names till stopped by the old gentleman's exclamation: "Deacon Bradley? The very man! Trust a deacon to keep a tight eye on his earthly treasure. Send for him at once."

Hauled out of meeting—where he had just declared the said treasure bestowed beyond corruption by "moth and rust"—the Deacon wrought mightily to justify this opinion. An elderly man whose lantern jaws formed the lower horn of a concave, parchment face, he raised hands of horror at David's tale, and five minutes later might have been seen flitting like a huge, dark bat through the dusk of the town, coat-tails flapping in his nervous haste. In twenty minutes he rounded up and herded a dozen resident shareholders into Mrs. Mann's back parlor, and about the time that Mr. Osgood rose to address the prayer-meeting, these also had received enlightenment on matters not included in the banker's modest testimony.

Of that long, lean, hard-headed type produced by the gruelling of Puritan stock in the hard, commercial struggle for existence, they listened either in dark silence to David's statement, or interposed, at most, single laconic remarks.

"If we only had the price at which they let themselves the contracts!" Mr. Ewing looked around when David finished. "Surely you must have an auditing committee?"

As aforesaid, the Deacon's face resembled nothing so much as an old-fashioned horn lantern, and it lit up a full candle-power at the question. "I'm the chairman." Shaving his lean chops with a meditative forefinger, he went on: "Not that we did much. You see, I was that sure of Osgood, I never more'n glanced at the books, an' the others left it all to me. I'd chance in once in a while, an' that was about all there was to it. But about them contrac's. Seein' as it was a new departure, the figgers kinder stuck in my mind—an even thousand a month, if I remember rightly."

"A thousand a month!" David whistled. "Exactly double my allowance."

"Yes?" The Deacon looked his surprise. "As much as that? Now I remember noticing an increase, but he explained that the expense grew with the plantation, an' would all come back in larger profits." With a touch of dry humor he added, "He didn't say to whom."

"And the stock-book?" Mr. Ewing pursued. "Do you know how many shares stand in his and Short's name?"

"Never thought of lookin' inter that. But I kin

find out when I go round to bid them to the meetin'
to-morrow. He's that used to havin' me pottering
round the books he'll never suspect."

"Well, find out if you can, though I feel certain
they don't own a share. Trust a rat to leave a sinking ship—especially if she's been scuttled by his own
sharp teeth. And you are certain that you can get
them to come to your house?"

This time the candle leaped into a sudden flare in
the Deacon's lantern. "Sure, for they often drop
in to pick a bone with me. I'll have 'em there at
eight. An' now we'll have to hurry out an' call the
others for seven."

As, unaware of these preparations on his behalf,
Mr. Osgood took his way home from meeting, the
Deacon and others passed him hurrying up the street
—some on their way to spread a quiet call through
the town, others to hitch steady nags to old buggies
and rattle through miles of black night to inject
financial nightmares into the sleep of tired farmers.
What time the financier turned over after his beauty sleep, the majority of Verda stockholders were
pledged to meet at the Deacon's house the following
night.

And they came. Long before the appointed hour,
a big room which had once served for a store was
filled to overflowing with small business men of the
town, farmers and hired hands, thrifty fellows who,
like their employers, sat very straight and stiff on
improvised benches, perspiringly aware of the creased

high boots which protruded from wrinkled trousers. In one corner a knot of country school-teachers sat on the Deacon's horse-hair chairs, men and women whose threadbare suits, dresses of cheap material, alike testified to the inadequacy of the pittances from which they had wrung their savings. The saw-mills, too, had contributed a quota, a boss-sawyer and several rough fellows whose muscles and raw joints punched knobs and bunches in their cheap store suits. A blacksmith, wagon-maker, two grocers, with a score or so of mechanics, added a leaven from the smaller trades. "Butcher, baker, candlestick-maker," they were all there, the little people upon whom the promoter battens, and of their number the most pitiable, the one upon which they seemed to centre, was a middle-aged woman in fusty black, a widow who took in washing.

"The inevitable widow!" Mr. Ewing whispered, as he and David looked in at the door. "She's always in evidence at every funeral. Look at her flustered face! Couldn't he have spared her mite? How quiet they are! And it isn't because they don't feel. See the sweat starting all over that old fellow's face! His little bit in Verda represents the expenditure of more energy than gains a million on Wall Street. And those poor girls—school-ma'ams, I take it, by their faded gentility. Tut, tut! Blind sheep for the shearers, sir, poor, blind sheep! And of such as these are the thousands who are being shorn by rubber promoters throughout the land."

THE SHEARLING DEVELOPS HORNS

Even their entrance caused only the slightest of stirs, a rustle such as attends the ascension of a minister to the pulpit. During the election of a chairman, and throughout David's long statement, they observed the decorum natural in those who come together but seldom and that principally at church, and when he closed their comments were passed in husky whispers. Indeed, but for their harassed, uneasy looks, troubled stares, occasional uneasy coughing, they might have been deemed unconcerned.

Bolder and more loquacious—perhaps by reason of much chaffering in his trade—a cattle-dealer was the first to find his voice. "So you didn't find no three hundred thousand trees, sir?"

"Less than fifty thousand," David answered. "Where there should have been a thousand acres of plantation, I found about a hundred that had survived the neglect of two seasons."

"And there's nothing else behind our stock?"

"Just that and the five hundred acres I replanted last rains."

A hard sigh greeted the answer, harsh suspiration which, escaping the guard of set teeth, conveyed bitterness of disappointment more eloquently than cries and lamentations. Again the cattleman broke a silence of consternation: "Then what's the prospects?"

And while they leaned forward taking the words from his mouth, David told—four years before the oldest rubber could be tapped; ten more before the replantings would come to bearing. Under careful management, the capital invested might be returned in from twelve to fifteen years—if the yield bore out theories and prices maintained? In the mean time—instalment payments till the stock was all paid up; whereafter it might be necessary to levy assessments on shares to bring the plantation along to its full yield.

"And if the payments are not kept up?" the Deacon asked.

"Plantation and investments will be a total loss."

Again the hard sigh went like a sough of dry wind through the room breathing of hope blasted in lives that had been, and were little more than a sustained effort to wring from the insufficient present a scant provision for the decrepit future. To this one end youth, beauty, pleasure had been ruthlessly sacrificed, marriage, children, every human relation made subservient; and whereas they had seen, for a moment, an easier path illumined by the golden promise of rubber, they now sat in darkness pitch-black as that which follows the lightning's flash. Their patient, oxlike pain, bewildered misery, touched David to the quick, resolved in his pitying eyes into a despairing, composite wave of pain which seemed to ebb and flow around the white, flustered face of the washerwoman.

"But I don't understand!" he heard her meekly complain to the cattleman. "Mr. Osgood said I'd get back my hun'red dollars along with two or three hun'red more. I'd like to ask him about it."

"And so you shall, mother," the man answered, with rough kindness. "He'll be here soon."

The banker was, indeed, even then doffing his overcoat in another room, for it had pleased the Fates to select this ripe moment for his entrance. Brought, or rather *shoved* in by the Deacon as he made to draw back at the door, he sustained the glower of angry eyes till his glance fell on David; then a sick, green pallor wiped out a first faint flush of surprise. Murmuring something about "intrusion," he tried again to withdraw—would have forced by and out if the cattleman had not reinforced the Deacon.

"No, you don't, mister, till you've answered this woman's question."

As, thus cut off, the banker stood, pale eyes blinking, dull red alternating with green pallors on his face, there recurred suddenly to David a vivid memory of the *iguana* at bay between himself and Consuela, and he experienced a repulsion strong as that excited by the chameleon changes of the ugly creature. Submerging bitter memories of the anxieties, annoyances, trouble, which this man had caused him personally, came a feeling of wonder that such a pitiable coward should have had power to ruin not only these, his fellows, but also a brown people in the far tropics not one of whom he had ever seen. Then this faded as the cattleman spoke.

"Now, mother!"

"'Twas only that Mr. Mann said I mightn't get back the money that took me five years to save, an' I just couldn't believe that Mr. Osgood, bein' a church-member, could rob a lone woman."

Out of the mouth of this, the least of his victims, had come his arraignment, and the faint hope on her face, last pale ray of a former faith, must have stabbed the man to his black heart, for he turned in preference from her mute distress to the cattleman's red scorn. "Then if you won't answer her, perhaps you can tell something about them contrac's?"

"Yes! Yes! Speak up! Explain, if you can!"

Finding its voice at last, the meeting gave tongue hoarsely, the louder because of its previous suppression. In their corner the school-teachers buzzed excitedly, emphasizing indignation by vigorous noddings. Farmers, business men, mill-hands, tradesmen were on their feet exclaiming, gesticulating with clenched fists as they voiced protest or denunciation. Once passion be loosed by an over-governed people, it becomes more dangerous because more irresponsible than a lawless community of which each unit is a law unto and acts for itself; and during a few minutes of wild disorder it seemed as though the banker would have no chance either for justification or to plead in court. Sensing the physical menace, he shrank and shook as with an ague while his mouth opened and shut, soundlessly, like that of a breathing fish, in a breathless struggle for words. But no sound issued in the midst of his agony.

THE SHEARLING DEVELOPS HORNS

The cattleman laid a heavy hand on the shoulder of Short, ushered in just then by the Deacon.

"Perhaps this gentleman will answer for you!"

Brutally aggressive as his partner was timid, Short angrily shook off the hand, then glanced defiantly around, gross head lowered and drawn in to his heavy shoulders in a manner eminently suggestive of a bull at bay. "Sneak meeting, eh?" His snarl broke on a sudden silence. "Just like you, Bradley, you canting old fraud! Come and pick a bone with you, eh? I will, too, before we finish—pick your old bones so clean there won't be a meal left for a starveling crow. What are you doing here, Osgood? Come along home." But as he turned to go the cattleman took him from behind, and with a movement too sudden for resistance, forced him down on a chair.

"You sit there!"

"Yes, sit there!" As, swelling with fury, he made to rise, a big hand gripped his shoulder with force that hurt the bone, and glaring round he came face to face with the boss-sawyer, a giant in stature and stockily built. To right and left farmers and millhands were rising, fists clenched, and their mutter of anger went like a growl through the room. Settling back again, he scowled at David, who began to speak:

"Sneak meeting or not, Mr. Short, now that you are here, perhaps you'll answer a few questions. How much Verda stock do you own?"

The scowl gave place to an ugly sneer. "You

haven't got your gall with you, have you? D'you think I've nothing better to do than answer silly questions from a discharged employé? You're not even a stockholder."

"If you won't answer—" David was going quietly on when the Deacon broke in:

"I will. He don't own none—neither him nor Osgood. Though their names still stand in the books, I found the numbers of their shares credited to new buyers." With a waspish glance at Short, he added: "Pick my bones, will you? Mr. Chairman, I move their removal from office."

It was done in a heat—one minute for the removal, a second to elect two of the business men in their place, a third saw David reinstated, in the glow of which hot moment he was carried back a week to Ewing's dining-room, felt small fingers softly caressing his face, heard Consuela's murmured comfort, "Soon you will come back, triumphant and reinstated." If mental telepathy had only been upon a practical basis, with what joy he would have flashed her the news! Instead, he indulged himself with a picture of her, reading or with graceful head bowed over a bit of sewing in the soft gloom of the Las Glorias dining-room—a picture that approached the reality only in the sewing; for at that moment she was sitting in the plantation-house at La Luna, watching Hertzer and Patricia at play with Carruthers.

From the moment's indulgence, David returned to the business in hand. "And now, sir"—he turned from Short to Osgood—"I should like to ask how you came to let out the work of the plantation at twice the present cost?"

Though still pale and shaky, the banker had recovered his voice, and, reassured by his partner's presence, he even attempted a stiff answer. "I recognize neither the legality of this meeting nor your right to question. The by-laws provide—"

"Yes, we know all about them," David quietly interrupted. "As for my right, I am voting a full third of Verda stock by proxy for my mother. Are you a partner in the Amarilla Labor Company?"

"No, sir, I am not."

"So you *will* answer—when it suits?" While a sudden blinking marked the other's realization of his mistake, he went on: "What about subsidiary companies? Have you an interest in any company to which the Amarilla may have sublet contracts? . . . Ah, now you are silent!"

"Double papers, as I thought," Mr. Ewing murmured.

"Look a-here!" His face livid with anger at his partner's mistake, Short sprang up. "We've already told you twice that we don't recognize this meeting and won't answer questions. Come on, Osgood, we ain't to be bluffed any more. There'll be a battery charge and heavy damages for the man that interferes." But, stopping dead, he glared at the town constable, who suddenly appeared at the door. Mopping his brow, he swung round again on David. "You

can't do that. A civil suit, perhaps, though a precious
lot of good it would do you. But this is criminal.
You haven't anything to go on—"

"The judge who issued the warrant thought differ-
ently."

At the cold interruption he blinked, but went
on: "What's the use? You haven't money enough
to—"

"It will be forthcoming." Though he had sat
quietly by David's side through all, nothing had
escaped Mr. Ewing. The banker's cowardice, anger,
and indignation which wiped out the patient distress of his victims, Short's defiance, every act and
emotion, set its reflection upon his fine face, and his
eyes, now looking at Short, glittered like points of
steel. "It will be forthcoming, sir."

"Hell! Who are you?"

"You know me, I believe."

Handing his card, the old gentleman assiduously
polished his pince-nez, while, after reading it with a
low whistle, Short passed the card on to his partner.
"Yes, we've done business with your firm. Glad to
meet you, sir."

Overlooking the proffered hand, Mr. Ewing continued: "Enough, I trust, for you to know that I
usually keep my word. . . . Then let me assure you
that if you do not instantly convey all of your title
and interest in the Amarilla or other labor corpora-
tion back to the Verda Company, this warrant will
be served."

THE SHEARLING DEVELOPS HORNS

"It will, will it?" Enraged by the snub, Short broke out in a defiant snarl. "Well, I guess you're good for damages. Go right ahead."

Quiet, as aforesaid, so far, the old gentleman now came to his feet, choleric with indignation. "You'll talk back, you scoundrel! Serve it we will, but, though to-morrow will see you gazetted in every paper throughout the United States for the rogues you are, don't harbor any illusions about damages. I'll furnish funds—enough to law you to a finish both here and in the Mexican courts—but suit will be entered on behalf of the Verda stockholders." Menacing him with the pince-nez, he concluded, "You have five minutes to come to a decision."

For the moment Short flinched, daunted by the suddenness of it; and while he stood, trembling with intense desire but afraid to utter a second defiance, his partner leaned to his ear, and he did not object when, after a minute of nervous whispering, the latter asked for a few minutes' private consultation in another room. Thoroughly cowed himself, the weaker rascal did not hesitate to add that the officer could stand at the door, a suggestion that provoked the old gentleman's comment.

"We've bluffed them!" he said, as the door closed on the three. "Even if that gross brute were willing, Osgood could never be got to face exposure. We've won, sir; we've won! . . . Hertzer?" he replied to David's surmise. "Hum! I don't think he'll press his share of the contract when he finds out who are his partners. Hullo, here's Osgood already!"

It had, indeed, required only a few seconds of cool reflection to bring Short around. Removed from the heat of conflict which made surrender next to impossible for his brutally obstinate nature, he gave immediate assent to Mr. Osgood's pallid counsel. "Yes, it's all off. Who'd have thought the young devil could have got such solid backing? It's lucky we didn't forward Hertzer that second thousand— and another month would have seen us stuck for at least five more. You go in, and if there's any papers to sign send them out here, for I'm damned if I face that congregation of fools again."

Thus it was that the banker appeared alone. On his entrance the hot buzz of conversation ceased, and while his thin fingers weaved in and out in the old, uncanny fashion, he made his shifty surrender. While they were not prepared to admit wrong-doing, or allow that any official act of theirs would furnish grounds for even a civil action, in order to avoid vexatious litigation and further the best interests of the company whose good they had had always at heart, they were willing to make any reasonable concession.

"Which means immunity from prosecution," the old man whispered.

"Well, let 'em have it." The Deacon, who caught the whisper, leaned across three of his neighbors to answer. "Prosecuted or not, they ain't agoing to do business in this town any more."

THE SHEARLING DEVELOPS HORNS

As, two days later, David entered his mother's front parlor, Mr. Ewing pushed back from the table, which was littered with papers, and fell to fanning himself.

"Warm?" he repeated. "I have just finished with the Deacon, the last and toughest of the lot. Looking into that room the other night, who would have thought such perfectly miserable persons could be changed into a rabid mob of speculators? They were quite canny in the beginning, but after it leaked out that I had paid the washerwoman in full for her shares"—he threw up his hands in comical despair— "Verda went soaring. They came at me like hungry wolves, mortgages, sheriff's sales, funerals—the variety and complexion of trouble spread out for my inspection the last two days is enough to make a man a pessimist for life. Of them all, only one seemed to think forty per cent. little enough for my risk and a five years' wait, and he, it seems, is not considered quite sane through the town. The Deacon thought a hundred and eight would be about the right price for his, and held out till he found that I really intended to close my books. Well, it's human nature, I suppose, and it is all over now. Lock, stock, and barrel, David, Verda now belongs to us. And how goes your business? Mamma still obdurate?"

David's gloomy nod testified to the futility of a day's struggle against his mother's religious prejudice. "When I once let out that she was a Catholic—" His eyebrows said the rest.

"Hum!" the old gentleman coughed. "Was it—er—necessary?"

"She asked me outright, sir."

"Of course, of course! What have you there?"

"Photos—pictures of her. I got them by this afternoon's mail, and I'm going in now to prove to mother that she really doesn't wear a blanket. . . . Certainly, if you wish it, sir."

Laying the series Mrs. Ewing had taken before him, the old gentleman looked long and earnestly before he spoke. "Well, well, you lucky fellow! And she nursed you through yellow-fever? I can well believe it. Of course you told your mother?"

"On the contrary, sir, I didn't, for I knew she'd worry dreadfully."

"What of it?" He laughed his rich laugh. "A bit of worry will do her good—supply a change of thought. With women of her age an opinion quickly crystallizes into a habit, and if she's been arguing against you all morning, she'll probably go on doing it till doomsday." Gathering up the pictures, he went on: "A touch of sex-jealousy usually figures in the objections of the best of mothers, and as they are chary of exhibiting it to strangers, argument from an outsider is generally more effective. So you'd better go for a walk while I try my luck. . . . No, thanks! Now—off with you."

Having thrust David with kindly force out of the front door, the old gentleman repaired at once to the back parlor, where Mrs. Mann sat with her Bible.

THE SHEARLING DEVELOPS HORNS

The touch of obstinacy in the face of mute misery she turned up to him told very plainly that she was killing two birds with one stone—fortifying her position while drawing comfort from the Scriptures—but, undismayed, he introduced the subject, then sat shuffling Consuela's pictures, while she descanted for a quarter of an hour upon David's incredible folly.

"Photographs?" she asked, at last, her curiosity stimulated by his frequent glances. "May I? . . . What a beautiful face!" And as, with natural intuitions which had been sharpened by long experience, he read meanings out of the wide-placing, open truth of the eyes, fine chiselling of the features, tender delicacy of mouth and chin, she eagerly affirmed his findings. "How proud you must be of her! Your daughter, is it—or perhaps the niece you mentioned yesterday?"

"No relation of mine, madam." He seized the opportunity. "But she may be of yours. This is the young lady who nursed David through yellow-fever."

"Yellow - fever?" Collapsing in her chair, she turned up a blanched face of horror. "*Yellow-fever?*"

"There, there!" Rather alarmed himself, he hastened to reassure her. "It is all over. He's immune —can never take it again." Noting her returning color, he continued: "But didn't he tell you? . . . Well, have it he did, and but for the devoted courage of this young lady you would now be childless."

THE PLANTER

As he ran on giving the particulars of David's illness, omitting no fact that would raise Consuela in her estimation, tears streamed from her eyes, and when he finished she burst out: "Oh, how can I thank her? I shall always remember her in my prayers, and—"

"Be kind to her when David brings her home?" he suggested, smiling. As flustered doubt repossessed her, he sternly added, "Or doesn't a mother's gratitude for the life of a son call for that?"

"Oh, it does! It does!" she cried, in distress. "But—she is a Catholic?"

Understanding as he did the narrowness of the life that had formed her, pity made it difficult for him to simulate offended gravity, but he did his best. "Madam, I am a Catholic."

"*You?*"

Noting the touch of reprobation in her surprise, he went on, with real sternness: "Three days, I know, is rather a short time to form an opinion, but I trust you have seen nothing in me that would cause you to advocate my active candidacy for hell?"

It was a good lead. Day and night, for those three days, had David sung the old gentleman's praises. In that very room the washerwoman had declaimed them over a hospitable cup of tea. Not to mention the saving of her own private fortune, she had seen a black cloud of despair lifted from several score of lives, and, rushing in upon her at once, the memory

430

of these things burst the shackles which fettered her soul.

"Oh, you good man!" she cried. "How small I must seem in your eyes! How little and dreadfully narrow! But see, I will do anything that you ask—write to her at once—my consent—grateful, loving thanks. I'll do it at once—if you will please find David."

As David was even then pacing impatiently up and down the garden walk, he was easily found. Coming in quietly upon her at her writing, he peeped over her shoulder. Then murmuring, "That's famous, mother, dear; keep right on," he slid an arm around her and looked on while the tide of motherly gratitude poured in unstinted stream from her pen. And glancing in as he went by to his room, Mr. Ewing muttered, "A pretty finish to a good day's work."

About the time the letter, with David's enclosure, was sealed, the old gentleman reappeared at the door, suit-case in hand. "We business men are ridden by perpetual devils of haste," he answered Mrs. Mann's protest. "I must catch the night train. David really ought to go with me, but you have been such a good little mother, we'll just have to let him stay out the week. Yes, yes, it's a short time, but then you'll have him for three months this summer when he brings you a lovely daughter. Now, if your letter is ready, I'll post it in New York to-night and gain a mail."

On the way to the station he explained his plans

for the reorganization of Verda. "I shall give Frank only half of my stock, which will give him, you, and me an equal interest in the plantation. Buying at sixty, I can afford to put up forty thousand, the difference between that and par value, to carry the work to completion, and I'm convinced that you'll have made the place self-supporting long before the money is exhausted. As regards Las Glorias, it can probably be bought in at a price that will enable you and Frank to come in as working partners, or, if extra money is needed, I can lend it on your Verda stock."

Worked out with a careful eye to David's stubborn independence, the plan contained nothing that could offend his sense of equity, and the fine old fellow cut him off when he tried to express his obligation. "Nonsense, nonsense, your stake in it is bigger, proportionately, than mine; and you forget that this is my hobby. I have made all the money that I need or can possibly use, and I tell you, sir, there's small comfort for the man who wakes up in the still, dark hours and looks back from the brink of the Unknown into which he must soon enter, upon a life which reads like a page in a business ledger. The man who uses a little of his substance in solving this problem of a world shortage in rubber is in a fair way to gain back to his natural sleep, for he stands next you, the pioneer, who gives up friends, pleasure, the luxuries and benefits of civilization to forward a noble work. I don't suppose you ever looked at it that way, but it's a fine thing you are doing; for however disastrous it may have proved to the individual, this experiment is bound to prove a social success. Let the plantations go back to jungle. The trees will still be there, immense forests of our planting, from which—in the event of our failure—Indians will bring out the supply of unborn generations. So we are simply partners, my dear boy, in a great enterprise, and let's have no more talk of gratitude."

Concealing strong feeling under a violent trumpeting into his handkerchief, he presently added: "I'll have all the papers ready when you come on, so that you can take them on down for Frank to sign. In the mean time possess your soul in patience—for the good mother's sake."

With the papers and a fat letter of credit buttoned over a high-beating heart, David took train south four days later. From New York to El Paso he passed the time alternately dreaming and planning, and not until he awoke in the middle of his first night out from the latter place did he realize the nature of the melancholy which had possessed him during the last slow days at home. Looking out at the scarlet *zarapes*, familiar brown faces under the *rebosas* of the women who brought milk, eggs, *tortillas* and *enchilados* to the train, he knew it for real, old-fashioned homesickness.

Because of this discovery he slept no more, but

sat propped against the Pullman window and watched while the train roared on through the night, for the intermittent fires at stations strung like a ruby necklace across the black breast of the desert. And when, from a flickering star, a bead would develop into a fire-lit *adobe* station, he made a feast of the women crouched over their clay pots, the peons in scarlet and white, whining beggars who fought and jostled with venders of food, opals, and lace the length of the train. Until the velvet east split into striped pennons of crimson and black, and day came with a puff of hot wind out of the far dust of the desert, he fed on that brilliant confusion; then after an hour's sleep awoke to a pageant of color.

Towns, hamlets, villages, adobe *haciendas* moved past his window in slow procession. Chihuahua, Zacatecas, Aguas Calientes, Silaoa, smouldering in purple, rose, umber, and gold, they passed in a day and night, the painted cities of the Plateau, and he awoke in the city of Mexico to the happy thought, "Consuela has my letter." Entraining once more at evening, the life, color, barbaric pomp, and pageantry of old Mexico passed with a brazen clangor of cathedral bells, and as his train swooped in hawk-circles down from the plateau into the ocean spread of the jungle, he raised his face to the soft wooing of the first tropical wind, drew such a breath as the returned wanderer takes of his native air. As, next morning, he saw the first *jacales* raise graceful peaks from a jungle clearing, a big lump rose in his throat, and he felt as never before the lure of the tropics, the soft call which had come on that scented wind. The comely women in their doorways, golden girls on their way to the river, *ollas* poised ahead, the nodding palms, great *sabers* that spread huge arms over the lower forest, every sight and sound of that fecund life presented the face or voice of welcome, and he realized with a great thrilling that he was come back to his own—the tropics had claimed him forever.

At Cordoba he met an old friend, the conductor with whom he had journeyed out of Vera Cruz just a year ago. "Been running on this branch almost ever sence," he said, shaking hands. "But I've heard of you from folks going up an' down. They tell me you're doing great things." And a subtle compliment inhered in the manner in which, putting his feet up on the opposite seat, he discussed between stations the news of the hot country with the freemasonry of an equal.

From the division-point where the friendly fellow left him, a night's run through the *tierra caliente* would bring David to his station. Nine hours from there to Carruthers', plus six with a fresh horse to Las Glorias, would put him with Consuela in twenty-four hours. Leaping at the thought, his pulses accelerated thereafter at the rate of a beat to every kilometer, but—he had omitted the inevitable derailment. Turning out at midnight, he slaved in muggy, sticky heat by the light of a bonfire, poured out his sweat and curses with the grimy train crew for two long hours before the engine consented to be led back to the track. And it bolted again through the malarial mists of the morning, setting an evil example to the baggage - car and one coach, which immediately followed. Wherefore it was late afternoon before the train pulled into his station, the ramshackle, mildewed village which had seen his first disembarkation.

"Hullo, Mann!" the American operator gave him hearty greeting. "Glad to see you back. I have news for you." Indicating the raffle of brown loafers that immediately cocked ears all over the platform, he added, "Some of them speak English. Come inside. . . . Ewing's moso brought this letter a couple of hours ago," he continued, after closing the door. "He didn't know much, and I packed him off home before he had time to spread it around, but I gathered that there was particular hell to pay up-river—Hertzer has half killed your mandador, and is holding Miss Robles a prisoner."

Excepting that it detailed Consuela's efforts to keep Hertzer in good humor, told of her entrance into his employment, and that she had opened a school at La Luna, the letter said little more. "Everything was going beautifully till Hertzer got wind of your letter yesterday," Ewing wrote in conclusion, "—just how he got it, I'll tell you later. Since then he has held her a close prisoner. When I went over there this morning, he was in the ugliest humor I ever saw. After his cabos had almost beaten the life out of poor old Magdaleno, he had had him locked up in his galera, and didn't hesitate to threaten me with the same dose if I didn't get off the place. Believing that I could do more good alive than dead, I left, and am sending mosos out up and down river to raise the white planters against him. They are to meet at Verda to-morrow, so come straight there."

High hopes, elation, the joy of home-coming utterly wiped out, David handed the letter to the agent ere he turned his face of despair to the wall.

Though lacking a year or two of forty, a grizzled stubble beard helped the attenuation of a hard, hot service to give the operator the appearance of sixty, and mighty disreputable at that. Nevertheless, a sound heart beat behind his grizzly front, nor had the violence, easy death, still easier living of the tropics destroyed his feeling. His hand dropped kindly on David's shoulder.

"Easy, my boy, easy does it. There ain't a thing to show that he's harmed her. I reckon you don't feel like eating? Then come right out to the stable."

While he pulled and hauled on straps and cinches in a record saddling, he explained, "The moso left a horse for you, but he ain't so fresh, an' I'm going to lend you mine." Backing the beast out, he said: "He can outrun anything around here. Kill him if you want; but remember it won't pay to have him drop half-way." As David rode away, he called after: "Good luck! and don't forget that my pistols are in the holsters. They shoot straight at ten-

score yards." And as, returning to the office, he recalled David's stern, white face, he muttered:
" 'Twasn't necessary to tell him to use 'em. If
he's only quick enough? With Hertzer, it's an even
chance between coroner and undertaker."

His caution against over-riding, also, was scarcely
necessary; for, though David rode in a nightmare,
his practical sense exercised automatic control over
his actions. Eleven hours easy going to La Luna
would require seven of killing riding, and *feeling*
rather than remembering this, he restrained sudden
lusts for speed. He rode steadily under the fiery
heat of afternoon, in the sunset's red glare, through
an incandescence of lantern-flies that rose in clouds
at dusk like sparks from a prairie fire—rode in and
out of pit blackness into the eye of a tawny moon
which presently sailed up and threw fantastic shadows, dwarfed twisted shapes across his path. Obsessed by the most awful of fears, he dashed along in
moonlight and shadow until, a long hour from La
Luna, the indigo sky ahead burst into sudden effulgence.

"Fire!" he exclaimed, after a startled glance. "At
La Luna!" And as the glow intensified and spread
from zenith to horizon: "The whole plantation!"

XXVI

WHEREIN THE "QUEEN" IS "CASTLED"

IN the dusk of the morning that would see David's train enter the City of Mexico, Consuela quietly opened the door of the *jacale* which she had occupied at La Luna every other night for the last three weeks. The Yaqui girl whom Hertzer had given her for a maid still slept in her *zarape* on the floor at the foot of the bed, and, closing the door quietly, Consuela moved with equal stealth past the dark house, down the garden-path in the gloom of shading rubber. From below, the low voice of the river rose out of dark mist; trees and buildings loomed dimly in a gray-ghost world; withal, old Tomas was already marshalling his Yaquis in front of the *galera*, and he exclaimed, as the gate clicked under her hand:

"It is you, señorita? Carambara!"

But his eyebrows came down when she explained that, as this was her day at Verda, she preferred to ride in the cool. Having, moreover, a hawk's eye to the future—which would see her his mistress if cook-house tattle were to be believed—he brought out coffee and *tortillas* from his own hut, nor would let her away till she had finished both, maintaining that *calenturas* were bred by empty stomachs, advice that would have been welcome as the coffee if she had been in less hurry. Sipping and eating, she nervously watched the house and sighed her relief as she rode away. Yet the sigh was not heavy, bespoke no fear. For she laughed, looking back from the turn of the trail; uttered a low, throaty chuckle like that of a mischievous child while whispering, "Henceforth, more care, Consuela!" an utterance which has its significance in that it revealed her knowledge, not only of Hertzer's love, but also of its development to the danger-point.

"Take care, my dear"—Mrs. Ewing had ridden over with warnings as soon as she heard of the new arrangement—"take care, he is madly in love with you, and if he should suspect— Better come home with me to Las Glorias?"

Consuela, of course, had refused, and Mrs. Ewing added a second reason to her plea of necessity in retailing their conversation to her husband. "I believe, Frank, she takes a wicked delight in managing him, and rather enjoys the danger." To which he laughingly assented.

"Did you just find that out? Under her demureness, Consuela is a dead game sport—spirited, if that suits you better — and your eternally feminine is fond as a child of playing with fire. However, I think Consuela is clever enough to take care of her fingers."

THE "QUEEN" IS "CASTLED"

Granting this small vanity—that she took pleasure in her ability to move a man who had proved savagely intractable to every other influence—it was dominated by bigger feelings. Riding back and forth between Verda and La Luna—he usually contrived to escort her part of the way—she gave him sympathetic encouragement when he discussed his plans, and, believing that with her help he might persist in and further the good with all of his great force, she was oppressed at all times with a torturing sense of responsibility, the very feeling which had caused her to utter words last night that made necessary this morning's flight.

"If I could *only* help you!" she had murmured, at the end of an after-supper talk, and, though the observation was borne of regret, the knowledge that David's return would snatch the foundations from under all these airy castles, he had interpreted by his own feeling; it had taken all her wit to stave off the consequences she saw leaping in his eyes.

"Yes, henceforth, more care," she now murmured once more, as she recalled his face. But she laughed again, with the assurance of safety, as she reined her horse from the main trail on to a by-path.

Leading in to a sugar *finca* where the coarse sweetening for *galera* use was made by a Zacateco family, the path had been heavily overgrown when last she passed that way, but, as more light broke down through the dim tracery of palms and *bejuca* tangle, she saw that it was now brushed out to twice its previous width, and wondered at such unusual industry on the part of the *ranchero*.

In the tropics your native does such work as he must in the cool of morning or evening, and the rumble, wooden creak of the crushing met her while still deep in the forest. Emerging at one end of a long clearing, as the sun's brazen disk rose out of the tree-tops at the other, she saw a naked boy goading on the mule whose endless circlings supplied the power. Primitive, rude of construction as the water-wheels of Egypt, the mill was built of wood throughout, power-arm, flat transverse wheel, the perpendiculars whose iron-wood cogs meshed with those of massive log rollers; even the moulds, which were simply holes in a log whittled to the size and shape of a Boston brown loaf. Indeed, a stack of cubes, yesterday's boiling, exactly resembled that edible. The boiling-pan, a big, flat kettle set in *adobe* bricks under an open *jacale* roof, was the one bit of iron about the place; and while the *ranchero* fed cane to the crusher, his wife, a mighty Zacateca, stirred the boiling sap. Because of the fire and exercise, she had thrown off her short bodice, and, with crimson skirt caught up and tied trunk-wise about wide hips, she stood forth in all her plenitudes, stood and stirred and stirred and stirred with a slow, easy motion that was the very poetry of strength.

While the *ranchero* was tying up in corn-husks the half-dozen sugar cubes she required for her children, Consuela sat her horse and looked on. The sun—

which would presently turn the clearing into an oven thrice heated—as yet diffused tempered heat and light over the sea-green spread of cane, darker florescences of the singing jungle. For its first ray had touched off an explosion of noise, calls of beast and bird, arguments of parrots and cockatoos, which still quarrelled as they winged it in flocks under the sky's enormous blue. Overhead, light cirrus clouds moved like feeding sheep toward a high snow mountain, towering cumulus, whose upper fleeces rose high above the trees. With time to spare, she found it very pleasant to sit there, bathed in warm sunshine, with the lazy creak of that old-world mill in her ears, and she yielded her senses to the charm of the moment with luxurious abandonment—sat and drank in the freshness of the morning; watched with delight, almost pagan, the easy strength, slow, unconscious grace of that big bronze goddess; might have sat longer but for the answer the *ranchero* returned to her question.

"You brushed out the trail?"

"No, señorita," he replied, as he finished wrapping her sugar in corn-husks. "It is the Señor Hertzer. From the platinas yonder he has also cut a path in to his new camp, and from there a trail runs out to the finca of Señor Phelps. From here you may go that way."

"And if it please thee to wait but a moment," the woman added, "the señor will show thee the way. He rides every morning to oversee the work before he breaks his fast."

THE PLANTER

Only part of this was news. The progress of his Zacateco builders had formed the text of their talk last night. But, whereas she knew of his early morning inspections, she had imagined that he always went by Phelps's trail, and now her little trick to give him the slip had turned out an undoubted trap. Any moment might bring him! And giving the *ranchero* a hasty *adios*, she rode on, but reined in again to call back:

"Tell him that I shall ride slowly."

Her prevision entailed one disadvantage: she had now to ride at a walk till out of sight. But she was thankful for it when, turning at a distant shout, she saw Hertzer galloping out from the mill. If he had seen her discovered colors? But she had time to school them, and met him with a little laugh. "You looked so tired last night, I thought to steal away. But already I had repented, and now you can show me the camp."

Following so closely upon the message, her solicitude and implied compliment completely allayed his suspicion, and his harsh facial lines flowed at once into the kindliness habitual with her. Replying that he would have been sorry to have her see it for the first time alone, he fell in at her side, but observed such silence thereafter that, out of sheer nervousness, she burst into a flood of talk, prattled of birds, flowers, the camp, any and everything as they rode along.

And she had grounds for alarm. At the sight of her, fresh and fair as the morning, waiting for him to

444

catch up, some suggestion of a tryst had caused him a shock of emotion, sudden fierce desire which now fed and fattened on every stealthy look. Anticipating heat, she had tucked her white blouse-waist in at the throat, a slight *décolleté* which yet accentuated sex, adding a touch of sensuousness to her pure beauty by the revelation of a rounded fulness of neck not to be expected from her delicate modelling; and when, in throwing off the last vestige of sleep, he caught a glimpse of a mouth red and sweet as a child's before her hand could stifle the yawn, he went blind.

She undoubtedly stood in great danger. An accidental word or girlish carelessness might have unstopped the flood of his passion, but, catching sight of his face, she froze, and rode thereafter in a flutter of fright. It was impossible to mistake the fear behind her sudden silence, and, as he sensed it, that queer æsthetic strain gave birth to one of his rare impulses. He began to talk. When she took courage to look again his way, she met the now familiar, friendly glance, and, desperately thankful, she broke again into sudden chatter, prattled, laughed, did her best to please him up to the moment they came in sight of the camp.

Though informed, as aforesaid, of the progress, she exclaimed at sight of the reality, for, just as he had seen them in his day-dream, two rows of *jacales* raised graceful peaks on either side of a long *galera*. Others in course of construction exhibited every stage of that curious building, from the planting of stout corner-posts to the tying on of the last rib of palm thatch. Here cross logs were being fitted into the crotches of the posts; there they already bore bamboo rafters, upon which, farther on, a half-dozen Zacatecores laid thatch, slitting each palm-leaf along the centre rib so that the fronds could be turned downward. Beyond them, still others were splitting pole-siding, and at every stage the invaluable *bejuca* was used to tie beams to posts, rafters to beams, to lace the thatch to ribs and all to the rafters.

"They'll soon be finished!" she cried.

"Hardly," he smiled, "though they've done pretty well—about six houses a day, which isn't so remarkable when you consider that I've hired about the entire Zacateco village. Pretty scene, isn't it?"

It was beautiful as cheerful. The jungle's variegated green lay about them in waves that now swelled over a distant rise, again sank into the trough, permitting glimpses of gilded roofs in sunlit clearings or shining bits of river; within which rich setting the plateau basked in warm sunshine, cheerful with cries and hammerings, musical babble of Spanish tongues, enriched with a crimson flutter of dresses, gold of satin skins; for, besides the half-hundred or so of men, an equal number of women worked about the buildings. Here a lithe girl trimmed palm ribs for bunk flooring with a deft *machete;* others bound on pole-siding; from all around they streamed in, dragging thirty-foot palm ribs for thatch, or walked uprightly beneath bundles of *bejuca* withes large as hay-ricks.

THE "QUEEN" IS "CASTLED"

"Another week will finish the buildings," Hertzer went on, "but there will still be a good deal to do—galeras to wire, compound to build, drainage. I've ordered galvanized pipe from Vera Cruz, to bring water in from the arroya above and let it out below. A month won't see it through. And this is only the beginning—the first camp."

Talking, his face had lit up to one of his enthusiasms, and while he now traced the run of Isthmus rivers on the open map of his hand, he called off a dozen plantations: "La Rosa, Trinidad, Tres Marias, Buena Ventura, Esperenza—I can lay my hand on fifty that can be bought in for a song. Some, of course, are no good—bad land or choked. But I can take my pick of those that will pay for clearing. In three more years the rubber on this river will shade the ground so that it can be left to take care of itself. Then this camp can be moved. But I shall not wait for that. I haven't put twenty years in here in the tropics for nothing, and if my own capital should prove insufficient I can easily raise more. I'll build a camp here—here—here." His big finger swooped from finger to finger between rivers. "One by one, I'll gather in those bankrupt plantations until"—he took a deep breath—"until I'm the biggest Mexican owner, big enough to control the rubber output."

While his sharp eyes searched the horizon as though it were the future he saw so vividly, he went on. "For it is useless to produce at random. The instant tame rubber comes on the market Goodyear and the

447

other big buyers will begin to force down prices. Whether it is corn, wheat, coal, or rubber, your little man stands as much chance with the monopolies these days as "—he smashed a fly on his horse's neck —"this! But the man who controls Mexican rubber can ask his own on the market."

Pausing to exchange a word with the Zacateco head man, he remained under the spell of his visioning and began again, went on planting out camps on his hand, reached further and further into the future, built warehouses and wharves for a steam-launch line to exploit the inland Indian trade; and as he proceeded, planning and explaining with that combination of prophecy and hard sense which has drawn the strings of the world's finances into the hands of the clever Jew, Consuela's fancy first followed, then outraced even his fierce enthusiasm. Vividly imaginative, she could not but be impressed by an audacity which paused only at the control of the Mexican tropics, a country immensely rich, large as an old-world kingdom. The romance of it set her aflame with kindred visions; only, where he saw boats, wharves, markets, warerooms, her fancy planted schools, churches, everything that would make for the good of the Isthmus peoples.

· "Señor," she breathed, as her mind flashed out to the possibilities of good and evil in his schemes— "señor, you would be master of the Isthmus."

"Master of the Isthmus."

Repeating it, he flung back his head with a move-

ment regal in its ineffable insolence, arrogant assertion of mastership over fate. In his eyes warm lights
were dancing, leaping, flashing like ripples on sun-
struck water. The flame of that great visioning had
melted the dross in his square Slav face, and for the
moment he sat invested with a nobility of force,
strength of masculinity, which always appeals to a
woman.

And Consuela, a true woman, felt the call—so
strongly that had he been ten years younger and of
better record, David might have had reason to tremble. As it was, she did not attempt to hide her admiration, and, warmed by its glow, he went on to put
her very thoughts into words.

"Master of the Isthmus, with power greater than
that of the governors of Vera Cruz, Oaxaca, Chiapas,
and Yucatan combined. Power great enough to
overawe the rascally jefe-politicos, abolish their
exactions. Wealth enough to build churches, schools,
hospitals. Powerful and wealthy enough to do all
that if—I had you at my elbow to point out what
should be done?"

It had come again, the crisis from which she had
fled, and, turning from the tumult, eager question of
his eyes, she tried to stave it off. "We shall always
be friends—"

"No, no!" he interrupted, with an emphatic shake
of the head. "A friend could not do that for me.
Let's be frank. Three months ago I should have
laughed at the very idea of having an interest outside

of flowers and fighting, for I understand myself—well
enough to be certain that if any good works are to
come out of me it will have to be through you. Don't
be afraid," he quickly added, as she glanced uneasily
toward the Zacatecores. "I am not asking you to
marry me—yet. We are already partners in work,
and the one will lead to the other. Only I want you
to think of it, to realize what it means to yourself and
others. Where a young man could only offer love,
I'll give you power as well, power to do the things you
like." With the rude eloquence natural to him in
moments of deep feeling, he finished, "I'll make you
mistress of the Isthmus. Where other women have
only babies, I'll give you peoples for your play-
things?"

As her head was turned away he could not see the
sudden distress that swept her face. All through he
had spoken with rude dignity born of restraint, and,
combining with the vibrant warmth the force of his
pleading, it quickened her remorse for the part she was
playing. Under urge of that Judas feeling, she was
tempted to speak out, to reply that, while love was out
of the question, she would always stand by him with
sympathy and encouragement. But just in time to
check the suicidal impulse, she caught a glint of gold,
the roofs of Verda, far off in the deep green of the
jungle, and remorse was swept out by flooding memories of his hard record, late treachery, the foundations of fraud upon which he expected to build these
shining castles. "If the good be in him, it will out

of itself—if not, of what avail thy efforts?" The wisdom of the old *mandador* was borne out by his own confession. "If good works are to come out of me, it will have to be through you." And the thought stiffened her to play out her rôle to the end.

But what to say?

"The idea seems strange?" To her immense relief, he lifted the burden of speech out of her hands. "Well, don't speak—just now. Give it time. Things will go very well as they are for a while. You can choose your own time to answer. Come over and look at the galera."

She was glad enough of the diversion, and put it to such good use that she was able to say good-bye quite gayly after they had examined the *galera*, with its wash-house and wooden troughs. "And now, señor, I must go, for I am late; a fine example to set my scholars. No, you cannot come one step farther."

"Why?" he asked, tickled by her pretty imperativeness.

"You have had no breakfast."

"Neither have you."

"But mine is waiting at Verda—just as is yours at La Luna. Go straight home."

The command, with its flattering suggestion of anxiety for his welfare, pleased him immensely, and he obeyed at once, pausing only on the edge of the jungle to make sure she had taken the right path. Reassured, he rode on at a footpace, plunged in reveries of a softness and sincerity hitherto alien to his hard nature, his craft, for once in abeyance, submerged beneath the glamours of love. Self-deceived or not, his intention had been honest. Meaning all that he had said, he now dreamed, dreamed, amplifying on the future, sketching in the details of that partnership of works with love; dreamed dreams the very memory of which would presently lash his raw pride with the sting of poisoned whips.

Busy with her own thoughts—and feelings, which alternated between thankfulness and pity—Consuela pursued the opposite direction. Now that the crisis was past and she felt sure of her ability to manage Hertzer to the end, she had more room for the latter feeling. Out of his sight and dominant influence, she knew that with him it must be either love or hate, and, seeing the impossibility of friendship between them, she was sorry, sorry that such force and strength as his should be doomed through her innocent default to flow in evil channels. Her conscience led her a miserable dance until her thought turned to David.

Where was he?—doing what?—with whom? The last was not necessarily least of the clauses, but if hypothetical *Americanas* of surpassing beauty hovered in her thought, they vanished before a sudden vision of David's honest face, leaving her free for the other questions. Travelling north, he had mailed a card from El Paso. A hasty scrawl from New York had drifted into some backwater of the Mexican post-office —to emerge three months later. Having experienced

the vagaries of that sluggish service, she had guessed
as much but was none the less anxious if not hurt.
For as this was the eighteenth day since his departure,
the fight for Verda must have been won or lost a week
ago, and though she quoted the Spanish equivalent
of the proverb, "It is ill news that travels fast," she
had sea-room and to spare for anxious speculation;
was tossing up and down in her cockle-shell of doubt
when Lola, Phelps's Tehuana wife, called to her from
the door as she passed the house.

Something in the woman's soft smile, touch of
sympathy mixed with mischief, caused her a flush as
Phelps came hurrying out with a bundle of letters
and papers, but her face fell when he said that they had
come up from San Juan with his corn and were all
for Ewing.   What of her frequent snubs, he stood a
little in awe of her these days, but while she stowed
the mail in her hempen saddle-bags, bending over to
hide her disappointment, he looked on with a mischievous smile.

"Now, what will you give me for this?" He
brought his hand suddenly out from behind his back.

A little gasping *"gracias"* was all that he got, or
deserved, for as she rode away he turned, grinning, to
Lola.   "If Hertzer could have seen her blush?   And
he believes that she never cared a rap for David—told
me so when I was chaffing him the other day.   Lordy,
how she's riding!"

"Ay, she cares."   And while her soft gaze followed
the flying figure, she whispered her own experience.

"The worse for it—for the woman that cares too much for a man."

Not until that mad gallop had buried her colors deep in the heart of the friendly jungle did Consuela pause to keep tryst with her letter. Of the two enclosures her eager fingers went of themselves to David's, and as she read—slowly, for written English was still a task—of his love and loneliness, which the young man's native wit had given precedence of even his great news, a quick dew spread rainbows across the page. Reading his mother's letter, the dew condensed in drops on her long lashes, bright tribute to its fervor of thanks. While giving the date set for his return, David had omitted, manlike, to state rhyme or reason for the delay; but this was supplied by the inevitable feminine postscript:

"I shall keep him a few days longer—an unwilling prisoner, I am afraid—but I feel that you won't begrudge him to his mother."

With which slight shadow removed from his otherwise bright eagerness, she gave answer aloud to his plea. "There are still the others, but—" David not being present in person to render delay delightful, she tossed a proud head in the face of La Señora, the *Americana* Grundy, "I will! will! will!"

Dropping again to his letter from a wistfully tender pause, she read, reread—indeed, read it so often that she arrived shamefully late at Verda, and had to call it a holiday to annul the force of the awful example. So, after distributing the good news and sugar respectively to Magdaleno and her children, she galloped on to Las Glorias.

Seeing her coming from the veranda—where he was cooling off for lunch—Ewing gauged news from her speed, good news, from the triumph in her clear call as she swept by the footlog to come round by the bridge, and his answering whoop brought his wife out just as Consuela dashed up to the door. As his mail contained a letter from his uncle, a quick scanning gave him precedence even of Consuela's excited Spanish, and, leaving his wife to dot its liquid flow with appropriate exclamations, he ran for the store, to presently return bearing a bottle, a left-over from Christmas.

"For this is a double occasion," he said, filling Consuela's glass at the meal. "Here's to you and Davy, wherever he may be. . . . And, by Jove! that's Ciudad Mexico," he added, after a rapid calculation. "He leaves there to-night . . . one . . . two . . . he ought to be here in three days."

"So you had better stay here till he comes," Mrs. Ewing said; and, having been informed of Hertzer's proposal while Consuela was washing her hands, she added, "I cannot bear to think of you going back to that man."

But Consuela shook her head, and when he had weighed her reasons Ewing took sides against his wife. "She's right, Nellie. In three days Hertzer could do an immense amount of damage—ship the people down-river, loot the stores, and it's a cinch that

455

he would if she didn't go back. But if she returns, as usual, to-morrow, teaches at La Luna the following day, and comes back here the next, she'll be in lots of time for Davy. With his reinstatement, of course, she goes naturally back into his employment, and even such an unreasonable man as Hertzer cannot suspect her of subterfuge. We shall only have his jealousy to reckon with."

Having received indignant enlightenment concerning the proposal, he still stuck to his guns. "Confound his cheek! Yet she's the safer for it. By all means, let her go."

And go she did—after a pitched battle next day with Magdaleno, who held to Mrs. Ewing's opinion. "'Twas on the last trip to the river the olla was broken," the faithful old fellow grumbled. "But so it was always with the Colonel, thy father. Forever poking the eagle nose of him into the place of danger. Scatter the people, sayest thou? Nay, but I can hold both thee and the place for three days till the coming of Don David."

And when she rode away he called after, "I feel it in my bones that this is folly, and if it be that thou breakest not thy fast here at Verda manana, thou wilt see my hot spurs at La Luna."

It was late in the afternoon that Consuela reined in on the very knoll from which David and Hertzer had overlooked La Luna more than a year ago. As then, the rubber lay at her feet, ruling off thousands of acres with dark-green lines like those on a sheet of foolscap. All around the jungle tossed its uneven masses, flecked here and there with a scum of wild *platinas*, brown of clump cedar, isles of palms in the lighter green of tree foliage. Luxuriously beautiful, it swam in the rich glow, tawny lights of a low sun; but, though she had paused to observe it, her eyes drew instead to Hertzer's Yaquis, whose line was strung a quarter-mile on either side of the hill.

In fulfilment of Hertzer's assertion that he would "clean La Luna an inch below ground before the rains," they had mowed a half-mile swath twice across the plantation in the last month, and the slaughtered *monte* cumbered the entire surface a foot deep. Fried to a crisp by the fierce sun, it loaded down the air with dank essences, odors of new-mown hay acrid in their strength.

Though Hertzer had given these, his slaves, treatment such as his miserable *enganchadores* had never heard of—even in dreams—allowing a three-hour *siesta* during the noon heat, giving them better food, dry clothing, and such care that he had brought them through the last rains with scarcely a death, the tropics had yet taken heavy toll of their flesh. Where their sweaty cottons had once stretched over bulging muscles, they now flapped loosely. Perpetual labor had humped square shoulders, bent straight backs; sullen eyes glowed like smouldering coals in sunken sockets. But if stripped to the foundations of bone, their hostile glances at the *cabos* who stood behind the line—one to every ten—with Winchesters cocked for use, told that the stubborn Yaqui spirit remained unbroken. Of them all, but one displayed his former physique—David's big Yaqui, who stood with his back turned half-way down the hill. Promoted through Hertzer's whim to the comparative ease of a caboship, he had regained his magnificence of flesh, upon which his thin *camisa* lay like a second skin, moving with the serpent play of muscle. The one *cabo* without a rifle—for the whim had stopped short of suicide—he leaned upon his *machete*, silent, motionless. Consuela thought he was lost in reverie till that occurred which permitted her to see—as David once saw in the fight in the glade—him spring, without a quiver of warning, out of absolute rest into violent action.

The *monte* always abounds with snakes which glide, a writhing brood, ahead of the cleaners: snakes big and little, *tethuanas*, *ashuadores*, fat and thin, from the deadly *vipero* to the twenty-foot python, one of which now suddenly loosed his battering-ram of a nose from low ambush and knocked a man head over heels. Echoing his yell, the men on his either side sprang, swinging their *machetes* as the serpent recoiled, jaws spread wide for the seizing stroke. But, quicker than they, the Yaqui leaped from his rest as it flashed out and took off the head with a single blow.

From first to last it passed in the wink of an eye, while Consuela opened her mouth to scream. Almost before she had time to close it, the fallen man returned with a grunt to his work, the Yaqui stilled the body's lashings with a few pounding blows along the spine and was back in his place, motionless, abstracted as ever—apparently, for he spoke as she rode by to look at the snake.

"Do not look this way, señorita. But tell me that it is a lie of the cabos that the Señor Hertzer has driven Don David away?"

A glance to her right revealed the reason for the caution—Patricia and Hertzer, who had just ridden around from behind a patch of uncut *monte;* and she had just time to answer, "It is a lie," and to catch his whispered "Sta'uena!" before they rode up.

"Hello, young lady! Back again?"

His welcoming smile caused her the usual compunction; she was glad when he turned to examine the snake. "Carambara! but he's big; a hundred pounds, at least. Hit that fellow, you say? Lucky for him that it didn't get a coil around him. One squeeze would stave in the ribs of an ox. I must have it skinned. Mounted on scarlet, it will make a gorgeous trophy for your room."

Coming up, Patricia had returned a cool nod to Consuela's greeting, and, while Hertzer rattled along with almost boyish eagerness, she sat her horse, sullenly pouting. Variable as vindictive, inheriting with her Indian blood the caprice natural in savage peoples, her manner in the last three weeks had oscillated between warmth almost affectionate, when alone with Consuela, to sullen jealousy in presence

459

of her father or, for matter of that, any other white planter. So, knowing that she would presently thaw, Consuela ignored her coldness.

This came to pass riding homeward. Bursting out in sudden laughter, the uncontrollable hilarity which the evil plight of another excites in a savage, she alternately tittered and shrieked while pointing at a reddish patch on the white of Consuela's skirt.

"Pinililleas," Hertzer answered the girl's puzzled glance. "You are covered with them."

Her first experience with the microscopic pests, which cling in their millions upon jungle foliage, Consuela tried to brush them off, whereupon Patricia redoubled her laughter. "You can't do it!" she cried. "It is a tub and a complete change for you, my lady—as quickly as you can make it." Yet she was quick to offer a change of her own when Consuela cried out in dismay that all her things were at Verda; moreover, on their arrival at the house, she hurried her into her own room, even helped her undress, exclaiming that the pests would be all over her.

As they already were. Sinking through her clothing in the few minutes required to gallop in, the atoms settled like sparks of fire upon her flesh; caused her such discomfort that she forgot David's letter—which she had pinned for safety on the inner side of her blouse—until, returning from her bath, she saw that her clothing was gone.

"Your things?" Patricia, who was exchanging her tight habit for cool white, carelessly repeated her question. "They were swarming, so I bundled them up for Pancha to take down to the river."

For the moment Consuela choked, then, realizing the need of hurry, she dressed quickly and ran for the river, where, after a vigorous sousing, she found Pancha beating the blouse on a bowlder. Held up for inspection, it still displayed the pin and piece of water-soaked envelope, so she returned to the house at ease, though greatly vexed—vexation that would have given place to active alarm had she known that the enclosures were even then in Patricia's hands.

Like the hum of their opposites, the busy bees, the drone of Consuela's lazy scholars floated across a band of fierce sunlight in through the window by which Patricia sat reading David's letter for the second time. Just what was her intention toward it would be hard to say. Most probably she had none. Her expression revealed an even mixture of amusement and contempt, with just a flavor of the relief which any girl would feel on being removed from the shadow of a stepmother; for if David's insensibility to her beauty had piqued a dominant jealousy which brooked no competition, demanded allegiance from every one, at this time and distance the feeling was not sufficiently strong to urge her to an act which she must have known would be fraught with serious consequences. If Hertzer had followed his custom and gone out to the camp instead of lounging with cigars and paper under her window, events would most likely have shaped toward a quiet conclusion. But when, glancing out, she saw that he was listening for Consuela's voice to punctuate the drone, her smile set in sudden scorn. When, sauntering over, he leaned in the doorway looking on with a pleased smile, the amber of her eyes deepened to red-brown, flared into actual red as, returning, he paused to scrape the python skin which was curing in the sun.

"You old fool!"

Unaware till then of her presence, he looked up quickly and caught the red glow, bitter scorn of her face through the dim veil of window-screen. In all their quarrels—which were frequent and furious in inverse proportion to the tiger affection that obtained between them—she had never used a tone so bitterly resentful. A trifle nonplussed, he stood, flushed and a little foolish, till she repeated it, throwing wide the screen: "You *old* fool!" Then he strode forward, the flush of discovered sentimentality deepening to the red of anger.

"What do you mean?"

"As if you didn't know!" She sustained his gray glare. "That look was worthy of old Tomas in sight of a new enganchada. It would be positively pathetic—if it was not so ridiculous. You and your schools! When you forced me to invite her here, I said that you'd get no good of it, that she was no Tehuana to be bought with a tin of sardines! And now—read that!"

As aforesaid, a man may measure others only by himself, and out of the fulness of his contempt he had scoffed at the very idea that a girl of Consuela's mettle could be in love with sober David. It was so unbelievable that even now his brain refused for the moment to accept the evidence of his eyes. Aware of the heat and glare beyond the brown shade of the eaves, he continued to stare down at the letter till Consuela's voice broke again on the somnolent drone. Then it came, the realization, and as he thought of the way in which he had been tricked, blinded, managed till the plot should be ripe for his thwarting, remembered his confidences, proposal, there flamed up within him the most furious passion of his furious life.

His *machete* hung with his belt and guns over the back of his chair, but the enormous impulse which swelled through every muscle permitted no thought of weapons. The letter crackled and tore under a fierce, unconscious clutch. Barehanded, bareheaded, blind, he strode from the veranda out into the sunlight, then paused, blinking, at a sudden hail.

"Hello, where are you going in such a hurry?"

It was Phelps, coming up the garden-path; and, conscious of his queer, inquisitive look, Hertzer thrust the letter into his pocket as he turned away. "I was going to cut a pineapple for your lunch. Come and choose it."

"Been fighting with Patricia again," Phelps thought. "I have good news," he said, aloud, as Hertzer stopped in the middle of the pineapples. "My folks have answered at last. They'll sublet the work at your price."

As the other was now stooped over the fruit, Phelps could not see the sudden sullen writhing of his face. It was the last insult of a humiliating fate to tender this empty husk of a petty success after robbing him of the ripe fruit. A curse rose to his lips, but he repressed it and heard himself answering, as in a hot dream:

"That's fine; we'll talk over the details after lunch."

Pleading a bilious headache, he refused to go in to the meal; lay at length on his bed, the big bulk of him quivering under gushes of passion, conscious of the talk at the table, which mixed in an odd jumble with angry memories, scraps of furious thought. Nor did he come out till Consuela had called in her afternoon school.

"I have to go over to the new camp," he then said to Phelps, who was smoking outside. "Come along; we can talk over your business on the way."

And talk he did, of this, that, the other—discussed an intention of buying in the sugar *finca* to supply his *galeras*, spoke of the number of men he would throw into Phelps's rubber, and came to an agreement as to the date of the first and periods between subsequent cleanings. At the camp he gave orders, settled small problems, seemed interested in Phelps's comments. But it was all superficial, overlaid the seething feeling which would send a shiver through his every limb in the middle of a sentence. Usually he paused, before leaving, to crack a rough joke with the women, who were not insensible to the vacancy at La Luna made by Rosa's dismissal. But whereas their glances—which ranged from the invitation of experience to the tentative timidity of virginity—had caused him much amusement, to-day he saw neither them, their fluttering pageant of color, always a delight to his eye, nor the sunset lights that shot the jungle with silken glamours as they journeyed homeward.

Coming out, he had entertained some dim notion that Phelps would ride on home from the camp, and those shivers of passion were premonitory of the flood that would burst the dams of his repression the moment he was alone. But he was doomed to harbor it longer, for Phelps turned with him.

"The relieving officer — that's my governor, you know—remitted my quarter's salary the other day, and I've a hunch to win back the hundred you robbed me of last week." Nor was he to be dissuaded by the dry answer:

"You'll be more likely to lose another."

Arrived at La Luna, they found the two girls, in cool white, waiting for them in the dusk under the eaves. Already a little repentant, Patricia studied her father's face with an anxiety which increased as, passing in, he returned only a nod to their greetings. If surprised at his sudden coldness, his pleasant manner all that morning prevented Consuela from divining the truth, and when he returned only monosyllables to her conversation at dinner without even looking her way, she jumped to the most probable conclusion — "Señor Phelps has told him about my letter"; a suspicion which was confirmed by an incident that occurred as they sat later at play.

Ordinarily, Phelps would not have done it. But if, as aforesaid, he now stood a little in awe of her, he had by no means forgiven her snubs, and when repeated losses had irritated his somewhat vixenish temper, he remembered and looked at her across the table, womanish resentment in his small, sparkling eyes.

"By the way," he asked, "who has heard from David?"

It came so suddenly that Consuela could not restrain her colors. Conscious of Hertzer's quick look, Patricia's face of angry alarm, she bent over the bit of sewing she was doing for her Yaqui maid till the red tide faded. When she looked up her eyes were full of scorn.

"Don't you know his writing?"

Aware, on his part, of Patricia's furious eyes, the touch of contempt in Hertzer's cold gaze, Phelps tried to carry it off with a forced laugh. "Oh, so it *was* from him? And how is the good boy?"

"Very well," she answered, quietly.

If he appreciated her quick understanding, the lightning intuition that steered her away from useless evasion, no glint of approval was revealed in Hertzer's expression.

"Your lead, Phelps," he broke in, with sharp impatience, and the game went on.

Despite her calmness, Consuela was dreadfully

shaken, and as she bent again to her sewing Patricia's woman's eyes detected the trembling of the needle that betrayed her whirl of frightened thought. A stealthy glance showed Hertzer's face, cold, gray, unwarmed by the gold of the lamp; the kindly lines gone; nothing left but the old suspicious mask, beneath which the delicate antennæ of her fears sensed his seething passion. What to do? The black jungle had fewer terrors than she read into his cold face, and at first she thought of trying to steal away on foot to Verda. But if the case were desperate as that, he would surely provide against her escape. Further reflection warned against any deviation from her usual programme. Ignorant as she was of the fulness of his knowledge, she reasoned that his spasm of jealousy would probably cool through the night; and much as she disliked Phelps, she thought with immense relief of his statement—made at dinner—that he would stay all night. For the present she must appear unconcerned. So, laying aside her needlework, she drew a chair close to Patricia's and laughed, gossiped, helped to play her hand, displaying animation beyond her usual; withal, took care to retire first, in view of a possible tête-à-tête.

"And we can ride together in the morning," she took care to add, saying good-night to Phelps.

Outside, a white moon rode brilliantly, etching in warm black the wandlike branches, pendent leaves of the shading rubber on the pale yellow ribbon of garden-path, barring the pit blackness inside her *jacale* with soft shafts of light. Tiptoeing to her *catre*, for the Yaqui maid's sleep-breathing pulsed through the darkness, she sat down, but had no more than undone the first button of her waist before Hertzer's harsh voice floated in from the house, and she hastily fastened it again.

"I've had enough. You two play on—if you like."

"No object to win from Patricia," came Phelps's cackling laugh. "Her hate more than balances the cash. Bed for me."

Followed a scrape of chairs, and, flying across the floor as the screen-door banged, she peeped through the pole-siding and saw them step out in the moonlight. So light it was she could see the smoke of Phelps's cigar ascending in a thin white spiral. She shrank as Hertzer glanced her way—shrank, but returned quickly and watched till his bulk faded among the shadowy buildings. She could still hear them talking, caught Phelps's "good-night." Then, while her heart thrummed like a low drum on the silence, she waited, waited, waited—waited till a dark figure formed again out of the shadows. Up the path he came as far as the veranda, then—her heart actually stopped beating—turned and headed straight for her door.

With a low gasp of fear she stepped to awaken her maid; with a quick change of intention she flew to the table upon which lay the knife Hertzer had lent her to sharpen pencils that morning. Two strokes cut

THE "QUEEN" IS "CASTLED"

the slim *bejucas* which bound the pole-siding in place, but, as she made to shove it aside, her hand recoiled from a prick sharper, more painful, than that of a thorn—once a storehouse, the *jacale* was wired from roof to ground.

Turning, knife in hand, she waited, back against the wall, eyes straining across the bars of moonlight to the door.

XXVII

THE TRAVAIL OF A NIGHT

FRESH gravel had been spread around the house in readiness for the rains, and Consuela heard it crunch under a heavy foot. But though the steps led up to her door, it neither moved nor shook during a half-minute of breathless waiting. Surprised, she then edged along, back flat against the wall, to the corner, and peeped through the siding. Nothing moved in the moonlight without. Another minute of strained listening, and she continued her sidling progress along that wall to the door, peeped, and— almost laughed in her relief; for there, rolled up in his *zarape*, lay old Tomas, face turned up to the light, gently snoring.

Hard on the heels of relief came weakness, so sudden and complete that she collapsed in a heap by the door. But with a return of nervousness, she sat up to renew her watch, and thus saw what she had nearly missed—a flutter of dull crimson, as Patricia slid from the dusk under the eaves into the shadows of the rubber along the path. With her disappearance among the buildings ensued a murmur of voices, too low for Consuela to catch the scorn with which the girl threw the responsibility for her own fault on to Phelps's shoulders.

"You know what the Padre is," she hissed, through a chink, answering his mumbled apologies, "and you shouldn't have done it. Now he has put Tomas on guard at her door. Well, you got her into it, and it is you that will have to get her out. The Padre is prowling around somewhere, so don't try it yet. Give him an hour to get to bed, then have the *veledor* bring out your horse—oh, tell him anything, that you prefer riding by moonlight, and don't wish to wake the house; he's stupid. Go softly, but, when you are once away, ride hard to Las Glorias and tell the Señor Ewing that I said he must come for her at once."

Thus it was that—long after Patricia had crept back to her bed with mind at ease concerning the complexion her own part would now wear in the affair—thus it was that Consuela came to hear the faint tramp of a horse an hour or so later. Crediting the sound, however, to the nervous exhaustion which was causing her to see a dozen Hertzers in every shadow, she stole back to her *catre* and lay down fully dressed, ears still trained to every sound. But though she waited, waited while the *galera* bell spaced off the hot black hours with recurrent melancholy tolling, waited till sleep like a soft thief mercifully stole her anxieties, she heard only the Yaqui girl's soft breathing, punctuated by an occasional snore from old Tomas.

THE PLANTER

For Hertzer was in the jungle.

After routing out Tomas, he struck straight down the plantation road to its end, then turned on to an overgrown path, black as a tunnel save where an occasional rift of moonlight sliced the thick darkness with a silver blade. Although he had thirsted all day for this moment, the solitude that would afford opportunity to pause, think, formulate the chaos of impulses behind his slow shivers, he did not cast off the leash at once. Though, moreover, he had realized in the mean time the consequences of David's victory, knew that it sapped his ambition in its foundations; though chagrin at his own blindness inflamed jealousy; though, lastly, the memories of that morning's hope, soft reflections, now lashed his raw pride, yet his habit of cold restraint held until, mounting with the blood of exercise, his passion overtopped, flooded out his dams of stony repression.

But when they went? As, just then, a narrow glade chanced to bisect his tunnel, a blaze of moonlight revealed his eyes, glazed and snapping like fire behind ice; coarse mouth working, face writhed, twisted in every line. Thrust pugnaciously forward, his heavy chin gave his profile a salience that was accentuated by the Jew-hang of his neck. With club arms upraised, thumbs hooked as though sunk in soft flesh, he was inexpressibly simian. Divested of human semblance, he loomed for a pause in that wonderful tropical moonlight, mouthing, clutching like some crazed gorilla ere the urge of his passion drove him on into the tunnel, — which presently emerged on a small clearing that was dotted with low mounds.

It was his secret cemetery, the dark annex—to be found on every plantation—established partly to avoid the trouble and expense of burial and registration at the nearest municipal graveyard, in accordance with the law, but principally to avoid the shock which might accrue to even a lax Mexican public opinion by exposure of the frightful plantation death rates. Full three hundred in number, harvest of scant five years, they lay under his eyes, the graves of his dead slaves, bathed in the soft peace of moonlight.

Coming with such suddenness upon them—for he had taken no heed of the path—he might have been expected to evince fright, nervousness, or awe. Only a few feet away—if rumor did not lie—lay one whom he had killed with a blow of his iron fist. Not one but had welcomed the death that gave ease from his oppressions. But though his vivid imagination peopled the glade with dim, haggard shapes, his sudden scowl displayed only an accentuation of anger during the pause he stood overlooking their shadowy number. Perhaps in that bitter moment he felt their quiet sleep as an affront which mocked his turmoil with its untroubled peace. Some emanation of reproach certainly penetrated through his whirl of passion, for, straining to his full height, he shook his big fist at the graves.

THE PLANTER

"I'd do it again! God d—— you all, I'd do it again!"

Here the path ended, but his *machete* hung at his shoulder; unsheathing it as he crossed the glade between graves, he crashed like a bull in pain through the light outer brush, and plunged on, mowing his way with right and left strokes. Usually he would have dropped into the bed of an *arroyo* to skirt around inextricable *bejuca* tangles, but in the fury that sought only an outlet for the passion that smothered thought, clogged purpose, he bored through dense thickets, pressed on, insensible of direction save that, bearing always toward the checkered light which bespoke the clear under tall trees, he unconsciously followed the circle of the moon. One hour, two, three, he followed her pale guidance; at first from choice, later with the idea of getting back home, followed until, dripping with sweat—for even his enormous strength felt the drain of such furious exertion in the thick hot night— he came out on a path and sat down to rest, the madness gone with the gorged blood from his brain.

Not that he was less angry, for if his passion had burned down to red coals, it burst again into flame under the slightest breath of his thought. As, after a short rest, he rose and pursued the path, anger, jealousy, rancor of disappointed ambition possessed him in turn. When, with a vicious "Heugh!" he sliced a six-inch *bejuca*, it was David's head that fell. The hands that shot up above the simian mask of lust, clutched Consuela's flesh. A scintillant blaze, green

474

as the blink of a wolf, defied David, Ewing, Fate itself to take her from him. Anger, jealousy, rancor, lust, they ruled him, the worst of his passions—all save avarice, for, to do him justice, this meanest of all had no place in their evil census. Not once had he paused to count the cost—of loss or revenge. And he needs this further justice. One by one the more ignoble were vanquished by the others. Desire and lust, with their wild imaginings, mental degradations, were consumed in the bright flame of his anger, leaving him possessed by a nobler, if deadlier hate, passion of revenge; burned out so completely that the ashes refused even a glow to a sight that might otherwise have raised a soaring flame—the pair of lovers whom he found by the trail.

Though the path had seemed familiar, there had been nothing in its dim succession of glades, tangles, long dark temples roofed with black lace and silver, to distinguish it from any of a dozen others, but now he knew. Since the pair stole out from his new camp to bed in the shadows on a couch of leaves, the moon had sailed a quarter circle, and now, breaking down through a rift in the foliage, betrayed their tryst, showed the man's arm lying across the girl's opulent bust. Unconscious of Hertzer's frown, they slept on in the full fruition of the love that had been denied his hope that day; for the carpet of leaves which had deadened his approach masked his passage as he went by to drain his cup of its dregs.

By what strange fate had he been guided—first to

the graves, next to this, the edifice he had tried to erect on their ghastly foundation, a ruin before completion? A minute, and they rose before him, the roofs of his new camp, pale gold fretted with sharp shadows, with here and there the red eye of a watch-fire winking in the midst of a duller inflammation, the crimson garments of sleeping women. There it lay, the great camp of his visionings—without a function. For well he knew that with Verda and Las Glorias gone, it would hardly pay to contract labor to the smaller plantations. True, the Isthmus, with scores of abandoned plantations, still remained? Equally true that every dollar so far expended had come out of the pockets of Osgood & Short? But the beginnings had been here, and a dozen years of scheming, saving, would be required to bring them again.

A dozen years? Forty-six—fifty-six—fifty-eight? He would then be nearly sixty—at the end of his prime? It wasn't worth while! And as, in opposition to this cruel fact, there flashed up in his memory the vision of wealth and power he had seen from this very spot less than a month ago, he was seized with a convulsion, agony of despairing hate, consuming desire for revenge.

Tall jungle masked the eastern sky, but as he stood overlooking the camp, steeped in thoughts of reprisals, the deep indigo above thinned out to dark gray, the moon's waxen pallor warned him that his passion had outworn the night. As he had come out of the jungle on the trail that led in to the plateau from Phelps's place, the camp lay between him and home, and having no stomach for the curiosity his presence on foot at that hour would excite in the Zacatecores, he footed softly back past the lovers to come round by the longer way.

A stiff walk of an hour and a half, daylight caught him at the forks of the main trail. The sun rose as he crossed the La Luna boundary. But, early as it was, other travellers were both before and behind him —Ewing, then coming along at a fast gallop a mile or so away; Magdaleno, who, roused by Phelps in the middle of the night, had taken horse at once without waiting for the morning.

Of the latter Hertzer now received news from the senior *cabo*, whom he met herding the Yaquis out to the field. "It is that he comes to Tomas in the dead of night with a tale that little Anita, the señorita's favorite scholar, is sick unto death, and when Tomas answers him that it is not meet to break the young mistress's sleep for a brat of an enganchador, he outs with the machete, this Magdaleno, and clouts Tomas over the head."

"And he took her away?" Now only half a mile away, Ewing heard the boom of the great voice.

"No, señor." The *cabo* touched a bloody cloth that bound his head. "At Tomas's yell we ran—and were needed. He fought like the seven devils of Quatla, and it took the six of us to beat him down. He now lies in the galera."

THE PLANTER

"And Tomas?"

The man grinned. "His thick head was none the worse of it, señor. He still guards the door."

Moving on, Hertzer had barely gained half-way home before Ewing overtook him. Ignorant, as yet, of Phelps's departure, he could not suspect the planter of having received warning; nor would it have made any difference if he had; ready, ay, thirsting for open war, he turned at the clatter of hoofs, blackly glowering.

"Fine morning, you say? Humph! You must have started in the middle of the night."

Now, if Ewing had known the extent of the other's knowledge, he would not have attempted further subterfuge. But as Phelps had taken care to paint the affair in the light of an uncomfortable situation following a careless jest, he was doing his best to justify his early appearance when Hertzer suddenly cut him off.

"Nonsense, you didn't come out this early to see me. Out with it! You are after the girl."

"I did think of"—riding back with her, he was going to say, but Hertzer again burst in—"carrying her off to Las Glorias to laugh with you at me?"

"What do I mean?" Swelling to his full height, he stood for a moment covering the other with his black glower, then out it came, the full knowledge he had from David's letter, in a breathless storm of words. Finishing, his voice dropped from its booming anger to a quiet that was wicked in its slow

478

suppression. "So you set her on to fool me with her smiles and soft sympathy while you stole Verda out of my hands? Weren't you afraid? Didn't you pause long enough to think of what a dangerous game she was playing? Man!" he boomed out again. "Man! I'd break you—break the two of you with my bare hands—if it wasn't that I can hurt you more through her. She's played? Now let her pay."

Though he flushed at the threat, Ewing restrained himself from active resentment, and answered with quiet good humor: "If you must have a victim, I would rather it were me. But come, come, Hertzer, be reasonable; look facts in the face. I don't know where you obtained your information, but granting it is true, I fail to see where you are wronged. You tried to do up David, to take Verda, in which every penny of his mother's fortune is invested, and you can't blame him for defending himself. As for my interest—it came naturally out of his efforts."

"David?" The glower drew into a sneer. "If he'd sat quiet when he first came down, instead of trying to teach old planters their business, I'd have been his good neighbor. Even when he was breeding discontent with his measly reforms and flouted his damned morals in my face, I let him alone. It wasn't until the prig refused me his hand after coming between me and my slave that I started to do him up. Looks as though I hadn't made much of a success," he added, with a sour grin, "but at least I've got the girl.

"What has she done?" he repeated, defiantly. "That is for me to know, and I don't have to chop logic with you about it. Sufficient that she's to pay."

His manner was so obstinately resolute that Ewing cried out, in sharp alarm: "Take care, Hertzer! If you mistreat her, you'll raise every planter on the Isthmus against you."

"Yes?" he sneered again. "They have all been so good to the Mexican women in their own galeras. Their cabores don't gamble for what's left after they've taken the pick for themselves?"

"Look here, Hertzer," Ewing earnestly reasoned, "Consuela is no enganchada, but a girl of good breeding, delicately reared."

"Good breeding?" He broke out in harsh mockery of laughter. "In other words, she possesses a trifle more than the ordinary greaser of the blood of the Spaniards, who debauched the Aztec mothers. Delicately reared, eh? by La Señora Morales, who has sold hundreds as good as herself to the slavery of the galeras? And now you raise hands of horror because she must travel their road."

"What!" Ewing gasped his unbelief of the suggestion. "You don't mean to say that you intend to enganchar her?"

"Maybe—and why not? A Mexican woman more or less doesn't cut much figure in the cook-house. In fact, I'm a trifle short-handed at present—only have five women to grind tortillas for fifty men."

His sudden sardonic grin prompted Ewing to try

again. "Oh, come, you know you're joking. What's done is done. Let's shake hands all round and settle down to be good friends and neighbors. I'll ride in with you to breakfast before I take her home?"

But the other drew back from his outstretched hand. "Joking or not, you won't ride in—unless you wish to join Magdaleno in the galera. As for taking her home?" His grin grew offensive with its evil suggestion. "Don't trouble. I'll send her home—after a while."

With a shrug of his big shoulders, he strode on, nor paused, though he answered Ewing's last warning. "Remember, you'll raise the Isthmus against you?"

"Let it rise. I'm short-handed, as I told you, and I'll enganchar the bunch to work in the fields."

Arrived at the buildings, he did not go near the house. Entering Tomas's *jacale*, he had the woman prepare coffee, then went to the store to wait on a Zacateco customer; thereafter served out the *galera* rations of corn, rice, and bones for soup to the cook-house women; busied himself throughout the morning with the usual affairs of the day. There was no hurry. Besides the malicious pleasure he took in the thought of Consuela's suspense, the coming of night was necessary to a refinement of the revenge he had in contemplation. So to guard against premature explosion of the passion that shook him at intervals, at noon he followed after the mule which carried *tortillas* and *frijoles* for the mid-day meal to the men in the field.

THE PLANTER

Sitting out there, in the shade of the rubber, he made a curious study of his *cabos'* faces as they grouped around the mule. Coarse brutes, the bad men of the Isthmus tribes who had drifted through sheer fitness into his service, their loose mouths, squat heads, distended nostrils of squat noses, indicated ineffable grossness, yet, studying them, his face evidenced a fierce satisfaction as though they fitted his purpose. He thrilled with an exultance so furiously savage that he had to turn away his face. And it seized him again, that fierce exultation. As, later, he sat on a stump overlooking the work in place of the *cabo* he had sent to relieve Tomas's watch, it seized and shook him at intervals with a frenzy that caused him to spring up and pace back and forth the length of the line.

It was while walking off one of these excesses that he paused opposite the Yaqui *cabo*. Observing him, a trifle of malevolence adulterated the speculation in his glance, the characteristic look of question, such a one as a hardened inquisitor might have bestowed on his victim ere he gave a last turn to the rack. Subtle insolence inhered in his remark:

"Thy men work well."

"They work well."

As, omitting the usual glib señor, and without even looking his way, the Yaqui gave answer, a flicker of approval lightened Hertzer's malevolence, but vanished as he spoke again. "Had they fought as well as they work—"

THE TRAVAIL OF A NIGHT

It returned, however, and in greater measure as, still looking to his front the other parried the taunt. "'We be greater than thou,' said the buzzards to the wounded hawk."

"But Mexicans?" Hertzer continued his malicious probing. "Had the gringo conquered thee, there could have been no question. But" — he used the contemptuous nickname of the American border — "greasers?"

"The coyotes in their swarms devoured the mountain-lion."

"I heard it the other way—that the coyote lay with the she-lion. Is it true, as the Mexicans say, that the cowardly Gentilos crept into the tents of the Yaquis and begot a base spawn while the hunters were away?"

Uttering the insult, a gleam of expectation replaced curiosity in his look, and gave way to disappointment when the other's stoicism withstood the insult. Receiving no answer, he suddenly asked, "What is that mark on thy neck?"

"Ask thy machete."

"And thy throat?"

"The teeth of the hound that saved thee thy head."

"Ah, yes, the hound." Head thrust out, eyes gleaming, teeth showing through his grin, he went on: "I had thought it a woman. The hound? Bueno! But see, here is no hound!" Interpreting the man's swift glance, he added: "The cabores, is it, with the rifles? But some day . . . when there are no cabores . . . neither a rifle—"

483

THE PLANTER

"I shall kill thee."

The conviction, absolute certainty in his sudden, dark glance would have given most men pause, but Hertzer only laughed as he walked away—to return again and again during the afternoon. Under urge of his freakish humor, he sometimes talked seriously of the Yaqui wars, plying the man with questions that revealed both knowledge and sympathetic understanding. "God!" he cried, once, "why did you do that? Couldn't you see they'd get you?" And again at the tale of a battle, "I'd have given a leg to be there!" Yet on the very next round he would renew the baiting, tempt mutiny with taunts and insults, in which curious alternation the afternoon slid away, for not until he followed the haggard line in through a hot red dusk did his mood change.

Then he relapsed into ominous quiet. Despatching the sick, feeding the well, he spoke hardly a word—was equally taciturn when, having eaten the meal Tomas's woman served in the store, he called four of his *cabos* before him.

"You can throw a riata?" he asked, and, receiving assent from all, gave his orders. "You, Angel, will go to the forks of Señor Carruthers' trail with Pedro—while Timoteo and Pancha lie in the madera across the ford. If the train be anywhere near its time, Don David should pass on one or other road in the next hour. To whosoever he falls, see that you make a sure cast about the arms, then bring him to me—alive."

THE TRAVAIL OF A NIGHT

Left alone, he relapsed into heavy brooding; sat for a long time, chin on hand, elbow propped on the rough table. His lamp threw a golden glow over tins of *chilis*, *galletas*, boxes and barrels ranged along the walls, with piles of maise and *frijoles* in sacks, showed the gay cottons that shared a few shelves with his small stock of American canned goods. Outside, a dull glare, barred with black, told that his women were still at work on the *tortillas* for the morrow's dark breakfast; and in through the open door came the noises of the night—confused mutter from the *galera*, wranglings of two *cabos* over a game of Mexican *monte*, laughter of Tomas's woman as he growled and grumbled at the tedium of his watch, the low singing in nasal falsetto of the *cabo* who had relieved him. But he neither saw nor heard. Turned to the light, his face showed a dark quiet, brows bent over eyes that were narrowed in retrospection; for by some process of association he was carried far back in the past. As in a series of moving pictures, he saw the current of his life flowing across the warm curtain of night at the open door.

Working, loving, spending, fighting, he saw himself doing one or another under urge of impulses and instinct that had come down to him from he knew not where, and which reacted against conditions that he had not made, could not control. He saw Hertzer, the boy, brawling in the hot, fetid slums of tropical ports; Hertzer the trader, cheating both for the love of it and lest he himself be cheated; Hertzer, the planter, extracting the life essences of his miserable contract slaves, bleeding the companies he served, trampling, in the instinct that shoved him forward, all who stood in the way. And to his hot mind it all seemed logical —for the boy to strike when he was stricken, to love when a woman smiled; for the man to mount on the bodies of those who would have made a stepping-stone of him; nor could he see an opening through which either might have escaped that set course. Granting those inherited instincts at work within fixed conditions, it was all inevitable as a doom; and with the thought of himself as a blind atom awhirl in a process of life, there arose within him, first a sense of injury at the fate which had cast his birth amid the fierce squalor of the Trieste boarding-house; then a feeling of justification for all that he had done or had it in mind to do.

"Nine o'clock." He rose and glanced at his watch after an hour of that black brooding. Then muttering, "He ought to be here now; I'll give him another hour," he went outside and stood for a while gazing at the moon, the red moon which had just peeped at David over the top of the trees.

It was the hour at which he invariably visited the *galera*, and after the moon's bronze paled to silver he walked over and entered the building. At one end a screen of barbed wire fenced off a few feet of the building into a sort of room, wherein the *veledor* could hold the night watch safe from the weather, and, peering through it, Hertzer saw a dim figure pacing and repacing the aisle between long rows of bunks.

"It is Magdaleno," the *veledor* whispered. "He walks it thus since morning."

Turning at the whisper, the *mandador's* face was revealed by the dim light of a single lantern, bruised and caked with dry blood, eyes burning hotly beneath a soiled bandage. For a space he stood, looking their way, but they were lost in thick darkness behind the screen, and, crediting the whisper to some dreamer, he walked on to the far end of the aisle. As, returning, he again approached the light, a man raised on his elbow in the upper tier of bunks, and Hertzer recognized the Yaqui *cabo*. Their voices came to him only as a murmur, but it was easy to read the sympathy in the man's dark face. A man less mad would have been impressed, at least, by that sinister whispering, but Hertzer merely grinned when, as the *mandador's* voice rose a tone, he caught the words "Don David" coupled with "*manana*."

"Nay," he muttered, going out. "If Timoteo has any luck, you shall have him with you to-night."

Returning to the store, he resumed his reverie, only this time his thought did not go back of the bitter present. Once more his passions swept him in unruled alternation, and as he sat staring at the lamp for the better part of an hour his face clearly mirrored their changes, now lighting to a flash of emotion, again darkening under a quick frown. At the close of the

hour a sudden gray writhing marked his realization
of a grim joke of fate.

Driven by centuries of oppression to build his
happiness within his family circle, domesticity has
become first nature with the Jew, and though hate
now possessed Hertzer in place of love, though the
very memory of his infatuation caused him angry
loathing, it had yet opened vistas of a softer life that
could not but appeal to the son of his Jew mother.
The stronger for that hate was it borne in upon him
that the succession of mistresses at his hearth had
sat there in default of the one, the wife who alone could
make his house a home with the prattle of herself and
children. Very clearly, he saw how the fates had
tangled him in the net he had spread for his enemy.
For while he had tried, first, to win Consuela in despite
of David, her small hands had reached down through
his feeling and unloosed an enormous domestic
instinct. Come what might, let him glut himself
with revenge, the hungers she had aroused would still
remain for his torture, the happiness he had glimpsed
through her was gone forever. With burning resentment he realized it, with a deadliness of hate that
brought him to his feet with a venomous oath.

"Half after ten." He glanced at his watch. "He's
stayed all night with Carruthers. I'll wait no longer."

His pistols lay with his *machete* upon the counter,
but in that sudden rush of feeling he forgot both
them and the light, which sent a yellow stream after
him out through the open door. Round the corner,

into the garden, he was borne on that angry tide—
there to receive a check, for at the click of the gate
Patricia moved out of the shadows under the rubber
and stood in his path.

All through that day the girl had lived in a hell of
mean fear, under a strain that had drawn haggard
lines about her full mouth and drained her healthy
colors. It was not that she repented her treachery or
was sorry for Consuela. Safe-guarded against remorse
by her natural vindictiveness, she would have looked
calmly on while events took their course if there had
been no after consequences. But, thinking of these,
she had cowered before the storm of her own raising,
strove vainly to avert its bursting.

The quality of her feeling displayed itself in her
pleading. "Padre! Padre! Please don't! If you
harm her, none of our white neighbors will ever speak
to us again."

Though the moonlight blanched her cold face until
the eyes shone dark and wide in the midst of its
whiteness, like the picture of some distressed saint, he
instantly detected the underlying selfishness. "The
neighbors, is it? Pity you didn't think of them
before. Is it only for them you plead? Off with you
to bed."

But as he thrust her aside she leaped upon him,
locked her fingers around his neck, babbling her
selfish fears. "You sha'n't! I tell you, you sha'n't
spoil my every chance. Only the other night the
Señor Boulton— You sha'n't! Sha'n't!"

THE PLANTER

His hands went up to break her grip, but, wheeling to a sudden change of purpose, he carried her back to the store, threw her in, and locked the door in the face of her rush. As he went back up the path, she ran across the store and called to him through the siding, renewed her prayers and pleadings, but he held right on. In another minute he was standing at Consuela's door watching the *cabo* shuffle through the moonlight toward his own *jacale*. When he was swallowed in the shadowy buildings Hertzer lifted the latch.

XXVIII

THE SINS OF THE FATHERS

AS the door swung under his hand, Hertzer found himself facing Consuela, for she had risen when he dismissed the *cabo*.

In his furious mental excesses he had lived this moment a thousand times over, feeding his passion fat with pictures of her in a hundred attitudes of nervous fear, but, as is usual, the reality differed widely from his imaginings—so widely that he gave pause, stood staring at the soft picture she made. For, straining up through a shade of crape paper, the light of her lamp diffused about her a mellow rose dusk that toned out the circles beneath her eyes and warmed her nervous pallors. The hand that rested lightly on the table did not shake.

Not that she was unafraid. Roused in the night by the cries and curses which attended Magdaleno's subjugation, she had lived through a day of tremors, rendered more unbearable by thoughts of David's return. Ignorant of the vexatious derailments that had delayed his train, she had pictured him in the crazy depot at early morning; thereafter had followed his ride in the sticky heat of the jungle, watched him at three-o'clock lunch with Carruthers—she felt sure he would come that way—accompanied him in thought every step of the way until, at sundown, her anxiety and disappointment found vent in a bitter cry:

"Now he is passing La Luna, far out on the trail! Soon he will be at Verda, and oh, I shall not be there!"

Nor had she derived much comfort from Patricia's consolations. When, with profuse apologies, Tomas, nevertheless, refused to permit even the Yaqui maid to pass his guard, Patricia had brought in their meals, remaining thereafter to lighten the burden of her own fears with attempts at reassurance.

"Don't be afraid," she had said, while trying to persuade Consuela to break her fast. "He stayed out in the jungle all night, and will come home tired and cured of his foolish anger."

"He is ashamed," she commented, as, later, they heard him booming his orders. "He will send orders presently for Tomas to let you free."

Though her own hope died when he went out to the fields, she simulated even greater confidence. "It is better so. He will have the longer to cool."

"Now I shall speak to him at dinner," she cried at night. "There will be a beautiful moon, so we shall ride, you and I, over to Las Glorias. Quien sabe? Don David may overtake us on the way."

Unable, however, to brazen it out any longer when his absence from dinner brought the end of her shifts, she sent their meal in, then stole out and down the path to lie in horrible fear under the shadowy rubber, the prey of her own revenge. So all evening Consuela had had for company only the little Yaqui maid, who squatted on the floor at her feet immersed in a picture-book, a position which emphasized her undersize.

She was, indeed, so small for her sixteen years that Hertzer had used her at odd work: to run errands, drive the water mule, weed in his garden. A milder slavery than that of the *metates*, it had yet taxed the limit of her small strength. From dawn to dark she either bent at the weeding till her small back ached and blood mixed with the dirt on her grubby fingers, or lifted leaden legs up and down the steep river-bank after the water mule, and always a cuff and curse from *cabo* or *mandador* waited at the end of her errands. And her small soul had hardened under the usage, the stubborn Yaqui soul that would not down even in this, a fledgling girl. Never a cuff—unless it came from Hertzer—that did not earn a well-flung stone; never a curse but drew her shrill malediction. So hard had she grown that Consuela had despaired at first of ever being able to get beneath her sullen exterior; and when she did begin to soften, her thawings had alternated with sudden freezings until to-day. As though she divined without understanding her mistress' trouble, she had been unusually thoughtful and gentle; the sloe eyes that now rose ever and anon from her book glowed with sympathy, and, catching her eye just before Hertzer entered, she had murmured in Spanish:

"I am still here to fight for thee."

Though she had smiled—just then—at the absurdity of it, Consuela had warmed to the little creature; for matter of that she had taken comfort out of her presence all day, far more than she had out of Patricia's high promises. Smiling, she had resumed her own thoughtful brooding.

Her reflections? Their key is to be found in Hertzer's sneer to Ewing, and they took naturally out her thoughts of David. "Was it for thee, a girl of such shameful upbringings, to marry with an honorable man?" she asked herself. "If thou hadst not seen the misery of the galeras, the intent might have been judged innocent. But, having seen, what word can be said for thee? Surely this is the punishment. And yet—" would come flooding a host of recollections, some arch, some merry, most tender, and all in justification of her weakness. But while she gave them soft indulgence, the text of that remembered sermon on "The Sins of the Fathers" uprose again and again to banish the smiles which leavened her distress. But, chiefest of all, the thought which gave her most comfort, lay back of her quiet composure under Hertzer's hard gaze—if she were now to suffer for her tender fault, at least she had been permitted to help in averting disaster from David and his people!

Her composure did not, however, obtain long, for

in the man before her she could see no moiety of either the Hertzer of their rides and talks or the sardonic planter of a year ago. Even the Hertzer of the night before—he of the gray face, sharp, cold glances—was absorbed by a savage whose every attribute reeked a coarse masculinity. Tucked in at the neck, his *camisa* revealed his breast's thick hair beneath the short neck. From rolled-up sleeves his arms protruded, equally hairy, knotted with muscle, streaked with swollen veins. The passion which swelled every great muscle had pulled him from his height to a slight crouch that accentuated his appearance of squatness. With every trace of his usual grim humor gone, burned out along with his curious æsthetic streak by deadly hate, he embodied grossness, loomed ferociously animal in her startled vision. Even the rose dusk could not hide her sudden blanching.

He saw it, the sudden fear, with a thrill of fierce satisfaction, first fruit of his revenge; to get his fill of it, wring the last drop out of the moment, he continued to look at her, unconscious of the black eyes which were returning his stare from under the table, feasted on her pallors till his smoking passion demanded further fuel.

"Well?"

The hot arrogance of the monosyllable touched her pride. She quickly answered: "It is for me to ask that, señor? Why do you hold me here a prisoner?"

His hand went to the pocket in which David's letter had lain since he crumpled it out of Phelps's sight. But it pleased him to play with her, fan his passion with breath of words. "Are you the first Mexican woman to suffer that in the tropics? La Señora Morales could tell you different."

But there his play ended; for, reading a judgment into his words, she remained mutely silent.

"You do not answer?" The suppression constricted his vocal chords so that he spoke in a gusty whine. "Must have rhyme and reason for it, must you? Well—there it is."

"Then Patricia did—" Astounded by this sudden revelation of the girl's treachery, she stared at the letter he threw on the table.

In the tense moment that followed she obtained flashing insight into his psychology; saw and understood all that had passed in the last two days; and, as he was already informed on hers further speech was unnecessary—events moved quickly on to a dramatic conclusion. As the familiar writing raised a vision of David's face, all aglow in its honest strength, she put out her hand to the letter, then tore herself with a mad wrench out of Hertzer's quick clutch, leaving her sleeve in his hands. Ripped away from throat to girdle, the flimsy mull of her waist fell down exposing her shoulder's soft pink to the lamp's rich light, and as she recoiled, gazing at him in dark horror, she made shift with the other hand to draw the shreds together.

"You would, would you?"

Girning between set teeth, he followed around the

end of the table, unmindful of, if he even saw, the little maid. Throughout she had watched him with catlike stealth, sliding forward upon her knees as he made that sudden clutch. Now her hand stole out to the knife he had lent Consuela to sharpen pencils, which still lay open upon the table, and as he paused, teetering between the impulses which urged him at once to go forward and stay to feed his passion fatter, the small thing rose and struck with all her might.

Lucky for him that it was not a case-knife. Delivered with knowledge of knives and anatomy gained in the skinning of many a beast on the Sonora plateau, having behind it the heft of her sinewy young body, it would have split through to his heart.

Lucky for her the smallness that saved her by contrast of her insignificance with the enormity of his anger. Swinging round with a roar, he gazed a pause in ludicrous surprise; then, picking her up by one arm as a child does a doll, he carried her to the door and tossed her outside.

"To the galera, you little devil, and tell the veledor to give you a spanking before he locks you in!"

Forgetting her own terror in her fear for the child, Consuela had run forward. As she now ran back again, a resumption of horror in her wide eyes, he broke out, in a sneering laugh: "Don't be afraid. The honor is not for you. That chance is gone forever." In black enjoyment of the puzzle that now mingled with her fright, he waited a full minute before going on: "But there! don't look so disappointed.

There are other fish in the sea. If I had not waited in the hope that David would grace the ceremony with his sanctimonious presence, you would have been mated ere this with one of my cabos. However, he will be able to view your completed happiness to-morrow."

Upon a strained silence, her answer issued in little gasps: "You would not . . . dare. There would be an inquiry . . . even here . . . in the tropics."

"An inquiry—by the Jefe of San Juan, who would take my report of you as a loose woman now safeguarded from further indiscretions by marriage."

Ensued another silence. Standing over her, he watched, with black triumph, despair wipe incredulous horror out of her wide, dark eyes. Over some thousand square miles of jungle country the Jefe of San Juan exercised corrupt jurisdiction, dealing out verdicts to the highest bidder. No crime but had its price in his court; and should there arise a stickler for justice, arrest upon misinformation was easy; more than one such had been thrust from the door of his *carcel* and shot under pretence of escape. And Hertzer was hand and glove with the man! As it all ran through her mind, her faith rose to a higher, if more primitive, law.

"David would kill thee!" she whispered.

He shrugged, laughing. "Would that mend thy case? Though I have no skill in religious matters, I am told that a broken reputation is beyond the tinkering of even a priest."

THE SINS OF THE FATHERS

There was little hope in that dry laugh, but now she was desperate enough to catch at any straw, and the fact that he was able to laugh encouraged her to attempt pleading. "Señor, is it the part of a man to frighten a woman? I had not thought this of him who spread his great visions before me the other morning. But you joke; I know that you joke. This is still that man, strong, self-reliant, not to be turned from a high purpose by one mistake. They are still there, the bright future, the plans which you will surely carry out. I am still to be permitted to lend sympathy and—"

"You remind me of that?" Eyes leaping, snapping in the midst of a dark suffusion, he went on, in the same gusty whine: "You, who laughed in your sleeve at my sentimental maunderings? By God! I'll—" His big fist came smashing down on the table, then, checked by the pain of his bruised knuckles, he stood glowering down upon her. "Pshaw! I'm keeping you from your lover."

Two strides and he gripped her bare arm with iron fingers that sunk in to the bone, extorting a low cry as he dragged her across the floor to the door. Flinging it wide open, he made to step out, then recoiled and stared blankly at the *veledor*, who stood, blinking, in the sudden lamplight.

"You sent for me, señor?"

"I—for you—"

"Si, señor. The little maid, she said that you—"

"What's that?" Hertzer broke in, sharply. A

499

twanging, like that of breaking harp - strings, but infinitely louder, resounded among the dark buildings; and as his mind flashed to the interpretation, he questioned, sharply, "Your machete, man—where is it?"

"In the galera, señor. When—"

"And she has thrust it through the screen! They are chopping down the wires!"

Even as he spoke the vibrance ceased. The shadows about the *galera* seemed to thicken, twitch with a convulsion of hidden life, and as he thrust by the *veledor*, they vomited a stream of running shapes into the vivid moonlight.

"Ola! Timotea! Pancho! Angel!"

With a sudden remembrance that he had sent most of the *cabos* to waylay David, he stopped running.

"Si, señor!" The sleepy voice in the *cabos' jacale* rose suddenly in a hoarse yell of fear, but he had no time to speculate on the struggle going on there in the dark, for, splitting at the store, half of the streaming shapes had turned on to the garden path. His hands went to his belt and came away empty, while a furious oath marked his rememberance that he had left both pistols and *machete* in the store.

"José, lend me your pistol!"

But, turning, he saw the man running hard for the jungle, and, at right angles to his direction, caught the flutter of white that marked Consuela's flight. For the moment he was minded to follow. But with a memory of Patricia, locked up in the store, there broke loose within him that furious parental instinct upon which Phelps had once commented to David. Turning again, he paused for a breath, eyes flashing insanely, face distorted, great bulk swelling to the impulse that launched him with a roar of rage at the van of streaming shapes.

Carried back or tossed aside by the thrust of his rush, the leaders closed again, for the stripes, insults, intolerable tyranny of his hard service had excoriated festering memories of tribal wrongs, rendered them desperate as he. And once at a standstill, they poured over him in a dark wave with a low moaning roar like that of a breaking sea; hung in twos, threes, as many as could obtain a hold on his every limb; piled upon him in a heap that slithered to and fro, writhed in the moonlight like a nest of fighting snakes. Sometimes a sudden convulsion from the centre would shift its base a yard. Splitting, it let Hertzer's face heave up for a second to the moonlight, desperately grim under a wet veil of sweat, to sink once more in the mass; for, with death at his heart, he fought as he never had in life—fought with teeth, nails, tearing fingers, butting head; even when a pain, sharp as the burn of a red-hot iron, shot through his ankles and he collapsed beneath the heap, each strong limb continued to fight an individual battle. But that was close to the end. Held down by dead weight of numbers, he felt a hair-cord bite his wrists to the bone; the heap dissolved, and, sitting up, he saw the Yaqui *cabo* looming above him against a red glare.

THE PLANTER

Through the blind smother of the fight he had been conscious of light, and now he saw that the *cabos' jacale* was on fire. Dried to a crisp in this the dry season, its palm roof burned like a huge torch, lifted a twisting spout of flame high above the peak painting the night sky with the effulgence which had just given David pause in the forest ten miles away. Even at his distance Hertzer could feel the heat, and when, at a sign from the Yaqui, he was lifted and carried down the path, he thought he divined his doom; his flesh shivered and crept to a premonition of licking flames. But, after setting him down with his back against the last tree at the foot of the path, they dispersed, some running to help their fellows retrieve *machetes*, rifles, *zarapes* from the burning building, others to follow their leader back to the house.

Sensing their purpose, Hertzer turned his face of despair to the store. Within forty feet of himself, and separated by a wider interval from the other buildings, he knew that Patricia must have watched the struggle, and after a stealthy glance around he threw a strained whisper at the siding.

"Si, padre."

Her quick answer proved his intuition, and after a second glance round he spoke out of his desperation. "Daughter, I am a prisoner and cannot help you; nor is it possible for you to escape. Just now they are busy sacking the house and jacales, but it is only a question of minutes till they break down your door.

Then—there are worse things than death. **My pistols** lie there on the table—"

Her cowardice leaped to his meaning. In a low wail her voice issued from the siding. "Oh, padre, I cannot, I cannot! To kill myself? I cannot! Oh, why didn't you listen to me? This would never have happened."

As, ignoring his "hush," she continued her low wail, mixing scraps of prayer with reproaches and demands for help, the cold sweat of despair stood out on Hertzer's face—if ever man felt the flame of hell, it was he in that minute. Looking around in that extremity of desperation which hopes only for hope, he saw the pillar of flame career under a breath of night wind toward the *galera*, and with the suddenness of an explosion, the great palm-leaf roof touched off, threw sheet flame a hundred feet in the air. Other buildings were catching, and, though such wind as there was blew away from the store, he saw that it also must soon go.

Under urge of the thought, he glanced around, looking for Magdaleno, whose voice he had heard during the fight—in what hope needs not to inquire, for he did not see him either among the Yaquis who were running among the burning buildings or those now coming back from the house. Realizing that it must be his last, he burdened his whisper with the strain of his awful despair.

"Child, they will presently burn me, but worse than twenty burnings would it be to have them capt-

ure you. There is still time to cheat them— Hush!
for God's sake, hush!"

But either she did not see the Yaqui *cabo* coming
down the path, or, seeing, wished to end the agony,
for she kept on crying, "I can't, padre, I can't!
can't! can't!"—cried it even when, passing Hertzer
on a swift run, the Yaqui came leaping out of the
shadowy rubber into the glare of the conflagration.

"The pistol! Quick! The pistol!"

"I can't! I can't!" She cried it once more, answering his mad shout. While he strained at his
bonds, came a crash; the piteous note changed to
quavering fear; then, as it rose to a scream, Hertzer's
head plunged forward upon his breast, a groan
bubbling upon his lips.

An hour later Hertzer sat up and looked around,
the screams of his daughter still in his ears; a vision
of her hanging across one of his horses in front of the
Yaqui, still splendid in her pallid dishevelment,
burned into his eyes.

In his rear the house and outbuildings still blazed;
the red embers of the store scorched his blistered face.
Galera, cook-house, stables, and storehouses, all were
gone, and among their glowing ashes loomed dim,
bulky shapes, the bodies of his slaughtered cattle.
Nor did his calamity give pause there. Touched off
by long trails of sparks, the *monte*, which cumbered
the ground a foot deep, had flamed into a wave of
fire that flowed across the plantation, licking every-

thing clean between opposite walls of green jungle. Through moonlit reek he could make out a black bristle of trees, a ghostly plantation litten here and there with sickly flames that leaped and flickered about dry stumps, pallid corpse lights in a pall of smoke. La Luna was gone, purged at last of the blood and sweat, immemorial suffering that had fertilized its green glories by the flame that burned it down to the stones. And as he overlooked it all, noted with dull eyes the completeness of his calamity, he realized not only why his life had been left him, but also the thorough manner in which fate had turned the tables he had spread for David. Yet neither thought brought recurrence of his passion. Thinking them, he fell into dull brooding, his eyes on his feet, which were soaked from the ankles down with blood; nor looked up again till a sudden splash rose out of the river's murmur.

A fish, he thought at first, but presently heard labored breathing, thud of shod feet ascending the bank, then, as a figure moved forward into the glare of the fires, he broke out in sudden laughter, harsh and mirthless—surely it had required only this to make the situation ridiculously complete. Pale from hard riding, and all dripping from his swim through the river, David stood looking down upon him.

"Hello! back again?" Absurd as it was under the circumstances, Hertzer heard himself give casual greeting without astonishment, for, apart from that sudden risibility, his mind was dead to all values—

David or Timoteo, it was all one. "Didn't you meet them?" he went on, in the same casual way; not noticed that David answered, though he had not named his *cabos*.

"Yes, on a run for the Zacateco village."

"I'll bet you. You are wet—and on foot?"

"Broke the heart of my horse two miles back. I swam the river."

Ensued a pause. While Hertzer resumed his dull brooding, David swept the desolation of fire and ashes, moonlit reek, with dark eyes of trouble. In him, also, the exhaustion of his hard ride had combined with the drain of emotion to induce a sort of coma. When he spoke again it was like a man in a dream.

"Where is Consuela?"

As he glanced up quickly, and took note for the first time of the other's pallid face, anxious preoccupation, a sinister gleam indicated a stir of passion under Hertzer's unnatural calm. In the following pause his every crooked power rallied to snatch some shred of revenge from calamity's grasp.

"Humph!" he sneered. "If you had happened along a few hours earlier you might have witnessed her marriage to one of my cabos. In fact, I sent out Timoteo and Angel to deliver an invitation. As for her whereabouts—as they were naturally wakeful, they escaped to finish their honeymoon out in the jungle."

"You lie! Your veledor swam the river and told me all. Get up!" Speaking, he cut the cords that bound Hertzer's wrists with the saddle *machete* he had carried, swimming, in his mouth. "Get up, or I'll strike you sitting!"

But Hertzer did not move, and as he looked up his eyes reflected the glare, glowed with a red malevolence. "You strike me? A clever bluff." His glance drooped again to the blood-soaked fringe of trousers. "You saw that I was hamstrung before you said it."

Hamstrung! Crippled for life! As a matter of fact, David had noticed the stain, and as its significance now burst upon him, and he realized what it meant to this man whose whole life had been one fury of action, pity cooled his anger.

"I didn't, Hertzer—and I'm sorry. If there's anything I can do—"

"Of course not!" the other jeeringly interrupted. "As for your help—the only thing you can do for me is to get out of my sight." Looking away, he added: "It isn't likely that the Yaquis will come back, but the fire may bring out some volunteer Zacatecores. They don't love me so well that I'd like to have them catch me unarmed, so, if you like, you can leave me a pistol."

Though he spoke carelessly, mentioning the pistol as an afterthought, he could not restrain an eager shiver. "To shoot me?" David quietly interpreted. "No. After you have answered my question I am going on to Phelps's place, and I'll send back help from there. When did you see Consuela last?"

But Hertzer's casual glance away had shown a

sudden effulgence far down the sky. Pointing, he exclaimed, "Look there!"

Even as David looked, the tops of the nearer trees stood blackly out as against a blood-red sunset, and while the effulgence quickened with pulsing blushes, they caught the roar of flames, faint in the distance, yet sufficiently loud to drown the approach of a sandalled foot.

"It's Phelps's place!"

Hertzer looked up with the old evil grin. "What's that old text about the rain falling on the just and the unjust? Seems to hold true of fire. Verda next, and with it all of our pretty plans go up in smoke. You really want to know where Consuela is? She is—" As he raised his hand, pointing at the sky-glare, a voice broke in from behind:

"Here!" And, swinging round, David found himself facing Magdaleno.

Besides its original bruises, the old fellow's grim face now bore innumerable scratches gained as he dashed after Consuela into the jungle, yet was in its blood and dirt the most welcome but one in David's sight. And that was not long withheld from his glad eyes; for, as he thrust out his hand, there came an echo of his joyful exclamation, and from behind a bush close by, Consuela came with a rush to his arms.

"Oh, it *is* thee! I knew it, but Magdaleno would have me wait."

Hertzer roused from a second dull doze of despair

to silence and ashes, mutter of falling embers, whisper of little winds. Westward the moon's spectral face loomed through a pall of smoke; eastward a fainter sky-blush attested fading fires. In the foreground the skeletons of his trees bristled blackly on every ridge; beyond them the dark line of jungle — the jungle, triumphant, insistent, whose ebb and flow had marked the rise and fall of Aztec and Toltec civilizations upon whose ruins its green life battened; the jungle, beside whose eternal recurrences the span of La Luna was as the amethyst flash of a fly out there in the murk; the jungle, which would presently flow in and wipe its very memory from the face of the earth. But while Consuela's glad cry rang in his ears in bitter alternation with his daughter's hysterical scream, no thought of mutability could arise to cheer him with suggestion of surcease from pain.

Standing there, so close that he glimpsed white flesh through the cloud of brown hair she had loosed to veil her shoulder, she had given herself up with the abandonment of perfect love to David's kisses; and, screw up his eyes as he might, Hertzer could not shut out the glory of tenderness which flooded her face as, nestling against his shoulder, she told of her flight into the jungle before Magdaleno found her. It was not to be shut out any more than David's happy glow or the fatherly indulgence of the *mandador's* grim visage; yet was perhaps less hard to bear than their consideration for himself, anxious inquiry after Patricia.

THE PLANTER

Thinking in his venomous madness to withhold this, the essence of his calamity, from their pity, he had replied that Patricia escaped with Tomas down-river in a canoe, and in his solitude had now leisure to rave over the lie that cut off immediate chance of rescue. And rave he did, turning a strained white face up to the night sky which mocked his passion with the untroubled peace of its great dark vault; raved first in hoarse whispers at the unnameable horrors that passed in vivid procession through his mind; then voicelessly—raved until, from sheer exhaustion, his head plunged forward, and he rolled over and lay in a stupor, half swoon, half sleep.

It was daybreak when he awoke again in the midst of a desolation of cold ashes. Under a cold dawn the rubber stood out, harsh and black, a dirty beard on the burned face of the plantation; stale, acrid odors burdened the heavy air.

In the gray light of early morning facts always slough off false glamours, stand out in their naked truth, and, looking across the gulf of sleep, he now obtained a perspective upon his calamity, saw and reviewed with a fresh mind its every consequence. Departing, David had called back that he would return with a canoe, and as he now pictured himself at Verda, a cripple subject to the pity of even the *enganchadores*, Hertzer broke out in a harsh laugh. Perhaps, more than anything else, the thought influenced him to the decision he attained long before a moving dot on the unburned strip of plantation road resolved into the figure of Phelps.

As he drew nearer a faint grin first disturbed the dark seriousness of Hertzer's face, for it was hard to recognize, in his wildly dishevelled figure, the precise Englishman, disciple of Spencer, Darwin, Kidd. From much rubbing, his face was one smudge through which canals of white meandered from his red and swollen eyes. In ludicrous contrast to the flannel pajamas in which he had escaped into the night, he carried a pistol in each hand, one of which he kept tucking under his arm while he wiped his eyes. Sooty, sweaty, tear-stained, it required only his air of injury, bewildered protest, to complete the picture that revived in Hertzer a brief recurrence of the old sardonic spirit.

"My God, Hertzer! Is that you?" he cried, running forward. "Isn't this terrible, terrible?" Then he stopped, staring at Hertzer's sudden boisterous laughter.

"What would Ben Kidd have to say about this?" Leaning back against his tree, he roared it between boisterous peals. "'Only those types survive that prove their fitness in the struggle for existence.' Isn't that it, Phelps? How do you like it yourself?" Then, with equal suddenness, he resumed his dark quiet, nor even grinned at Phelps's pathetic protest.

"Hertzer, Hertzer, don't talk that way! It's too serious. My throat might have been cut in my bed —would have, if the veledor hadn't rung the galera bell." Shuddering at the thought of it, he ran on without waiting for questions: "As it was, they nearly got me. Thinking that some scrap had arisen in the galera over a woman, I grabbed my pistols and ran out, and I had just time to make the banana-patch before they surrounded the house, with Lola—and the kiddies—still there in bed." Pausing, he swallowed painfully, trying to conquer the lump that was threatening his English reserve, but failed, and, while the tears washed new channels through the smudge, he continued, wildly, "My God, Hertzer, I'd always taken them as a matter of course, and when I think of them now—Felice, with her little curly head; Lola, so quiet and thoughtful; and the boy was such a manly little chap—I—" He stopped, and while he choked and blubbered, Hertzer observed him with eyes that pierced down through his shallow grief to the wounded selfishness beneath.

"They killed them?"

Harsh, matter of fact, the question checked Phelps's emotion. He looked up in injured surprise. "No, carried them off—after they'd gutted the place and turned loose my enganchars. I saw them go from where I lay in the skirts of the jungle—"

"And you with a Colt in either hand?"

Phelps stared. "Why, you wouldn't expect one man to—"

"No, I wouldn't expect it—of you. Did you see Patricia?"

Passing over, if he noticed the scorn of the first

sentence, Phelps burst out. "Then it *was* she? I couldn't trust my eyes. She, also? My God, Hertzer, what shall we do?"

"Which way were they heading when you saw them last?" And when Phelps replied that they had taken a path that led south to the next river, he darkly commented, "Where they'll seize canoes, and once on the water they leave no trace."

Rousing from a fit of black musing, during which Phelps had looked helplessly down upon him, he began, "Did you see—" but stopped as he remembered that if Phelps *had* seen David he would not now be here. What was more to, or, rather, against his purpose, if he found out that David was at Verda, nothing would stop him from heading back that way.

"What shall we do?" He repeated Phelps's question. "First you'll go down-river to warn Boulton and Carruthers. Though their wives and children have not been carried off "— the pause was worse than a sneer—"they will know what to do. Later you will take the first ship back home. Yes, you will." He savagely overrode Phelps's protest. "It hurts just now, of course.' Even a cow requires a week to forget her calf. You will go back to school-mastering in England, marry and settle down, to birch other folks' children while you raise a smug brood of your own. You'll grow fat, bald, and respectable, and, if ever you remember your Indian wife, it will be with a shudder of thankfulness for the accident that rid you of her and your brown children. As for me . . . all I need is the loan of a pistol?"

As he extended his hand, Phelps, who had opened his mouth to a second weak protest, recoiled and stood, open-mouthed, staring, chilled by a premonition. "No, Hertzer, no; not—that!"

"What's the matter with the man?" With a wonderful effort he veiled his face in surprise. "It will be hours before Carruthers can get up here with a canoe, and do you mean to say that you'll leave me here, hamstrung and unarmed, while fifty of your enganchars are floating round in the jungle?"

The first mention of his hurt. Phelps exclaimed his horror. "*Hamstrung!*"

"Hamstrung, I said. Did you think I was sitting here for fun—taking a siesta? Give me that gun?"

Reassured, Phelps handed him the weapon, or, rather, yielded it to his quick clutch, then shrank in sudden fear before the fierce joy that leaped in the other's eyes. His nerve completely gone, he stood for a space as before, blanched, open-mouthed, staring, then turned and ran, squealing his fear.

Until he disappeared in the jungle, Hertzer watched him with contemptous amusement which, fading, left his face grimly calm. Returning, his glance circled the burned plantation from west to east, and there paused, arrested by a crimson crescent, burnished tip of the rising sun. Overhead the mists of night trailed out in long, diaphanous veils of scarlet. From below rose the murmur of the river, spaced by the

splash of leaping fish; across from the other shore
floated chirrups and chirpings, the overture of sunrise
song. Until the great red orb heaved clear of the
forest horizon, he watched with sombre eyes in
which was no reflection of the peace of that fair
morning; then, as at a signal, he raised the pistol.

Hearing the report far off in the jungle, Phelps
hastened his breathless run.

XXIX

THE REALIZATION OF A DREAM

AT the close of day some five weeks later, David
stood looking out on the camp from his veranda
at Verda—not that of the old *jacale*, which was merely an extension of the eaves supported on posts, but
a really truly veranda, wire-screened against *rodedores* or other ferocious pests, floored with fair boards
painfully whip-sawed out of the log, a fit appurte-
nance of the new plantation house it encircled.

A low bungalow wide and roomy, this was in
construction a compromise between Northern ideals
and tropical necessities; for while the floors, siding,
and partitions were all of lumber, the cunning of the
Zacateco had supplied the palm-leaf roof.   From the
veranda edge its sere surfaces swept up to the custom-
ary peak, and David had omitted the usual ceiling
of cotton which would have hidden the graceful inner
curve.   Crossing at an even height with the walls,
the partitions allowed the evening breeze free play
in the brown gloom of rafters and ribs above before
it slid out through an open window freighted with
perfume of cedar chests and cupboards.   The native

516

carpenter who built these had also wrought from seasoned mahogany—flotsam and jetsam of the last rains—chairs, lounges, tables, whose massive beauty was unspoiled by taint of veneer. Only half an hour ago David had given them a last touch with oil and soft cloth as he moved them to their places. Now the house stood ready for its mistress, clean, wholesome, airy as the nests of the forest.

And it did not sum the month's improvements. As the report of his service had long ago travelled from plantation to plantation, penetrating even the hopeless darkness of the *galeras*, there is nothing surprising in the fact that, the morning after the fire, all Phelps' people—both free folk and *enganchadores* —descended upon him in a body demanding employment. To house, feed, allot land, and task work for them would have been a sufficient labor without the dozen extra families which Ewing had transferred from the Las Glorias *galera* two weeks later, but this evening saw all done. Under his thoughtful eyes lay the camp of Hertzer's visionings—in fact as well as figurately, for even death had not stayed the ironical reversions of fate; in lieu of unpaid wages, the Zacatecores had razed the new camp to furnish material for David's houses. Just as Hertzer had dreamed, uprose serried rows of *jacales* with brown people coming and going between; only instead of the harsh commands of *cabo* and *mandador*, the evening air pulsed to snatches of song, shrill treble of children, musical laughter of women. As on the day that David received his dismissal, it basked, this palm city of his building, in fluid golds that flowed out in quivering waves to stain the dark. environing rubber with sunset hues. Small wonder if its peace and beauty caused him a thrill of pride; or that he stood looking at it all till the skyglows faded and Ewing's voice roused him from pleasant musings.

"Hello, young man! Come out of your dreams. . . . Didn't expect to be here myself," he went on, answering David's greeting. "But, you see, these days the voice of the sewing-machine is heard in the land, every blessed table at Las Glorias is piled high with filmy things—they haven't left me even my writing-desk—and do I but poke my nose anywhere near the mysteries, Nell ruffles like an irate hen and shoos me promptly away. Positively, I was driven out." Laughing, he continued: "I really cannot conceive why a girl should think it necessary to rig herself out anew from top to toe simply because she's going to be married. Men don't. You, for instance, have not increased your wardrobe by so much as a pair of suspenders. But they all do, and I can assure you that the present rumpus isn't a circumstance to the convulsions which preceded my marriage. Must be instinct, however, for I notice that even the Tehuanas deem it necessary to put on a little extra side, and if the facts of the first marriage were accessible, I'd be willing to lay odds that Eve not only trimmed her leaves with flowers, but also stuck a rose in her hair. But don't be

alarmed," he finished, grinning. "I am to assure
you that all will be done in good time—also that
you never *saw* such needlework! Nell boxed my
ears for suggesting that I didn't believe you had,
another grievance. But how about your end?
When did you get back from San Juan?"

"Late this morning. I had all kinds of trouble."
Its very remembrance spread David's face with a
rueful grin. "No sooner did I mention marriage
license, than official San Juan rose in a body with its
hand stuck out behind its back. The Jefe, the Jefe's
clerk, and the rurale who guards the court, the
Registrar, his Deputy, and the moso who runs their
errands, their faces clouded with doubt as to whether
it were even legal for an alien—Gringo in particular—
to wed a daughter of the soil, nor cleared till every
last man had got his bit. And where the law stopped
the church began—not quite so unblushingly, of
course, still the poor of San Juan ought to live out
the year very comfortably on my contribution to
the box. Altogether, it cost me two days' hard talking and three months' salary to get what I could
have for three dollars in two minutes at home.
However, the graft had its advantages. You could
have knocked the priest's eyes off with sticks when
I showed him the license; assured me that it would
have required at least three weeks to procure it by
the usual method. What are you grinning at?"

"Only at the idea of our Davy bribing his way
through thick and thin. And the house? Done?

That's fine. Well, lock up and come over to the old jacale. I brought my own cigars, and if you have a drop of that old Scotch left, we can celebrate your fall from freedom and be very comfy over a glass of toddy. By-the-way, I brought over the last *El Imparcial*."

"More about the Yaquis?" David inquired, as he led the way.

"Yes, telegraphic despatch from Honduras. Exterminated once more — makes the fourth time, doesn't it?"

"*Honduras?*"

Ewing nodded. "Travelling, aren't they? Makes three hundred miles easting along the Isthmus since we lost their trail at the Chiapas line."

He alluded to the pursuit which he, David, and other half-dozen planters had made after the Yaquis — hopeless from the beginning through Hertzer's lie. For Boulton and Carruthers had both answered Ewing's call to assemble at Verda on Consuela's behalf, and when — after Hertzer had been found and laid with his dead slaves out in the jungle — they returned home to receive news of Patricia's abduction from Phelps, two days had gone by. A third was used organizing the pursuit, and though burned plantations blazed the trail southeast through Oaxaca and Chiapas, it went blind at every river, faded altogether in the deep jungles of Guatemala. Excepting Carruthers and Boulton — who had waited till the report of another burning should furnish a fresh clew

—they had returned to glimpse further of that wild journeying in the telegraphic reports of *El Imparcial* and other Mexican papers. Now a Guatemalian coffee *finca* had been fed to the flames. Again, the Yaquis were reported wiped out by the massed forces of a dozen *haciendas;* and, while they were reading, far to the southeast the night skies would be blushing for the lie.

"I don't believe it," David now commented on the article. "If it wasn't for Patricia, my sympathies would be entirely with them. Wonder what's become of Carrie and Boulton? Looks as if they had picked up the trail again?"

"Must have, or they would have been back before now. But they'd lose it again. What can you do with a trail that takes a hop, skip, and jump every other day down fifty miles of river? They might just as well have come back with us, but you couldn't tell that to Boulton. He surprised me. Of course, I knew that he fancied the girl, but never expected he would have taken it as hard as he did. Though it sounds cruel, it is really the best thing that could have happened for him. She'd have made him most beautifully miserable, and he'll soon get over it—that is, if they don't overtake them. If they do—" He shook a grave head. "It is only in story books that a lover succeeds in stealing his sweetheart out of an Indian camp."

"Yes, I wish we had news of them," David echoed his doubt.

They had not long to wait, for as, after supper, Ewing busied himself over the brew of punch, a shout rose outs de, and Carruthers reined in at the door. Streaming out through the doorway, the lamplight showed his face thin and deep-graven with haggard lines. His eyes shone fever-bright. But his cheery spirit remained undiminished, and he laughed protestingly against their welcoming punches.

"Here, here, that's no way to treat a fellow who has lost the ability to cast a shadow! Quit it before I get spinal curvature!" But he sobered when they demanded news. "Yes, yes, I'll tell you all about it after my horse is stabled—too long to give it out here."

With its details of forced marches, heart-breaking waits, détours, and back-tracking upon false scents, not to mention frequent digressions upon the teak, mahogany, and other rare woods which had excited his American instinct for commerce, it *was* a long tale that he told while sipping his punch. The brew stood low in the bowl, and from its first fresh brightness the lamp burned smoky gold before he came to its climax.

"Nonsense." He dismissed *El Imparcial*. "They were frontier guards, ran at the first shot, and were still shivering when we saw them two days later. In their imaginations your big Yaqui, Davy, loomed as a demon of enormous size, and they plead with us not to go on, swearing that he would kill us, which I felt to be likely enough. To tell you the truth, what of hunger and heat—we didn't average much more than a meal a day—I was willing enough to quit, but Boulton would have gone on alone, and of course I couldn't leave him.

"It wasn't that he was so deeply in love. They used to scuffle a bit at La Luna, with a few kisses thrown in for luck when nobody looked, but if she'd gone in the usual way, married the other fellow or left the country, I don't believe he'd have fallen off in his eating. It was the way she went. In novels it is quite the usual thing, I know, for young women to be carried away and return from a long sojourn among Indians in a state of pristine innocence; but he labored under no such hallucinations, and the horror of it drove him stark staring mad for the time being. Indeed, I don't believe that anything else but that which actually occurred could have given him back his senses.

"It was this way. Crossing into Honduras, we were guided by a Guatemala Indian at whose village the Yaquis had camped the week before; for down there, as up here, the volunteers have no love for the planter, helped them along from village to village. It took fifty dollars to persuade this man to our service, nor would he go a step farther, when, after three days' fast going in a hill country sparsely forested, we came, one night, on the warm ashes of their last camp. Because the few rivers we had lately crossed ran without exception west, they were now travelling slowly, hunting and fishing as they went; and if the

Guatemalian had remained with us—but he didn't, and so, shoving hotly forward through the dusk of the following evening, we almost walked into their camp, would have but for a sudden burst of woman's laughter.

"I will say this much for ourselves—the camp was pitched on a sand playa under the bank of a wide river which effectually hid their cooking-fires. Heavy thickets screened us from view, and we dropped like dead men flat on our bellies. My impulse was to crawl away, but Boulton had already wormed into the thicket, and nothing remained but to follow.

"I suppose one can never escape the influence of the Indian yarns he reads in his youth—scalpings, torture, and all that; but I can assure you that the scene which opened before us after a few minutes' crawling lacked even a taint of Fenimore Cooper. Imagine a smooth playa with a gleam of wide water beyond fading into brown dusk at the opposite shore. On its edge a score or so of Yaquis were at work on a raft, and about the same number of women were grouped about the fires, for in addition to the squaws who had worked in Hertzer's cook-house they had taken their pick out of a dozen galeras. Yet, looking them over, a stranger could not have singled out the prisoners, for they moved with perfect freedom in and out of the jungle, over to the water's edge, back to the fires, laughing and chatting, apparently contented. And small wonder if they were. After the slavery of the plantations, the peace, ease, freedom of that warm gloaming must have seemed like heaven itself. I felt it, then, without having time to think, for my eyes had gone at once to Patricia, who sat with Phelps' Lola and two Yaqui women at the nearest fire.

"It was their laughter we had heard, and while we lay there looking on, so close that I could have pitched a stone in Patricia's lap, they broke out again at a point in the story one of the Yaquis was telling with hands, eyes, irradiance of brown smiles, as much as by words; and, to my utter astonishment, Patricia laughed the loudest. Rocking back and forth, she slapped her thighs in one of the old uncontrollable fits of mirth, rocked and slapped until little Felice— with whom she had evidently been playing—tagged her shoulder from behind.

"Rising, she then chased the little thing, shrieking with laughter, across the playa toward the raft-builders, who paused to observe their play. Instead of returning at once when she caught her, they stood for a while, hand in hand, looking on at the work, and though I could not see her face, her whole attitude bespoke keen interest. Once she spoke, and here my ideas of Indian nature underwent further reconstruction. There was no hate in the face of the man who looked up to answer. Stooping, he patted the child's head, and when, at last, Patricia returned to the fire, neither fear nor aversion showed on her face. Its calm, on the contrary, bordered on content, and as I lay there studying her, I sensed, without being able to locate it, a radical change.

THE PLANTER

"It wasn't that she was sunburned or thinner—that would have made toward refinement, for you'll remember that she erred toward voluptousness. Neither was it due to the white chemisette and red Tehauna skirt which replaced her own clothing; nor homesickness, for, as I say, her calm bordered on content. But while I watched she solved the puzzle herself. When, suddenly squatting, she began to tear a piece of meat she had fished from a cooking-pot into bits with her fingers, I knew—the squaw habit and posture told their tale—that the blood had asserted itself, she had gone back to her mother's people. After that her every gesture breathed of meaning—the toss that sent her hair in a wave back from her face over naked arms and shoulders, her easy flexures reaching to the pot, her laugh which, always wild, had lowered a full tone and issued with a throaty coo. In the splendor of her savagery she was infinitely wilder than Lola, the Tehuana, who sat by her side. That, however, did not total the change. Beyond it I sensed something other, a something so subtle that it defied my analysis until, glancing sideways, I glimpsed Boulton's eyes, sick and uneasy in the midst of his red shamed face. Then it flashed upon me—it was the content of a mated woman, soft sensuousness of young wifehood that enveloped her like a mist.

"'Come away!' his eyes said, and as I crawled after him back through the thicket, I knew that we were turned toward home.

THE REALIZATION OF A DREAM

"And now I'll have to confess to a second foolishness. Because of its density, we had left our rifles on the outer edge of the thicket, and though the dusk had thickened, there was still light enough to see, not only that they were gone, but also the ugly black muzzles that stared us from every bush.

"I'll confess to a mortal funk. It came so blamed sudden I hadn't time to grip my nerves, and every muscle contracted anticipating the tearing shock of heavy bullets. Each second I expected a burst of flame, but the muzzles held us with their unblinking stare until, just as I was dying my seventh death, your big Yaqui, Davy, came sauntering out from behind a bush.

"You had him here at Verda for a long time, but you never really saw him. The difference between the silent hulk you knew and this man who towered above me in the dusk was wider than that between the tame cats of a menagerie and a royal tiger loose in the jungle. He moved with the easy swing of authority. Loomed so large that I felt small, and shrank a couple more sizes when he spoke.

"'So it is you, Señor Carruthers, who makes such a noise in the forest, scaring the deer for miles around?'

"Think of it! And we priding ourselves all the while on our Injun stealth! But I was too busy wondering whether we were to be plain shot or have our necks twisted, after the fashion of Hertzer's veledor, to feel the insult. When, turning, he bade us follow, I made up my mind for the latter, already felt the crick in my neck. But it was merely preliminary to the hardest walk of my life. Striding ahead, he led on hour after hour through the dark forest, nor paused until, at midnight, we emerged on a trail that led down through a moonlit valley. In all that time he had not looked back, nor was it necessary, for if either of us lagged, the thrust of a rifle barrel from behind admonished him forward. Now he spoke for the second and last time.

"'You were friendly to Don David. Take your lives back to him.' Then, while we stood staring, all blown and sweating, he turned and vanished in the forest."

In spite of his light tone, the suspense of that black march had made itself felt in Carruthers' manner, and now, concluding, he sat staring at the lamp. Even for the tropics, where romance and reality are wedded and death lies ever in ambush, the matter of his tale was out of the ordinary, and for a long while the three sat in silence, each busy with his thoughts.

"Well," Ewing spoke at last, "she has gone back to her own. Nell always said that she would. Do you remember, Davy, the day we saw her in the La Luna cook-house?"

It was even then in his mind—Patricia squatted opposite the swart headwoman, long hair flowing down the fire of her kimona to sweep the dust as she leaned to scoop *frijoles* out of the dish; and to complete the barbaric picture, came a vivid memory of her garrulous speech, unlike in both tone and accent the spaced cadence of her convent speech.

"And what's to be the end?" he asked, nodding.

Carruthers came out of his brown study. "They'll join with some Central American tribe, or make a place for themselves; plenty of room down there."

"And Hertzer's blood will help them to hold it," Ewing musingly added. "Queer to think of, isn't it?"

It was—strange to think that a mixture of his strong blood might stiffen a people to hold back for a space, perhaps a generation, the van of a greedy commercialism. The thought held them for another silence.

"I don't know but that it has all worked out for the best," Ewing finally commented. "Now for one last glass and then to bed. To-morrow is Davy's busy day."

"His happy day," Carruthers added. "To you both, Davy!"

Morning saw the three on the way to Las Glorias, riding through heat that caused Ewing to exclaim at David's luck in vacations.

"None of your pity, sir," he said, mopping his parboiled face. "Only one more month before the blessed rains, and think of the fun that Nell and I will have up North after you come back. Fancy us at supper some night after the play—Sherry's, Delmonico's, any old place that the good uncle may take a notion to blow himself—fancy me jogging Nell's elbow, 'Hum, my dear, just think of Davy stewing in his own grease down there in the tropics.' To all men revenge cometh in its own good time."

In that the last stitch was taken as they rode up to the house, Mrs. Ewing may be held to have lived in the strict letter of her promise. It remained only to parade Consuela in a neat travelling dress, jacket and skirt of cream serge, innocent of any other trimming than the shy smiles which glowed in the shadow of a soft unblocked Panama hat.

"So simple and yet so stylish." As she turned the girl round and round before the three pairs of admiring eyes, Mrs. Ewing sighed her satisfaction. "And a *perfect* fit. But she's not to wear it down-river, Davy. Khaki is good enough for that. She can slip it on before you go to church, but see that she changes it when you go back to the boat. It is all she has to wear on the steamer." Which little speech foreshadows plans that were to be the realization of a dream; that which David dreamed the night he lay in the roots of the great *saber* awaiting the runaway Yaqui out in the jungle.

Alone they two would drift down to the priest at San Juan; then re-embark and drift or tie-up to the bank as the mood suited, drift at the will of the river, follow its myriad sinuosities past the sand *playas* where saurians take their torrid *siesta*, with always the broidered screen of the jungle on either hand; drift, drift lazy days down to the Gulf, from where a coasting-steamer would take them to the Ward Liner at Vera Cruz for passage to New York.

THE REALIZATION OF A DREAM

It began, the dream, three hours later, for though the travelling would be done thereafter principally by moonlight, they wished to pass Verda by day. It began with the usual tribute of bright tears from the women, the vigorous handshakes which belied the superb indifference of the men. Indeed, David's hand still tingled when, at sundown, a blast of his conch-shell brought out Verda, men, maids, women, and children, to illumine the bank with sunshine of brown smiles. All the way down David had cast a vigorous pole, but now he let the dugout drift; and as he stood leaning upon his pole a sweet voice came from astern quivering with pride beneath its archness.

"And now, señor, look at your work."

Warmed by the sunset, the long array of happy faces was surely worth a glance, and small wonder if David's face reflected their glow. Not that he either overestimated accomplishment or belittled that which remained to do. Well he knew the pains by which these good beginnings could alone be brought to fruition; the patience, care, love seasoned with severity; given which, in fullest measure, time would still be required to root them to the soil. But foreseeing it all, he had faith in himself and them, and while the boat drifted, he stood, the man face to face with his work and able to call it good.

Just as they floated opposite, came a splash like that of alighting ducks, and, naked and unashamed, Consuela's pupils came shooting out from the bank with Anita, the future bookkeeper, well in the lead.

531

THE PLANTER

Not one would turn till Consuela had caressed each of twenty small wet heads. Indeed, the *Buena fortunas*, *Felicidadis*, *Hasta luegos*, even Magdaleno's roaring *Vivas!* were growing faint in the distance before they shot like a school of brown minnows back to the bank.

Once around the bend, David struck in his pole again; but though he was long ago broken to its use, it cannot be urged that he made any records. For temptation sat astern. Progress was delayed by frequent rests when, nestling in to his shoulder, Consuela chattered, planning for their future, or prattled of their house, indulging her woman's humor by arranging its furniture in a hundred different ways. With many such lapses they glided down-stream, sometimes poling, sometimes drifting through the blood-red sunset reflections which presently deepened into gleaming sable. Out of the clamor of twilight they drifted into the silence of night, then the moon peeped at them over the trees; thereafter laid a silver path for their guidance across the dark waters, down which they glided until Consuela's sudden shiver brought a pause to the dream—industrious while David was idle, the current had brought them to La Luna.

High above them the bank upreared, a monolithic mass crowned with a bristle of dead trees. Moving elsewhere softly as a sigh, perfumed breath of the jungle, the night wind here rustled harshly, laden with stale odors of burning. As he drew her closer, David saw that Consuela's lips were moving and sensed her prayer for the hard man who lay out there in the peace of moonlight, and while they drifted its length, they came again, he and his dead slaves, to people the ghostly plantation.

As on his first evening at La Luna, David heard Hertzer's stern voice booming out orders for Carmen; saw him come swinging down the path to the landing with Phelps—Phelps, who was now thousands of miles away in England. He could see the log upon which he had sat while Ewing gave him first warning; he heard Patricia's laugh stir hollow echos in the dark silence of the *galera*. A long succession of memories brought him again upon the veranda in company with Patricia. Now he was looking down upon Consuela in the freight canoe below.

"It was here that I caught thy kiss."

He awoke to knowledge of the river, a stream of silver flowing once more between dark walls of jungle—La Luna lay behind. "Then you did catch it?" he laughed. "You told me—"

A small hand smothered further speech. "Some things may be told to husbands that are not good for lovers to hear. Surely I caught it—and kept it all this time to give it back to thee. There! And now for some more poling—if ever we are to reach San Juan?"

"And you must go to sleep, or I shall have a wan bride in the morning," he said, rising; and albeit with many protestations that she would rather stay out in the moonlight, she went to her rest under the tent cover he rigged across the dugout.

For hours thereafter he drove on down the silver river, pausing only on occasion to catch her gentle breathing. Carruthers' place, Boulton's, Yerba Buena, and other plantations flashed pale gold roofs out of the black jungle, to sink again in his rear. Oblivious of time in his happy dreaming, he watched the moon sail round her circle and dip down behind the trees. Even then he drove on through the darkness, nor rested till he saw that the pace would fetch San Juan before morning. Sitting down then, one hand on the steering sweep that was lashed in the crotch astern, he continued his dreaming. He did not feel sleepy, yet, awakening at a shy touch, he found Consuela smiling down upon him, not she of the khaki dress, but a delicate dark beauty in the cream serge of Mrs. Ewing's solemn warning; and there, dead ahead, the parti-colored *adobes* of San Juan were flaming in the sun.

Situated on a grassy plain at the confluence of two rivers, the town was still within call of the jungle, and as they made their way to the church, the wood-dove's gentle call thrilled out on the fresh morning air. Arriving a quarter-hour before first mass, there was just time for Consuela to make her confession, and while she kneeled at the grating, David stood at a distance wondering, after the fashion of true lovers, what she could possibly find to confess. Perhaps the priest, too, smiled at her list of small vanities; at least, he did her a service by lifting a remorseful doubt from her heart.

"That surely was sin, daughter," he chid her when

she told of having exulted in her power over Hertzer, "but of all else thou art free. He died of his own evil."

So she brought back to David a face so calmly serene that while he might still have his doubts as to her need, he was obliged to admit the efficacy of her confession. Taking his seat beside her, he sat with bowed head in the grotto cool of the church, aware of the perfume of incense, shuffling of naked feet, intoning of the priest celebrating the mass, silver crash of bells that announced the "consecration." It was a strange atmosphere for the son of his Puritan mother, yet when, at the close of the mass, they followed the priest into the sacristy, he experienced in full measure the feeling of cleanness, purification of sense he had felt after many a good sermon at home.

Half an hour later they walked hand in hand down the steps, and as they passed through the streets, retraced the grassy plain to the boat, they smiled, whenever their eyes met, with the shy happiness of children. They had still three hours before the heat would drive them off the river, and during the last hour David looked continually for a suitable landing. But Consuela spied it first. Turning at her exclamation, he saw a backwater open up behind them, a long strip of green water, smooth as silk ribbon, with a diminutive *playa* at its end running back into the black shade of a *banyan*. Eden itself could not have furnished a pleasanter bower, or its first inhabitants have been happier than they in setting up their first housekeeping. While David built a fire, she carried utensils and packages up from the boat—all save one which caused him a grunt of surprise by its unsuspected weight.

"Presently, presently," she put him off, laughing, when he asked what it was, and sent him away to spread their *zarapes* far back in the shade on a soft cool couch of sand; and when he came back—there was she, sleeves rolled above white elbows, on her knees before a stone *metate*. "To grind the tortillas for thee, my husband!" she cried, with a happy laugh that did not hide her serious intent. Looking down upon her, he knew it for a consecration, offering of the service without which love is naught.

And while he watched the dimples come and go with her rubbing, she told how she had dreamed of this the day she sat beside him while he rested after their hunting in the jungle. "I shall leave it here," she said, patting the *metate*, at the close of her labors; adding, with piercing sweetness of look and voice, "And when, some day, my husband forgets that he was once a lover, we shall come again, thou and I, to this dear place and live again these sweet hours."

"Then we shall never come," he stoutly assured her; and as lover's faith dominated woman's wisdom, she went with a sigh of content to his arms.

THE END